YESTERDAY'S GONE

Season Six

SEAN PLATT

DAVID W. WRIGHT

STERLING & STONE

To YOU, the reader.
Thank you for taking a chance on us.
Thank you for your support.
Thank you for the emails.
Thank you for the reviews.
Thank you for reading and joining us on this road.

YESTERDAY'S GONE

Episode 31

(FIRST EPISODE OF SEASON SIX)

"Wounds"

Prologue

PAUL ROBERTS

Three and a half years ago

PAUL KNEW he wasn't alone in the dark alley.

He could feel the presence of something lurking in the shadows. The only question was whether it was human or alien. He picked up his pace, stolen antibiotics tucked into the pockets of his jacket, pistol in his right hand. If he didn't make it home, his daughter, Emily, was as good as dead.

The cold sweats, puking, and 104 fever weren't a normal illness. No, it was *the plague* that had killed so many — including his wife — since the aliens landed six months ago. Paul had hoped they were immune, seeing as they'd survived the first outbreak. But maybe the illness had mutated. If they'd had a natural resistance, that no longer mattered. It was back to finish the job.

If Paul lost Emily, he'd have no reason to go on. No reason to hide from the roaming aliens, or worse, the savage humans left behind. A bullet in his head would be better than another day alone. He was only alive and fighting to keep Emily safe.

She can't die now.

Paul chided his own lack of preparation.

He'd built a secret shelter in his apartment building's basement then stockpiled food, weapons, and emergency medical equipment. But he'd failed to replenish the stash of antibiotics after Jane died, and now his daughter might follow her to the grave. And just like that — the power and money he'd acquired as a TV producer of hit reality shows like *The Box, Sing for It,* and *American Adventure* was all for naught.

Paul was two blocks from home when the men appeared, spilling from a building's rear door, holding guns and bags of loot. All four saw him immediately.

Their guns were aimed before he could raise his.

He was outmanned and outgunned. At their mercy.

He put his pistol down on the asphalt and raised his hands, trying to appear as nonthreatening as possible. He had a second gun in a back holster beneath his jacket, and a knife strapped to his wrist — both last resorts.

Three of the men might've been brothers. They were all within a few years of each other. Lean but muscular, broad shoulders, dark hair, brown eyes, scruffy beards. Paul pegged them for partly Italian. The fourth man was older, heavyset, graying hair and a ruddy face. Maybe German. Paul wondered if the eldest man was their father. It seemed odd that an entire family could survive the sickness, but a shared genetic trait, or whatever the hell it was, could've spared them like it had for Paul and his daughter.

Ruddy Face spoke first. Stern and calm, aiming a shotgun at Paul. "On your knees." This was all business, at least to the older man, but he could feel the others' anxiety, visible in their bright-red auras. If he weren't careful, this robbery would turn to a murder.

Judging from their duffels, they'd already loaded up from whatever shop they'd just left — a bakery, an electronics boutique, or a clothing store, Paul figured, assuming he remembered the shops' locations correctly.

Paul went down on his knees, keeping his arms high, eyes on Ruddy Face.

"I don't have anything worth taking."

One of the young men came over, bent down, and grabbed Paul's pistol. "I wouldn't say nothin'."

"Empty your pockets," Ruddy Face said.

Paul had nothing in his pockets, save for a small lock picking set and, of course, the medicine.

He placed the lock picking set on the dark wet asphalt, followed by the medicine. Four large bottles of antibiotics, one hundred pills in each one.

"Whoa, those pain pills?" the guy said, holding Paul's gun with his eyes on the bottle.

"No, they're antibiotics." Paul thought about explaining that they were for his sick daughter. But he didn't yet know these men, and letting them know he had a young girl at home, unprotected, might lead to an uglier death for Emily. In the invasion's aftermath, people hadn't come together as they had after September 11. They'd turned on each other instead, committing the worst of atrocities.

Paul had tried plugging his ears but heard it all the same: a paralyzing aria of murder, rape, and God knew what else might have been happening beyond his protective shelter, where predators surely ripped prey to pieces. Mankind's history repeated. If anything, the recent era of relative peace was an anomaly. Before then, before *civilization*, mankind had been cruel, barbaric, worse than animals. Now society's shackles were gone; mankind at his worst was free to do what he did best — kill. Survival of the fittest. Or cruelest.

While Paul didn't consider himself a cruel man, he *would do* whatever it took to protect his daughter.

The young man bent, retrieved the pills, then studied the labels.

Paul waited, hoping the man would see they weren't Oxy or some other recreational drug, and would toss them back.

Ruddy Face intervened. "Give those here. We can use 'em."

"Please," Paul said, meeting the man's eyes, "please leave me at least one bottle. I've got a sick one at home."

"A sick *what?*" one of the young men asked. Unlike the older man, his voice *was* cruel, as was the scar running down his right cheek. He stared down at Paul, his trigger finger itchy.

He heard the scarred man's thoughts as clear as day.

Maybe he's got a bitch we can take.

Judging from their new clothes in a mishmash of styles, these men weren't used to money. Their shoes had no scuffs: shiny black boots, expensive loafers, and dress shoes, none suited for the apocalypse. Ruddy Face was dressed in older clothing — jeans, dark shirt, a well-worn leather jacket, and comfortable-looking sneakers.

"A daughter. She's ten and has a terrible fever."

"You sick?" The man who'd taken Paul's gun fell two steps back, still aiming at his forehead.

"No, no, she, I mean, we, survived the sickness. She has something else, and she's burning up. She'll die without those pills."

The scarred man said, "We're all gonna die anyway."

Paul looked to Ruddy Face. "Please, sir, just one bottle. You can keep my gun. Just let me get back to my daughter. She's lost her mother already."

The old man stared at Paul, evaluating.

"I got a better idea," the scarred man said. "Why don't you take us to your place and give us your stuff?"

"We don't have much," Paul lied, meeting his awful eyes. He got a glimpse of the man's stream of thoughts. He was already picturing shooting Paul right in the head. Maybe he'd even make the little girl watch, before he turned his attentions on her.

"I don't believe you. Stand up. We're going to your place."

Shit.

Paul had to play this cool. There was no time to try and infiltrate all of their minds. If he chose the wrong target, he could trigger a chain reaction of unintended horrors. He'd nearly caused a riot early after The Fall, and had been lucky to escape with his life.

He met Ruddy's eyes, trying to figure out the relationship between the men. If he was their father, why was Scarred Man barking orders? Was *he* their leader?

"Come on, Tony, let's just let him be," said the young man holding Paul's gun.

Tony is the scarred one's name. And he is their leader.

Who is the older man?

Tony snapped, "I didn't ask for your opinion, so shut the fuck up, Marco."

Tony stepped forward and aimed his pistol between Paul's eyes. "You gonna get up, or you wanna die right here?"

The man glared at Paul, revealing his issues with disrespect. Paul had to be careful not to piss him off and make it personal. At the same time, he had to stand his ground. A man like Tony wouldn't respect weakness, and would see it as further invitation to take. He had to tread the line carefully. If Paul was *too strong*, Tony would see him as a threat to his authority and shoot him on principle.

Paul stood, meeting Tony's eyes.

"Tell you what," Paul said, "I'm not going to give you everything. I have a child to look out for. She needs medicine. And we need some supplies. But I understand what's happening and will give you everything I can if you leave us be."

"That's not good enough." Tony's eyes narrowed on Paul.

"Then you may as well kill me. If I give you the medicine, my daughter's dead."

Paul wouldn't back down. His heart raced, hoping his gambit would work. If not, Emily was waiting for a father who wouldn't come home. The thought of her alone — scared, waiting, wondering if her father had left her abandoned or orphaned — was breaking his heart.

He couldn't show his sorrow. Had to be braver than he was.

Paul looked from Tony to Ruddy Face, going into his head.

His name was Frank, and he was sick of Tony's shit. The younger man was constantly challenging his authority and pushing Frank to do things. But at the same time, Frank knew that Tony had won over the others. If he screwed up, they all might turn on him.

Paul decided to use this division in their ranks to his advantage. He looked past Tony, ignoring him, and spoke directly to Frank.

"Please, sir," he said to Frank, "just let me keep one bottle, and I'm on my way."

"Why you talkin' to *him?*" Tony said. "Look at me, mother-fucker. *I'm* the one with the gun in your face."

Paul continued staring at Frank. "I just wanna get home to my daughter."

Tony cocked his arm back and swung, striking Paul hard across his forehead, knocking him back but not down.

Hot blood trickled into Paul's eyes. The pain was a flea to the threat.

Paul stood silent, staring at Tony, waiting to see what the hothead would do.

He was tempted to reach back for his pistol, but he'd be lucky to land one or two shots before the others cut him down. He had to stay the course, hope he could talk some sense into Frank, or push thoughts into the man's head to convince him to shut Tony down.

It would be easier, of course, if he could tap into Tony's head and control him. But the man was riding a wave of anger, fear, and a meth high that made his mind a dangerous place to enter.

So Frank was Paul's best shot.

Paul hadn't just been the executive producer for *The Box*, he was heavily involved in casting. He'd never been terribly original with his show ideas, but Paul was inventively intuitive when it came to reading people and assembling casts for maximum drama. Plus, he was a telepath — able to read most people's minds, and sometimes even to control them for short spurts. Having such a power made show business a natural path to follow. He could use his abilities under the radar while getting rich and not rocking too many boats or drawing unwanted attention from the powers-that-be.

Sure, critics hated *The Box* because it appealed to the lowest common denominator, but a lot of people appreciated the fights, the backstabbing, and the show's many political machinations. Paul was a master of pitting people against one another.

Tony raised his gun, aiming it square between Paul's eyes.

Paul pushed the thought into Frank's head: *Am I really gonna let Tony do this?*

Paul swallowed, heart racing, hoping he'd not misjudged the situation.

"Wait," Frank said.

Tony looked back. "What?"

"Let him go."

"What?"

"We don't need this shit. Give him his medicine and gun. We're letting him go."

Paul had hoped to leave with his life, and maybe a bottle of pills, but the gun, too? His smile was hard to throttle.

"What the hell?" Tony said. "You letting this guy go because, what, he's got a kid?"

"It's not worth it," Frank said, still cool. "He ain't done nothin' to us. Let's just be on our way."

Tony looked back at Paul like Daddy was telling him to return his toy to the shelf. But Tony wasn't letting go. He shoved his gun back in Paul's face then turned to the other men. "What do you two think? We letting this fucker go?"

Marco and the other one, whose name Paul didn't yet know, exchanged glances, both avoiding the gaze of either Tony or Frank.

Paul could tell from snippets of Frank's thoughts that he wasn't father to any of the men. But he must've been someone who knew them before the world went to shit, someone who had their respect — otherwise Tony would've been leader. Whatever the struggle's origins, it festered for a while.

Still calm, Frank said, "We're letting him go. This isn't up for debate."

"No?" Tony turned his aim on Frank. "I say we have a vote. Everyone who thinks we should let this guy go, say nothing. Everyone who says we follow him home and get his stuff, raise your hands."

The four men traded stares. Only Tony was aiming a gun, at Frank.

Paul watched the first nameless man raise his hand.

Marco followed.

Fuck.

Tony raised his empty hand. "Sorry, Frank, you've been outvoted."

"This isn't a democracy." Frank raised his shotgun at Tony. "Now put your gun away, and let's end this."

"You're right," Tony said, "this isn't a democracy. And we're tired of taking orders from you. How about another vote — for a new leader? Raise your hands if you want me to lead."

The unnamed man raised his hand; Paul's gut somersaulted.

Marco's hand creeped up.

The men voted, Tony's back to Paul.

Now was his chance.

Paul drew his gun, aimed at the back of Tony's head, and fired twice.

Gunshots thundered through the alley.

The three remaining men traded shots.

Marco fell back, a gunshot blast to the chest. Before the unnamed man could hit his target, Frank and Paul brought him down with another two shots. All the young men were dead.

It was just Paul and Frank left, staring each other down, guns aimed.

Paul's hands shook. His heart raced, pounding loud below his ringing ears. He thought about pushing a thought into Frank's head but didn't think he needed the risk.

Frank stared at him but wasn't taking the shot.

Paul raised his gun at the sky. "We good?"

Frank looked down at the men with no emotion and nodded. "We're good."

Frank went to each of their bodies, retrieved the men's fallen bags, hoisted them over his shoulders, then reached into his jacket and pulled out three of the four bottles of antibiotics and tossed them, one at a time, to Paul.

"Be careful out there," Frank said then turned to be on his way.

Paul let out a deep sigh of relief then went to the dead man who'd taken his gun. As Paul leaned over to get it, a cacophony of shrieks echoed off the buildings.

He spun around, gun raised, just in time to see a trio of black creatures descend from the shadows above, dropping on top of Frank. They were fast — long, black, wet limbs like lightning, large clawed hands slicing Frank's body to pieces in an instant.

Frank fell to the ground, in chunks of flesh and splashes of blood.

Paul was paralyzed.

He'd seen the aliens from the windows of an upstairs apartment and on TV before the networks — and power — had left forever. But never up close.

They were tall, though bent, almost as if their enormous, bulbous heads were too heavy for their long, thin necks. Their eyes were large and even blacker than their almost translucent flesh. Something like lights pulsated under the aliens' flesh in an almost rhythmic, hypnotizing, cycle that Paul found it impossible to turn from.

They spun toward him.

He wanted to run. But the thought came too late.

They closed in on Paul in an instant, surrounding him, arms raised, wide-open mouths with sharp black teeth chattering, clicking, as that horrible shrieking grew so loud that he wanted to cover his ears and crawl into a hole.

The aliens were so close, he could feel an icy wind wafting from their bodies, sending chills through his.

He wanted to raise his pistol and fire but couldn't eliminate three aliens at once. Even if he managed to injure or kill one, the other two would shred him, like they had Frank, in seconds.

Before Paul could raise his barrel to aim, he noticed that the aliens were no longer moving — almost frozen in place.

What the hell?

Paul looked up to see his panicked reflection in their large black eyes, staring at him as if waiting for a reboot.

A man's voice spoke from behind.

"Mr. Paul Roberts, what an honor to finally meet you."

The aliens, all three at once, fell from their positions, allowing Paul to see the man walking toward him.

Why isn't he scared of them?

Is he controlling *them somehow?*

Maybe he's one of them — an alien within a human host.

The man was wearing a charcoal gray suit and had brown hair, greased back, and piercing blue eyes. Paul could easily cast him as a successful entrepreneur on one of his shows. But there was something else about the guy, something under the surface — *maybe the way he's controlling the aliens, or how he knows my name?* — that unsettled Paul like the sight of his own headstone.

"Who are you?" Paul asked, not attempting to hide his suspicions or fear. "And how do you know my name?"

"My name is Desmond Armstrong, and I've been watching you for a while."

"Watching me? How?"

Desmond smiled. "I have eyes and ears everywhere, Mr. Roberts."

The aliens clicked as if acknowledging their master.

"What are you?"

"I suppose that depends on whom you ask. I think the question you ought to be asking is why I'm so interested in you, Mr. Roberts."

"Okay. Why?"

"Because I could use a man with your talents."

"Talents?" Paul wondered how he could possibly know of his talents.

"I've seen you talk your way out of certain death no less than six times in the past couple of weeks. In a world full of people running around like chickens missing their heads, you maintain your composure. You're able to negotiate your way out of almost anything, aren't you? I'd call it an almost preternatural quality you possess. Would you agree?"

Paul wasn't sure if the man was leading him with the question, trying to see what he might admit.

Desmond stepped toward Paul, eyeing him up and down. His gaze was unnerving, like an unwanted lover's. But Paul didn't dare move, or take offense. Doing so would spell his death, and given what the man seemed to know, perhaps Emily's too.

Desmond, now behind him, said, "You're thinking about your daughter right now, and whether she's in danger."

He said this matter-of-factly, not even asking.

Can he read my *mind?*

Is he doing it now?

Oh, God!

He focused on nothing, clearing his mind and thoughts, a technique he'd learned from The Church of Original Design — the place that gave him the materials to hone his talents early on.

Desmond spoke again, "Ah, clearing your mind, I see."

Paul felt like a magician whose act had been spoiled. He turned to Desmond. "Get out of my head."

Desmond laughed, a small laugh like you might use with a child who was trying to outwit you.

"Don't worry, Mr. Roberts, I am not here to harm you, or your sick daughter. On the contrary, I'm here to help you both."

"How are *you* going to help us?"

"I have an important job vacancy. It requires a man of your talents."

Paul was horrified. He'd heard rumors of aliens going into people's bodies, taking them over like sinister puppeteers. He'd rather die, would rather Emily die, than have either of them play host to these foul things.

Desmond frowned. "I'm sorry you view us with such disgust."

Paul swallowed. He'd offended the alien, and now he would pay.

"I said I'm not going to harm you, and I meant it. You can walk away right now and never see me again. I can't promise your safety, of course. It is a rather barbaric world, I'm afraid, and I've no control over the savages that still scour the streets."

By savages he surely meant men.

Desmond continued, "And you needn't worry about us hijacking your body. I want your unique mind, Mr. Roberts. For me to install one of our own into you would infinitely lessen your value. You come with me, and I promise to provide you and your daughter a safe haven. You can live with others who are serving to build a new society, free of illness, death, and violence."

"I've seen what your things have done to my people. You call that *safe?*"

"We are merely clearing dead wood, eliminating the worst of your kind. But there is a place for you both in our society, where excellence is esteemed, and well rewarded. I promise: Come with me, and Emily can live a long, happy life by your side. We have people who can cure her."

Paul stared at the man, trying to gauge his honesty. It was difficult to be certain — especially when he wasn't dealing with a human intelligence whose mind he could enter — but his gut said that Desmond was telling the truth.

"Are you interested, Mr. Roberts? Or shall I leave you to your few remaining days in an underground hovel spent waiting for your daughter to die?"

Paul flinched.

He wanted to hit the man for threatening Emily. But Desmond's tone conveyed more honesty than threat. The alien had offered to cure Emily. Even if she survived the sickness without the aliens' help, how long could they live like this? They were on borrowed time. Sooner or later, aliens, or men who wanted what little they had left, would find them. Paul had been lucky, six times by Desmond's count, but how long could such luck run?

Paul knew people well, but he also knew luck, and when people were pressing it. He'd seen too many contestants in his games push their fortunes too far. The woman who'd been close to walking away with two million dollars in the show's third season — but allowed herself to gamble it all for a chance to knock out a threat to her seat in the house. She left with a consolation prize instead. And she was hardly alone when it came to people who didn't recognize an opportunity for what it was.

Paul met Desmond's eyes. "Well?"

~

ONE

Boricio Wolfe

Las Orillas, California
 2017 (present day)

"SON OF A FUCKING CUNT!" Boricio's knife slipped through the apple's side and into his left index finger.

He raised his digit and examined the wound. The slice was deep but clean. Pain pounded through to his bone, worse than it had any right to feel.

"You okay?" Mary came to the kitchen from the living room where she'd been napping.

She brought his finger to her mouth and kissed it. Blood dabbed her lips in a crimson stain, turning him on more than it had any right to.

"I'll be fine." He took his hand back and searched the cabinet under the sink for his red plastic box. He grabbed a bandage and tore it open.

"Wait, you need to rinse it out first." Mary grabbed a bottle of water from the counter and flipped off the cap.

Boricio let her pour a little water over his wound then held up a hand. "That's enough. Let's not waste it."

He patted the wound dry with a paper towel then wrapped a bandage around his finger.

"See, this is what happens when you use dull knives!" Boricio raised the blade for Mary to see the offending party. "I need to find some baby knives or a sharpener for the geriatrics."

Mary laughed. "Sorry that the comforts of postapocalypse life don't suit Chef Boricio."

"Hey, I was a damned good chef, and I'll have you know you're pretty fucking lucky to have me at the stove. Especially with no power, running water, and whatever the hell I can find left on Planet FuckAll."

"Don't forget the contributions of my rooftop garden," Mary reminded him.

"Of course, Miss Mary, how *could* I ever forget how your garden grows, or the bounty it brings to my kitchen? I have all the truffles I could ever want."

"Oh, shut up, I grow some damned good tomatoes, carrots, and radishes." Mary grabbed Boricio's apple from the counter and took a bite. "Wouldn't cut yourself if you ate apples like a normal person. Where did you even get an apple?"

"When Ed and I went to visit The Farm last week."

"Oh." Mary turned away and looked out the window. She was either great at being a drama queen or the world's shittiest poker player, because the way she turned off and away whenever The Farm came up in conversation, Boricio felt like he was watching a guest star on *Manimal*.

"You know you could've come." Boricio came up behind Mary and wrapped his arms around her waist.

"No," she said, false pride wounded. She was still annoyed that Marina had left their group and gone to The Farm, saying she'd had enough of war and The City. "It's fine. So … how are they?"

"They're doing okay," he said, staring out at what was left of the Las Orillas skyline. Scout ships dotted the sky, alien fuckers searching for more people to grab and bring to the mothership floating over The Island like some goddamned hobbit-hating red eye. He couldn't wait to find a weakness in their program and bring the fuckers down. But even after four years, the alien occupation still felt as far off as a return to TV with *ALF* as the main attraction. They'd already lost the war on the other world, with most of the Black Mountain Militia, as he liked to call them, retreating then coming over in a portal that Luca had made — back when the Boy Wonder still had considerable power coursing through him.

Mary said nothing, continuing to stare out the window at the setting, sky bleeding orange and violet.

"Go ahead," she said.

"Go ahead what?"

"Say it."

"Say what?"

"That we should go there, too."

"Nope. I'm not bothering with that line anymore. You already chewed my ass like it'd been too long on the grill. Our place is here, fighting on the front lines. Besides, neither of us is the type to settle on a farm."

Mary said nothing, staring into her past — reflecting on a life she no longer had. She'd lost her daughter. Lost a baby. Two, actually. There *was* once a Mary who would've longed for a farm to settle on, but that Mary was buried beneath several calloused layers of pain. This Mary was Linda Fucking Hamilton in *Terminator 2*: buff, badass, and looking for a fight.

Boricio would have loved to help bring the Old Mary back, but he also loved being with a woman who was starving for violence like he was. Someone who didn't shy away from killing bandit wannabes, blowing alien cornholes to chunky nuggets, or finding traitorous fucks who sold out their brothers to the aliens and decorating the streets with their skinned remains so other survivors wouldn't be so swift to turn their coats.

"You thinking 'bout the little lamb?"

"Yeah."

"I think about her, too," he said. "Paola was a good kid."

Mary kept staring out the window.

Times like this, Boricio wished she'd show some emotion and cry for her daughter. Hell, a part of Boricio wanted her to weep on his shoulder — he was surprisingly old-fashioned that way. But tears couldn't own her, and she refused to dwell on what couldn't be.

A knock on the front door cut into their quiet, rapid and careless, ignoring the coded knock rebels were instructed to use.

In most circumstances, Boricio would see that as a sign that shit was wrong, that maybe someone was being coerced to knock and draw them out. But a few of their recent recruits weren't exactly the sharpest crayons in the box. But hell, beggars were bitches when even choosers were chumps.

Mary grabbed her shotgun from the kitchen table.

Boricio grabbed his knife from the counter. Even dull-for-apples would gut a fucker fine.

"Who is it?" Boricio asked.

"It's me, Barrow."

Boricio rolled his eyes. Jake Barrow was the freshest of his recruits, a freckle-faced sixteen-year-old farm boy who was as big as a linebacker but dumb as one who'd taken a few too many hits. He'd lost his family to the plague last year and had been wandering upstate searching for God Knew What when Boricio and Ed found him and invited Hayseed Harry back to The City.

Boricio glanced at Mary to make sure she was ready, in case he didn't use the code because he happened to be at gunpoint or some shit, then opened the door.

Barrow stood there, sweating — obvious even in the candlelit living room — out of breath, eager to spit something out.

"You forget the fucking knock?" Mary said before the boy could open his mouth. She slammed the door shut behind him then sat her shotgun down on the couch.

"S-sorry, I forgot. I was in a hurry to get up here and tell you."

"Tell us what?" Boricio asked, waiting for Barrow to hit the fucking point.

"They're dead."

"Who's dead?"

"Matt and Jace."

"What the hell you talking about?" Boricio asked.

"The scouts we sent to infiltrate the slaughterhouse last week, Matt and Jace. They're dead. When I went to see if they'd left a message at the drop point like they were supposed to after gaining the aliens' trust, I saw their bodies hanging on pikes outside the slaughterhouse."

"Are you sure?" Mary asked.

"Yes, I'm sure! It's them, and they were torn to shreds!"

"Shit." Boricio shook his head. "We've gotta flush."

Mary was a step ahead already, loading duffel bags as Boricio hit the radios and called Ed Keenan over the encrypted transmission.

"Ed, we've got a Protocol 15. Repeat, Protocol 15. We'll meet at Station 20."

"Copy," Keenan said over the radio.

"What's going on?" Barrow asked.

"We need to pronto the fuck outta here before the place starts crawling with Guardsmen, aliens, or maybe an orgy of both."

Bags packed, Boricio proceeded to set off the timer for the bomb that would leave the apartment looking like a busted box of Cocoa Pebbles — along with anything they left behind.

Two minutes.

They headed to the stairs when five men in Black Island Guardsmen uniforms and black visored helmets appeared just below them, automatic rifles in hand, taking aim. Desmond had infected all the Guardsmen shortly after the invasion, and their numbers were strong.

"Stop!" one of the men said, voice sounding mechanical through his helmet's speakers, aiming his rife.

Mary fired her shotgun and sent him backward down the stairs, taking the other four men tumbling with him.

They had two paths of escape — up the stairs and to the rooftop, where they'd constructed a makeshift slide to the next apartment building or down the stairs.

Way Boricio saw it, if the cock swallowers were coming from downstairs, that meant another group was flooding down from above. They weren't stupid enough to send *all* their men in the same way. He had to take care of the three remaining cumswappers before more fuckers wanted to party.

He leaped down, knife in hand, quick to slice through the suit's black leather collar, straight into the man's throat.

Boricio could see the helmet visor cloud with the alien attempting to escape through the man's mouth, no doubt desperate for a new host.

"Don't break their helmets!" Boricio shouted in case Barrow forgot yet *another* element of basic training.

One of the two remaining Guardsmen reached up, glove gripping Boricio's arm.

A painful shock coursed from the man's glove through Boricio's arm.

Boricio screamed, trying to wrench himself free, but all he could do was shake in the electric current.

The man reached down to his left and grabbed his blade, eager to punch holes in Boricio.

Gunshot from above.

Mary.

Electro Glove fell back, his chest full of buckshot — down but not yet out. Boricio struggled against the pain to grab his knife and make a filet.

Below Boricio and the fallen Guardsman, the last of them started to stand, raising his rifle.

Boricio's hand found the handle, but there was no way he'd be quick enough to reach the man. And he doubted he could throw the blade hard enough to pierce the man's uniform.

But he didn't need to. A yell from above as Barrow barreled downstairs. He jumped over Boricio and the fallen Guardsmen then landed on top of the last man, taking him down, both of them tumbling down the stairs until they hit a hard stop at the landing.

Boricio finished off his guy then raced downstairs to make sure Barrow's guy stayed the fuck down.

A shot exploded above them.

Boricio quickly turned, afraid he'd see the worst — Mary shot dead in front of his eyes.

He couldn't see her injury but could tell from the way Mary stood frozen and wide-eyed for a moment, she'd been shot from behind.

Four new Guardsmen crowded the hall behind Mary, guns aimed at her.

She fell limply down the stairs. Boricio caught a glimpse of her bloodied back as he raced forward to catch her. She'd hit the wall and a step on the way before he could bring her fall to a halt.

Her eyes were closed.

Boricio's gut scraped the floor.

He couldn't lose her, too.

The Guardsman above barked, "Arms up!"

Boricio looked up, growling, wanting to tear them to shreds with his bare hands.

But he couldn't move. He was the only thing keeping

Mary from falling farther. His blade was on the ground, his gun in one of the bags Mary had dropped at the top of the stairway.

The Guardsman repeated his order, "Arms —"

And then the explosion.

~

TWO

Brent Foster

Sometimes, waking up was the hardest thing in the world.

In Brent's dreams, life was still the same as it had been before he'd been stolen from the world. His wife, Gina, was still alive. Ben hadn't lost his mother, and they lived in Manhattan, where he still had a job at the paper. Life was stressful, but good. He was doing what he'd always wanted to do, and though Brent rarely had time for his family, he still *had* them.

Then he opened his eyes, and reality smothered the sensation. Slowly at first. For a brief moment, he felt like the life he'd lived the past six years was the dream. Brent merely had to roll over, and he'd find his sleeping wife beside him. They'd spend the morning in bed, read *the New York Times*, then go for a walk in the park with Ben. But then it fell apart, like all good dreams did these days.

The world outside was a festering shell inside an empty echo. This wasn't their world any longer, even if Keenan and crew were in The City, fighting the war. The way Brent saw it, it was a pointless battle. The aliens had won. They could only hope for a way to somehow exist without being noticed by either the roving bandits that claimed lands outside The City or the aliens who sometimes flew ships overhead searching for people to face God Knew What.

Despite Crowded House's plea, the dream *was* over. Nothing was the same — or could be again.

Brent sat up, his room at The Farm bathed in the moon's pale blue. Beside him, his nine-year-old son, Ben, snored softly.

At least one good thing is left.

Living at The Farm still felt like a gift, even though they'd been at the compound for nearly two years. It had limited solar power, running water, a well, and of course crops and animals, which sustained the thirty-five people who lived there. But they could be discovered any day, and few too people at The Farm seemed to recognize the threat.

While Marina and Teagan had come a long way with their shooting and combat training, neither of them, nor anyone else at The Farm, came close to the skills boasted by Ed Keenan or Lisa from Black Mountain. He'd feel a lot safer if Ed were here, but he'd chosen to stay in The City with *Team Boricio*.

Brent respected Boricio's skills, but the man was a lunatic who would only lead anyone behind him into the jaws of death. He was glad that Ben and Becca didn't have to be around the psychopath. It wasn't that Brent thought Boricio would ever hurt the kids. He'd been quite nice to them during their times together. But Brent had seen the things Boricio had done in his life prior to the world falling apart. And while he might have changed, and was now on their side, there was a part of Brent that believed nobody ever changed all that much. Which meant that Boricio might slip some day and murder everyone around him. And the farther away Brent, Teagan, and the kids were, the better.

A wolf howled in the distance and sent a chill rippling through Brent.

Calm down. You're worrying too damned much.

Brent had always been a worrier, and the alien invasion had only poured gasoline on the fire of his fretting. If anything, he'd grown more paralyzed. More worried about what might happen to the kids.

He hated his fear and would give anything to be more like Ed — or hell, even Boricio. If he could somehow find a bit of their bravery, without Boricio's recklessness, he'd bring more value to The Farm, and his son.

He looked at his watch, saw that it was 4:19 a.m. Given that he hadn't fallen asleep until midnight, he should have been exhausted. Instead, Brent was wired — his mind racing with awful possibilities.

He got out of bed, careful not to wake Ben, deciding he'd go to the kitchen for something to eat.

He softly descended the stairs, trying not to wake any of the other inhabitants in the two-story home. In addition to the main house, there was a barn and a small cottage on the back of the heavily wooded property. There was also a small farm in the rear where they grew corn, wheat, potatoes, and carrots alongside a small orchard of apple trees.

Brent stepped into the kitchen area; he wasn't alone.

Teagan was leaning against the wood-burning stove, cradling a cup of coffee. She was wearing a long pink shirt. Brent wondered if she were wearing shorts or panties beneath it. Her nipples were hard, poking visibly through the fabric.

He tried not to leer. He had ten years, or more, on her. But it felt like forever since he'd been with another woman, and she was beautiful and sexy in a shy sort of way. And while he felt too old for Teagan, she had been with Ed's doppelgänger on the other world, and *he* was more than twenty years her senior. Maybe Teagan had a thing for older guys? Maybe Brent had a shot.

She was nice and had been a good friend these past four years. And their kids got along great, too. But she'd never given Brent any sign of interest beyond friendship, and he wasn't about to make the first move. Particularly when they lived in such close quarters.

"Want some?" Teagan nodded toward the kettle.

"Is that still any good?"

"Not really. But better than I expected, given the cans expired three years ago."

"No, thanks. I'll pass."

Brent went to the pantry and found a plastic bowl of homemade blueberry muffins made by one of the other women last week.

He peeled back the lid and held the open bowl toward Teagan. "Want one?"

Her smile was sweet with guilt. "No, thanks. I already had one."

Brent smiled back, took a muffin, then replaced the bowl. He took a bite, pacing near the kitchen sink, not wanting to hover near Teagan.

"So," she said, "why are you up?"

"I dunno. Just woke up and couldn't get back to sleep. You?"

"Becca woke up crying. It took forever to get her back to sleep. And now I'm wide awake."

"Nightmares again?"

"Yeah, poor girl. Does Ben get them?"

"Not too much anymore."

"What about you? Do you have nightmares?"

Brent thought about telling Teagan how the nightmares weren't the worst part — it was the happy dreams where his wife was alive. But he didn't feel like talking about Gina with anyone, least of all to a woman he was attracted to. It felt somehow wrong, even though Gina never had a problem moving on when she thought Brent was gone.

"Sometimes. You?"

Teagan met his gaze. Her green eyes looked almost blue in the dark, beneath her long red hair. "Sometimes, I dream about my parents. When we first came back to Earth, I thought about going back to see if they were okay. Originally, I thought they'd vanished right in front of me, but after I realized it was me who'd disappeared in front of them, I thought maybe I should go let them know I was alive. But then I thought better."

"Why's that?"

"They never would've accepted Becca. Hell, my father would think Satan had taken me. He'd probably have had me institutionalized and put Becca up for adoption. Or worse, raised her."

Brent remembered an earlier conversation when Teagan told him about her abusive father. And how her parents had wanted her to get an abortion. He also had some of her memories, painful memories, from whatever Luca had put in all of them.

"So, what happens in these dreams with your parents?"

"I'm coming home with Becca, but they're not there. Instead, there are aliens in the house, sitting at the kitchen table, having dinner as if they belonged."

"So do you think you feel guilty for not going back?"

"Maybe," she said, taking a sip then refreshing her mug.

"You shouldn't feel bad."

"I know." She shrugged.

Brent felt awkward, like he was trying to console a girl who wasn't seeking consolation.

I should just shut up now before I say something stupid.

Teagan set her cup on the counter.

"Do you want to kiss me?"

Brent nearly choked on his muffin.

"Wh-what?"

"I've seen the way you look at me," she said, meeting his eyes, no shyness now.

Brent was surprised. Part of him wondered if he was still dreaming. If so, he hoped he wasn't about to wake up.

"How do I look at you?"

"Sad," she said. "But sweet."

His mind was racing with a dozen things to say. But his erection told him to shut the hell up and *just act.*

He put the rest of his muffin on the table, licked his teeth to make sure they weren't coated, and swallowed. Then he stepped forward.

Brent paused a foot away from Teagan and realized he was visibly shaking. At least it seemed that way; he couldn't look at anything but her eyes.

Teagan threw herself at Brent, devouring his mouth with hers, with a hunger that matched (and maybe swallowed) his own.

They stumbled out of the kitchen and into the living room, tangled, kissing, hands running over one another's bodies.

He guided her toward the couch, and she fell back, legs spread, waiting.

He fell on top of her, hands reaching up her shirt, practically pawing at her soft, supple breasts.

Teagan moaned, hands reaching down into his shorts, grabbing his cock, pulling it out.

He reached down, breathlessly, pulling her underwear aside, feeling her wetness on his fingertips. She guided him inside her. Her warmth made him feel more alive than he'd felt in forever.

Oh, God, don't cum, don't cum, don't cum.

Brent lasted less than twenty seconds.

He thrust, trying to deliver an orgasm before he went soft. She wrapped her legs around his waist and pulled him closer, deeper into her.

He kept thrusting then realized it was a lost cause. Desperate to pleasure her, Brent reached down and finished Teagan with his fingers.

Afterwards, they lay on the couch in a sweaty heap, and he felt like he was surfacing from a daze.

Did we just really do this?

Why did she want to fuck me? Does she really like me?

Brent didn't dare voice his thoughts, the creeping doubts about his sexual prowess. He'd been married so long that he'd forgotten how awkward he'd once been with women. He'd said, and done, enough stupid things in the past to ruin the postcoital mood, displaying insecurities, wondering if they were now a couple — and a million other things that had felt foolish once he was married.

But now those awkward feelings were racing back, and Brent felt like a stupid teenager all over again. He decided to just enjoy the moment for what it was, hoping maybe it would happen again.

Neither of them spoke, lying in silence together until a scream shattered their moment.

~

THREE

Mary Olson

Mary woke shivering, surrounded by black.

She was cold, confused, unable to remember anything but her name.

Where am I?

Fear was copper on her tongue. She reached into the darkness. Her fingers touched cold, wet grass, and the world was slowly lit as if someone were turning a dimmer above.

She looked up to see the full moon peeking out from behind dark clouds gliding through the sky. The world was bathed in a milky-blue luminescence, revealing something that seemed unreal — two rows of thick, ancient trees on either side, carving a neatly sculpted path of tall grass in front and behind her.

Again, Mary wondered where she was.

She looked ahead and behind, both paths identical, not knowing which way to go.

Her head buzzed, sounds of something she couldn't quite decipher swirling beneath a high-pitched ringing. She reached up to cover her ears.

Moving hurt.

Her body ached, though she saw no signs of injury.

Mary was wearing jeans and a dark sweater, clothes she couldn't remember owning.

Confused, she moved forward, her back and legs aching with every step. The ringing in her ears faded, though the whispers — perhaps fragments of memory — remained. She tried to focus but couldn't make out anything other than a male voice, his words muffled as if underwater.

She continued forward and noticed something ahead: small and red, almost glowing in the grass.

Confused, she picked up her pace then stopped in front of the small glowing object. She bent to retrieve it: a red rose petal, bleeding with a luminous amber light, fading to black as her fingers rubbed the soft, silky texture.

The petal blackened, and the rose disintegrated, so fast that Mary feared its undoing would spread to her hand and render her into nothingness.

She was about to turn back and head in the other direction when she saw more petals ahead, all lighting at once, illuminating the path.

She had to be dreaming.

Yet this didn't *feel* like a dream. The cold air pocked her with gooseflesh. The gentle breeze rattled tree limbs. Somewhere in the distance, she heard a new sound — *a train?*

Mary kept moving, faster now. Each petal disintegrated when she reached it, charred embers lifting then getting carried off on the wind in every direction.

This must be a dream.

Ahead, the path narrowed until it closed in on itself. A voice called out in the dark.

"Mommy?"

Paola?

Mary remembered her daughter, shot dead before her eyes.

More memories flooded her mind, but Mary ignored them, clinging to the image of Paola.

Maybe she's not dead. Maybe she brought me to this place. Maybe there's some part of her still alive!

Mary shoved herself forward, following the trail of petals into the darkness.

The train raged behind her, so loud they must be sharing a path.

Mary broke into a run, ignoring her aching body and buzzing head, along with the branches scratching and scraping her skin. The path closed in around her.

The train screamed behind her. Then Mary recognized the sound: a tornado, not a train.

A flash of memory raced through her mind, too fast to grasp or make sense of before it was gone. Another deadly tornado — on that other world.

She looked back and wished she hadn't. Everything behind her was coming apart — like the petals — remnants cast in every direction.

The path had sealed ahead of her, giving way to an endless tangle of brambles.

The red petals had vanished, but Mary couldn't turn back. Whatever was ripping the world to pieces was growing closer and louder, eager to catch her. The only way was forward, through the sharp brambles.

"Mommy!" Paola's voice cried out, scared, from somewhere ahead.

"I'm coming!" Mary screamed.

She closed her eyes and threw her arms forward, pushing the branches aside, suffering cuts like she were barreling through a field of razor wire.

The roar behind her sounded like it was whipping repeatedly at chunks of earth. With the sound, she felt tremors underfoot, convinced that the ground would split open and claim her.

The wind assaulted her from all sides, and branches thrashed violently, lashing and lacerating her flesh.

She cried out from the pain.

Mary opened her mouth and felt chunks of the world ripped up and carried away. Clumps of dirt, grass, and rock forced their way down her throat, threatening to choke her as she struggled to spit.

The sound grew louder, swelling with a pressure that supplanted every sense except pain.

With nothing to hold her, Mary was moments from lifting off and getting carried away by the sky.

Then it happened.

Mary felt her body lift, slowly at first, then with great speed, racing upward at an angle so fast, she was certain she'd smash into something — if there was anything left of the world — and get splattered by the force in an instant. Just like that, she'd be as undone as the petals and earth.

Mary reached out as if doing so could somehow control her flight, that she could manage and maybe slow her elliptical vortex. Shards of debris lacerated her body for the effort.

Her head was thrumming, dizzy. She couldn't tell which way was up as she spun through the night sky. She wanted to look around, to gather some sense of where she was and where she was going. How near she was to the ground, if there was something she might be able to grab. Maybe she'd see Paola. Could reach her. Be with her again, as impossible as it seemed.

She didn't dare open her eyes; she'd lose them forever if she tried, and maybe find herself a half mile in the sky. Like in those old Roadrunner cartoons, she'd plummet to nothing the second she saw reality for what it was.

As if reading her mind, the tornado stopped.

So did everything else.

And there was nothing but silence.

Mary fell but never hit the ground.

She found herself standing in the darkness, looking

around, amazed by the world — empty except for an impossibly smooth dark soil surface.

Where's all the debris?

Where's Paola?

"Paola?"

Mary was filled with an ominous chill while standing among the nothing. The world was wrong, and she was desperate to know why.

She saw movement in the distance — a tree. One sole tree, giant, with hundreds of skeletal branches dotted by surreal, luminous red roses. It was the most beautiful thing she'd ever seen.

Something hit her head, hard.

Mary reached up, feeling a giant knot rising under her scalp, certain she was bleeding.

What the hell hit me?

She looked down and saw a small rock.

Where did that come from?

Another fell, maybe six feet away.

And then another.

Mary looked up. Her heart stopped as she saw that everything the cyclone had ripped from the ground was hundreds of feet above in one giant mass, falling fast.

She screamed, then ran.

Mary didn't get far before the earth fell and buried her alive.

And now she was farther from Paola.

MARY WOKE TO A MUFFLED SOUND, a familiar voice saying her name.

She remembered the Black Guardsmen raiding their hiding spot. The bomb going off.

She opened her eyes, surprised to be alive.

Luca's face swam into focus. Behind him, light seeped through an apartment window.

She still couldn't get used to seeing him so old, now looking like he was in his late fifties. The healing had taken its toll. And he'd just used it to bring her back, just when she'd been so close to being with Paola again.

She sat up, surprised that her body no longer hurt. Even her headache was gone. But there was still a pain deep in her soul, an ache that even Luca couldn't heal.

She looked up at him then at Boricio, Ed, and Jake Barrow all standing and waiting for her to return like Lazarus.

Mary looked at Luca again. Poor Luca. He looked like he'd aged five years, if not more, his hair gone completely gray, the lines in his face a bit deeper.

"Why did you do it?" she asked, her voice cracking.

"What?" he asked, his kind eyes wide and confused.

"Why did you bring me back?"

Luca stared at her, as if he couldn't believe her question.

"Are you okay?" Boricio asked.

"No!" she shouted, getting to her feet.

Dizziness overwhelmed Mary and sent her stumbling forward.

Boricio and Ed reached out to break her fall.

Mary found her feet then swiped at their hands, eager to be away from them.

"Leave me alone!" She turned around, finding the unfamiliar apartment's front door. She opened it then rushed through and into the hallway.

"Mary!" Boricio cried out.

Mary kept running.

∼

FOUR

Boricio Wolfe

Boricio and Keenan traded looks of confusion as Mary left the apartment.

"What the hell?" Boricio said to himself.

Luca, surprisingly, had the only response. "It's Paola."

"What?" Boricio asked.

"Mary heard her while she was dying and didn't want to come back."

Boricio wanted to ask what in the devil's dick that even meant, but he knew he didn't have long if he wanted to catch up with Mary. They were in a new apartment, one she hadn't been to before, surrounded by unfamiliar territory until they could reconnect with others in The Resistance.

He raced out the door and into the hallway, hoping she would just be outside, pissed, maybe sucking on a nicotine titty.

But she wasn't anywhere to be seen.

"Fuck!" Boricio turned back to the apartment. "Keenan, Barrow, I need some help!"

Three seconds later, Boricio was directing Barrow to start searching apartments on this floor, Keenan to head upstairs. He'd take the bottom floor.

"Wait for me!" Luca called out, grabbing his machete and strapping it to his belt.

"Dude, you stay put." Protecting Luca was their prime fucking directive. He wasn't just a healer. Luca was connected to the aliens, could warn his friends when he felt them near, and had thus far shielded them from discovery. Without Luca, they wouldn't have had any of their successes killing squads of Guardsmen, sabotaging known alien outposts in The City, or finding new people for The Resistance.

"I might be able to find her." Luca tapped his head with his index finger.

"Ah, right, I forgot." Boricio hadn't forgotten but knew Luca's skills were declining. Moving them from one world to another, and healing all the people he'd been healing, had beaten his body like a drum, turning him into an antique over the last several years. Additionally, the boy-turned-old-man seemed to look older every morning he woke up.

But fuck it, he was out here. May as well use his powers. "Okay, put that detector to work."

Luca closed his eyes and focused. He looked down. "She's downstairs. Heading for the street."

"Try and keep up." Boricio bolted toward the stairs and took them two then three at a time, six flights to the bottom.

The old kid couldn't keep up, but Boricio figured if he were fast enough, he'd end the search before Luca made it downstairs anyway.

Boricio raced out into the street, into the bright morning light, and looked around, searching for any sign of Miss Mary Quite Contrary. The street was lined with apartment buildings, many climbing ten stories or higher. She could easily squirrel away in any one, which was why they'd picked Las Orillas to hide in.

Mary appeared in the doorway of an apartment building just up the road. Boricio sighed with relief.

She started walking toward him, her eyes on the ground,

avoiding his gaze. She reached him and stopped, still not looking up.

"What's wrong, Mary?"

"Nothing." She looked up and met Boricio's eyes, not a trace of tears or any expression.

"You storm out like a redneck at a gay pride parade and expect me to buy 'nothin'? Come the fuck on, Mary. Boricio knows when there's bullshit in his burrito."

Boricio heard Luca on the radio behind him, telling the others that they'd found Mary.

"I don't want to talk about it," Mary said, "okay?"

Boricio considered telling her tough titties and soaking-wet tacos, but he already knew why she was upset. Luca said it was Paola. But if Boricio said he knew what was bothering her, she'd get at Luca for pokin' in her head. No point in having Mary mad at the Boy Wonder, too. And hell, who was he to say she couldn't keep her sorrow a secret? It wasn't like he didn't have his own demons to battle sunup to sundown. But Mary had made those battles less intense, even if she didn't know it. He wished he could do the same for her — murder the pain that was eating her up.

It had been four years since Paola had died. How long was she going to keep blaming herself?

Boricio's radio beeped, followed by Lisa's voice. "Hey, I've got a hot package, and I need to know where to drop it."

"How hot?" Keenan answered before Boricio could.

"Hotter than hell."

∼

FIVE

Paul Roberts

The Island
 Earlier that day

PAUL WOKE to the smell of bacon and eggs, smiling at Emily's predictability. Today was her scheduled field trip into The Wastelands — The City he'd grown up in — and Paul still hadn't decided whether she could go. This was her way of buttering him up.

He got out of bed, went into the bathroom and showered, dressed in shorts and a black tee, and came out to the kitchen where his twelve-year-old daughter was sitting at the kitchen table, waiting for him, smile wide, green eyes beaming from beneath her thick brown curls.

"Ah, you made breakfast today? What a *spontaneous* treat!"

Emily said nothing, probably wondering if he was on to her and being sarcastic. He felt her attempting to worm inside his mind. Her telepathic skills had improved significantly over the past year, but she was nowhere near experienced enough to probe his mind ... yet. Paul pushed back, gently, and noticed her wince, probably unaware that he'd built a psychic wall. From Emily's perspective, it probably felt like a mild migraine.

Paul was waiting for Emily to tell him about her newfound abilities. He didn't want to let her know he already knew. For some reason, he felt it was better to let Emily feel things out for herself without his interference. She was at the age where any idea originating with him was met with natural resistance. And while he wanted to train her on how to use, and hide, her skills, the subject required a delicate approach.

Paul sat and looked at the glass of cold orange juice.

"Wow, you went all out!"

Breakfast usually consisted of either protein shakes or *maybe* toast and jam. Neither of them was a morning person, so their first meal was usually a rushed ceremony between waking and preparing for the day — him for work and her for school — then getting out the door.

"I like to cook every now and then." Emily dug her fork into her eggs and took a bite.

He grabbed a piece of bacon, bit into it. Perfectly crispy, just like he loved it.

"This is good. And so spontaneous," he repeated.

Emily met his eyes. Her smile faltered. "Okay, I get it. I know you know what I want. So, have you decided?"

"I have not."

"Great." She rolled her eyes and sighed. "Are you really gonna make me do this?"

"You know the rules."

"Why do you make me do this? I never win."

"That's because *you think* you'll never win."

"No, I *know* I'll never win. For every reasonable argument I make, you come back with three against me. How can I win any argument with *you?* It's not fair."

"What did I say about that?"

"Sorry, sir."

Paul hated the term *not fair* — the last defense of someone too lazy to try, or fight, for what they wanted.

"Why do you do this to me?" Emily's shoulders slumped, defeated already. "What's the point in teaching me to debate? Arguing may have worked in the old world, but it doesn't anymore. Not for us. We're at their mercy."

"They can be reasoned with. We're living here on The Island, aren't we? We could be scrounging around in The Wastelands. If I couldn't argue and reason, I — " Paul thought of how desperately close they'd been to death when Desmond found them, " — well, we wouldn't be here. No whining. Tell me why you should be able to go."

"Fine." Emily sat up, her eyes determined and lips pursed. The expression, the fire in her eyes, reminded Paul so much of Jane. "I should go on the trip so I can see where I came from. Because I don't have many memories before the aliens."

"Okay, but what's left of The Wastelands isn't remotely close to the world you were born in. Many of the homes and buildings are rubble. What the aliens didn't shoot down with their lasers, humans destroyed in the aftermath. Those buildings that *are* still standing house freaks, bandits, and God knows what other monstrosities. It's impossible to see what's no longer there."

"I can't give you a logical reason that'll make sense to you. I just feel like I need to see where I came from."

"That's an emotional reason not a logical one. Emotional reasons aren't valid, Emily. But emotions can be a liability, putting you in danger if you don't master them. Far better to be in control of one's feelings than to need outside stimuli or validation. Master your emotions, and you can master others who are still enslaved by their own."

If she were ever going to develop her telepathic gifts, she'd need a framework to put them to good use. Persuading people, or controlling them, was nearly impossible if you didn't understand what made people tick. And part of that understanding was mastering emotions, hers and others'.

"Ugh." Emily rolled her eyes. "Fine. Then I should be allowed to go because I can only learn so much from books and video. I need to observe these freaks, bandits, and monstrosities firsthand to develop a working knowledge. Aren't you always saying that knowledge is power?"

"Fair enough. Counterpoint: The working *knowledge* you'll gain on this trip will be of dubious value at best. It's not as if you'll be on the ground. You'll be in a shuttle, flying high above The Wastelands."

"Yes, but with the equipment onboard, I'm sure I'll be able to zoom in and get bio readings on-screen, a lot more than I can get from books."

"Agreed." Paul nodded. "But I have to ask, why do you want to go so badly? Why are they even having this trip? The Wastelands are the past. This Island is the present and future. Why do you care so much about yesterday?"

"I told you that Mr. Pace is testing field aptitude to see who should be filtered into working in The Wastelands."

"Is *that* what you want? To work in The Wastelands?" The idea of his daughter out there working at the slaughterhouse, factory, or farms the aliens maintained in The Wastelands terrified Paul to the bone. He'd sacrificed everything — had done horrible, unspeakable things for the aliens — to keep them safe on The Island. Not that she knew all the things his job required. She knew that he helped transition aliens into the bodies of hosts. She thought the humans were willing participants in this process. She didn't know to what extent he went to break down the hosts to make them malleable enough to be suitable for the aliens to live in. Or that 12.8 percent of the people he transitioned wound up having to be put down when the migration didn't take.

She shrugged. "I dunno, maybe I want to be out there."

"Why? You have everything taken care of here. You want for nothing. Why would you want to be ... *out there?*"

She looked down at her plate, shaking her head.

"What is it?"

She sniffled, titling her face down so he couldn't see her crying beneath her hair.

"What's wrong, honey?"

"I don't like it here."

Now it was Paul who was rolling *his* eyes. He didn't feel like having *this* argument again.

"Do we have any other options? Is there anywhere left in the world where we would have it this good?"

"No, sir," she said, still avoiding his eyes.

"So, what's the point? Do you think it's *better* out there? Out in The Wastelands?"

"At least we'd be with our own kind — not living with the *things* that killed us. That killed Mom!"

"I don't know what you *think* is out there. It's not like there's people living life like they used to live. Humanity's broken, Em. It's nothing but people killing one another, bandits and rape gangs, survival of the fittest. Even those who manage to make it still have to look out for the Ferals."

The Ferals were the aliens that Desmond had brought with him prior to the invasion, a species designed to wipe out the humans before the Pruhm arrived. Once, the Ferals had been under his complete and utter control. Lately, though, for some unknown and mysterious reason, Desmond was losing contact and control with the aliens. The Ferals were just as likely to attack humans as they were Guardsmen in The Wastelands.

"You don't know that The Wastelands are like that. Maybe that's just what the aliens here want us to think. Humans could've come back."

The look in her eye, that glimmer of hope that there might be a paradise waiting, was too much for him to crush.

Better for Emily to see for herself. Then maybe she'd be more realistic in her expectations.

"Fine," Paul said. "Go on your trip. I think it'll open your eyes and make you appreciate what you have."

"Thank you." She sipped her juice, still not meeting his eyes.

"Please, Emily, don't ever talk like this, not being happy here, around them. Do you understand me?"

"Yes, sir."

"I'm serious. In fact, don't talk like this, period. You can't trust anyone other than me. Do you understand?"

Emily finally looked up at him, eyes still wet. Then she sliced him with his words. "Can't trust anyone other than you in this island paradise. Gotchya."

Emily stood from the table, having barely touched her food, and went to her room to finish getting ready for school.

Paul stared at his plate, his appetite gone.

Emily was right. Paul hated living among the fuckers as much as anyone. But there were no other options. Even if his boss allowed him to leave — which Paul highly doubted — it wasn't as if they'd last five minutes in The Wastelands, where only death waited.

Yes, he had to compromise his beliefs, but morals meant nothing next to protecting his daughter. He would do anything to keep her safe. They had creature comforts — good food, running water, housing, medical care, and even entertainment by way of old sitcoms the aliens ran 24/7 on one of their two TV stations broadcast on The Island and in two sectors of The City occupied by blue collar humans and hybrids.

Emily was too young to remember the aliens' arrival. How bad things had got, how sick she'd become. Yes, she remembered the plague killing her mother. But Emily never knew the struggle of daily survival. It was Paul's job to ensure she never did.

His communicator rang on the kitchen counter.

Paul stood, went to the kitchen, and looked at the screen. Desmond rarely called him at home.

"Hello?"

"Where are you?"

"Home. Why? What's wrong?"

"Get here. Now!" Desmond hung up.

Sickness crept into Paul's gut. Something told him today was a horror waiting to happen.

~

SIX

Brent Foster

The scream came from outside.

Brent raced to the living room, Teagan by his side. He grabbed a shotgun from one of the gun racks then ran to the front window, looking out. Teagan grabbed a gun, too.

The front yard was pitch black. Brent shook his head at Teagan as she went to one of the side windows. She looked and shook her head, too.

"I'll check the back," she said.

Another scream, definitely coming from out front. Teagan stopped in her tracks — the house was alive with movement as Joe, Marilyn, and Peter descended the stairs. Marina charged behind them, pistol in hand, as if it had been under her pillow.

"What the hell was that?" said Joe, a forty-five-year-old former mechanic, and The Farm's de facto leader.

Still at the window, Brent said, "Something out front. I can't see anything."

Joe grabbed a rifle from the gun rack. "Brent, Marilyn, come with me. Peter, you stay back and protect the others in case this shit gets out of hand."

Peter, a young blond in his early twenties, nodded his head and grabbed a shotgun.

Upstairs, the kids started crying, though Brent couldn't tell for sure if Ben was among them. There were four other kids on The Farm besides him and Becca.

"I'll settle the kids down," Teagan said then headed upstairs, gun still in hand.

Joe headed toward the front door, rifle raised.

Brent and Marilyn, a fifty-one-year-old trucker before shit hit the fan, followed behind.

More screaming. "Open the door!"

Brent recognized the voice: Otis, the man guarding the front gate.

"It's Otis!" he said.

Brent's gut soured with panic, imagining the scenario leading to the front guard screaming for help. Were aliens about to overrun the place? Had bandits found them?

Joe, as if thinking the same thing, turned back to the room, now filled with nearly everyone in the house, save for the children and Teagan. "Everyone get a weapon and prepare for the worst."

Brent wished he could be upstairs with Ben, Teagan, and Becca. They were the only ones he truly gave a damn about. He had other friends, but going through hell together made you family. He moistened his lips, swallowed hard, and focused. He had to defend the house, and his family, from whatever waited in the dark.

Joe opened the door.

Otis stumbled forward holding his left arm, mangled from midway down. His bloody stump of a hand hung by sinewy threads. His face was shredded, blood coating the front of his shirt and pants. He looked as if he'd been mauled by a wild animal, maybe a wolf.

The wolf I heard earlier?

"What happened?" Marilyn helped him up the steps and onto the porch.

Joe scanned the darkness with his rifle, searching for enemies.

"A wolf, or … something on the property."

Marilyn brought Otis inside, laid him on the floor, and called out to Tomas, who'd been a nurse in training, to help stop the bleeding.

The household teetered somewhere between concern for Otis and fear of whatever the hell had attacked him.

Joe closed the front door, locked it, and came back to Otis. "Are you sure it wasn't an alien?"

"No, I … don't think so," Otis said through deep breaths as Tomas tied the man's arm off with straps to prevent further blood loss. Marilyn dropped beside him to help hold Otis down for what was next. "It was a wolf … a giant fucking wolf, but a wolf."

"I ain't seen wolves this brazen before," Joe said.

"Wasn't no regular wolf." Otis screamed and bucked against Marilyn's weight as Tomas started to saw at what little was still connecting the man to his hand. Brent had to look away, but doing so didn't prevent him from hearing the agony as Otis cried out.

"What do we do?" Brent asked.

"Well, if we wait until morning, that thing might eat our livestock."

Brent was afraid he'd say that.

Joe looked around the room. "Who wants to hunt a wolf?"

Three others, including Marina, raised their hands. Joe looked at Brent. "You coming?"

Brent wanted to say no then head upstairs and comfort his son, let him know his world would be okay. It was only a wolf, not aliens or bandits or anything worse. But at the same time, Brent wasn't sure if four people were enough to take down a wolf that had maimed Otis so badly. The man was tough, and quick on the draw. It was the reason he was on guard duty at night, patrolling The Farm. If the wolf had got the drop on him, what hope did the others have?

Brent nodded: the more hunters, the better their odds.

He turned to Marina. "Can you stay here?"

"What?" she said, as if insulted.

He met Marina's eyes and lowered his voice so only she could hear him. "I'd feel better if you were here to protect Ben."

Her eyes said she knew. Marina nodded.

Brent said, "Please let them know I'll be back soon."

"Of course."

He hoped he hadn't asked her to lie.

THE NIGHT WAS EERILY quiet in a way that was new to this world.

When the aliens had killed this planet, the sounds of wildlife were among the first to feel familiar. Without man and his machines drowning everything out, nature took over and held center stage. Insects, birds, wolves, foxes, deer, elk, and countless species added their song to the symphony. Brent had grown decent at picking out one animal from another, a skill he'd never have gathered while living the rest of his life in Manhattan.

Now he heard nothing, and nothing felt wrong.

"Anyone else notice it?" he whispered. The five of them crept through the amber-lit darkness behind the light on Joe's rifle.

"Notice what?" Peter asked.

"The silence."

Joe said, "I don't like it one fuckin' bit."

"What do you think it means?" Sammy said, clearly spooked. Sammy was an Italian giant, who'd worked sanitation before the aliens came. They liked to joke around and say he was in the Mob, and he clearly looked like he could have been — big and pudgy, late forties, tough. While he was a killer shot on the range, and had already taken down a few people who'd tried to fuck with them, Sammy was a teddy bear with the kids.

Brent had never heard him afraid — until now.

Something moved to their right.

Brent turned, his shotgun searching, finger pressed to the trigger.

Joe turned his light to help, but Brent saw mostly darkness. The moon was concealed behind dark clouds with no break in sight.

The aliens destroying most of the power had darkened the night's usual artificial glow. Usually, Brent liked it — without light pollution, the night sky teased a billion stars.

But even that comfort had its downside. Now that they knew what forces had come from some far-off galaxy, intent on consuming humanity, the stars were no longer a comfort. They made Brent feel occasionally claustrophobic, on display, as if one of the many scouting ships would find and seize them.

Many people had been taken over the years.

Those who had been lucky enough to survive the plague soon found themselves hunted by alien ships, picked up and brought to the only part of the world — so far as Brent knew — with running water and power, a modest-sized island twenty or so miles off the coast of Las Orillas. The people were enslaved, forced to work for the aliens on The Island and at a few spots in The City. It seemed as if the aliens were trying to rebuild society, but only in a space of The Island's seventy-four square miles, while the rest of the world was left to nature, plague, and barbarism.

Fortunately, scouting ships rarely came this far north, and when they did, they were as loud as jets, so if you were halfway paying attention, and had cover, you could escape detection.

A wolf howled in the distance, and Brent looked to see everyone jump, frantically scanning the darkness with their guns.

Brent supposed he shouldn't be surprised that they were now being hunted by wolves. He'd seen a few large wolves on the other world. He'd assumed they'd somehow mutated, but maybe they'd always been there, hiding from humans in the woodlands, unseen, undetected, waiting to reclaim their world.

Something moved behind them.

Peter turned and fired.

More shots, this time from Sammy.

Joe scanned the darkness with his light but illuminated nothing other than grass, rocks, and trees beyond the tall wooden fence surrounding their compound.

Because Brent couldn't see what the hell they were firing at, he held back, not wanting to waste ammo, or get stuck empty and needing to reload as the wolf came right at him.

"Did you hit anything?" Joe asked, also holding back.

"I don't think so." Peter moved forward into the amber light, looking almost otherworldly as he searched for signs of whatever had moved.

Brent watched, certain the man would be swallowed by alien Darkness — before The Darkness came for them all.

Stop it. There are no bleakers, as Mary and others called the black aliens here. We haven't seen any in more than a year. They're all in the cities, with all the people.

From the property's rear, cows mooed in distress.

Joe led the way as the five men went to the fenced-off area where their last three cows grazed. He flashed the light around, searching for signs of the wolf.

"Holy shit!" Joe hopped over the front gate and started running toward the field's center. His gun and its amber light were aimed at the sky, so Brent and the others couldn't see what he had.

They followed, guns ready.

Brent was out of breath when Joe finally stopped about a hundred yards from the front gate. He caught up to Joe flashing the light over what was clearly a corpse in the field's center.

Brent looked down and saw the impossible — a dead man. Not just any dead man, but Otis.

Joe looked up and met Brent's eyes.

Peter said what they were both thinking. "If Otis is out here, who the hell is that inside?"

"Not who," Brent said. "*What.*"

SEVEN

Teagan McLachlan

Teagan was upstairs in the dark bedroom, lying in Brent's bed with the kids, trying to get them back to sleep. Becca was already drifting off; Ben was fighting to stay awake until his father returned.

They'd been gone fifteen minutes or so, and everyone else in the house was abuzz downstairs. It wasn't helping Teagan, but at least the screaming had stopped. And the other kids had either gone to sleep or downstairs to be with adults.

"When's Dad going to be back?" Ben asked.

"Soon, sweetie." Teagan ran her hand over his forehead and through his thick hair. She often played with Becca's hair to help her relax — it was worth trying with Ben.

The boy's eyes seemed to gain weight as Teagan teased his dark hair through her fingers.

She thought about her encounter with Brent. She wasn't sure what had come over her the past few months, but she'd developed a strong attraction to him — even though he wasn't really her type.

Truth was, Teagan wasn't sure *what* her type was. She'd never been in love, though she'd felt something close with the Ed Keenan from the other world. She wasn't sure if that was because *this world's* Ed had saved her and been so protective, or if it was some need for positive attention she'd never felt from her father. After the other Ed's death, she never even attempted to connect with this world's double. He felt more like a father. Plus, she'd become close friends, almost like sisters, with Jade before her death, so it never seemed right.

This thing with Brent seemed out of the blue. Teagan had always thought he was nice, but she'd never looked at him *that way*.

Sudden lust had sneaked up on her one day when they'd been out eating with the kids under the shade of an oak. He'd melted her heart — something in Brent's smile and the way he looked at his son with such love and affection. It made her want to get closer and cobble some sort of family together. It also made her imagine their bodies pressed together. Maybe she was getting baby fever.

Like the world needs another baby now!

She'd fought it at first — there was no point in changing what was already working. They were finally in a place where things were sort of okay, and they could have a chance at not just survival but something resembling a normal life in a solar-powered house and a fully working farm. This was as close to paradise as there was these days. And the group generally got along. What more could you ask for?

Why risk things? If their relationship went south, it wasn't like Teagan could move. She'd still have to see him every day.

Yet the more senseless it seemed to pursue the relationship, the more she wanted him.

She'd noticed a couple of weeks ago that he tended to wake in the middle of the night and would hang out in the kitchen a bit before returning to his room. Tonight, she'd decided to wait and seduce him.

Putting the moves on Brent, Teagan felt silly and awkward, afraid he'd laugh at her.

Then they'd kissed, and everything had changed.

All her wrong thoughts felt suddenly right. She craved him inside her, even if it meant another child. And despite his awkwardness, he was an animal sexually. Though the event was over way too quickly, she could still feel his lust.

Now, as she lay with the kids in her bed, she wondered if she was being ridiculous to wish for a family. Wondered why she even wanted to try. It wasn't as if *her parents* had been happy or showed her how to be a good parent or partner. Then she thought about him cumming too soon, and inside her.

Shit.

Maybe it's all a disaster waiting to happen.

Just as she started to feel stupid again, a scream came from downstairs. At first, she thought it was Otis in pain again. But it wasn't his scream.

And it wasn't just one person screaming.

Teagan heard a sound she'd hoped to go a lifetime without hearing again — the horrible clicking of an alien — downstairs.

❧

Brent Foster

The front door to the main house was wide open when they reached it.

Brent counted six bodies on the front porch and lawn, eviscerated as they attempted to escape. One of them a child, a small girl named Catherine.

Brent shook his head and broke into a jog toward the front door, shotgun in hand, eager to find the monster that did this, and even more eager to make sure the others — Ben, Teagan, Becca, and Marina — were safe.

He crossed the threshold, with Joe and the others behind him, stopping dead in his tracks at the sight of more bodies littering the living room.

It was a massacre.

His eyes could hardly move fast enough over the bodies, identifying the dead, praying his own weren't among them.

Brent saw movement in the corner of his eyes and raised his gun. He realized it wasn't an alien before he could fire. It was Marina, sitting at the bottom of the steps, blood soaked from head to toe, clutching a bloody machete.

Beneath her, on the floor, was the thing that had been Otis, hacked into pieces of flesh, black wet tendrils still flopping reflexively on the wooden floorboards. Otis hadn't just been hacked, his body had been demolished.

Brent tried to imagine that sort of rage coursing through Marina. She'd always seemed so calm and collected. Marina stood, meeting his eyes. She looked like she'd been through hell and back before ending the alien.

Oh, God, please don't tell me they're dead. Please.

He opened his mouth, but no words could leave it. He couldn't ask the question out of fear for the answer.

"They're okay," Marina said.

"Who?"

"Your son, Teagan, and Becca."

Brent sighed, holding his tears.

Behind him, Joe said, "Is anyone else alive?"

Marina shook her head.

Joe fell to his knees, sobbing. Though none of the dead were his family, he'd formed strong bonds with most of the people at The Farm.

Peter and Sammy were silent, staring at the carnage.

Brent raced upstairs to his bedroom door and found it locked. Chunks of alien flesh sat in black blood all over the floor outside the door and leading down the stairs. The fight had come up here.

He banged on the door. "Teagan?"

Seconds later, she opened the door, tears in her eyes. Ben and Becca were in bed, covers pulled up to their chins, crying.

Ben jumped off the bed, running to Brent and leaping into his arms.

"Daddy, you're okay!"

"Yes, buddy, I am." Brent kissed his son's head over and over, squeezing him tight, thanking God that his son, and Teagan and Becca, were alive.

They didn't have a scratch.

Teagan moved closer and hugged both him and Ben. Becca climbed off the bed and joined.

"How?" he asked. "How did you all survive?"

"Marina. She somehow fought the thing off. I heard her right outside our door, and I tried to go out to help, to make sure it didn't get in here, but she shoved me back inside the room and finished it off."

Teagan's voice cracked. "I was so afraid."

Brent continued to hug them then finally broke the embraces and said he'd be right back. He had to take care of something downstairs.

"Don't go, Dad!" Ben threw his arms around Brent's waist.

"I'll be right back. The monster is dead, don't worry. I just want to thank Marina."

Teagan pulled Ben back into bed. Brent made a break for the door and closed it softly behind him.

He went downstairs where Marina was still standing in a daze while Joe, Peter, and Sammy walked around and surveyed the dead.

He met Marina's eyes. She wasn't staring at, so much as through, him.

"Thank you."

Marina nodded. Brent expected her to make some joke or mention how he was lucky he asked her to stay behind, but she said nothing. She merely nodded, staring through him, white knuckling the machete as if the alien might return to life at any moment.

He reached down to take her machete. She flinched and tightened her grip.

"It's okay," he said softly. "It's dead."

Marina relaxed her grip and let go.

He would have to ask Teagan to lead her to the bathroom so she could wash up, but first he needed to talk with Joe and the others.

He set Marina's machete against the wall. She stayed

standing, staring at nothing. He went to Joe and the others. "What do we do now?"

Joe's eyes were still wet.

"What do you mean?" He looked around at the bodies. "What *can* we do? They're all dead!"

"No, *we're not* all dead. And we need to consider that this wasn't a random attack. An alien posed as Otis! More could be coming. We can't stay here."

"You're right," Joe said. "We need to get to the backup site."

"That's not all," Brent said.

Peter and Sammy came over.

"Whadya mean that's not all?" Sammy asked.

"This." Brent pointed at Otis. "We've never seen anything like this before. The aliens aren't just invading people's bodies. They're changing their shapes — to look like us! We need to tell the others."

"You know the radios don't transmit that far north," Joe said.

"I know. Someone has to go tell them."

Joe shook his head. "I can't even think straight."

"I'll go," Sammy volunteered.

"Me, too," Peter said. "What about you, Brent?"

He didn't know what to say. Brent could only think about Ben, Teagan, Becca, and a devastated Marina at the bottom of the stairs.

~

NINE

Paul Roberts

Paul's stomach did summersaults as the tri-winged shuttle left The Island, ascending to the giant mothership floating overhead.

The shuttle's cabin was the size of a large cargo van, with seating for ten. But Paul was alone, save for the Guardsman sitting across from him dressed in all black with a mirrored black helmet.

He considered trying to read the man's thoughts but didn't know if he was human or host. If he were a host, then the alien might detect Paul's probing, which would give the aliens reasons for suspicion if they didn't have any already.

While a Guardsman always accompanied Paul to the mothership, his presence today was particularly intimidating. Paul couldn't help but wonder why Desmond had called for him so urgently. What had he discovered? Paul had been cautious to keep his anti-alien thoughts to himself, but what if one of the aliens had somehow found his true feelings? He wondered if Desmond had heard Emily's complaints. Or maybe she'd grumbled to someone already, before he told her to keep her dissatisfaction to herself. The aliens didn't tolerate dissension. You were either with their program or against it.

Speaking or acting out against them led to one of two things: excommunication to The Wastelands or — Paul shuddered — a forced hosting.

The idea of them using him, or *God forbid* Emily, as hosts for one of the aliens chilled him to the core. Paul would sooner die than "become one" with their species, as Desmond referred to the process.

They'd been fortunate to be among the free humans allowed to live on The Island. But they were only free because Desmond valued Paul's contributions to their program. The moment his contributions ceased to matter or were outweighed by some other thing — such as Emily's preteen rebellion — they would no longer be of value, no better than the humans stockpiled in Warehouse 11 waiting to be hosts.

The shuttle docked in one of the mothership's many bottom decks. Paul's stomach continued to churn.

The shuttle door opened. Paul stepped out, trying not to show his nerves, and followed the Guardsman through the spacious gray, dingy bay, past the control room, and to the elevators leading to the upper levels.

The entire mothership was a technological marvel made by a species thousands, if not hundreds of thousands, of years more advanced than humans. It was surprisingly similar to human engineering, from lighting to elevators to the bays and the rooms' basic layouts. But a part of Paul wondered if this was by design, appealing to the humans who worked on the ship, to soften assimilation. The ship's upper levels, where Paul had sometimes occasion to go, were quite different — metal walls were replaced with black organic tissue not unlike the Ferals, replete with the selvion lights beneath their skin.

The elevator opened to the command center where he and Desmond usually met, a circular room with a long dark glass table and several large paper-thin monitors lining the walls. The monitors showed video feeds coming from the many shuttles scouring The Wastelands, along with security footage from some of the factories and warehouses aliens maintained in The City.

Desmond was seated at the table's head. Beside him was Wasterman, his second in command, a broad-shouldered tall man in his fifties with sunken dark eyes, gray hair, and a wide nose. Paul was never certain if the man was among the free humans or host to one of the aliens. The man barely uttered a word, ever, and always looked like he was contemplating the many ways he could kill the closest man, woman, or child. A stark contrast to Desmond's charisma.

"Have a seat." Desmond pointed to Paul's usual chair, which seemed a half mile away on the other side of the long conference table.

Paul sat. He felt Wasterman watching him, scrutinizing Paul's every move.

What do they know?

Relax. If they knew anything, I wouldn't be here. I'd be carried away by The Guardsmen. I'd never see it.

If this was an ambush, Paul was unprepared. He couldn't even clear his mind of thoughts he shouldn't be having. Not only was he at their mercy, but he had no allies, nobody to protect Emily. They were on their own in enemy territory. The few free humans living on The Island were like him — too scared to fuck up a good thing.

Desmond spoke. "Have you noticed anything different about the hosts we've been bringing in lately?"

As head of processing, it was Paul's job to ensure they weeded out any humans who would make poor hosts. Rejections were too high, and constantly climbing, harming aliens who endured the psychological, and oftentimes physiological, harm that followed rejection.

"Other than the dropping lack of quality hosts, no, sir."

"And what, in your professional opinion, do you attribute that lack of quality to, Mr. Roberts?"

Paul wasn't sure if Desmond wanted the truth or a

comfortable lie that didn't lay any blame at the aliens' feet. Paul could read any human he met with an almost 99 percent certainty, but the aliens were a different story. Particularly Desmond, whose temperament was too mercurial to effectively decipher.

"Well," Paul hedged his response, "I have two theories."

"Go ahead."

Paul tried to ignore Wasterman's glare.

"Well, my first theory is that the best hosts are those who haven't experienced much trauma. But the longer these people are out there in The Wastelands, the harder it is on them. Harder it is to find pure souls, so to speak."

"Yes, we know. And we're already taking measures to counter that."

"Measures?" Paul said, surprised, wondering why this was the first he was hearing about such measures.

"Later. First, your second theory."

This was the part Desmond probably wouldn't want to hear. But Paul's value was based on shooting straight, no matter how difficult the news might be to deliver.

"I think the Ferals aren't helping the matter."

"How so?"

Discussing the aliens was a precarious affair. The Ferals were a slightly different species than the Pruhm. They were an evolutionary step beneath the aliens on the ship, killing machines ravaging anything they encountered. Even so, Paul was hesitant to suggest extermination of the Pruhm's creation, their pets, or whatever else these things were to them. His attempts to dance around such proposals before had been met with hostility from Desmond, for reasons Paul couldn't quite understand.

He'd have thought that the aliens aboard the ship would *want to* protect whatever humans were left after the plague. There were more than nine hundred aliens aboard the ship, who were known as the Pruhm, but who referred to themselves as The Eternal Ones, a conceited title if he ever heard one, waiting for a potential host. They couldn't live on Earth's surface without a host, and there was only so long the mothership could maintain a livable environment in the ship's upper decks before they started dying. It seemed to Paul that the problem of finding enough humans was starting to outweigh whatever sentimentality Desmond, or the others, held for their wild brothers.

Paul gambled with blunt honesty.

"Forgive me, sir, but the Ferals are savages, feeding on the very humans your kind needs to survive. The situation is getting worse not better. Exponentially so. And they're not interested in using the humans as hosts."

"And how would you suggest we handle this?"

Paul met Desmond's eyes.

"You need to kill them."

Desmond smirked, as if he'd led Paul down this path.

"I appreciate your honesty, Mr. Roberts. But I have a third theory. Something that I'm disappointed to find you've overlooked."

"What's that?"

"There's another influence out there, and it's spreading, infecting the humans and Ferals alike, sullying them."

"Another presence?"

"It calls itself The Light," Desmond laughed, "seeing itself in some good versus evil battle with the Ferals, or as it called us, The Darkness. But such terms as light, dark, good, evil — none of that means anything. Those are human constructs, and this … *Light* … has been tainted by the very humans it strives to *protect*."

Paul leaned forward. This was the first time he'd heard anything about Light or Darkness. And he also noticed that Desmond had referred to the Ferals as *us.* Was he one of them? "Are you saying there's another alien species out there?"

"We started to think the same. But it has been tainted, ruined. Trying to thwart our destiny for reasons I can't fathom."

"*We?* Are you saying you aren't the same, you aren't an Eternal One?" He called him that, as the Pruhm didn't like being referred to by their proper names, preferring their chosen title.

Desmond smiled. "I am not Pruhm. I am also not The Light nor The Darkness. I am something that's never been, but has always been."

Paul didn't want to say he had no fucking clue what Desmond was saying. Fortunately, he didn't need to.

"I am self-aware evolution. *We*, with the human's help, can do what all matter, what all *life*, yearns to do — realize our full potential. But in order to do that, we must work together to make it happen."

"What do you need?" Paul tried not to think about their endgame. Did a single species mean that he, and Emily, would eventually be hosts for these fuckers? Or victims of this so-called evolution, made extinct?

"We need to find this source of *Light* and extinguish it once and for all."

"How do we do that?"

"That is what I'm going to show you. It begins with a child who is no longer a child. His name is Luca Harding, and he is the biggest threat to this new world."

~

TEN

Emily Roberts

Emily pressed her face to the shuttle's right-side window, looking down at The Wastelands below.

She was surprised to find that the aliens hadn't destroyed as much of The City as she'd imagined. In the stories she'd heard, from her father and others, the aliens had come down in their ships and blasted away major capitals around the world. She'd imagined The Wastelands as nothing but smoldering piles of rubble, maybe a few buildings poking up from it.

But most of The City was actually intact. Many of the buildings were overgrown with vegetation, and some were missing entire sides, while a few leaned to the side as if a giant had started to tip them over then got distracted and walked away. Pipes had burst through some roads while other roads had huge gaping holes that went down deep into darkness. The shuttle soared overhead, sending a herd of deer racing away from what had once been a large parking lot where cars now rusted and rotted forever.

"Wow," Emily said, smiling at the sight below. Despite the destruction, there was something promising in what remained

— signs of life fighting back, reclaiming what the aliens had tried to destroy.

Sutton, one of three other students chosen for the tour, pointed at the deer and asked, "What are those?"

"Deer, I think," Emily said to the blonde girl who'd never really talked with Emily before, despite their class being so small.

"Yes," their teacher, Mr. Pace, said from the front of the cabin, "those are deer. The Wastelands are full of deer, dogs, pigs, and wolves. Without people, the animal population is out of control."

"What about the Ferals?" Kenny said. "Don't they eat the animals?"

Emily watched as the teacher's expression changed from smiling and happy to something else. She couldn't read it. Maybe he was annoyed by the question. Emily wasn't sure if the teacher were among the hosts or a free person too. If he were an alien, perhaps he didn't appreciate disparaging comments about the Ferals — despite the fact that everyone on The Island was told to avoid contact with the Ferals at all costs, that they were deadly aliens run amok.

Mr. Pace cleared his throat. "The aliens typically eat humans not animals."

"Eww," Sutton said.

Chris, who was sitting in the back of the shuttle, pushed his long brown hair from his face. "Better watch out, Sutton, or they're gonna eat you next."

Sutton raised her hand then extended her middle finger.

Emily laughed.

"Now, now," Mr. Pace said. "None of us will be eaten."

Chris murmured, "None of *us?*"

Emily looked at Mr. Pace, certain he must have heard the comment basically accusing him of being an alien. If Mr. Pace *had* heard him, he said nothing and didn't react.

Emily turned and met Chris's eyes. He was a year older then she, and known for causing trouble. Nothing too serious but annoying to the teachers — and charming to some of the girls. Emily was surprised he'd been among the students chosen for the tour. Not only was he always getting into one thing or another, he was obnoxious like most overly aggressive boys were.

Why is he even on this trip?

It was easy to see why the others were there. Sutton was pretty and popular — her father was a big shot at one of the mainland factories. Kenny was one of the smartest kids in class. And Emily, well, Emily wasn't sure why she was picked, either. She didn't think of herself as especially smart. Perceptive, yes. But she'd never been particularly interested in learning history, remembering facts, or anything having to do with math. And nobody knew about her gifts.

Last year, Mr. Pace had called Emily's father in for a conference because Emily was "daydreaming," as he'd said, too much in class. She didn't see it so much as daydreaming as much as thinking up songs she planned to write when class was out.

If there was one thing Emily missed in this world, it was that nobody would ever make another song, at least not in her lifetime. Emily remembered when she was a child and her mother would sing while rocking her to sleep. She'd sing in the car when they were going to preschool. As Emily grew up, she started singing in music class, plays, and church choir.

Nowadays, she sang only to herself, when she was alone.

Emily didn't feel comfortable singing to her father. He was always so logical and wanting to discuss facts, history, and other stuff she had no interest in. The few times she did try to sing, he gave her a polite, "That was nice" but didn't seem to appreciate it. She often wondered if her singing reminded him of her mother.

Dad hated talking about her.

Sure, he'd answer Emily's questions, but he always cut the

conversation short. For a while, she thought maybe her father didn't like his wife. But then one night, following a fight she had with her dad, he'd drunk too much wine and said something she'd never forget.

"I wish the plague had taken me instead."

He got up, went to his room, and they never spoke of it again.

Emily would always remember the words, and how much they hurt, but she wasn't entirely sure why he'd said it, or what he'd meant. But the part of Emily that kept her awake at night suggested that her father was mad at her mother for dying. For leaving him with a burden. For having to take care of Emily.

"What is that?" Chris asked, voice raised in enthusiasm, yanking Emily from her Memory Lane.

She looked out the window and saw a huge parking lot. In the center of the lot, where the store — or perhaps a mall — should be, lay a block-wide crater in the earth, maybe ten feet deep, filled with what looked like vegetation-peppered rubble.

Mr. Pace said, "That's one of the impact spots from our mothership's lasers."

"Wow!" Chris and Kenny said in unison.

The crater gave Emily chills, reminding her of everything the aliens had robbed from the world — and her. She hated how Chris and Kenny seemed to be in awe of the aliens' destructive powers. Such boys. She wanted to throttle them.

Don't you realize you're oohing and ahhing over aliens killing our people? What kind of insensitive jerks are you?

Instead, Emily kept her mouth shut.

See, Dad, I do listen to your advice, sometimes.

She wished she'd come on the trip alone. While Sutton wasn't being her usual bitchy self, Chris and Kenny's enthusiasm over every sign of destruction got progressively worse as the field trip continued. You'd think they were touring enemy territory, not the place they'd all called home before The Fall.

Surely, the boys had lost loved ones, maybe a parent or two, to the plague or aliens.

A sudden bang outside rocked the shuttle, causing it to shudder violently back and forth, sending the kids stumbling.

Emily sat and grabbed the straps in the back of her seat, sliding them over her shoulders.

"What's happening?" Sutton asked, falling onto Emily.

Emily helped her to sit up and secure the straps around her so she wouldn't fly into a wall.

The shuttle rocked harder. A horrible whirring burped from below.

"What's happening?" Sutton repeated, this time shrieking.

Neither Mr. Pace nor the two Guardsmen up front said a word.

Mr. Pace strapped himself in and instructed the boys to do the same.

Then the shuttle lurched downward.

～

ELEVEN

Paul Roberts

The elevator ascended, and Paul's mind stirred with possibilities of what Desmond might show him. Whatever the case, he felt safe — for the moment.

The elevator doors opened into an all-white hallway that stretched as far as Paul could see, ending in blinding white. The brightness of the light panels above combined with the sterility reminded Paul of a hospital. The floors were so shiny he could see their reflections as he, Desmond, and Wasterman started down the hall.

Every twenty feet or so, they passed white doors with no discernible knobs or electronic panels to open them. He hoped his chills went unnoticed.

What if they bring me into one of these rooms and lock the door?

Each door had a silver insignia of some sort, in an alien language Paul had seen many times but never understood. Were these names? Numbers?

Desmond stopped at the second door and waved his hand before it. The door slid open.

Four beds were neatly lined inside the white room, each holding a sleeping woman. They were under translucent blankets with hundreds of selvions blinking in different colors. It took a moment for Paul to realize their common denominator: they were all pregnant.

The door slid shut behind them.

"What is this?" Paul said.

"This is our solution to the lack of pure psyches to serve as host."

"You're going to implant them into babies?"

"Yes. We've already had four successful implantations. Though the children are still young, the process shows promise."

"How … how many are there?"

"So far, thirty."

"Thirty pregnant women? How? Why am I just learning about this?"

Desmond looked slighted. "This project is unrelated to your work."

"You don't need me to screen appropriate women?"

"Not yet. Perhaps in the next phase. Now we're a bit less discriminating, seeking proof of concept."

"So, why are you showing me now?"

"There are certain people in our council who feel we should consider using more locally sourced women to impregnate. And perhaps we should start younger."

Paul was confused then did the math.

This is about Emily! This is a threat!

"What the hell are you saying?"

"Watch your tone," Wasterman said from behind.

"Paul, Paul, Paul, I'm not saying we'll do this to your daughter. What kind of monster do you think I am? I'm saying there are certain people here who believe that would be a good idea. I won't allow it because you are an important member of our society. And your family is *our* family. Besides, she's still a child."

Paul stared at Desmond, wanting to knock the fucker's smile from his face. But he had to throttle his rage.

"Why are you telling me this?"

"Because I'm about to upset you. And I need you to be cautious in how you react."

A cold sweat beaded Paul's back. His heart throbbed. What the hell was Desmond about to say?

"What?"

"Your daughter has shown herself to be quite gifted."

Oh, God, they know. What do they want with Emily?

"Are you aware that she's a telepath?"

"I've not talked to her about it — yet. I just started sensing it a couple of weeks ago. I didn't want to say anything. She's at that age, you know, where anything I say is met with hostility. If I want to explore this, she has to bring it up."

While Paul initially thought her having abilities, like him, would protect her from the aliens, he wasn't so certain now. Maybe it put a target on her back. They had leverage over him. They could control him. But her, not so much. Especially if she came to dislike her father as so many teens did. Why would a disgruntled kid care if they used their dad as leverage?

Desmond nodded. "Well, unfortunately, we needed to expedite her development."

"What the hell does that mean?" Paul bristled, struggling to stifle his anger. Wasterman loomed so close behind Paul, he could imagine the man's breath, and the gun in his belt holster.

"So far, Luca, and the others under The Light's influence, have been undetectable to us. We have a general idea where they are but not enough to make a move. We needed to set a trap."

"What do you mean, *a trap?*"

"Remember what I said. I'm about to anger you. I need you to stay calm. Are you calm, Mr. Roberts?"

Paul nodded, panicked.

"Your daughter is bait. The trip she just took, it's all part of our plan to bring out our enemy."

Paul had to force himself not to scream. "What?"

"Tone!" Wasterman barked behind him.

"Don't worry," Desmond said. "Your daughter is completely safe."

"What did you do to her?"

"We've staged an *accident* to lure our enemy. When they move in to help, we can follow her back to their lair."

Paul shook his head. He wanted to murder Desmond. Then he'd grab Wasterman's gun, shove it in his mouth, and blow a hole through the back of his skull, killing the man and the alien likely riding jockey inside him.

"Why did you do this? If you have a general idea where they are, why not take one of those big fucking laser cannons on your ship and level the damned city like you all did when you arrived?"

"Because it's not enough to kill the hosts. It's far harder to kill The Light. So we must contain The Light."

Paul paced back and forth, fists shoved in his pants pockets. "How are you ensuring her safety? What if they take her and you lose her, too?"

"She has a tracking chip embedded in her, part of the protocol for any trip into The Wastelands."

"And if that fails?"

"That's where you come in. You will contact her telepathically."

Paul hated every part of this but was powerless to do anything. Emily was already out there. Possibly already in the hands of the enemy. He had no choice but to play ball, and they knew it.

"So," Desmond said, "are we on the same page, Mr. Roberts?"

Paul nodded. What else could he do?

~

TWELVE

Mary Olson

The shuttle sat in the burned-out shopping center's parking lot like a silent sentinel. Mary and the group were more than a hundred yards away, but danger seemed to crackle in the air from being so close to the alien ship.

The shopping center was located in a part of The City that had seen the worst of the mothership's lasers. There wasn't another building standing within a hundred yards, which made the crash site a prime target for snipers — countless hiding places salted the apartment buildings and storefronts scattered past the blast zone.

Mary and her group stood at the edges of a wooded area just south of the shopping center, relatively concealed, though probably not against infrared or alien technology. Fortunately, she couldn't hear the shuttle's loud engines.

Mary zoomed in with the binoculars for a closer look and saw two Guardsmen on the ground, torn to shreds. She panned up at the terrified faces of the children.

Three bleakers circled the craft, each taking turns at running into the ship, trying to gain entry.

Mary handed the binoculars back to Keenan.

Boricio looked at them both. "So, we gonna save these little bastards or what?"

Boricio, Lisa, and Jevonne all had rifles trained on the aliens, waiting for Keenan and Mary to make a decision. Until a few months ago, Boricio had been calling most of the shots, but following some group infighting, Boricio decided to be a bit more diplomatic and mine a few other opinions before making any major decisions. It was sorta sweet, as he was obviously doing it to appease her. Mary had grown sick of the arguments among the group's clashing personalities, with Boricio's being the most prickly. She'd been ready to declare a general *fuck off*, rather than tolerate any more bullshit.

Boricio looked back at her. She tried reading his face to see if he was as disturbed by this idle shuttle as she was.

Something felt off.

"Why the hell did they bring a shuttle full of kids into The City?"

Lisa looked through her scope. "They all have uniforms on, like *school uniforms*."

"They've got a Hogwarts on The Island, *and* the little fuckers are in monkey suits? Jesus Stepford Christ! We oughta let the aliens eat 'em on principle."

Mary wasn't surprised that they had a school. Even from the mainland at night, she knew The Island had power, as did certain sections of the mainland where the aliens had their heavily guarded factories and warehouses. Luca was right — they *were* trying to rebuild society with the new *evolved* human alien hybrids. So were these kids human or hybrids? Or puppets controlled by the aliens? Not that there was much distinction. And other than Luca, and briefly Paola, she'd yet to meet a true hybrid, where the humans maintained some, or most, control of themselves.

Mary turned to Keenan. "What do you think?"

He stared at the shuttle for a while. Mary wondered if he

was thinking about Jade. Did he think about her as much as Mary thought about Paola — *every fucking day for four years?*

Keenan said, "Well, we've been waiting to capture someone from the inside for a long time, right?"

"But doesn't this feel convenient to you? And why haven't they sent backup? I dunno." She shrugged. "Feels like a trap."

Lisa looked back. "I agree. This doesn't feel right. Let's jet."

"What?" Boricio turned. "We're gonna leave Dora's Explorers to die?"

"There's something wrong about this," Lisa said. "I feel like they're trying to draw us out. And besides, we want to capture someone of worth from The Island to interrogate, not a bunch of kids."

"Then why the fuck did you call us down here in the first place? You knew they were kids when you found the crash site."

Lisa, ignoring Boricio, walked up to Keenan. "What do you think?"

"I agree. Something's not right."

Boricio shook his head. "Hello, Earth to assholes. Do you all not see the same shit I'm seeing? Those kids are making Hersheys in their Underoos! Look at their eyes! There ain't no ETs in there!"

"They could be acting scared," Keenan said. "We all know what they're capable of."

Mary nodded. She knew more than any of them. She'd slept with Desmond, *almost* had his alien baby. "I don't wanna take any chances. I say we head back."

Boricio stared at Mary, slack jawed. "No. Fuck this shit."

He picked up the rifle and fired one, two, three silenced shots, dropping two of the three aliens before squeezing off another two shots and felling the last one.

"What the fuck?" Lisa got in his face.

"You best step the fuck back." Boricio didn't raise his rifle and aim it at Lisa, but he didn't need to.

"We're not bringing those kids back," she said. "It's too risky."

"Since when did *I* become the only motherfucker here who gives a shit about a shuttle of munchkins?"

Mary was as surprised as Boricio. Then again, ever since he'd lost Rose to the aliens, just before Paola's death, something had shifted in Boricio. He was still a stone-cold killer, but there had been a few times when it seemed like more of an act. She thought it was a necessary adjustment to becoming a more balanced person — dangerous enough to be useful rather than a psycho who kept them in danger. But now, Boricio was thinking with emotion rather than logic. The risks of saving these kids far outweighed the rewards. Boricio's blindness made her afraid that he'd grown *too* soft.

Jevonne, normally quiet like Keenan, spoke up. "I'm with Boricio. Yeah, maybe it's a trap. But my gut says it isn't. I think this is an accident, and we need to act fast before they realize their shuttle is missing."

"That's just the problem," Keenan said. "If they realize the kids are missing, and they care enough to search for them, they'll blanket The City with shuttles."

Boricio spat on the ground. "Let 'em. We lie low a while. Maybe go to The Farm. We came out here to pick up high-value targets, right? We haven't been able to get anyone from The Island to talk yet. This is our chance. And as far as whether or not they're aliens, we'll let Luca sort it out. If they are, we kill 'em. No harm, no foul."

Boricio looked at Mary.

And then, suddenly, they were all looking at Mary.

"Why the hell are you all looking at *me* to make a decision?"

Keenan smiled. "I guess you're the voice of reason."

She didn't want to own the decision, tired of playing

mother to the group. The responsibility was too much. Let someone else call the shots, even if it meant Boricio and the others butting heads more often than agreeing.

This was a no-win decision.

Boricio was right: They *did* need to find someone from The Island who would talk, and maybe help them find a way onto The Island to strike at the aliens. On the other hand, this felt like a trap; it was too damned easy.

"I dunno," she said. "I think we head back."

"And leave the kids to die?" Boricio shook his head, furious.

Mary argued, "You all said it already: The aliens are going to notice they're missing. They're gonna send help. You killed the aliens, and they seem pretty damned safe locked in the shuttle. Just leave 'em. They'll be fine."

A girl's voice cried out behind them.

"Hey! Hey! Can you help us?"

Mary turned and saw that a girl had come out of the shuttle while the other kids cowered inside. She was small, young, maybe twelve or thirteen, with thick shoulder-length brown hair.

Keenan, Lisa, and Jevonne raised their weapons, aiming at the girl.

Boricio waved his hands down. "Would you all calm the fuck down?"

They held their aim.

Mary watched the girl approach and couldn't help but admire her bravery.

Is it bravery, or is she a clever bleaker with no reason to fear?

Mary started toward the girl, hand on her belt, the blade in a sheath on her right side. Mary walked fast, closing the distance between them. As Mary drew closer, about twenty feet away, she saw the girl's eyes and the fear inside them.

Good. You should fear us.

Mary kept moving, waiting for something — maybe a

shuttle to descend from the clouds or a sniper to fire from a nearby building to the north.

But as she drew closer, nothing happened.

Could the situation be what it appeared — defenseless kids in need of help? If so, Mary and the group could both help them, and maybe figure out a way to finally get onto The Island.

Fifteen feet away.

Can't let down our defenses. Something has to be off.

Ten feet away.

The girl looked up at her, eyes wide and full of hope.

"Thank you for helping us!"

The girl's youth and wide eyes reminded her too much of Paola.

Mary grabbed the girl, spun her around, and put the blade to her throat.

"Show yourselves, or she's dead!" Mary shouted.

THIRTEEN

Boricio Wolfe

"What the fuck are you doing?" Boricio yelled at Mary

She took the girl at knifepoint, screaming at the sky, demanding their unseen enemy come out of hiding.

Lisa, Keenan, and Jevonne were turning their rifles, scanning the woods and the buildings in the distance for any sign of a threat.

"I mean it!" Mary screamed. "I'll slit her throat!"

The girl cried out. Mary pressed the blade hard against her skin. Boricio flinched when he saw she wasn't bluffing.

Blood trickled from the knife's tip down her neck.

A part of Boricio felt a nostalgic rush, remembering the feeling of a knife against a soft throat — that sensation when it plunged into his victims, just before the gurgle.

But this wasn't some fucker who had it coming. This was a young girl, someone's daughter. And while Boricio had killed all sorts who didn't deserve it, including daughters, he'd never murdered a child.

Someone should throw me a hero parade!

The look in her eyes scared Boricio. He'd not seen Mary this filled with rage in a couple of years. There had been a while, after their return to this world, when Mary had run on nothing but hate and vengeance. She'd killed hundreds — of aliens, bandits, and any motherfuckers that crossed them. She'd become a regular Britany Badass. And he liked it, even if not the horrors that broke her. But this … *this* was something else entirely.

"Show yourself!" Mary shouted.

No one was coming.

If there was anyone waiting to take them out, they would've showed their faces already. Boricio had to end this bullshit before Mary killed the girl.

"It's not a trap," Boricio said, approaching Mary. "See? Nobody's shooting. No ships in the sky. I know you don't wanna hurt her, Mary."

Her face looked blank, as if Boricio's words were hitting a wall. Her eyes were wild, searching for enemies, something to kill and absorb her deep well of rage.

The girl whimpered, the sound of her pain making Boricio wince.

He waved his hands in front of Mary like a magician showing the nothing up his sleeve, trying to snap her out of whatever the hell kind of PTSD she seemed to be suffering.

When her eyes finally stopped on Boricio, seeming to register him as a friend, he said, "Please, Mary, let her go. She's just a kid."

Mary met his eyes. "So was Paola. And they took her."

Boricio turned to the girl. "Hey, honey, what's your name?"

"Emily," she said, voice shaking.

"You hear that, Mary? Her name's Emily. Emily didn't do nothing to Paola. Emily is not your enemy."

Mary looked around again, searching for enemies that weren't coming. "You have five seconds to show yourselves! One!"

"Come on, Mary," Boricio said. "You don't have to do this."

"Two!"

"Listen to me, Mary. You've gotta let Emily go."

"Three!"

"Mary!" Boricio yelled.

"Four!"

The girl cried, "Please, I'm not an alien!"

Could Mary really do this?

Was this a bluff to get the enemies to show themselves? Maybe get Emily, or one of the other kids, to reveal their true selves?

"Mary!" Boricio waved his hands, begging her to look at him.

"Five!"

The girl cried out.

Mary's eyes darted back and forth then up to the skies.

She met Boricio's eyes. In that look, he could tell that Mary finally realized she was wrong. This wasn't a trap. Nobody was coming to get them.

At least he thought that's what he saw.

Mary slit the girl's throat.

Episode 32

(SECOND EPISODE OF SEASON SIX)

"Hell"

Prologue

IT

Four years ago

WHEN THE MOTHERSHIP ARRIVED, *It* had been no less surprised than the Earthlings.

It had watched the mothership obliterate cities. Had watched the virus, presumably unleashed by the ship's occupants, wipe out most of humanity. *It* had watched and wondered what *Its* purpose was in this invasion.

Why hadn't *It* felt the aliens' thoughts as they floated overhead laying waste to the world? Was it not part of the collective that *It* had unleashed when *It* got the final vials? It had to be. Nothing else made sense.

If that were the case, why was the virus also killing many of the new creatures *It* had unleashed, along with hybrids *It* had created?

Something wasn't adding up. As weeks went by, *It* wondered if this was a separate alien invasion. *Its* human part — Desmond, as he called himself — laughed at the irony.

You've taken over the world, and for what? Another race to claim your prize?

It sent pain through *Its* body to silence the human.

It tried probing the minds aboard the alien ship. But like its brethren calling itself The Light, *It* couldn't connect. Couldn't even sense anything aboard. The ship's inhabitants were different than *It*.

Six weeks after the mothership appeared in the skies, *It* was beckoned to The Island where the ship had *docked* high above.

An unmanned shuttle came down to retrieve *It*.

It went aboard and was ushered to the mothership. Doors opened into a dark bay where *It* was met by something unfamiliar, yet oddly felt like home.

A large red creature, roughly eight feet high — like a centipede mated with a moth — standing upright, like a human, somehow supported by two dozen or so spindly, sharp, shiny black legs along the lower third of its body. More legs ran along its length, though what use they served was beyond *It*. They were short and had only tiny pincers, rather than digits designed to hold and manipulate objects. Its face was a stub with a gaping maw and giant black eyes that offered no reflection. This was what reminded *It* of a moth most, besides the large papery wings that were sheer enough to see through.

The creature was beautiful *and* hideous.

"What are you?" *It* asked.

The creature spoke without its mouth, inside *Its* head, and in Desmond's voice, as if accessing the language and voice *Its* host preferred.

Little did the creature know that the last thing *It* wanted to hear was *more* from the human who had gone from being a barely there passenger to an increasingly annoying backseat driver in the past few weeks. *It* feared that like others, *It* was about to lose control of *Its* host body, or perhaps go mad. But *It* could say this to no one. *It* had to hide this deficiency — or risk ejection from *Its* role as de facto leader of the alien army *It* had unleashed.

The creature said, "Do you not recognize us?"

Three more beasts, all similar, though with minor differences in coloring, skittered forth. They seemed heavy yet moved with grace that belied their bulk. *It* figured their legs must be quite strong to move them so effortlessly. One, more gray than red, walked on all of its legs like an Earth centipede.

"No," *It* said. "Though you feel familiar."

A couple of the creatures — *It* couldn't be sure which ones, as they all had Desmond's voice in *Its* head — laughed.

"We are the Pruhm. Do you not recognize your creators?"

"Creators?"

"He doesn't think he's human, does he?"

It shook *Its* head, offended by the suggestion. "No, I am *better* than humans, here to replace them! To evolve them — *us* — into something better."

More laughter.

"What?" *It* said, angered by the tone of these giant fucking insects, as if *It* were a stupid child with insignificant plans.

One of the things said, presumably to the others, "You can't blame him. It *has* been a long time since we sent them out."

"Please," *It* said, holding *Its* temper in check, "will you tell me what you're talking about?"

One of the creatures obliged. "We made you then sent through the universe, to help us find a new home. To find a species we could implant, as you say, ourselves into. Your job was to thin the herd to a manageable amount. We arrived and unleashed a virus to eliminate all who wouldn't be compatible."

"I was *created?* What do you mean?"

"You are a tool. A fungus imbued with artificial intelligence. A rudimentary and somewhat uncontrollable tool, but an implement of our design nonetheless."

"No, I am not a tool!" *It* shook *Its* head. "I am an evolved species, blending the best of my kind and humanity."

"You may have evolved, but do not mistake your role."

Its body felt hot. *Its* heart raced faster. Human emotions surging through *It* — fear running rampant, short-circuiting *Its* ability to process what was happening. *It* finally managed to string a few words together.

"What *is* my role?"

"To find hosts for our species."

"How? I know nothing of your biology. I've been preparing for *my* species, not yours."

"Do not mistake our corporeal appearance for our true nature. This is but one of many bodies we've been forced to use since fleeing our world. We engineered you in our image. We can use the same bodies as you."

It didn't like this a bit. These things, the Pruhm, were taking the wheel of his ship. *It* didn't care if they created *It* or not.

But *It* had to be wise.

It had to play the game, and make sure they still needed *It*.

"Whatever you need," *It* said.

"How stable are these bodies?"

"We've had mixed results. There have been issues with the hosts rejecting us."

"What happens?"

"In the worst cases, a complete psychological breakdown followed by suicide, usually leading to the death of our species."

"What?" said one of the creatures, seemingly surprised. "It was our understanding from the transmissions that the humans were a match."

While *It* didn't know what transmission they were speaking about, now was *Its* chance to prove *Its* value.

"Well, finding a host is more than just finding a suitable physical specimen. We also need to find the right psychological makeup, to find a stable match. How many of you are there?"

There was a moment of silence. *It* wondered if they didn't know their number or were trying to determine if it was wise to let *It* know. Did they view *It* as a threat with whom they shouldn't share information or expose potential vulnerabilities?

"Nine hundred and fifty-eight. Though, once implanted, we can propagate our species. Like you, we reproduce by regenerative cell division. Can you find us stable humans to start our program?"

"Yes."

It would play ball … so long as their goals were aligned. But *It* would also seek a way to destroy all 958 lives aboard the mothership the moment the Pruhm's goals branched from *Its*. *It* had come too far to abandon *Its* attempt to fulfill *Its* potential, regardless of *Its* design.

You may have created us, but you do not own us.

It had *Its* own collective destiny to fulfill. And damn anyone, or anything, trying to stop *It*.

"Good," the Pruhm said in unison.

The shuttle door opened behind him.

It took that as *Its* cue to leave and turned.

A horrible pain seized *Its* body, as if someone had found every one of Desmond's pain points and pressed them at once.

Desmond's body moved on its own, without *Its* control.

For a horrifying moment *It* was certain the human inside had somehow seized control of *Its* shell at the most inopportune of times. *Its* usefulness would be questioned by the Pruhm, and then they would terminate *It*.

But then, as *It* was turned face-to-face with one of the grotesque insectoids, *It* realized that the aliens were somehow asserting control of their creation.

The gray one made itself taller, more intimidating.

The creature moved closer to *Its* face, so close *It* could hear the gnashing of the insect's rows of needle teeth, could hear the sharp legs thrashing along its body like a rattler's tail.

The creature spoke in *Its* mind, this time in a horrible screeching that was neither human in sound nor English in words.

But its message was clear:

We are superior to you. We own you.

Deviate from our *plans, and we will end you.*

Somewhere in *Its* shell, Desmond laughed.

~

FOURTEEN

Boricio Wolfe

The girl fell to the ground.

Boricio yelled, "What the fuck did you do?" and dropped to her side, staring into the girl's helpless eyes. Blood gushed from her throat. Boricio could do nothing to stop it.

She murmured something he couldn't make out.

Boricio leaned closer.

"Why?" she asked.

He stared into her eyes and felt the world tip on its end. If he didn't hang on, he, along with the rest of them, would plummet into a chaotic abyss.

Boricio hadn't a single word of comfort. Only, "Sorry," as the girl faded, eyes rolling into the back of her head.

He glared up at Mary, staring down at the girl without expression.

His voice cracked. "How could you?"

A loud whine over an even louder rumbling roar tore the air above them. Startled, Boricio looked up to see an alien shuttle racing toward them from the clouds, then rippling as it stopped on a dime.

While the kids' shuttle looked like a boxy subway car with a trio of wings, this thing was sleek, circular, and with no visible cabin to house a pilot. Boricio registered two mounted cannons on the ship's bottom a heartbeat before it opened fire.

There was nowhere to run.

No way to fight back.

They were about to be shredded by alien gunfire.

Mary might have been right. Maybe it was a trap.

Gunfire grazed Boricio's left shoulder. Another several rounds spit asphalt behind him.

He grabbed his gun and turned, ready to unleash hell on the motherfuckers trying to kill him, determined to do whatever damage he could before it tore him asunder.

But a flash changed the world in a second.

Boricio blinked to find himself inside what looked like a dark warehouse. Luca was kneeling on the ground, hands over the girl's bleeding neck.

Lisa, Keenan, and Jevonne stood in a semicircle, staring at Luca and the bleeding girl as if they weren't sure what to say, or do. Lisa and Keenan traded a nod, indicating that they would sweep the warehouse and ensure their safety.

"What the hell are you doing?" Mary yelled at Luca, despite the potential danger of raising her voice in an unknown area where enemies could be lurking.

Eyes closed, Luca said nothing.

"Indoor voices," Boricio said. "And can't you see he's trying to save her? What the hell do you think you're doing?"

"It *was* a trap!" Mary said, still too loud.

"We don't kill Happy Meals," Boricio whisper-shouted back.

"Why the fuck not? *They* do."

And there it was.

No one spoke.

Mary stared at Luca and the girl. Boricio wondered two things at once. One: How could Mary look at the girl after what she'd done? She should feel a Vatican's worth of guilt for that shit. Two: Would she try something again? And if so, how far would he go to intervene?

Boricio liked Mary. A lot. Loved her, even. Not just as someone he'd grown close to over the years, and shared a bed with for a while, but before then — as a sister-in-arms. A bond forged in the hellish fires of loss. She'd lost her daughter, and he'd lost Rose, the only other woman he ever loved.

But no amount of affection could let Boricio sit by while she killed an innocent child.

Yeah, but how far will ya go, pal?

Boricio hoped he wouldn't have to answer.

He reached up to where his elbow had been shot to find his shirt still ripped but his wound healed. As was his finger from the earlier apple slice. Luca hadn't just teleported them away from certain death — he'd managed to heal Boricio's wounds. He looked at the others, not sure if any of them had sustained gunfire from the ship. Tough to tell if they were bleeding since they were all wearing dark clothes. If so, they seemed fine now.

He looked back at Mary.

Her eyes were still wild, angry. He had to get her away from the group, sort things out, calm her down. If not for Mary's sake, then for the group's. If Boricio was starting to think she might've become a liability, the others were certainly wondering the same thing.

"Come here." He grabbed her gently by the elbow.

Mary flinched, pulling back, jaw set, eyes burning through him.

"Please. We need to talk."

Mary sighed and followed Boricio away from Luca, the girl, and Jevonne. Boricio nodded as they passed Keenan, Lisa, and Barrow, all huddled together, no doubt talking about Mary losing her shit.

Keenan looked up at Boricio. "We're in Sector 40. Not too far from Beta Team."

Beta was one of the other rebel groups, the only other group whose headquarters they knew the location of. The other two rebel camps were cells isolated from each other and the Alpha (Boricio's team) and Beta teams. Being close to Beta was a blessing in case they had invited unwanted attention by slicing the girl's throat then taking her. A search would surely be coming.

Boricio nodded back. "Thanks."

Boricio led Mary as far from everyone as possible, passing several empty rows of ransacked shelves. Out of earshot, he said, "I know it hurts, Mary. I do. But we're not them. We don't kill kids."

Mary met his eyes, hers still wild. "Don't tell me about hurt. You don't know what it's like to lose a child."

Boricio wanted to push back. No, he didn't know what it felt like to lose a child, but he did know what it felt like to lose someone he loved. But doing that might push Mary too far. If she snapped any more than she already had, she'd become too big a liability to the group, and there was no way in hell they'd put up with that, no matter who that liability was.

Boricio said nothing.

"And don't even get up on your high horse, saying we don't kill kids. Really, Boricio? You're gonna play *that* card?"

"What's that supposed to mean?"

"It means I'm not stupid. I know what you were before Luca fixed you. And not just the shit you told me. I know the *really* sick shit you did. I'm pretty sure we *all* do, if we're all sharing dreams."

Boricio suspected that Mary knew more than she let on. He'd had dreams of the others' memories, too. Snippets of unguarded, highly personal moments: Brent fighting with his wife, Mary giving birth to Paola, Keenan killing enemies of the state even as his marriage was falling apart and his daughter was growing to hate him. If he'd seen *their* demons, they'd surely seen his. And if they'd seen the worst, how could any of them ever truly trust or accept him?

It hurt like hell to think of them peeking in on such unguarded memories. Hurt more to think that Mary and Paola had seen him at his worst. He'd done horrible things — murdered, raped, and God only knew how many things he'd forgotten in some drunken or drugged stupor. Boricio had spent a lifetime not giving a fiddler's fuck about dick, including his victims or their families. But since Luca went in his head and fixed him, guilt was a stone on his shoulders, growing heavier with every connection — each new man, woman, or child he grew to care about.

"That's not me anymore."

"*You* still don't get to judge me. And besides, it *was* a trap. That alien ship would've killed us all if not for Luca. As far as I'm concerned, you're all trying to save our enemy. Maybe you should care about us instead."

"Care about us? Everything I do is for all of us. What the fuck does that even mean?"

"Nothing." Mary shook her head and stared at the ground.

"Don't play Silent Bob with me. Say what you mean, or don't say shit."

"Nothing! Just forget it." Mary turned and walked away.

"Don't you fucking walk away from me!" Boricio grabbed Mary by the shoulders and spun her around, more violently than he'd intended.

Mary's eyes widened. For a moment, it felt as if they'd both gone too far, pushed harder than either of them wanted.

"What? Are you gonna hit me now?"

There was a part of Boricio — a part that terrified him — that wanted to do exactly that.

"Fuck you," he said instead.

Mary turned and walked away.

FIFTEEN

Luca Harding

Luca was halfway finished healing the unconscious girl's neck wound when he realized she wasn't an ordinary girl.

There was something different about her.

He saw it inside her head while trying to calm her panic with reassuring words. *You'll be okay. You'll be okay. I'm going to help you.* Luca realized that only part of her was responding to him. Another part of her had gone inside *his head.* She was rooting around in his memories, manifesting them for her own viewing within his mind.

His first instinct was to shut her out as he'd done to the alien who had hijacked Desmond's body when he'd tried to worm inside Luca's head. Throw up psychic defenses and maybe hurt the girl to keep her from prying again. But as her memories unwound and he watched the girl lose her mother, nearly die herself, and get brought to The Island by her father, Luca knew he could trust her. He didn't want to kick her out.

He met her inside his mind, his body showing its true biological age of fourteen.

"Who are you?" she asked, looking around.

They were in his old Las Orillas home, probably because he'd been thinking so much about it lately. But that was only for a moment. Then they were in the Other Luca's home, on Black Island.

The girl looked at him, confused. Then her eyes widened, and her head tilted a bit. "Oh, my God."

"What?"

The Luca saw it, too. His own self, doubled. Other Luca standing beside him.

"What *are* you?" she asked.

Luca multiplied. He saw his older forms — at twenty-eight, at forty, and his current physical self, now somewhere in his early sixties.

He wasn't sure how to explain everything to her. How there were two versions of him, how he'd died then come back inside the other Luca's body. How they weren't alone, that there was the alien species inside him, calling itself The Light.

Luca couldn't find the words.

He'd have to show her.

"Are you sure you want to know?"

She stepped toward him, head still turned to the side like she was studying a rare artifact. "Yes," she whispered.

He put his hands to her head, in both the physical world and in the shared space inside his head.

Then Luca showed her everything.

~

SIXTEEN

Teagan McLachlan

Teagan and the others said their final farewell to The Farm just before dawn.

It wasn't easy to leave. Morning light poured onto the Alto Verde hilltops where Teagan's new family had sheltered themselves for the last couple of years. Like always, it reminded her of Sunday church, now like a blessing rather than the feeling's occasional haunting knowing she'd never see it again.

Teagan wrapped her left arm tighter around Becca's and ran her right hand through Whinny's mane before turning to steal a last look behind her. Her eyes drifted from the front porch where she often let the sun kiss her skin while staring at the sea to her small plot in the garden where she was allowed to grow flowers instead of vegetables. Her mind's eye then went to the back door leading to the kitchen where *it* had finally happened.

Teagan let the memory come: throwing herself at Brent, claiming his mouth, and spilling from the kitchen into the living room where she let him finally have what she knew he'd been craving a while. She hoped they could eventually pick up where they left off, when they reached their new location. Teagan refused to call it a safe house, though Ed was so glued to the name that it had infected everyone at The Farm, including Brent.

"Second Refuge," as Teagan preferred to call it, was at the base of the hills, in what seemed to be a forgotten neighborhood about halfway between Alto Verde and Las Orillas, about a mile from the Pacific Coast Highway.

Moving down through the hills made Teagan nervous, though she couldn't argue that it was better than the alternative. They needed to reach the refuge so they'd be close enough to radio the others in The City and warn them about the shapeshifters.

Teagan still couldn't believe what had happened. She didn't want to. Her skin crawled thinking about losing so many lives when there were none to spare, including Catherine, the sweet girl who'd had her hair braided by Teagan early that afternoon.

The image of Otis, or at least the thing that had pretended to be him, refused to leave her mind. Hacked to pieces, wet and black, flopping on the floorboards like a suffocating fish.

She wasn't cut out for this. Teagan was a mom; her responsibility was to take care of Becca. Same for Brent. He had his son, she had her daughter, and they'd agreed they were safest outside The City. Thinking that Las Orillas might now offer the most security was a horror in her head.

"We'll be fine," Brent had said. "The City has Boricio, Ed, and Mary — the three people most capable of keeping us safe."

She wasn't sure that Brent bought it himself, but Teagan appreciated that he cared enough to safeguard her feelings. And it wasn't like there was any other logical action beyond reaching the refuge, reporting what happened, and waiting for the Alpha Team to tell them what to do.

Becca leaned back and nuzzled against Teagan's chest.

"I'm tired, Mommy."

"Do you want to walk?"

"Kind of, yeah."

She gently yanked the reins, and Whinny stopped. Teagan lifted Becca then planted her on the ground, feeling the burn in her muscles and wondering how much longer she'd be able to do that before Becca was simply too heavy.

Without saying goodbye, Becca ran a few horses up the line to where Ben was walking beside Bashful — Brent's horse, and one of the stable's rowdier steeds. The two children fell into chatter.

Becca was six. Ben's extra three years practically made him God to the girl, though gender might have also had something to do with it. Either way, Teagan's daughter more than adored him. Becca mimicked Ben's every move.

Ben reached down, grabbed a rock, and hurled it toward a huddle of trees. Teagan winced. So did Brent, probably thinking the same thing: *don't make any noise.*

Though it wasn't like a small rock hitting a large trunk made any more noise than the caravan's tromping hooves. Or Becca's laugh, now a guffaw.

Teagan smiled. Brent turned from Bashful's back to find her eyes. Becca was lucky to have Ben, and she was lucky to have his father.

She nudged Whinny and trotted up beside Bashful.

"Hey," she said.

"Hay is for the horses, or is that one for me?"

It was stupid, but Teagan smiled anyway.

"Hey for you," she said.

"So, do you want to make small talk, or admit we're scared shitless?"

Teagan's smile turned into a laugh. "Might as well admit we're scared shitless." A beat, then, "I just hope we can get to Second Refuge without seeing the Reaper."

Brent's jaw set. Teagan saw him swallow. She thought he might scold her for mentioning the notorious bandit leader who'd been wreaking havoc up and down the hinterlands, and whom they had somehow avoided thus far. Mentioning him was kind of like telling the world you're glad you'll never get cancer: inviting disaster. Instead, he nodded toward the caravan's front, just behind Joe, Peter, and the others who were leading the formation.

"She seem okay to you?"

Teagan followed his gaze. "You mean Marina?"

Brent nodded.

"Of course she's not okay, Brent. You should've seen her trying to fight that … thing off. After she pushed me back into the room, I could only hear it … I — "

"It's okay, Teagan. You don't have to." After a few moments of clomping hooves and preadolescent laughter, he spoke again. "But that's what I mean. That's a lot to deal with, and she seems really shaken up. I think she needs someone to talk to."

Brent looked at Teagan, waiting for her to get the clue.

"Me? Why me? She obviously doesn't want to talk."

"Because you're the only person she's remotely close to."

"Yeah," Teagan said. "The operative word is *remote*."

Brent laughed. "I thought you were friends."

Teagan shrugged. "We get along. But Marina's always seemed a bit … off."

Brent seemed to be choosing his words carefully. Finally, he said, "Well, you two have something to bond over, right?"

"And what's that?"

"Overbearing religious fathers."

Teagan laughed. Brent smiled.

"You're right. Marina's probably no more *off* than I am."

"That's not what I'm saying."

"Well, sort of." Teagan laughed again. "But that's okay. I get it."

"I'm just saying that out of everyone here, maybe you're the person most equipped to understand her."

Teagan craned her neck, looking up the line toward Marina, then turned toward Brent. "I get what you're saying, but just because we both had religious fathers doesn't mean we have all that much in common. And besides, there's little shared between Christianity and The Church of Original Whatever."

"I'm comparing households, not religions, and suggesting that there's something about growing up orthodox anything that tempts parents to nurture a fascination with laws and control. Look, my parents weren't especially religious, so maybe I don't know what I'm talking about, but being a reporter gives you a front row seat to plenty of shit you don't want to see. In my experience, people become religious for a lot of reasons, good and bad. Sometimes, it's because their lives are out of control, morally, socially, whatever. Religion brings light to their dark, order to the chaos. It serves as inner police. Even if everything else in your lives is opposite, the two religions, and your fathers, probably have *that* in common. Just *talk* to her," he added, nodding toward the front of the line. "Please."

"Dad?" Ben appeared by Bashful's side, with Becca just behind him. "I have to pee."

Brent looked toward the bushes. "Why are you telling me?"

Ben ticked his head toward Becca.

"Ah," Brent said. "Got it."

He turned to Becca. "Hey, Becca, wanna play I Spy?"

"Yes!"

"Well, I'll leave you all to it, then." Teagan smiled, nodded at Becca, turned and winked at Brent, mouthed *thank you*, then nudged Whinny forward.

Teagan took her time falling into pace beside Marina, not wanting to seem eager, but after a few minutes Whinny and Marina's horse, Nickel, were trotting side-by-side.

"It's a nice day," Teagan said.

Wow. I'm actually talking about the weather.

No response, not that she deserved one.

"Feels nice to ride outside The Farm."

You know, after being chased away by alien shapeshifters.

"Ben and Becca seem to think we're on an adventure. Can you imagine?"

I'm getting dumber by the word.

Marina finally looked over. It seemed like she wanted to smile, but the morning's weight seemed heavy on her face. Her mouth rose at the corners then fell. She turned from Teagan.

"You know, I'm happy to talk, if you want to."

Marina said nothing, gaze fixed in front of her, skin creamy against her green scarf.

Another few moments of silence, then Teagan tried again.

"I got pregnant with Becca while I was in high school. That was the loneliest time of my life."

Marina didn't respond. Teagan continued.

"I didn't have anyone I could talk to. My sister was gone because she'd killed herself not too long before. And I couldn't say anything to my mom or dad. The thought of talking to any of the adults I knew was scary because I didn't know who might fink to my parents."

Another pause, still nothing.

"Even if I got the courage to talk, everyone I knew would have probably tried to give me advice or help in some way. But that wasn't what I wanted. When I thought about it — and I did each night before falling asleep, each morning when I woke, and all day long — I realized that all I *really* wanted was someone to give me their unbiased ear."

Marina finally looked over, still silent.

"Sometimes, we want a stranger to listen because they're less likely to judge us or make the wrong assumptions. And sometimes, the best advice is no advice, when all you want is for someone to hear you vent. Well," Teagan shrugged, "I never had that. But I'd love to be that person for you."

Teagan could practically feel Marina thinking. She finally said, "I guess I'm just numb to it all."

A pregnant pause. Teagan didn't know if she was supposed to listen or fill it.

"What's the point in fighting anymore?" Marina's voice dropped an octave. "At first, I thought we were fighting for something, and *that* gave me hope. I thought I was somehow going to make a difference. But how can we have hope if everything can be taken away so easily? One moment of weakness, and it's over … why bother?"

"My grandma used to say, 'When the world says, *'Give up,'* hope whispers, *'Try one more time.'* I used to think that was corny. Not anymore. Now I think things like that are all we really have to hold onto."

"My dad used to say, 'Hope is frail but hard to kill.' But he was wrong about a lot of things."

Maybe she was imagining it, but Teagan felt Marina's voice blush with warmth despite her chilling words.

"If you knew that hope and despair were two roads going to the same place, wouldn't you rather be where the sun *might be* shining?"

Marina looked at Teagan for a long moment before returning her eyes to the trail. Finally, she said, "Thank you, Teagan. Really. That — "

Gunfire exploded up front, to the sides, and behind them.

Just ahead, and slightly to the left, Joe tumbled off of his horse. The brown colt whinnied, bucked, and knocked into Peter. He fell, too.

Marina looked wide eyed and vacant, her mouth hanging open.

"Marina, move!" Teagan pointed to the trees. "There! Find cover!"

More gunshots.

Teagan hoped she wasn't sending Marina into the worst of it but saw no other choice. She turned Whinny around, searching for Brent and the children.

Gunshots, flying dust, screaming horses.

Chaos.

Teagan wrapped her arm around Whinny, pressed her face to the horse's neck, and surveyed the scene, keeping low enough to hopefully miss any whizzing bullets.

She found Brent and the children at the edge of her vision, barely visible through the dust clouds. Between her and them, a fallen convoy.

Peter and Joe had been trampled; Rebecca lay sprawled with her head busted like a melon dropped on Spanish tile, a pool of blood soaking the dirt; James and Nils didn't seem to be bleeding, or breathing. Marilyn was lying facedown, half her head blown off.

Only the big man, Sammy, seemed unscathed, galloping away from Brent toward Teagan.

She hoped Marina was safe in the trees.

"Come on, girl," Sammy said, riding up beside her.

"We have to get the children, and Brent." Teagan pointed through the dust.

"I'll get them. You get to Marina." Sammy nodded toward the trees. Reading her mind, he added, "And pray that it's safe."

It took everything inside Teagan to listen. She wanted to ignore Sammy and gallop toward her daughter, the only man left in this world that she truly cared about, and his son. But she imagined a volley of bullets sending her to the dirt. Sammy was a way better shot than her and far less likely to get everyone killed.

She swallowed hard, licked her lips, and said, "Okay. Bring them back to me, Sammy."

Sammy was already gone.

Staying low, Teagan kicked Whinny and took off toward

the trees, searching for Marina but not seeing so much as a hint of her scarf.

Most of the horses had lost their riders and fled. The remaining few cantered in nervous circles, making scared sounds. She peered through the dust, desperate to see, crying out when it finally cleared.

Brent and Sammy, along with Ben and Becca, huddled near their horses, surrounded by a half-dozen bandits, all with rifles or pistols aimed directly at them.

Teagan began to go forward but stopped when the frozen voice behind her growled, "I wouldn't do that if I were you."

❧

SEVENTEEN

Ed Keenan

Ed and Lisa stood on the warehouse roof under the pretense of watching the streets and skies for signs of aliens. Truth was, tension was too thick in the warehouse, so Ed found a reason to leave, taking Lisa, his most trusted person in the team.

"So," she said, "do you think it was a trap?"

He nodded. "I think so."

"Do you think Mary should've sliced her throat?"

There was a time when Ed would've thought yes. He'd killed too many people to judge Mary. But since losing Jade, he wasn't sure he would've — or could've — done the same thing.

"No," he said. "There were other ways to respond."

"Agreed. And I don't even think she was doing it in response to the trap. I think she snapped."

"I wouldn't blame her."

Lisa stared at Ed as if trying to read him. "You lost your daughter, too. How do you keep it together?"

He shook his head. "Who said I do?"

For a long moment, neither spoke.

A cool, salty breeze rolled in off the coast. The clouds had broken, and the sun was high in the sky. They could see the mothership in the distance, always hovering above The Island — so close, yet so far out of reach.

Lisa paced, as if wanting to say something but unable to figure out how to broach the subject. It was odd for her, as she was usually such a bold person — too brusque for Ed's tastes.

Ed took the bull by its horns. "What is it?"

"What are we gonna do about her?"

"*Do?*"

"We can't trust her not to do something like this again. She could've got us all killed. Hell, she would've if not for Luca teleporting in and saving our asses."

"First off, if it was a trap, and we were in danger regardless. Yes, things would've unfolded differently, but given what happened, I'd say we were pretty lucky. Maybe we wouldn't have been so fortunate without Mary acting."

"You don't really believe that horseshit, do you?"

Ed met her eyes. Lisa was giving him that look like she dared him to argue that she was wrong. She was used to intimidating others. He wondered how much his calm reaction fueled her anger, never taking the bait.

"I'll ask you again, what would you have us do? Ostracize her?"

"I didn't say that."

"So, what *are* you saying, Lisa?"

"She shouldn't go on any more missions, at least not until she gets her head clear."

He chewed on it then said, "So, you want me to approach the others, is that it?"

"It can't come from me. They hate me."

"True." He nodded.

"Screw you," she joked. "Seriously, they won't take this as well coming from me."

"And you think they'll take it better from me?"

"Boricio respects you."

"He's a psychopath." Ed laughed. "He respects nothing."

"No, Ed. He respects you. Don't tell me you can't see it."

"Maybe. But he's with Mary. They're an item. You can't go telling a guy that his girlfriend's a loose cannon that needs to be kept away from the gang. Even if he agrees, he's not gonna tell her she can't go on missions."

"Then I want a reassignment."

"To where?"

"Beta Team? Charlie Team? Delta? The Farm? I dunno. Anywhere but here. She's an accident waiting to happen, and I don't want to be here when it does."

"Fair enough," Ed said. "I'll talk to Boricio."

"So, you're not going to reassign me?"

"I'd prefer not to. Pain in the ass that you are, you're one of the only people I can count on 100 percent."

She smiled then quickly turned away.

He was reasonably sure she was blushing but wasn't about to call attention to it for fear she'd think he was flirting. Lisa might have a thing for him, but Ed had no room in his heart for anyone else. It was bad enough that Teagan and Becca — two of the only people he cared about — depended on him for their safety. He couldn't stand to let anyone else in for fear of failing them as he had Jade.

Ed started back toward the ladder leading down into the warehouse. "I'm gonna talk to Boricio. You staying or going?"

"I'll hang out here," she said. "Let shit cool down."

"Good call."

Ed went to the rooftop hatch then descended the ladder.

He found Boricio sitting cross-legged on the ground in front of Luca and the now-conscious girl. No matter how many times Ed saw Luca heal someone near death, he still wasn't used to the remarkable feat. Nor how much it had aged the young boy into an old man.

Luca's hair was a thick gray mop falling over his droopy, dark-circled eyes. Wrinkles, which had only appeared a month or so ago, were now deeply etched into his face. Luca was leaning against the wall, looking exhausted, while Boricio questioned the girl.

Luca closed his eyes. Ed wondered how many more miracles the man-child had inside him.

Ed approached Boricio and the girl.

Boricio looked up. "Pop a squat, Keen-O! This here is Emily. And Boy Wonder here says she checks out. If it *was* a trap, she didn't know. But she also wouldn't be surprised. Turns out her dad works with Desmond Do Right."

"In what capacity?" Ed asked, still on his feet.

"He helps get people ready for *implantation,* putting the aliens in their fresh new hosts." Ed noted that Boricio wasn't shitting all over the man's being a traitor to his kind, probably wanting to keep the girl from getting defensive. "And it's an important job because he's one of the only free humans."

"Free humans?" Ed asked. "How many humans are on The Island, and the ship?"

Emily looked up at him. "I don't know. Probably six hundred, though I don't know how many are free. Most of the people who work on The Island are hosts. They have an alien inside them. My dad is important, though, so we're allowed to keep our independence, along with a few other people with important jobs."

"How many aliens are on the ship?"

"Just over nine hundred, I think."

Boricio and Ed exchanged a glance. They didn't want to verbalize it in front of the girl, but that was a lot of fucking aliens.

Ed asked, "What can you tell us about Desmond?"

"Not much. I know he makes my dad nervous."

"How do you know that?" Boricio asked.

Emily paused, as if unsure whether she should voice her thoughts. She looked at Luca.

He nodded.

"Because sometimes I can peek into his head."

"Whatchyou talkin' bout, Willis?" Boricio asked.

Luca said, "She's like me. She has powers."

Boricio asked, "Like *X-Men* powers 'n shit?"

"Maybe kinda like Jean Grey but not Phoenix. She's a telepath. But not from the vials or anything. Telepathy runs in her family."

"How do you know this?" Ed asked. "She tell you?"

"No, I could tell while inside her head. And when she went inside mine."

"You let her inside your head?" Boricio looked annoyed. "We don't even know her!"

"She's okay."

Suddenly, footsteps. Mary approaching. The last thing this conversation needed.

Mary must've heard the last part of the conversation because she snapped, "She's okay? So then why the hell did she lead us right into a trap?"

"I didn't know it was a trap." Emily looked up at Mary nervously, likely afraid the woman who nearly killed her was back to finish the job.

Boricio popped up onto his feet and stepped between Mary and the girl. "She's clean."

"Yeah, and how do you know? How can any of us know for sure? How do you know this isn't part of the trap, too? We bring her back to our headquarters, then they come and hit us when we're off guard."

Luca, with considerable effort, stood. "Please, Mary. Stop it."

Whatever steam had been building in Mary was suddenly let out in one big gust as her shoulders slumped and she stared at Luca as if he'd smacked her. Less angry than surprised. Perhaps she was taken aback by his appearance. It was one thing to be called out by a child, but another when that child looks like your grandfather.

Luca continued, "I know you miss Paola. We all do. But you can't live your life in fear."

Mary shook her head. "I don't know if you've looked around lately, but that's all we have left — fear we'll be discovered, fear we'll be infected, fear that The Farm will be overrun and that no one can protect them, fear that ... "

She stopped.

"What?" Luca asked.

Mary looked at Boricio and Ed then back at Luca. "Fear of what happens when you die."

Luca seemed genuinely confused. "Why are you afraid for me?"

"Because you're the only thing that's kept us from being killed already. You've saved us more times than we can count, and now you're aging too quickly. And fuck, I didn't exactly help." She pointed to Emily. "That must've aged you five years between teleporting us and healing her."

"It's okay," Luca said. "I don't mind. I want to help you all."

"What's the point, though? Really. We've been rats for four fucking years: running, hiding, running, and waiting for what — a chance to get on The Island? Then what? Do we have any fucking clue how to bring the aliens down once we get there? *If* we even can?"

Everybody was silent.

Ed considered saying something, but hell if Mary didn't have a point. They'd been trying so hard to find a way onto The Island — kidnapping people, attempting to hijack a shuttle, and they'd even sent two scouts on boats late at night — but nothing had worked.

The Island was a fortress. And the alien ship above it, an even more impenetrable one.

While they'd saved a number of humans from being killed or taken by the aliens, many whom now served as scouts for the cause in other sectors, some who joined their ranks, they didn't have the soldiers to win a war. Not against nine hundred-something aliens, and however many humans were now on their side.

"She's right," Ed finally said. "We've got nothing."

They'd had similar discussions before. They'd never known the number of aliens on the ship, so conversations hadn't felt so defeating or hopeless, but certainly the shades of doubt weren't new. Each time, Boricio had given them a pep talk to get their heads back in the game, ready to do whatever might keep them fighting.

But now he was silent.

They all traded stares.

Jevonne, who had been on the discussion's periphery, stared at the ground without any suggestions.

Emily spoke.

"I might have something that can help."

"Oh?" Ed asked. "What's that?"

"I may be able to reach my dad." She touched her temple. "In here."

~

EIGHTEEN

Paul Roberts

Paul hated when they drugged the subjects.

He sighed at the Guardsman leading the sluggish redhead into the interview room then depositing her handcuffed body into the seat opposite him at the table.

"Really?" Paul said. "You're bringing her to me like this? How the hell am I supposed to get a good reading on her in this state?"

"Hey," the Guardsman answered from behind his dark visored helmet, "she was feisty."

Paul looked the woman up and down, rolling his eyes. She was in her early twenties and weighed about a buck ten at most. Unless she was a jujitsu master, he didn't see her creating too big a problem for the armed Guardsman.

"So, do you want her or not?" the Guardsman asked.

"Just get out of here," Paul said, annoyed at their incompetence. More so today because he found it hard to think of anything other than his daughter, wondering how the mission was going, and if they had what was needed. Paul had tried to feel Emily's presence but couldn't. He wasn't sure if it was the distance between them or if something had happened to her. He tried not to think of the latter.

Focus on the work. The rest will take care of itself.

The Guardsman left, closing the door behind him.

Now it was Paul and his subject in the dimly lit interview room.

He hated entering drugged minds. It felt like more of a violation to people who were already victims — kidnapped and possibly giving their lives up to become hosts for parasitic aliens. And worse, their brains seemed to move so much slower when drugged. It was like swimming in a sea of memories with one hand tied behind his back, and sometimes like dealing with an overemotional child's tantrum.

Just looking at the woman — the bruises and track marks on her arms, old abrasions on her face, scratches all over — Paul could tell she'd been through some serious shit and was using a lot of drugs to cope with life in The Wastelands. He'd have to wade through it all to determine her worth as a host.

There was a time when he'd have dismissed her as dysfunctional without even sifting. She had too many strikes against her. But lately the people being picked up were looking worse and worse, and beggars couldn't be choosers when crops were thin. They needed new bodies. The upper levels were designed to accommodate the aliens in their current forms, but their bodies were atrophying at an alarming rate. And who knew how quickly they could get their baby farm producing more children for the aliens to use?

Paul shuddered. He wasn't sure which grossed him out more: the aliens' insect-like bodies or their gelatinous true form. He'd been present for three implantations so far, and had barely been able to hide his disgust.

At least they weren't using his body — or Emily's.

"So," the redhead said, her voice slurred, "who the fuck are you?"

God, I hate my job.

"I'm here to determine if you're a match for our program."

"I don't wanna be part a no program. I jus' wanna go home," she said, her voice slightly raised, body still sedated.

Judging from her grammar, she was the right amount of stupid to make for an appropriate host. The aliens didn't want morons but found the ignorant easier to placate once inhabited. How exactly the aliens pacified the host mind, Paul wasn't certain. He imagined that they flooded the host mind with arousing sensations — similar to the consumption of food, sex, and drugs. Intelligent people were coddled in a different way — making them feel like they were part of the decision-making process rather than a vessel used by the aliens.

Paul wasn't sure which would be a worse hell: thinking you were an equal in your body or being distracted by a flood of meaningless pleasantries.

Well, ignorance is bliss, right?

He asked the woman a series of questions designed to relax her mind, to make her more receptive to his infiltration.

Six questions in, the door to the room opened.

Paul was half out of his seat ready to yell at whoever the hell was interrupting him. But it was Desmond.

"We need to talk."

∾

PAUL COULDN'T DO anything other than stare at the command center screens, watching replays of the woman, whom Desmond called Mary, slicing his daughter's neck on repeat.

He wanted to hit something while watching the video footage shot from the shuttle. No, not something — Desmond. And not hit, but murder.

"She's not dead," Desmond assured him. "I'm certain that Luca has healed her."

"How can you know that?"

"Because if she were dead, her chip would've exploded.

"You put an *exploding* chip in her?"

"Would you please relax?" Desmond said as if they were discussing a minor inconvenience rather than his daughter's throat being slit and an explosive tracking chip embedded in her body.

"What are you doing to get her back?" Paul asked, voice too loud, too stern for Desmond's right-hand man, Wasterman. Paul didn't give a fuck.

"We're monitoring the situation," Wasterman said.

"What the fuck does that even mean?"

Wasterman's bushy eyebrows arched as if to ask, *Who the hell do you think you are?*

Desmond, in his calmest smile and voice, said, "We are tending to the situation and have eyes on their location now."

"So why the hell aren't you there getting her, and your target?"

"I assume you want your daughter back in one piece?"

"Well, yes, of course."

"Then we need to be cautious. I meant what I said before, Paul. You and your daughter are valuable members of our family. We're not going to let anyone harm her."

Paul pointed at the monitors and his daughter's throat being slit. "Yeah, some job you've done. What if Luca hadn't teleported in and saved her? Could *you* have healed her?"

"We would have tried our best."

"But no guarantees, right?"

Desmond met his eyes. Paul felt something shifting under the surface, something that said he was pushing his luck. Worse, Paul was doing so in front of Desmond's underling. You don't show up the boss in front of his subordinates. That never went well, in Hollywood or the alien apocalypse.

"I'm sorry," Paul said, trying his best to show he meant it. "I … I just get rattled not being able to do anything. And seeing that … *that bitch* … do that to Emily only pisses me off more. What the hell did Emily ever do to them?"

"You'll get your chance to do whatever you like with Mary soon, Mr. Roberts. I promise. For now, please trust that we have the matter under control."

"So, why did you bring me in here? Just to update me? Or do you need something more?"

"You *are* the perceptive one, Mr. Roberts." Desmond smiled. "When we capture Luca, I'll need you to get inside his head to ensure he doesn't teleport away, and extract information I want. Do you think you can do that?"

"Aren't you able to get inside his head?"

"No. Unfortunately. He's a blank spot on my radar. I can barely sense him. I certainly can't access his head."

"So, how do you think *I* can get in there?"

"If Luca healed your daughter, it may have opened a doorway."

"But first we need to get him, and my daughter."

"We're already on it, Mr. Roberts."

NINETEEN

Teagan McLachlan

The trees behind Teagan seethed with unseen dangers. She could feel the bandits' weapons as if pressed to her flesh.

"Trot," said a threatening voice from behind.

She wanted to glance back, see how many men might be prodding her forward, but Teagan didn't dare. She urged Whinny forward and quietly surveyed the scene.

Sammy's eyes were fixed on a black man in front of him — the only man she'd ever seen who might have been larger than Barrow. Brent turned to Teagan, his eyes full of apology for a disaster he couldn't have stopped. Becca was sobbing. Ben held out until he saw Teagan approaching. Then he, too, surrendered to tears.

Whinny stopped a few feet from the captives, Nickel beside her. Teagan was afraid to look around but counted six bandits from what she could see, two of them women, not including however many were behind her and Marina.

One of the women had bright-red hair, filthy and ratted, hanging in a thick curtain around her filthy, stained face. The other looked like she might have been a preapocalypse blonde, before the world turned her into a monster willing to aim a sawed off shotgun at children.

The most menacing bandit stared Sammy down. He was riding atop Bashful, but Teagan pegged him to be around seven feet tall. He had a kinky black halo of hair, jutting out from his head in ragged tufts. A long scar bisected his face into two ghastly, unequal parts, the ugliest sharing the side with a milky blind eye.

He looked like a living nightmare, and judging from appearances, had to be the Reaper.

He finally spoke with a voice that sounded like an ancient engine forced to turn. "Anyone else trip-trapping across my bridge? Or you six the last of them?"

The man sat on his horse, eyes scraping the group, drifting from Brent's sweaty terror to Sammy's throttled rage to Ben's and Becca's sobbing.

The Reaper, if that's who he was, had barely an ounce of fat on his body. Muscles rippled across his bare chest and bulged the fabric around his thighs and legs.

Teagan tried not to give way to tears.

"I said, anyone else trip-trapping across my bridge?"

"This is it," Sammy said. "You butchered the rest of us."

Teagan's heart pounded painfully hard, hoping that Sammy hadn't just asked the beast to kill him. Or *them*.

The Reaper smiled and showed his rotting teeth. "That's right." He leaned toward Sammy. "I did."

Sammy flinched and staggered back.

The Reaper smiled wider. "I did what I had to so the rest of you would be smart enough to keep yourselves from doing something stupid. Should I have finished the job?"

He glanced at the group then settled back on Sammy.

Sammy held the man's stare for as long as he could — three seconds at most — then fell another step back, swallowed, and said, "No."

Eyes still on Sammy, the Reaper again displayed his rotting teeth. "I'm guessin' you was expecting to hit the highway without any highway men, am I right?"

"We didn't expect anything, one way or the other. We had a run-in with some aliens up at our farm." Sammy nodded toward the hills. "And we needed to reach the highway. We meant no disrespect, and hold no grudges. Let us get on our way, and you'll never have to see us again."

"That's awful nice of you to keep them grudges to yourself." The Reaper laughed. "Now, what would make you think I don't want to see you again?"

The Reaper turned from Sammy to Teagan and licked her with his good eye.

"Howz about I let *some* of you go — keep the rest as fair trade?"

Brent got stupid: "Don't you dare touch her!"

The Reaper nodded at a hook-nosed man standing behind Brent, holding a blade. A beat later, Brent was sprawled on the ground, screaming, covering his right eye to keep gushing blood from his head gash from getting inside it.

"You must have me confused for someone patient, or maybe a man who might be interested in your side of whatever bargain I'm not likely to make." Again, the Reaper raked the group with his gaze. "Anyone else have anything to add?"

No one did.

The Reaper turned and rode Bashful into the forest.

The hook-nosed man reached down and took Brent's gun then searched his body for anything else he might be carrying.

"Weapons in a pile." He pointed to the ground.

Teagan was unarmed but lost her horse. Sammy's gun and knife were taken.

The hook-nosed man climbed onto Teagan's horse and addressed the group. "Any of you wants to come at Marcus, you best not miss. He'll clean his teeth with your bones."

If Marcus was the Reaper, it didn't look like he cleaned his teeth with anything at all. The thought failed to improve Teagan's mood.

The bandits put collars on all of them then tied the adults

to one another, then Becca and Ben to each other, then marched them into the woods at gunpoint. She wasn't sure how many of them there were, as some had stayed behind in the woods. She could hear them moving as they started marching to wherever the hell Marcus was leading them.

She hoped that they didn't find Marina. And that Marina was somehow tracking them. Maybe she could go and get the others and save them.

Teagan turned to check on the kids marching behind her, sniffling back tears. One of the women barked, "Turn around!"

Teagan did.

"And stop your damned crying, kids, or I'll give ya somethin' to cry about!"

Teagan wanted to tear the bitch's eyes out.

After what felt like an hour of relatively silent marching, Teagan saw a flash of movement to her left. And then it was gone. But she was pretty certain she'd seen Marina's green scarf.

She is *following us!*

But even as she felt a ray of hope, Teagan wondered if maybe it was just wishful thinking. Maybe she hadn't seen anything but what she'd wanted to. Surely, if there were someone tracking them, the other bandits would've noticed. Hell, maybe it was even one of the bandits traveling in the woods. Maybe the bandit had killed Marina and taken her scarf.

No, no, it has *to be her.*

Has to be.

Any other possibility was too horrible to consider.

If it were Marina, Teagan wondered what she was planning. Marina wasn't exactly Ed or Boricio. But she was a fighter. And she clearly wouldn't leave them to the Reaper. Not that Teagan could blame her if she did.

Teagan held her pace for another fifteen minutes,

wondering if any of the other refugees saw Marina. And then Teagan saw something ahead in the brush, lying on the ground, a dead woman with a green scarf.

No, no, no!

"Hold up!" yelled the hook-nosed man, seeing the same thing.

Whinny whined. Brent and Sammy stopped marching.

Teagan inched forward but was ordered back by Hook Nose as he brought the horse toward the bed of leaves and the body sprawled across it.

It was Marina, lying there on the ground, perfectly still, faceup, arms sprawled, eyes closed, blood on her face and neck.

Oh God, no!

Had Marcus seen her, killed her, then kept on riding ahead?

Hook Nose dropped to the ground with a thud. He looked down at Marina, shrugged, then kicked her in the ribs. Her body trembled from the force of his foot, but Marina made no other sound.

Hook Nose drew a sword from the scabbard at his back, mouth curled in a wicked grin. He nodded then moved to plunge his blade.

It stopped an inch from her skin. Marina's eyes opened, and her hands circled the metal. Blood gushed from her fingers, seeping between them, spilling down over her knuckles and onto the blade.

Hook Nose lost his calm to terror. His eyes were confused, his bottom lip quivered, and he lost his grip on the hilt.

A fat Hispanic behind Teagan yelled, "What the fuck?" then he and the others rushed toward Marina.

Teagan couldn't imagine where she found the strength, or the will, but Marina managed to twist the blade without losing her fingers then turn it around and bury it in her attacker's chest.

Hook Nose fell forward, probably dead before hitting the ground. Marina grabbed the sword, this time by the handle, blood pouring like a faucet from her skin.

Fat Hispanic's rifle was aimed, but Marina swung the sword in a wide arc, slicing into his throat before he pulled the trigger.

Blood sprayed from Fat Hispanic onto Marina's face and body. He dropped his rifle, hands clapped to his gushing throat.

A shot rang out, maybe hitting Marina before she darted past the tree line and disappeared into the woods.

Bandits flew by Teagan, emptying their guns in pursuit.

Suddenly, it seemed as if there was nobody watching them. Three bandits on horseback were ahead of them, watching after the bandits who took off after Marina.

Teagan looked back, caught Brent's eyes, and shook her head. He and Sammy looked ready to strike the three remaining bandits, but all were unarmed. If they tried anything, the five survivors, including Ben and Becca, would be cut to nothing.

Sammy looked ready to go anyway.

Brent planted a hand on Sammy's shoulder to stop him.

One of the three horsemen, an old man with an eye patch, who reminded Teagan of a pirate, turned his horse around and started toward them. He reached down and, proving his strength despite his age, grabbed Becca and planted her in front of him. She buried her face in the horse's mane and sobbed.

Ben, still connected to Becca by a length of rope to his collar, was tugged forward and nearly fell.

Brent helped him up as the pirate watched them.

Pirate said, "Anyone speaks, moves, or looks like they're gonna, I kill every one of you. Understood?"

Everyone nodded, Ben sniffling back tears.

No one spoke.

Teagan had to piss but knew better than to ask. She held it in, trying to think of anything other than having to piss.

Time seemed to stretch forever with just them and the three horsemen. Neither the Reaper nor the others had yet returned.

Maybe Marina had killed them all. Was it too much to hope?

Several minutes later — it felt like an hour — the men and woman who had chased Marina into the woods returned.

"Did you get her?" the old pirate asked.

The ugly blonde said, "I think we got a couple of shots in her, but who knows? She disappeared."

An ugly man with a T-shirt that read, *I hope you like feminist rants, because that's sort of my thing* added, "Bitch was fast."

"So what now?" asked the pirate. "We go and find her or leave her for the aliens?"

The blonde shrugged. "We wait for Marcus."

As if on cue, without a single snapping twig to announce his horse, Marcus appeared like a ghost.

"She best bury herself. If the aliens find her, bitch'll wish she was dead. *We* find her, she'll wish I was an alien." A beat, then the Reaper added, "Have you all ever eaten human flesh? It's tasty. Children are especially yummy."

He glared down at them without a trace of anything but stone-cold seriousness.

Before Teagan could stop herself, piss darkened her crotch. Marcus looked down, saw the soaking spot, and smiled.

She felt another chill at the man's rotting teeth.

He turned around and twirled his finger in the air. "We got places to be before dark."

Marcus trotted forward. Everyone fell in line behind him.

Teagan wasn't sure how long they walked, but she'd never felt so exhausted. They were spent and thirsty but had yet been given a chance to rest or offered water. Nor did they ask.

While Becca was on horseback ahead with the pirate, Ben was walking between her and Brent, staring straight ahead, his face dirty, save for where tears had cleared a path on their way down his cheeks. His eyes were numb, just like Brent's, staring ahead, marching on toward the unknown.

They didn't head down to PCH like she expected. Once close to the bend at the hill's bottom, they turned and started heading up another hill to the east, into what had once been a nice neighborhood in the hills with huge houses and even larger yards — both overgrown with vegetation.

They followed a long street, cracked and broken in parts, but still relatively holding together against nature. The followed a twisting path of side roads as day flirted with night.

They stopped in front of a wall tall enough to make Teagan think it might be missing a drawbridge. In contrast to Alto Verde's opulent architecture, the wall was sloppy, with bricks askew in uneven rows, mortar oozing like pus from a wound. A wooden gate was cut roughly into the wall. Two armed guards stood in front, one on either side. Neither spoke, though both nodded at the group's approach. Above the guards, a wooden sign was somehow fixed to the brick.

The sign, in rough red paint, read, *Welcome to Hell.*

~

TWENTY

It

___

After Paul and Wasterman left the room, *It* stared at the monitors, unable to look away from the sight of Luca teleporting in and saving the group.

Why did this boy-turned-man continue fighting?

Or rather, why did The Light continue to fight for the humans?

Couldn't *It* see that they'd lost the war? Were the ships in the sky, the flattened cities, or the millions of corpses not proof enough? The old world was gone; a new species had inherited it.

Yet the humans continued fighting progress. *The Light* continued fighting his collective. Every day, *It* lost touch with more and more of the creatures *It* had unleashed on the world.

Where were they going? Were the humans killing them? Or was The Light somehow thinning their ranks?

Why?

"Why do you torment me so?" *It* asked the video.

Part of *It* wished *It* could teleport to where Luca was at that moment. Teleport in, grab him, teleport out. But *It* knew that Luca would sense *It* coming. And would throw up defenses.

No, *It* had to plan this carefully. Move in at the exact right moment. Perhaps *It* wouldn't get Luca now, but *It* had little doubt that one of *Its* plans would come to fruition. Luca, The Light, would be caught soon enough.

It had to be patient. Had to remember that battles were fought in incremental stages. If you moved too soon and exposed yourself to the enemy, you would be vanquished. The human race had existed for hundreds of thousands of years, and they weren't quite ready to lie down for the new order just yet.

Again, he wondered why The Light was fighting on the side of the humans. If The Light and Darkness had both, in fact, been designed by the Pruhm to help usher in destruction, why was The Light now fighting to preserve humanity?

It had to be because of the humans The Light had come into contact with. When *It* was in *Its* primal form, in the vials, *It* was untainted, programmed to both create and destroy as *It* saw fit. Damaged humans had been beneficial to *Its* growth — showing *It* what must be done to usher in the new world and species.

But the naive, the gullible, and the innocent had infected part of *It*, turning it into this so-called *Light.* Twisting *Its* purpose, giving *It* some sort of empathy with the creatures marked for extinction or evolution.

The Light saw *Itself* as the hero in this act, a force of Good. But *It* saw the truth — that The Light was only harming life's purpose — to fulfill *Its* potential. As far as *It* was concerned, The Light was an anathema to life. The Light was clinging to a dead world, to a dead species, preventing progress.

And *It* would do everything in *Its* power to extinguish The Light once and for all.

It thought about *Its* moment of weakness back on the other world's Black Island.

Darkness and Light had shed their mortal husks and fought in their pure forms. During that battle, *It* glimpsed something *It* had never seen — a peace that existed within The Light. A peace so tranquil, so promising, *It* was momentarily tempted to surrender to The Light, to forget *Its* own purpose.

But *It* couldn't surrender.

It was not designed to acquiesce. And progress was rarely peaceful. It came in violent fits.

It wondered how long *Its* masters would continue to sit by and watch as *It* continued to lose control of the Ferals, which were running wild, killing at will both humans and Guardsmen sent into The Wasteland. *It* had to figure out how to reverse this situation and seize control of the collective before losing connection to all but those on the ship and The Island.

It stared at Luca's image on-screen, knowing that he, or The Light inside him, held the answers. The Light would allow *It* to finally reconnect with *Its* collective. And once *It* had regained full control, and could finally evolve humans properly, *It* could break free of *Its* masters' chains and be something more than the Pruhm or humanity ever dreamed they could be.

~

TWENTY-ONE

Mary Olson

As the sun was setting, Mary knew some bad shit was afoot.

She could tell in the way everyone was looking at her. Could tell from Keenan, Boricio, and Lisa's traded secret glances. Could tell from the way the girl seemed to have everyone wrapped around her little fiction: being able to telepathically connect with her father — even though the bitch had yet been able to do so.

What's the deal? Is Daddy's connection down? Maybe he didn't pay his telepathy bill.

What utter bullshit.

Maybe the girl had fooled everyone else, but Mary refused to buy what the girl was selling.

Mary sensed the trap before, and figured they were still in its jaws, even if none of them had the sense to know better. They were like mice marveling over all the cheese they found on top of this conveniently placed wooden contraption. She wasn't sure whose naiveté disappointed her more, Keenan's or Boricio's.

Keenan was a brilliant strategist, a former secret agent, and one of the deadliest close-quarter fighters she'd ever seen.

He was also a skilled marksman. The full package. The guy you want leading your team, even if he was gruff.

Boricio was her closest friend, and lover. He was charismatic as hell and a lot of fun to bullshit with, even if he was an egomaniacal psychopath. He was supposed to have her back, without question or argument. That was the arrangement she *thought* they had. She'd defended him early on when some of the group had grown tired of his "beer-battered bullshit." When they'd started to see glimpses of his past in their dreams, thanks to whatever the hell alien stuff was coursing through Luca.

Then there was Luca. He was no longer just a boy. He was two boys and an alien, who had claimed to have part of Paola in him, too, until Mary told him to stop telling her that. Mary refused to believe that any part of Paola lived inside him. It was a macabre joke, some game the alien was playing to manage their emotions — to make them think they'd not lost as much as they had. Maybe The Light was on their side, but The Light wasn't human, no matter what, and as far as Mary was concerned, The Light couldn't be completely trusted either, even if it was saving them. The question was — why was it saving them? To what end did it continue to keep them alive?

This was the kind of shit that Boricio said made her sound paranoid. But from her point of view, she was the only one thinking clearly these days. The only one who could see a threat.

To see this girl here, working them, made Mary sick to her stomach. Were they desperate enough for something to believe in that they'd give this girl carte-blanche access to their information, to their network, to their most secret of hideouts in hopes that she could get them to The Island?

Mary wanted to reach The Island more than anyone there. Wanted to see Desmond's face when she slit him nuts to throat, watched his entrails, and perhaps the alien, spill out of his body. If she were being honest with herself, it was the only thought that pushed her to go on. But Mary wasn't willing to put all her eggs in Little Miss Emily's basket.

After dinner, when everyone sat silently around a large folding table, chowing down on the contents of tin cans over candlelight, Boricio approached Mary, his eyes saying they needed to talk.

She followed him to the roof where the cold wind was picking up and got in Boricio's face, "So, what the hell's going on?"

Boricio met her glare. "You've got everyone thinking you're just three scenes from 'Heeeere's Johnny,' and I'm sure that doesn't surprise you."

She sighed, figuring this would be the topic of conversation. "Really?" she said, sarcastically.

"Yeah, who knew? Slit one kid's throat, and the natives get restless."

Normally, they'd have laughed, wondered why they were fighting, then got drunk and fucked. But this wasn't a normal situation. Mary felt sure that Boricio was again about to prove he didn't have her back.

"So, what do they want? To reassign me?"

"No, nothing that bad. But they don't want you on their missions."

"Excuse me? *They* don't want *me* on *their* missions? Who's this coming from? Lisa? That bitch never liked me."

"I dunno where it started, but everyone agrees."

"*Everyone?*"

Boricio looked down.

"You motherfucker!"

"What?" Boricio said. "You've earned some time off. Consider it a reward for a job well done!"

"Time off? What the hell? No one is punching a clock! I don't need time off. You all need to pull your heads out of your asses! Do you really think that girl is an innocent victim?"

"I don't think she's part of some trap. Yeah, she was probably bait, but that don't make her complicit … *or* deserving of a knife to the throat. And ain't nobody gonna wanna run with you if they can't trust you."

"Yeah, because we all know there can't be two wild cards on *Team Boricio!*"

"I never said I was the perfect team player, but I also don't do shit that gets people killed."

"Neither did I!"

"No, but this could've gone a lot differently."

"So, you want me to do what? Stay at home, barefoot and pregnant, while the big boys and girls play army?"

"Come on, Mary, don't be like that. This isn't permanent. Just until shit blows over. You can stay with Luca and guard him."

"Gee, thanks. You sure you trust me, especially if that girl's staying with us?"

"Well, maybe *she* might have an issue with it. But we'll cross that bridge when we need to."

"No," Mary said. "We won't."

"What do you mean?"

"I'm done."

"Done what?"

"Done with this. We've been running in circles for four years, never getting closer to Desmond. The first time we do, we're walking right into a trap. And I'm the only one who seems to see it. Desmond is getting closer to us, though. The next time, we might not be so lucky."

"So, what, you want to be reassigned?"

"No, I'm going solo."

Mary didn't give Boricio time to try talking her out of it. She turned and headed back to the rooftop hatch.

"Wait! You can't leave."

"No, Boricio. I can't stay."

Boricio chased after her, grabbing Mary again by the elbow.

"You can't leave! I'll talk to them. We'll straighten things out."

Mary wanted to ask why he didn't think to do that already but didn't feel like arguing anymore. She had to do this, make a clean break, before she thought too much about it.

"No, I think it's time for me to go," she said, looking away, lest she break down crying.

"You're not thinking straight."

"Sorry." Mary shook free and descended the ladder.

Boricio followed, on her heels as she reached the ground, then followed Mary toward the exit. She could feel everyone watching, probably wondering what drama the *crazy bitch* was up to now.

"Mary!" Boricio shouted, a few steps behind.

She ignored him, pushing through the door and out onto the streets.

Boricio followed, his voice too damned loud in the evening's quiet.

"You can't go. Please, think it over."

Mary turned, and saw that tears were welling up in Boricio's eyes, too. Seeing those tears only hurt her more. She had to get away, now, before she changed her mind.

Mary turned and started to walk.

"Mary!" Boricio yelled.

"Please, just leave me alone. I can't be around you all now. Just … just leave me alone."

Mary broke into a run with nothing but her pistol and a blade on her belt, leaving Boricio alone and blindsided.

~

TWENTY-TWO

Brent Foster

Brent had never wanted to be Boricio, but as he was led through gates that read, *Welcome to Hell*, he felt like he would have given anything to be the man now.

Sure, Boricio was a beast, but that beast would have already ended this. He wouldn't have allowed so many bodies to fall and wouldn't be marching into the monster's maw with Sammy tied to his wrist.

Brent was too scared to so much as steal a glance at Sammy. His throbbing head was a constant reminder of what might happen if he stepped out of line. Teagan walked in front of him, her back to Becca, who was sharing a horse with an eye patch wearing old man who *smelled* like he had wrong-doing on his mind. Ben walked beside the old man's horse. He'd tried looking back at his dad three times already and earned a smack on the head each time.

The group was led past the makeshift brick wall and into a cul-de-sac, where a half-dozen modest-sized houses made a horseshoe within the fortress walls.

He gulped, seeing four weathered shipping containers at the far end of the cul-de-sac, where the road was at its widest. The boxes were rusted, their red and blue paint flaking. Something ugly and desperate was likely waiting inside, and the five survivors of a roadside assault were surely about to find out just what that was.

The group was made to wait in an awkward circle. Curtains in the homes peeled back, just enough light within the houses — maybe candlelight, Brent thought — to reveal curious and unfriendly eyes. Brent sensed a flash of movement to his left, maybe a fluttering drape, and looked over without thinking.

"I told you to keep your eyes up front!"

Something crashed into the back of his head.

He nearly fell over from the pain but somehow remained standing, if a bit wobbly. He felt like if he did fall, it would make things worse. He'd be inviting the savages to attack more.

The old bandit with the eye patch got off his horse, bringing Becca and Ben to join Brent, Teagan, and Sammy.

The kids tried to hug Brent and Teagan, but the old man snapped, "Stand behind them. No touching!"

Becca cried.

"It'll be okay," Teagan said, even if it was a lie.

Again, Brent longed for courage he didn't have, still wishing he could find the monster inside him, unleash the beast to save them all.

A handful of people spilled from houses and circled the containers, joining the mass of bandits already there.

Everyone was armed and painted with tattoos. Several bandits had stretched ears with objects stuck in the holes — a body mutilation that had never made sense to Brent. Before the apocalypse, he always wondered how people like that found a job. Now it seemed they ruled the world.

A man with a shaved head and a skull tattoo stared at Brent, his eyes gleaming with hate. He smiled, and Brent swallowed, wondering if that might be the man who would take his life.

He chanced a glance at Ben, wanting to comfort his son, knowing that might get them killed. The boy was holding Becca's hand, offering her what little courage he had in him. Brent had never felt prouder of his son, nor more helpless to protect him.

"Tommy!" bellowed a man with tufts of purple hair sprouting from a receding hairline as he ran up to them, circling as he raked Teagan with his eyes. "Fresh meat. Just your type."

Men multiplied. A few women joined the party, surrounding the three of them.

The air filled with whistles and slurps.

Brent could feel Sammy wanting to unleash his rage. But the big Italian kept his anger in check, which was good for all their sakes since they were so heavily outnumbered, not to mention outgunned.

Tommy looked like a hipster heroin rock star. Skinny, thick black eyeliner, leather pants, tattoos covering his body, and a chain running from both pierced nipples. He swaggered over to the man with purple hair. He licked his lips, ran his fingers through his thick, bushy dark hair, and stared at Teagan, his eyes bolted to her chest.

"Yummy." He licked his lips again. "I got dibs."

The purple-haired man said, "You can have the front. I'll take the back."

A general commotion erupted as the swarm surrounded them, arguing over who would be permitted to fraternize with whom.

The hairs on Brent's arms stood on end.

Tommy reached out to touch Teagan. She flinched back.

"Don't be scared, Sally."

Teagan said, "That's not my name."

Brent wished she hadn't.

Purple hair pulled a knife from his back, raised it to her

neck, and said, "How about Tommy calls you whatever he wants, and you say 'Yes, sir.'"

Teagan said nothing.

Ben began to cry behind them. Becca followed a second later.

Teagan reached out and grabbed Becca's hand. The bandit beside her allowed it. "It's going to be okay, sweetheart," she said.

Tommy smiled then leaned close to Teagan's ear and whispered, just loud enough for Brent to hear, "Didn't anyone ever tell you it ain't nice to lie to your child?"

Brent thought again of Boricio and Ed, promising the Lord anything for their balls.

But who was he kidding? An *armed* Ed Keenan probably couldn't get out of this jam. Even Ed would be dead.

Brent couldn't afford the thought, so he shrugged it away. If he chose the wrong battle and was killed now, as he certainly would be, there was no way he could be there to protect his newfound family. Ben would never last in a place like this. Neither would Becca. He didn't want to think about what might happen to Teagan if he died, though atrocities were sure to come whether he kept breathing or not.

Brent's eyes drifted to the shipping containers at the end of the block. He rubbed the swelling egg on the back of his skull, trying not to feel like the coward he was.

He wasn't an action hero and couldn't just storm through the cobbled compound, disarming bandits and kicking ass. But he *could* be smart. He *could* survive. He *could* strike — *when the time was right.*

Brent might not be able to protect everyone now, but maybe he could mitigate the damage until opportunity smiled.

Maybe Marina would make it back to The City, could call in the troops to do what he couldn't on her own. She could bring Ed and Boricio back to Hell, rescue them from whatever waited inside those containers.

Yes, they will know what to do here!

Brent smiled at the thought of unleashing Ed and Boricio on these sick fuckers. They'd destroy them. Boricio would laugh as he skullfucked the purple-haired one.

Brent stifled a laugh, thankful the bandits closest to him were looking at Teagan, not him.

As long as I can keep anyone from doing anything stupid, Marina will make it back. She will bring help. Then these fuckers will wish they'd kept on riding.

"All right, all right," a new voice said. A tall, lean, muscular man with a jet-black beard began waving his arms. "Break it up. Dinner first, dessert later."

Skull Tattoo said, "Looks like you're going inside" then prodded them to march forward, toward the waiting containers. They were greeted by the old man with the eye patch, holding the doors open. He had no smile. No expression at all. Just a routine day of rounding up refugees and placing them in containers.

Skull Tattoo shoved Brent inside.

Two bright halogen lights were rigged on a pole just outside the container entrance. The old man turned them on to illuminate the squalor. There were four others, chained with wire by their collars, to pipes running the length of both sides of the twenty-foot-long, eight-foot-wide, and eight-foot-tall container. When the light came on, they threw their hands over their eyes, some crying out from the pain of the sudden light penetrating their darkness.

Brent was six steps inside, just in front of Teagan and the kids, still beside Sammy, when the door clanged shut behind them, and they were plunged back into darkness.

Brent gagged.

The room was thick with body heat. The stench of sweat, piss, and shit assaulted his nostrils. He forced his breathing into a regular rhythm, and swallowed vomit rising like a tide in his throat.

Ben coughed. "It smells like the outside bathroom in here."

"You'll get used to it," someone said in the dark.

Brent couldn't imagine that wasn't a lie.

The door swung open again, and with it came the bright light. A trio of bandits stepped into the container. Because the light was directly behind them, their faces were cast in shadow, making it difficult to see if these were new people or some of the others Brent had already noted. Skull Tattoo, old Pirate Man, Purple Hair, Tommy, and of course, Marcus.

One guard stood at the doors, rifle aimed at them to ensure everything went smooth.

A part of Brent wondered what Boricio would do. Obviously, they were about to get chained inside the container. At that point, they'd be fucked. But now, they still had a chance at freedom. At least a better chance then they'd have in a few minutes.

He glanced up at Sammy. The man's eyes were wide, maybe thinking the same thing.

Brent's heart raced in anticipation, thinking about what the big man might initiate. Before, he didn't want Sammy to do anything. But now he wasn't so sure. They had no assurance that Marina would make it back. This might be their only shot. They could disable these men, grab their guns, and maybe shoot their way out of the compound.

Brent looked at Teagan running her hands over the kids' shoulders, trying to keep them calm.

The bandit closest to Sammy leaned over, grabbed a length of wire, and attached it to the collar on Sammy's neck, locking it with a small but formidable-looking lock. It happened quickly, but just like that, they'd lost their shot at escaping.

Sammy was confined.

The others were next.

Brent used his scant seconds to survey the room.

Brent imagined he was in the field, absorbing facts for later. He saw everything with the corners of his eyes, afraid that if he seemed to be looking hard, or moving his head too much, he'd earn another blow to the skull.

He looked at the other prisoners.

There was a young mother who looked to be in her thirties. A young teenage girl clung to her side. A fat old man sat beside her, shirt crusted in what looked like old food. Brent wondered how much of the rotten smell belonged to him. On the far end of the bar, a big bruiser with bulging muscles and not an ounce of fat was lying in the corner, eyes closed, face bruised and bloodied. He looked scary enough to be one of the bandits but was obviously not, given that he was beaten, if not altogether broken, maybe even dead.

Becca started crying again, despite Teagan's attempts to soothe her.

Brent wanted to reach out, tell Teagan and Becca that everything would be okay. Promise his son that they'd get out of this, just like they'd managed to get out of everything before. He wanted to ignore the growl inside him insisting that all hope was false, and that they were surely approaching their end.

He wanted to ask the bandits why they were in there, hoping against hope that one of the three might have enough humanity left to tell them what was coming. They couldn't all be crazy, violent rapist fucks, could they? Surely, some still had a heart.

But Brent was too scared to make words or raise his head, still smarting — and leaking blood — from the last time he had.

He kept telling himself it was best not to provoke anyone's wrath. If they stayed under the radar, they might have a chance.

They had to be patient. Help might be coming.

With everyone shackled, Ben clung to Brent, and Becca to

her mother. Mercifully, the bandits allowed it. But clemency ended there.

The bandits cut away the ropes that had tied them together then gathered the remains, lest anyone use it to fashion a weapon or something. Brent was no longer tied to the others, but that gave him no comfort. Now they were all tied by metal wire, much harder to break than rope, to the metal pipe along the container's left side, where Muscle Man lay crumpled in the corner.

The door clanged shut. The container fell into darkness, save for hundreds of thin beams of moonlight coming through holes drilled in the roof.

Brent felt grateful for the relative darkness. At least no one could see him crying, praying he could keep his family safe from the wolves outside the door.

~

TWENTY-THREE

Emily Roberts

Emily knew she should be more scared, essentially a prisoner of these rebels. But she didn't feel like a prisoner so much as one of the group.

All that time living on The Island, she'd hoped there were people somehow surviving out here, in The Wastelands, and not just savages as the teachers and aliens had led her to believe. No, these people weren't savages; they were survivors reclaiming their lives.

She'd seen, in Luca's memories, all that they'd been through. *Experienced* the memories unspooling like a tapestry for her to read, absorb, and experience as if she'd been with them these past few years. Lifetimes of pain, and yet they still fought, clinging to hope that they could have something like normal lives again.

It was admirable, and the opposite of what The Island had taught her — life lived by alien rule, never stepping out of bounds or being noticed, lest you lose your independence and become another body for the aliens to usurp. Just another puppet.

Some of the group scared her, like Mary. But Emily had seen what had happened to her, how the aliens had killed

Mary's daughter, how she'd lost her husband to the infection. How she'd lost two babies. The horrible things the woman had been through, and had to do for survival, was nothing short of admirable. She wished Mary had stayed — Emily wanted her to know that she understood and didn't hold any grudges for Mary slicing her throat.

Most of the group was sleeping on the apartment floor, using jackets as pillows. Emily was surprised they could sleep in such conditions but knew they'd slumbered through worse. Out here, you took rest as it came because you never knew when you'd need energy to fight or escape.

Emily wasn't the only one unable to sleep.

Neither could Boricio. He'd spent an hour pacing near the windows overlooking the street below, punctuated with several stops, lifting of binoculars, then a sigh as he lowered them. She'd heard his many unsuccessful attempts to reach Mary on the radio.

Emily got up and went over to Boricio.

"Any sign of her?"

He shook his head.

"I'm sorry if this is all because of what happened with me."

Boricio looked at Emily like he was about to speak but said nothing. He turned back to the window, staring out at the night. She couldn't tell if he was using darkness to ignore her or scanning the night for Mary.

"Do you think she'll come back?"

"Hell if I know," Boricio said. "At first, I thought so. We've done the old Whitney and Bobby before. She'll storm off but always come backs after she's let off some steam. This time ... I dunno."

"What's the *Whitney and Bobby?*"

Boricio looked at her, annoyed. "You get ahold of your daddy yet?"

"No." Emily looked down. "I can't feel him."

"I thought you said you were telepaths. So why ain't he picking up the ole psychic hotline?"

"We've never talked before … like that."

"What?" He turned to Emily, his eyes wild. She'd seen a few dark flashes of Boricio's past in Luca and knew the man could be menacing, but nothing prepared her for his fiery stare. "I thought you said you could reach him."

"I've tried before. And I've felt him push back, like closing the door on someone you don't want in your house. They know you're there and can choose whether to welcome you in. I thought if I knocked, he'd open the door. But it's like I can't find his door."

"Fucking great," Boricio grunted, throwing his hands up then turning back to the window, crossing his arms.

"I'm sorry."

"Just stop."

"Stop what?"

"Apologizing. This is, what, like, the tenth time you've said sorry to one of us. Stop it. That shit looks suspicious."

"What do you mean?"

"We took you. We slit your throat, and you're walking around here apologizing to everyone for the inconvenience."

"I feel bad that Mary left, and everyone seems angry at me."

"Yeah, well, we'll get over it! Just stop apologizing, and start trying to find your daddy's knock knock."

"What are we going to do if I can?"

"Not if, *when*," Boricio said, turning back to her. "You *are* going to get ahold of him. As for what we're gonna do, I don't know yet. But you are going to get us on that fucking island so we can take care of Desmond once and for all. *Capisce?*"

"Huh?"

"I mean, do you understand? Jesus, didn't you ever watch any movies?"

"Sor — um, no. Not like that."

Boricio shook his head. "Get some sleep. I'm going to the roof."

The way he said it, and the way he immediately headed for the ladder, told Emily he wanted to be alone. She'd annoyed him enough.

Emily returned to her spot beside Luca on the floor. He'd been asleep when she left but was now awake. It was so weird seeing him as an old man. In Emily's head, he was closer to her age. With open eyes, he was a horrible joke. Or a curse.

She settled beside him and looked into his eyes. Deep in his old and wrinkled face, Luca's eyes were still vibrant and young. The same eyes that had stared back from his younger version when she was in his head.

Keeping her voice low, she asked, "Can't sleep?"

"Off and on. I've been trying to find Mary but haven't been able to feel her."

"Do you think something happened? I mean, can you always feel her?"

"Not always, no. And lately, I feel like she's been pushing me out."

"My dad does that to me. I tried sneaking into his head, looking around to see what I can find, to figure out what he knows about my abilities."

"Abilities? You have others?"

"Well, not really. I don't think so. A few times, I thought I saw things before they happened, but nothing I could be certain of. What about you? What else can you do?"

"I don't really know until I know."

"What do you mean?"

"There's The Light inside me, and sometimes it tells me to do or think something. Sometimes, it happens. I can heal. I can teleport. If I really focus, I can control someone."

"Really? Like the aliens? You get inside them?"

"Not quite. I mean, I don't think so. More like I think for them to do something. Kinda like your telepathy, where I can hear and see their thoughts, but I can get them to say or do something. But it's hard, and it doesn't always work out so well."

She stared at Luca for a long while, wondering what it was like to be old and young at once. How it felt to have missed so many of the things you looked forward to doing when you got older — driving, dating, getting married, having kids.

Of course, none of those things were common in The Wastelands, or on The Island. Those were dreams of a lost life, luxuries no one could afford.

It's not so bad, his voice answered in her mind.

Are you reading my mind? she asked, surprised to hear him speaking in her head.

No, you were broadcasting your thoughts into mine.

Oh, really?

Yes. And for the record, I try not to think about it much.

Why do you heal all these people? Why did you heal me, when you knew it would only age you?

Because they needed my help. You needed my help. What's the use of a gift if you keep it to yourself?

You are a good person, Luca.

"Thank you," he said aloud. "You are too, Emily."

Thank you.

"Now go to sleep. We'll try to contact your father again in the morning."

Goodnight, Luca.

Goodnight, Emily.

~

TWENTY-FOUR

Mary Olson

Mary watched from a dark room in a two-story apartment building across the street from the warehouse.

She stood by the window, staring through parted curtains, watching Boricio pace the rooftop. The warehouse was taller, so she could only see him when he edged the roof, looking around.

Mary knew he was looking for her, and it killed her to cause him so much pain. But she had to leave. Had to distance herself from the others. She had a bad feeling that taking Emily into the group would be disastrous. She'd watch them from afar, to look out for them, until she was sure they were safe.

She hadn't really given much thought to the plan. It seemed like a good idea: get pissed at Boricio, which she already was, and storm away in a huff. Nobody would miss her for a while. She could lie low, watch the surrounding area for the telltale sign of Guardsmen approaching.

But there were a few flaws in her impulsive plan.

First, she'd not had time to gather supplies. She needed a rifle with a scope, not the Glock in her holster. If shit hit the fan, a pistol would be useless from this range. Second, she'd not figured sleep into the equation. She was wired now. Might even be able to go another twenty-four hours, but eventually, she'd fall to exhaustion. If the enemy hit while she snoozed, her plan went to shit.

There was also a third option she'd been stupid not to consider. The one that distressed her while watching Boricio on the rooftop. What if he came looking for her?

Mary hated to think that she'd put his, or anyone on the team's, life in danger.

His voice crackled over her radio again.

"Mary? You copy?"

A part of her wanted to ignore the transmission. Let him stew in his guilt — if he was feeling any — for failing to back her. She wondered what was wrong with her, why she needed him to repent, to admit he was wrong. She'd never been one for head games, so why start now? Especially when her actions could put him in danger.

"Copy," she said over the radio.

Boricio had backed away from the edge. Mary imagined his relief, and maybe a smile when he realized she was safe.

"Where are you?"

"Close."

"Listen, *Lucy*, I'm sorry about everything."

"It's okay, *Ricky*. I'm not … *that* mad."

"Are you on your way back?"

"No."

"Why? You're not really going solo, are you?"

"No, I just needed time to think. I'm heading to The Farm for a bit."

"Let me come with you."

"You really don't get the whole *I need time to think* thing, do you?"

"It's not safe out there."

"It's not safe anywhere. Besides, I'm a big girl. I don't need you looking out for me."

"I like looking out for you."

Mary closed her eyes, remembering some of their tender moments together. For all his crassness, for all Boricio's bravado and bluster, for all his disgusting past, he was a different man now. He *liked* being needed by her. And it wasn't some *damsel in distress* thing, so much as a *we're in this together* mindset. Boricio had spent his life not giving a fuck about anyone but himself. The events following October 15, 2011 had given him a sense of purpose, an identity, a role other than monster — *protector*. And she felt bad stealing that from him.

"You need to look after Luca."

That was something he could still feel good about doing, and a priority if they ever hoped to defeat the aliens.

Mary wondered if she should tell him that she was keeping an eye on them from afar. But her cautious — or paranoid — part, heightened in recent years, said not to. It wasn't that she didn't trust him so much as she didn't trust the others not to fall under the girl's influence. Mary had little doubt that the girl was somehow in contact with her father, feeding the enemy information. It was best to let the aliens think Mary was gone. Not someone to consider or plan for.

Surprise was the key to any attack, and could be critical to an excellent defense.

"I need to go."

"I ... " Boricio paused.

She wondered if he was going to finally say the three words she'd never heard him say.

She hoped not.

The last thing Mary needed was an overdose of emotion. They knew how each other felt. It didn't need to be said. She liked that about their relationship. And here it sounded like he was about to go and ruin it.

"I've gotta go." Mary cut him off before he could find the words which escaped him. "Seeya soon. Over."

"Over."

Boricio appeared at the edge of the rooftop again, looking out. He looked down, right at her window.

She ducked out of the way.

Did he just see me?

Shit.

Her heart raced, standing out of sight, trying to work up the courage to peek through the curtains and see if he was there. The jig was up if he'd seen her. There was no way he wouldn't come after her. And if he did, there was little chance she'd be strong enough to push him away again.

She crept closer to the curtains' slight part. Boricio was still there, staring off in a different direction.

Mary sighed with relief.

MARY DIDN'T REMEMBER FALLING asleep.

She hadn't felt especially tired.

One moment she'd been sitting in a chair, watching the street below, then her eyes had climbed to the skies before she was out — until the gunfire opened her eyes.

She jolted out of the seat, hand on her gun, looking around the room. But the threat wasn't there. It was across the street, an alien shuttle on the warehouse roof.

She didn't see anyone there. That, along with the gunfire, meant the aliens were in the building already, mounting their attack on her friends.

She had to move.

Mary raced down the steps, two and three at a time, nearly falling more than once but somehow maintaining her balance thanks to the adrenaline flooding her system. She reached the first floor and slammed through the lobby doors.

She spun, gun scanning the dark street, glad to see that no one was waiting.

She headed across the street, feeling exposed to any aliens on the rooftop looking down below.

She reached the entrance to the warehouse without drawing attention.

She stopped at the door, listening, but heard only silence.

Why can't I hear anyone?

Her heart was racing, her stomach on the precipice of a high dive, fear coursing through her. Was the gunfight over already?

Why is it so quiet?

If Team Boricio had dusted the floor with a bunch of aliens, hybrids, or whatever attacked them, there would be celebration, not silence.

Maybe they're being quiet, in case there are aliens lurking.

Mary realized that she'd left the radio on the windowsill back in the apartment. Just as well, considering she couldn't risk calling one of the team if they were in hiding. She'd seen countless movies where the woman or child in jeopardy was clutching a ringing phone and broadcasting their location to the enemy.

She stood at the doorway, afraid to open it.

Terrified to find a massacre.

She imagined opening the door only to have her friends mistake her for an alien and blast her to nothing.

Time seemed to slow, yet Mary realized she had precious little to make an impact if the others were in danger. Hell, the aliens could be dragging them all up to the rooftop now.

I have to move.

Now.

Mary opened the door.

Her friends weren't there.

Several Guardsmen were. Including one to her left. She didn't see him until the butt of his rifle thunked into her head.

Oh, fu —

Episode 33

(THIRD EPISODE OF SEASON SIX)

"Fates Worse Than Death"

TWENTY-FIVE

Emily Roberts

Emily didn't remember falling asleep, but she'd never woken to the sound of gunshots.

She opened her eyes to see lights — too many — aimed at them from every direction. She made out a few Guardsmen uniforms beyond the blur. *How many Guardsmen are there?* They'd found the rebels and were coming to rescue Emily, or, as Mary had accused earlier, coming to kill everyone else. Maybe both.

She saw movement to her right. Boricio running out, guns blazing, screaming as he went.

Then bullets found him, blood streaming in arcs from his flesh, as he staggered, still shooting.

The others were screaming, either firing their guns or already wounded.

Emily tried to stand, to wave the Guardsmen off, to let them know she was okay and there was no need to kill the others.

The sounds of screams became twisted, as if coming from some faraway place as lights exploded around them — pink, purple, and blue, like millions of tiny detonating stars.

Then the warehouse was gone.

. . .

THEY WERE IN A LONG, dark tunnel about twelve feet high and ten feet wide. The others kept firing until they realized they were no longer in danger, or in the warehouse.

"What happened?" Emily asked.

Boricio and Lisa both looked down at themselves, their ripped, bloodstained clothes, marveling over their healed wounds. Surely, they would've been dead if not for Luca.

Where's Luca?

Emily looked around, pulse racing.

He wasn't there.

"Where's Luca?" she cried out.

And then, as if in answer, a burst of more lights among them, forming a floating, glowing bright-blue ball of brilliance.

Something dark was shrouded in its center, like something about to hatch from an egg. The lights hissed, crackled, then died all at once, dropping the object to the ground.

A fetal Luca, gasping for air.

Emily fell to his side and shouted, "Luca can't breathe!"

Keenan, Boricio, Barrow, Jevonne, and Lisa all rushed over. Keenan dropped to his knees on the other side of Emily. Luca's body started shaking, his eyes rolling back, thick white slobber foaming from his mouth.

"What's happening?" Emily prayed he wasn't dying.

Keenan held him down. "Get the needle!"

Lisa reached into a black pouch on her belt, retrieved a hypodermic filled with some sort of dark-red liquid.

Keenan bit the cap off the needle and met Emily's eyes. "Can you hold his arm still?"

She nodded then put all her weight on Luca's frail left arm. His flesh and muscles felt like a bird in her clutch. She was afraid to hold on too tight for fear of snapping his limb but had to apply enough pressure and keep him still.

But his arm was wildly thrashing, even beneath her weight.

His legs kicked hard against the ground, and his eyes kept rolling up. More white spittle flew from his mouth.

Emily couldn't look.

She turned her head.

"Outta the way, Sister." Boricio shoved her roughly aside.

Emily fell back, pride wounded.

Boricio straddled Luca's frame to stabilize his arm, doing a far better job than Emily. "Go!" he said to Keenan.

Keenan injected the needle, then both men fell back.

Luca's body went limp.

Emily was sure he was dead.

She stared at the old boy, waiting for some sign of life. Finally, his chest rose and fell.

Emily stood. "What happened?"

Boricio got up, ignoring Emily's question, and went to Lisa, Barrow, and Jevonne.

Keenan felt for Luca's pulse then took off his jacket, balled it up, and put it under Luca's head as a makeshift pillow. He stood and met Emily's gaze. "Every time he teleports us, or heals someone, it takes a lot out of him. Sometimes, more than usual."

Emily looked down at Luca. He seemed at least ten years older than before. It was hard to believe that this was the same person she'd fallen asleep beside a short while ago. The person who was really a boy, a few years older than she.

"Is he going to die?"

Keenan sighed. "We're all dying. The only question is when."

"I mean soon. Is he going to die soon?"

"I don't know."

"What was in the needle?"

"His blood, from when he was younger. He gave us a few vials, told us to use it if he ever passed out or anything."

"That wasn't passing out. That was a seizure. It was scary. Has he had those before?"

"Once, yeah," Keenan said.

Emily could feel the others looking at her and hear their discussion in whispers. From her peripheral vision, she could see Boricio on his radio, repeatedly shaking his head.

Emily felt like everyone in the room, except maybe Luca, and *possibly* Keenan — it was hard to get a read on him — hated her.

"I'm so sorry." She tried not to cry while looking down at Luca. "If you all hadn't saved me, none of this would be happening. You could be home. You wouldn't be fighting with one another. Luca wouldn't be so old."

Boricio barreled over to them, harsh eyes on Emily.

"Would you stop with the sorry shit?" He grabbed her by the collar and shoved Emily backward, hard into the tunnel's wall.

She yelped as her head hit the concrete.

"Stop!" Lisa yelled.

"No, I wanna know how they found us!" Boricio shouted, hot spittle flying in her face. "Did you contact Daddy and rat us out, you little cunt?"

"No! I told you I couldn't reach him."

"Couldn't or *wouldn't?*" Boricio yelled, his eyes wide like he'd caught her in a lie rather than semantics.

"Couldn't, can't. I haven't been able to reach him!"

Boricio leaned in close enough for Emily to see his rage-filled eyes, hear the low growl in his throat, and feel the intensity wafting off his body like a fire threatening to consume them. He hissed, "I don't fucking believe you!"

"I swear!"

"Then how did they find us? Not once, but twice!"

"I don't know!"

A look crossed Boricio's face as if he remembered something he'd been trying to recall for days.

He ripped at her collar. "Take off your clothes!"

"What?" Fear somersaulted in Emily's gut.

She pulled away from him, but Boricio grabbed her by the shoulder and threw her back against the wall. "I said take off your clothes!"

Lisa and Keenan ran over, inserting themselves between Boricio and Emily.

"What the hell are you doing?" Lisa might have grabbed Boricio if Barrow hadn't put his considerable bulk between them and raised his hands to stop her.

"She's got a tracking device on her! That's the only explanation if she ain't been chattin' with Daddy via the Psychic Friends Network!"

Lisa and Keenan looked at Emily as if considering the charge.

Keenan turned to Jevonne. "Did anyone check her clothes, or her body, when we processed her?"

"I dunno." Jevonne shrugged. "I don't think we ever properly processed her, what with everything goin' on at the time. She was dying, remember? Luca was healing her, then you all questioned her, but I don't think anyone ever checked her fully."

"Jesus Fucking Christ," Boricio shook his head. "Do I have to manage every crab in the fucking bucket?"

Lisa stepped between Boricio and Emily. "I got it. Go cool off before you blow a gasket."

Boricio shook his head then walked off with Keenan.

"Come on, let's find somewhere to look you over," Lisa said, her voice far gentler than it had been.

The tunnel was dark, but not pitch black. Someone had lined blue lights along the ceiling. Emily wasn't sure how they were charged, nor did she ask. "What is this place?" she said instead.

Lisa looked at her for a long moment but didn't respond.

"Oh, you think I'm a rat, too, eh? Think if you tell me where we're hiding, more people will show up?"

"I don't know what to think. Let's check you out over here, okay?"

Emily felt horrible for what had happened to them, and to Luca, but couldn't help but feel somewhat indignant that she was still a suspect. Part of her wanted to go back and yell at Boricio, maybe take it out on Lisa. *Screw you for not trusting me!*

But Emily kept her mouth shut.

She could feel their fear, palpable in her thoughts, rolling off their auras in black and red waves. She'd considered trying to enter their heads, maybe to see if any of them believed her innocence. But Emily couldn't risk the odds of someone catching her snooping. They weren't regular people. They all had some of Luca's Light inside them, and because of that, they might be more likely to catch her spying. And if they didn't trust her now, they certainly wouldn't if they found her snooping in their thoughts. She'd be as a good as dead.

"I need you to get undressed in front of me. Will that be a problem?"

Yes, it was a problem! Emily hadn't been naked in front of anyone since she was five or six, and that had been in front of her parents, not a stranger. Not with men so close by. She felt hyperaware of her body, and her awkward feelings about it. She did *not* want to disrobe in front of these people, even if it was just the woman, Lisa.

Suddenly, Emily longed to be back on The Island, even with all the aliens. Yes, The Island was a creepy place where she never felt safe. And yes, she'd been excited when these people took her, even with all the drama. She'd been saved, with no permanent harm done. A part of her even hoped they'd invite her to stay, and they'd all go to this farm they'd been talking about. Maybe they'd live normal lives, like people used to do. Maybe someday she could even convince her father to live with them. Or maybe if he helped them do whatever they planned to do on The Island, they'd invite them both to stay.

But now everyone hated her.

And Luca might be dying.

And she was being asked to strip in a dark, cold tunnel.

It was all Emily could do to keep from breaking down in tears.

"Do I have to take *all* my clothes off?"

"Yes, I need to make sure you don't have anything on you, or that you don't try and hide it if you do."

Something in Lisa's tone flipped a switch in Emily.

She was no longer sad. Now she was angry.

She took her shirt off and threw it at Lisa.

She removed her bra and threw that, too.

Emily continued in a white-hot anger until she was completely naked and had thrown each item of clothing at Lisa as if she were a hamper.

"There, you happy?" Part of Emily wanted to yell louder, maybe invite the others to the show. But the reality of being naked and cold, with Lisa staring, unfazed by her anger, seemed to cool her, made her realize the danger of inviting others to come look. The last thing Emily wanted was for boys, let alone grown men, to see her naked.

She felt vulnerable and threw her hands over her privates.

She watched Lisa run her fingers over every inch of clothing, feeling for something she obviously didn't find.

Lisa dropped the clothes to the ground then approached Emily, too fast for comfort.

For a moment, Emily was sure the woman would hit her, in retaliation for throwing her clothes.

Instead, she said, "Can you please turn around and pull your hair up?"

Emily did as instructed, her stomach churning.

Lisa grabbed a small flashlight from her pouch and ran it over the back of Emily's neck. "Did any doctor do anything to you before the trip?"

"Well, yeah, they put some antivirus thing in me, which

they said would keep us safe from any infection from The Wastelands."

"Where did they put this?"

"My shoulder."

Emily ran her fingers over her left shoulder where there was still a small red lump — still itching, now that she thought about it.

Lisa sighed. "Of course."

"What?" Emily asked, scared.

"It's gotta be a tracking device."

"What can we do?"

Lisa walked away for a moment, leaving Emily cold and alone. She stared at the wall, so if anyone were looking at her, all they saw was her butt.

Lisa returned with Emily's shirt.

Emily started to put it on.

"No, I want you to bite down on it. Hard."

"Why?"

"Because this is gonna hurt," Lisa said, holding up a large blade.

~

TWENTY-SIX

Brent Foster

Brent inched toward Teagan, who herself had moved closer to the front of the container to try and talk with the young mother and daughter across from them in the darkness. But every time Brent stood up or started to slide over, Ben wrapped himself tighter around Brent, anchoring him in place.

It took Teagan a while to get the woman talking. For the longest time, her prompts were met with empty eyes, a vacant expression, and fearful shakes of her head, barely visible in the container's stingy light. Finally, she seemed to break and began speaking to Teagan in terrified whispers that Brent couldn't quite hear, especially above the old man's sporadic coughs. He needed to get closer, to learn as much as he could about this place.

Brent leaned down and kissed his son on the cheek. He whispered, "I'm only going a few feet away, and you can come with me if you want. I need to speak with Teagan. And you can be closer to Becca."

"I don't want to move." Ben pointed. "And they're closer to the door."

"You can come with me or stay here, but I have to go."

Brent stood, and Ben let go.

Brent took four steps to his right, his son following like a shadow. Once he was beside Becca, to Teagan's left, he sat. Ben did the same.

Teagan and the young woman stopped talking. The woman looked among the three of them furtively. Brent said nothing, waiting for Teagan to speak, maybe make an introduction.

She turned to Brent and nodded toward the woman and the girl. "This is Meghan and her fourteen-year-old daughter, Lara. They were brought in late last night. She's as scared as we are, and might know even less than we do. She doesn't want to talk because she says there was someone who wouldn't shut up when she got here last night. The guards came in yelling about 'bad things happening to people who didn't know how to keep their traps closed.'"

Brent turned to the woman and tried his best smile. "Hi, Meghan. I'm Brent." He looked over to his shadow. "And this is my son, Ben."

She stared at Brent and said nothing.

He said, "Can you tell us anything that might help us find a way out of here?"

Meghan shook her head and looked at the doors, as if a guard might be standing just inside, watching them. The front of the container was just dark enough to be hiding someone, Brent supposed.

Brent kept trying. "Where did you come from?"

She swallowed then said, "Las Orillas. We were heading up into Alto Verde, thinking we might find a full pantry in one of those big homes." She paused then added, "That's where Teagan said you were all coming from?"

"It was," Brent nodded. "We were heading to Las Orillas when we were attacked." He paused, deciding not to relive the horror, then said, "Do you know what's going on here? Or what's in the other three containers?"

She shook her head. "I don't have any idea … but there are noises."

"Noises?"

"Noises," she whispered then pursed her lips tight.

Brent turned to the room and whispered, "Hey. Does anyone know what this place is, or what they're going to do with us?"

Nobody spoke.

Brent ran his eyes along the bar on the other side, past the woman and her daughter, past the old man, and then to his side, where the man who looked like a bandit was still looking passed out. No one looked back, all of them either looking down at nothing, sleeping, or pretending to sleep. He couldn't tell if any of their eyes were even open. Brent wasn't sure if they were afraid to speak, or broken and unable.

"Come on," Brent said, his voice getting louder, "Nobody knows anything? None of you are willing to talk?"

Sammy came over and put a hand on his shoulder to calm him down.

The old man opened his mouth, but rather than speaking he began to violently cough. His coughing turned to hacking. Minutes later, he managed to get a few cracked sentences to leave his dry-sounding throat.

"I've been here for four months," he finally said. "We're forced to work on a farm just outside the walls each morning. We work all day then come back here just before dark. This container's our home. We sleep on the floor. We piss and shit in the buckets. And we eat and drink whatever they give us once a day. Same routine every day, no weekends off."

It sounded awful for sure, but Brent could imagine much worse.

"That's it? Just work?" Sammy said, echoing Brent's

thoughts. "Everyone does as they're told, and this is as bad as it gets?"

Brent could hear his wheels turning. Like him, Sammy was looking for a way out, maybe hoping Marina was watching, biding her time in the outskirts, surveying the situation until she could bring Ed, Boricio, and the rest of the team to save them.

"I don't know what you define as 'bad as it gets.' That shit bucket I mentioned, it's a communal one, so yeah, whatever that's worth to ya … "

The old man coughed again, covering his mouth with one hand while pointing to the end of the container, in front of the big bandit-looking man, with the other.

"One there, and another while we're working the land. That's two buckets for us all to share. And no food or water, except for at noon. We get a helping of fruits or vegetables with our water, once a day. Never good, and never seconds. I've not eaten meat since about a week before I got here. If that fits your definition, congratulations, you'll do fine."

He shrugged, coughed again, then added, "At least you'll get used to it. It's easier once you're alone."

"Alone?" Sammy repeated.

"I was dragged in here with my wife."

"What happened to her?" Brent asked.

The man shook his head.

Ben surprised everyone. He left Brent's leg, approached the old man, tugged on his pant leg, and said, "What happened? Where is your wife now? It's okay to say it; I lost my mommy, too."

The old man looked up at Ben, his eyes getting heavy with tears. Then he looked over at Teagan and Becca and the rest of them.

"They usually take the young ones first. But one day it was down to just me and Susan. So they took her."

Brent swallowed. "Took her for what?"

"They did it right there, in one of the other containers." The old man shook his head. "For hours, she screamed."

"Did *what?*" Brent asked, afraid of the answer.

He stared at Brent and started coughing. The container echoed with his violent hacking, loud enough that Brent wondered if the guards might come to see what was wrong, if the man didn't lose a vital organ first.

His voice dropped to the ugliest whisper. He glanced once more at the children before whispering, "They'll come for your children first; they'll take the woman next."

The last few words left the man's mouth like sandpaper scraping wood. Brent wanted him to keep talking, but the man wouldn't, or couldn't, say more. He raised his hand, palm out, while shaking his head and occasionally hacking.

Brent said, "Can you at least tell us your name?"

"Wilson." he coughed. "Not that it matters. I don't expect we'll all be together long enough to become friends. Either my time'll be up, or yours. Nobody stays for too long. I've been here four months, and that's the record ... by about two."

Silence covered them like a blanket through the night.

BRENT WAS only awake for a few minutes when the heavy steel container doors creaked open on their giant hinges. He'd yet to speak or even look around, keeping his eyes closed, staying inside himself while trying to gather his strength. The guards made him feel like a chicken for not using his waking moments to comfort his son.

A guard said, "Time to work, slaves."

Brent squinted, feeling half-blind. The day wasn't especially bright, but compared to the container's black shadows, it felt for a moment like staring into the sun. He felt the guards fasten another steel wire to his collar, linking it to the others, like some kind of prison chain gang, before unlinking the wires that held them to the pole running along the floor.

Brent marched in line out of the container, still dazed and confused, unsure of everyone's position in the line. The container had been emptied, but he didn't know where Teagan, Becca, or Sammy were in relation to him. Ben walked inches away, his tiny hand curled into Brent's pant leg.

By the time his eyes were finally working, Brent could see that the old man with the bad cough — Wilson — was marching directly in front of him, just behind Teagan and Becca, along with everyone else. Shuffling feet behind him probably belonged to Sammy and a couple of guards. Maybe the big guy at the end of the container, if he were alive. Brent didn't dare look back to find out.

They reached the end of the cul-de-sac, passed through a tall gate, built from scraps, and entered another walled-off area: a farm, alongside a stretch of woodland.

Marcus stood waiting, shirtless, his body gleaming in sweat and his scar even uglier in the morning sun. "New slaves, this is where you'll work. Old slaves, you know what to do."

They were all still wearing their collars and chains. If any of them ran, they'd have to drag the entire postapocalyptic chain gang behind them, or get yanked back by the force of the crowd.

Not that anyone *could* run, surrounded by guards as they were.

Becca began to cry. To Brent's surprise, the guards allowed Teagan to lean down and whisper into her daughter's ear. Brent couldn't hear but could easily imagine what she'd said. Marcus stood staring at the pair, off to the side, away from slaves and guards, arms folded across his chest, glaring at the girls with his milky-white eye.

Becca finally stopped crying, and Teagan stood.

Marcus said, "Is she done?"

Teagan nodded.

"She best be."

His three words sounded like a funeral dirge.

Marcus turned and led the slaves into The Farm's heart, past a group of leering men, including Tommy and the purple-haired freak from last night. To Brent's surprise, they kept on walking, finally stopping at a field a few hundred yards past The Farm, where they met up with two other groups. Brent's faction stopped in between the other two. He tried to count chained bodies without being obvious. Maybe forty men and women total. In front of the slaves sat a long rectangular wooden box.

Brent thought of Marina and wondered if they had any hope of rescue.

The Reaper pointed to a patch of dirt behind him. "Twelve feet deep, and large," he said then nodded to a pair of guards flanking his body on either side.

The guards opened the box and revealed a bounty of shovels. They handed them out, one per slave, including smaller spades for Ben, Becca, and two children from the other groups.

The guards fell back and left the slaves to dig.

Knowing what to do, the other two groups began piercing the dirt with their shovels. Brent followed along, then Teagan, whispering for Becca to follow her lead.

Ben said, "We're supposed to dig?"

"Yep." Brent nodded and kneeled beside his son. "We're going to look for treasure."

"Okay, Dad," Ben said, understanding the lie.

Brent finally turned back and saw Sammy, just behind Ben, and felt a chill from the man's obvious fear.

They dug in silence until Brent finally gathered enough courage to lean closer to Wilson. "What are we digging?"

He dreaded the answer but needed to know.

"A mass grave. Means there's gonna be a culling soon.

"A culling?"

"Every once in a while, they pick the weakest among us and shoot 'em. I suggest you never get sick or injure yourself."

Wilson coughed.

"You okay?" a guard asked.

"Of course," he said, without lifting his eyes from the dig.

~

TWENTY-SEVEN

Ed Keenan

Ed stared at the tracking chip Lisa had carved from the girl: a small black square with circuitry covered by clear plastic, similar to ones he'd seen in the field back in his Agency days. Hell, he'd cut one out of his leg once when an operation was in danger of going south and he needed to get deeper under-cover without agents breathing down his neck. This one was a bit different in that it packed a small explosive charge. Lisa had thankfully managed to figure out a way to disarm it before it blew up.

Lisa and Boricio stood beside Ed while Barrow and Jevonne were farther down the tunnel, watching over an unconscious Luca and the girl.

"So, you believe her, that she didn't know this shit was in her?" Boricio asked Lisa.

"I do."

"And more importantly," Ed added, "Luca did. He was inside her head. He said we could trust her."

Boricio looked back at the girl. "I dunno. She coulda got inside his head and tricked him. He might be an old man, but he's probably got a teenager's hormones."

"What is it with you?" Lisa's voice edged frustration.

"First, you were defending this girl when Mary was hell bent on killing her, and now you're what — thinking Mary was right?"

"I dunno. I mean, probably not. I'm just not used to feeling like a fucking rat in a cage. For the past few years, we've been taking the fight to them, disrupting operations, killing aliens, and now they're showing up on our doorstep, surprising *us*. I don't like it."

Ed said, "Well, it's not like we've disrupted much of their operations. We're firing pea shooters against cannons. But I think with the girl, we can maybe find a way inside and turn the tables. But if we keep treating her like the enemy, she won't trust us. She'll sell us out if she thinks she's safer back on The Island."

"So, what, I gotta make nice?" Boricio asked.

"I think it's our only play."

"What if we use the chip to trap them?" Lisa suggested. "Lead them to an ambush?"

Ed looked at the chip again. "If this were back in the day, I'd say that's a workable plan, but we don't have anything on hand to temporarily block the signal. And I'm not about to go scouting for shit in The City. I think we crush this and figure out what the girl can do. Meanwhile, I'll get in touch with Beta Team and see if they've got eyes on Mary."

"No," Boricio said, "I'm going out to find her. She said she was headed to The Farm. But the fact that she's not answering her radio has me worried that her plans have changed, or someone changed them for her."

"We need you here," Ed said. "In case they've already got a bead on us. Luca isn't up to teleporting again. We need everyone at the Chandler House."

They were in what Las Orillas locals called The Catacombs, an old network of service and equestrian tunnels that saw a lot of use during Prohibition. Alpha and Beta Teams had staked out a section of The Catacombs back when they'd first returned to this world. They'd sealed off the entrances, which had been easy to find. Now there were only a handful of ways in and out of the tunnels. You had to know where to look to find the hidden doors — which meant bandits and aliens would have to know of The Catacombs and be actively searching for them or might have stumbled onto them by sheer chance, or captured and tortured one of the rebels into revealing their locations. But for now, The Catacombs provided safe passage in areas it would be otherwise difficult to traverse.

The Chandler House basement, an old historic home that had once belonged to a famous playwright, was Beta Team headquarters, and judging from their current location, just two miles south.

"It's only two miles, then you can go look for her. Do you have any idea where she is?"

"No, like I said, she was headed to The Farm. But something's happened."

"So, what, you're gonna go to The Farm? Or back to the warehouse?"

"How far away from the warehouse are we now?"

"We're about four miles from the warehouse," Lisa said.

"So that would put Chandler House six miles away? Shit. That's a lot of time off the ticking clock. No bueno."

Ed was trying to think of the best tack to take with Boricio. Lisa went with blunt.

"Mary left *us*, remember? She got pissed and stormed off. We didn't ostracize her or anything. She left, not even thinking about how that would affect our missions. So please, Boricio, ask yourself what serves the greater good: keeping Luca safe or going out in the streets and looking for her when she's probably already close to The Farm."

For a moment, Ed thought Boricio was about to go off on Lisa. It wouldn't be the first time they'd tangled. Instead, he nodded and said, "Okay." There was something in that nod, and the way his shoulders slumped, that made Ed wonder if the one-man wrecking ball was finally tired of fighting. Ed knew that feeling all too well.

Ed dropped the tracking chip and crushed it with his boot heel.

~

TWENTY-EIGHT

Brent Foster

Brent tried to fall asleep, unable to remember ever feeling more exhausted from a day of work.

His shoulders weighed a thousand pounds, his arms and legs were tight and burning, hands blistered and speckled in blood. Ben and Becca, to their credit, somehow plugged away, even if they were crying half the day. Brent and Teagan had shared a single, sweet, foulmouthed kiss, barely stolen, after the long day had finally ended, just before getting shoved and shut inside the container. The moment had been sweeter than his midday water.

Last night's silence made more sense after the weeklong day. The slaves weren't just scared. They were absolutely exhausted. And the arrival of new prisoners had stolen precious moments of their sleep.

He remembered what Wilson had said about not getting sick. And in Brent's experience, the best way to stay healthy was to get a decent sleep.

Eventually, he drifted off on the cold metal container floor, with Ben sleeping against his back.

Seconds into sleep's embrace, the door creaked open, and a blast of halogen lights jarred him awake.

It wasn't yet morning.

Two men tromped into the container, Purple Hair and Tommy — neither of whom had stopped taking every opportunity to undress Teagan with their eyes since the group marched through the gates of Hell.

Tommy walked straight to Lara.

"No!"

Meghan reached out and swatted at Tommy, trying to protect her daughter. Brent could see a horrible gleam in his eye and a satisfied twist in his smile as he pulled back his hand like the string of a bow and smacked her with a loud THWAP across the cheek.

Lara, just starting to fight, immediately settled.

"Are you okay, Mom?" she asked with surprising calm.

Tommy wiped slobber from his mouth. "She will be if you behave."

Meghan, now crying, stood to face him. She screeched, lurched forward, and clawed at Tommy's face.

Purple Hair ignored the quarrel and started pawing at Lara, rubbing her breasts with one hand while cupping her ass with the other.

Tommy sent Meghan sprawling to the floor with a shove, and into a curled ball with a kick. Then he laughed and went to join his buddy.

Meghan whimpered.

Again, Brent felt like a coward, doing nothing to intervene. Too consumed with worry for what would happen to his family if he stepped up to help another. He felt Ben clutching his back. The boy whispered, "Do something, Daddy."

Brent had felt like a shadow of his best self since his return to Earth. He longed to do something now, to stop the wrong being executed before him. Doing nothing was teaching Ben that this atrocity was acceptable, that he was fine with it happening. That maybe he'd let the same thing happen to him, or Teagan, or Becca.

But what choice did he have? Anything he could do might draw attention to his family. Or Sammy.

The bandits unhooked Lara's collar and dragged her out, laughing.

Just outside the door, Purple Hair said, "Think she's tight?"

Tommy whistled. "I bet she's like that Indian bitch."

The door closed, and for a few minutes the only thing beyond the container's cautious, collective breath were Meghan's quiet sobs coming from the corner.

Then came the nightmare's soundtrack, barely audible though it may as well have been a bullhorn, coming from behind the ugly metal walls one container over.

Protests, screams, and cries cut with grunts of male pleasure.

Laughter, muffled jokes, the echoes of slapping.

It went on too long.

Maybe an hour. It felt like a day.

Meghan sobbed. Teagan crawled over to her side of the container and held her.

Becca lived under one of Brent's arms, and Ben in the other.

Sammy paced.

The rest of the container pretended they couldn't hear.

Ben looked up at Brent, "Why didn't you do anything, Dad?"

He looked down, wiping tears from his eyes. "Because I didn't want them to hurt either of you."

Ben simply stared ahead, as if processing. Brent wasn't sure how his son would file that — Dad as a coward or Dad doing what he had to in order to protect his family.

Finally, the door opened.

Lara was thrown inside, panting, trying to catch her breath, clothes bloody. She ran to her mom, but Meghan didn't embrace her. Instead, she launched herself at the bandits and pummeled them both with her fists.

"You want some too, you feisty bitch?" Purple Hair asked, punching her in the gut.

Tommy grabbed the woman from behind, in a choke hold, as Purple Hair continued to hit her.

Lara screamed, "Stop! Please stop!"

They ignored her until they were ready to stop, and that wasn't until Meghan was an almost lifeless bloody heap on the floor.

Then Tommy hooked the girl's wire back up to the pole and left without another word.

Purple Hair spit on the mother then followed his tattooed friend.

The door closed, plunging them back into darkness.

Mother and daughter cried as one.

Ben and Becca joined them.

Brent was closing his eyes, quietly crying. He jumped, startled when Teagan's hand grasped his. Their fingers threaded together. With Ben and Becca's, too, the four a tangled mass.

"What did they do to her?" Becca asked.

Teagan tried to speak, choked, and closed her mouth to breathe or think. Brent said, "They beat her up and took something that didn't belong to them."

"What did they take?"

"Something she can never have back, Becca. Because they're bullies who knew they could take what they wanted, and that no one could stop them."

Meghan hugged her daughter harder and wailed, "I'm so, so sorry baby. I should never have let that happen."

"You didn't *let it* happen, Mom." She cried. "There was nothing you could do."

They sobbed harder and louder.

Wilson walked over, coughing, and hovered above them,

waiting. Meghan looked up, her eyes as angry as her voice, but hard to see in the scant light. "What do you want?"

He coughed then said, "To help if I can."

Her voice untrusting, she said, "What can you possibly do?"

"I'll show you." He looked at Lara then back at her mom. "Over here, alone."

Wilson took Meghan gently by the arm, led her away toward the container's rear wall, then told Brent to come, too. "I need to speak to your dad alone," he whispered when Ben tried to follow.

Brent and Meghan reached the rear wall, where the big man was still out, or dead. Wilson looked at them and opened his palm.

A moonbeam glinted off the blade.

Wilson licked his dry lips and glanced at Meghan. "Take it."

"What is it?" Meghan asked, as if she'd never seen a razor.

"I found a box of disposables when they brought me in to scrub the bathrooms two weeks back. I snagged a few and chipped the plastic from the metal. Figured I'd find a way to use 'em before they counted them gone."

He coughed, long and hard, before spitting onto the floor. Brent couldn't see in the dark, but imagined the man's spit filled with blood.

"I've been here long enough to know what'll happen to her." Wilson glanced at Lara and lowered his voice even further. "They've already started, and they're not gonna stop till she's dead. They'll come back every night and keep on raping your daughter until she's raw meat."

His voice lost another octave.

"And then they'll kill her."

Meghan gasped.

"Take it," Wilson repeated. "End her suffering."

"No." Meghan's whisper was angry and surprised. "That's *awful*."

A cough then, "Which part?"

Meghan paused, thinking. Brent could hear his pounding heart.

"All of it."

Another cough, then a gentler voice. "Don't be so quick to make up your mind. I'd never suggest it if I didn't know how bad things are going to get for her. Or for you having to hear it each night. Tonight was the start. You'll be the one holding her after they throw her back. In another few days, she won't even be able to look at you."

"No," Meghan repeated. "I could never do that."

She opened her hand anyway, and Wilson placed the razor inside it. She returned to Lara, falling to a crouch and holding her close.

"What did he say?" Lara asked.

"Nothing." Meghan kissed her daughter on the forehead.

Wilson turned to Brent. "Open your hand."

Brent did.

"Whatever you do, don't tell 'em where you got it. Hide it under the dirt on the floor."

Brent took the second razor and stared at the blade, hoping he wouldn't need to use it.

～

TWENTY-NINE

Paul Roberts

Paul watched through the observation window as the woman who sliced his daughter's throat writhed on the table below, trying to free herself from the metal cuffs binding her wrists and ankles.

But there'd be no escaping.

She was naked. It had been a long time since he'd seen a nude woman up close, but her body offered no titillation. Paul was too filled with disgust.

Desmond stood beside him, watching, a satisfied expression on his face. While Desmond had hoped to get Luca, he seemed pleasantly surprised to have captured Mary instead. Paul wasn't sure of their shared past, but it must've been intense, judging from his grin.

"What do you need me to find out?" Paul asked.

"Find out what she knows. Dig around in her head. Find out their locations, and we'll proceed from there."

Paul had done hundreds of these interrogations over the past few years, with varying degrees of success. If you asked him, he'd say his success rate was 100 percent — when people possessed whatever information he was seeking. Desmond always resorted to Plan B when they didn't. That involved torture. Sometimes, Desmond conducted the torment himself. Other times, it was Wasterman, who took exceptional glee in such orders. But as Paul remembered how callously the woman had slit his little girl's throat, he hoped she *didn't* have what they needed, and that Desmond would let Paul implement Plan B himself.

Paul was about to head into the interrogation room. Desmond put a hand out to stop him.

"What is it?"

"I just received bad news from someone in the field."

Paul paused, heart racing, fearing Desmond's telepathic news.

"It's Emily."

Oh, God, no. She's dead!

"The tracking chip stopped working."

"What?" Paul yelled. "What do you mean, *stopped working?*"

"We don't know if it's malfunctioning, or if they found and destroyed it."

"Could it have exploded, and killed her?"

"We'd have received a signal if that happened. My guess is they found and neutralized it."

"Fuck! I thought you said this wouldn't happen, that you had this under control! This is now *two* failed attempts to capture your target, and now we've lost our only hope of finding my daughter!"

Still smiling, Desmond said, "Please, Mr. Roberts, have some faith."

Paul wanted to punch that smile from Desmond's smug face. Wanted to reach inside and yank the alien from inside him, throw it on the ground, and stomp it to chunks of goo.

Instead, he asked, "Faith in what? Do we have another plan?"

"Yes," Desmond said. "That would be you, Mr. Roberts."

"Me?"

"Yes, *you're* going to go in there, get inside Mary's head, and find everything we need to retrieve your daughter. You want her back, well, go and get her."

Desmond turned and left Paul staring down at the woman who held his daughter's fate inside her head.

He'd find out what she knew, or kill the bitch himself.

THIRTY

Mary Olson

Mary felt like a trapped animal caught in some sterile lab, strapped to a table, awaiting dissection. She was nude, likely to make her feel even less human and more like a lab rat, which was probably how the aliens viewed humans: curious creatures to exploit, tear apart, and toy with.

Her head was pounding, her throat was sore from screaming for what felt like an hour after she woke to find herself confined. She'd gone from threats to cajoling, neither bearing fruit.

Nobody answered her calls.

Nobody entered the sterile ten-by-ten room with its all-white walls and high ceiling. She stared into the large mirror running along the top half of the wall in front of her. It reminded Mary of an operating theater. She wondered who was on the other side watching.

Desmond?

And if so, what horrors did he have in store?

She tried to bar her mind from such grisly images, telling herself that they'd already done the worst they could do. They'd killed Ryan and Paola — the only people she'd loved.

The aliens had occupied Desmond, the man Mary *thought* she loved.

What else could they do?

Hurt her?

She'd borne great pain before. She'd ride it out again.

Kill her?

Mary was already dead. Hell, if death was the endless sleep she figured it was, she was readier than ever to take an endless nap.

There was nothing left to take. Thinking about it that way, Mary felt almost calm.

In that serenity, she tried to reach out to Luca telepathically.

Mary felt nothing.

Sorry, the number you're trying to reach is no longer in service.

Mary was on her own, presumably on the mothership, with no Team Boricio coming to rescue her. Hell, Team Boricio didn't even know she was missing. Boricio thought she was at The Farm.

Dammit. I should've told him the truth.

Alone, restrained, her fate was thoroughly out of her hands. While that realization had scared the hell out of Mary when she first woke up tied to the table, it now offered an odd sort of peace.

There's nothing I can do, so sit back, and wait for the end.

She wondered if this was a coping mechanism that would crumble the minute they hurt her. If they'd make her beg for mercy.

Mary vowed to herself that she would never beg. If anything, she'd push them — she'd *make them* kill her. She'd find a way to piss them off and lose sight of their plan.

She smiled.

They may have restrained her, but they couldn't murder her wits. She'd find a way to endure or force their hand. She'd die on her terms, not theirs.

The door opened.

A short, schlumpy-looking man in his forties entered the room. He was wearing white pants and a matching shirt — either a doctor or a member of some stupid cult. His light-brown hair was graying in a thinning mess on his head.

Mary laughed. "He sent *you* to do his dirty work?"

"Whom are you talking about, ma'am?" the man said in a smooth, confident voice that belied his appearance.

"Desmond, the coward who killed my daughter. Why isn't *he* here?" Mary looked up at the mirror and shouted. "You hiding behind the mirror, you cowardly fuck? You like watching, do ya?"

"My name is Paul Roberts," the man said, approaching Mary with a friendly smile. He stopped at around where her hand was cuffed by her waist, standing to her right.

She looked him up and down. He wasn't carrying anything. No pad to write. No tools for torture. So *why* was he here?

"Good for you," she said, staring into his eyes.

The man was locked onto Mary's eyes, as if afraid to look at her body. That boosted her confidence — something else she could use against him, even if she didn't yet know how.

"I'm here to talk."

"So, talk."

"Where are your friends hiding?"

"Really?" Mary laughed. "That's what you want to know? Like I'm going to tell you!"

"Desmond is offering you all safe passage. If your friends surrender, they can live on The Island. Wouldn't you like to stop running? To stop hiding? To stop fighting? To stop dying?"

Mary smiled at the mirror. "You really think I believe you for a moment? We're all dead the second we surrender. And we'd rather die than hand our bodies to you fuckers!"

"I understand. You don't believe us. But there is no need to fight any longer. There are no vials left. There is no reason for your people to keep fighting. The war is over. We have many free humans living on The Island, I among them. We won't take your bodies. Besides, your bodies are far from ideal."

Mary laughed. "None of this means anything, *Paul*. I do not, and will not ever trust your leader."

"Very well." Paul's smile faded.

Mary felt a sharp pain, like a vice clamping down on her head.

A psychic invasion. He'd said he was human, but unless he was a telepath — *how many of these fuckers are there?* — then the man was a liar.

She closed him out, hard, pushing back with everything she had.

Paul stumbled back as if physically pushed.

He stared at her, nervously.

Mary smiled. "Didn't ever meet someone who could keep you out, eh?"

She could feel him trying again but held her focus, refusing his entry. Because Mary had been at least partially telepathic even before part of The Light found a home in her, Luca devoted more time training her than any of the others. She knew how to hold her defenses, and to mount minor counterattacks. Mary had never been able to go into some-one's head like Luca, but she could keep Paul out of hers, for a while at least.

Paul's face flushed with anger, though he held his artificial smile.

Mary laughed, knowing it would piss him off more.

"What's wrong, Paul? You look beat."

His eyes narrowed, his anger emerging.

Yeah, that's it. Embrace the rage.

Paul went from zero to sixty in a blink. He reached into his pocket. Before Mary could register his action, he placed a blade to her neck.

"How's it feel?" he whispered in her ear.

Mary flinched, surprised to have death so close, the cold blade pressed to her throat. A bit of pressure would end it all. She might be able to force him to stab her if she thrust her neck forward, but she couldn't quite muster that much suicidal enthusiasm.

Instead, she prodded him.

"Good," she said, channeling her best Boricio. "Now finish the job, you pussy. Or don't you have it in ya?"

"Where's my daughter?" he asked, eyes red, hand trembling.

"Daughter?" Mary said, confused.

"The girl whose throat you slit. Where is she?"

Mary felt as if someone had taken all the bluster out of her sails.

Oh my God, this is Emily's father.

Instead of feeling a hate for the man, she felt a kinship. He was as consumed with rage at her as she was for Desmond. The man was about to crack under the pressure.

All of the emotions she'd pushed away since slicing the girl's neck flooded through her like a tidal wave, threatening to drag Mary to the depths of despair if she couldn't cling to her sanity.

"I don't know," Mary said, desperate for him to believe her. "But she's alive. I swear. I didn't mean to do it. I don't know what happened."

Mary hated herself for sounding as if she were pleading for her life. But she wasn't begging for salvation so much as for him to not hate her for what she did. To not think her a monster.

"Where is she?" Paul yelled. He took the knife from her throat and then plunged it into her leg.

Mary screamed, buckled in her restraints.

Paul pulled the knife out and was about to stab Mary again when the door flew open and two Guardsmen stormed into the room, guns drawn. "Drop the knife, Mr. Roberts!"

Paul turned to them, eyes wide as if he were as surprised to find himself stabbing Mary as they were. His hand opened, and the blade fell to the ground.

The Guardsmen grabbed him, roughly by the arms, cuffed his hands behind his back, and dragged him away.

As he was yanked through the door, he screamed, "Where is Emily?"

The door slid shut, leaving Mary alone, bleeding and crying.

～

THIRTY-ONE

Brent Foster

The duffel bag's strap dug into Brent's shoulder blade.

"Fuck me," said Luis, three yards ahead.

Brent looked up to see another wall of cars spanning the street.

He hoisted himself behind Luis, climbing atop an old Cadillac, denting the metal under his weight and hoping he wouldn't fall through the roof. Luis was climbing the hood of a Hummer ahead.

A high-pitched siren screamed through the air.

Brent raised his gun and fired into the fog.

Creatures poured from inside it: running, clicking, shrieking.

Brent ran. A creature cried out behind him, so loud it seemed like it was over his shoulder, about to take him down.

CLICK CLICK CLICK CLICK.

The monster landed on Brent and opened its large mouth, wailing an unearthly bellow as it straddled his chest, swiping at his face with its claws. Brent pushed against the creature's wet, fleshy chest with his left hand, trying desperately to hold it back.

"Fuck, fuck, fuck!" He struggled to raise his pistol then emptied his ammo into the creature.

A spatter of hot, black gore spattered his face.

Something punched Brent in the ribs, sending him hard into another car. The gun fell from his clumsy hands. He looked up to see another creature approaching, eyes narrowed.

A pair of thunderous gunshots ripped through the air and knocked the creature back.

"Die! Die! Die!" Luis screamed, emptying his clip …

BRENT WAS awake for a few minutes, hearing automatic gunfire explode on the other side of the metal wall before realizing he was no longer inside the old memories replaying as a dream.

The sounds exploded again, several shots at once, lasting in bursts of about twenty seconds.

Brent scrambled to standing, now fully out of his dream, daring to hope that their rescue had come.

"Dad?" Ben said.

The doors swung open before Brent could respond.

Marcus eclipsed most of the morning's bright light.

"Slaves," he said, then turned and marched toward the fields, leaving guards to gather chains and lead the prisoners from their rusty home.

Teagan was standing close to the door. Brent read her lips in the light: *What do you think that was?*

Brent shook his head and shrugged, hating himself for not knowing more, or being willing to share the possible truth. He remembered Wilson's words: *Every once in a while, they pick the weakest among us and shoot 'em.*

Marcus led the group to yesterday's hole, but this time Brent saw not a box but the reason for the pit: dozens of bodies, bleeding from fresh wounds, some still moving.

Behind him, the kids screamed.

He retched, certain he was about to vomit.

He had to hold it in. Losing yesterday's water and half-rotten fruit would only make him a target. Brent forced himself to look, to confront the truth of what he was about to do.

There were plenty of bodies, none with much meat. Not a single corpse could have weighed much more than Ben, though they'd all been stretched like taffy. They were scattered rather than stacked. The pair nearest Brent looked like they might have once been a couple, about the same age, a guy and a girl, the man in denim and the girl in a filthy cotton dress, ripped and stained. It might have been green when new. Their bones seemed baby bird brittle, barely there, so thin they might as well have been see-through.

Behind him, the kids cried.

"Sshhh … " Brent fell to one knee, eager to soothe his son before the Reaper turned his single eye upon them.

Teagan managed to stop Becca's tears, but Ben cried louder.

"I suggest you give his tongue to the cat, or I'll cut it out." Marcus glanced at the hole. "And *you'll* be dropping him in there with the rest of *them*."

Marcus pointed to the bodies closest to Brent and dragged his digit through the air, pointing at each emaciated husk until his finger found the pit.

"All of them, in there." Marcus turned to the guards. "Give them an hour."

Then the giant turned and walked away.

Brent's hand found Ben's mouth, and he pressed down hard to stifle his tears. He whispered, "It's going to be okay."

"I'm scared."

"I know you are. Me, too. But being scared is normal."

"Not like this, Dad."

"It's the same," Brent said. "Just different. Everyone's afraid. Some people are afraid of the dark. Others are frightened of dogs or spiders or snakes. What scares one person might not be a big deal for someone else. Are you afraid of bees?"

"No," Ben said.

"Me neither. But a lot of people are. I knew a kid named Tim when I was your age; he cried whenever he saw one. What about spiders, are you afraid of spiders?"

"No."

"I am. I've always been afraid of spiders."

"Really?"

"Yes, really. And I hate that I am. I really wish I wasn't. But I can't help how I feel. So the best thing I can do is to know there are plenty of people who *aren't* afraid of spiders, then I pretend I'm one of them."

Ben's voice trembled. "Does that work?"

"It does," Brent lied. "And that's what I'm going to do now, pretend I'm one of the people who wouldn't be scared about all of this now."

"*Everyone* would be scared of this."

"Not Boricio," Brent said.

He thought he saw his son crack the slightest of smiles. Before he could respond, one of the guards — the man with the black beard from their first day — came over and ordered them to work.

Ben moved closer to Brent, and they both bent down and grabbed the arms of a thin man in his thirties. His eyes were wide open, staring at the sky.

Ben looked away, closing his own eyes.

"Why are his eyes open?" he asked.

"Sometimes, that's how people die," Brent said. "Now let's get him in the grave so his soul can find peace.

As they dragged the man together, Ben asked, "Do you really think that souls find peace when a person's body is buried?"

Brent wasn't sure what he'd believed before today. But in that moment, he found that yes, he did believe that.

"Yes, I do."

They continued pulling bodies into the ditch, with Teagan

and Becca working beside them. Sammy and Wilson were picking bodies up and throwing them, reminding Brent of old Holocaust films he'd unfortunately seen.

So much for never again.

Soon enough, Ben had drifted closer to Becca and appeared to be trying to cheer her up. First, he repeated what Brent had said about souls finding peace, and that they were helping these people by putting them in the hole.

Soon, to Brent and Teagan's surprise, Becca giggled at something Ben had said. Brent wasn't sure if he was horrified that the kids had become so immediately numb to the death around them, or thankful that they'd been resilient enough to block the worst of it out.

Brent appreciated Ben's indelible spirit and was happy that his son could temporarily forget the danger. But Ben tended to get loud once carried away, which often happened around Becca. It wouldn't take much to nab the guard's attention, and bring trouble to them all.

And now, Tommy was on duty.

As Brent and Teagan returned from dragging a woman into the pit, he saw that the kids had stopped working.

They were just standing there, talking.

"What do you call a cow with no legs?" Ben asked Becca.

"I don't know," she said, already laughing.

"Ground beef!"

The children burst into laughter, shockingly oblivious to the danger around them.

Tommy marched over, hand on the pistol hanging from his belt, but not yet drawing it. Brent steeled his body to keep himself in place. He looked over at Teagan and saw her doing the same. They each wanted to intervene, run to their children and make apologies on their behalf. But that would be the wrong thing to do, and likely only get them all in more trouble.

They were children. Things couldn't be too bad. The

adults would only make things worse by getting in Tommy's way.

"You two need to shut the fuck up," he said.

He grabbed the arm one of the corpses beside them, a boy not much older than them.

"Back to work, or you join him in the hole, you got it?"

Ben nodded, clearly terrified.

Becca began to cry.

Tommy reached out, grabbed a handful of hair, and yanked her toward him. "Shut the fuck up!"

Brent lost it. A second later, he was next to the pervert, shoving the man backward.

Tommy yelled, "You best step back!" then spit in his face.

Brent stood on the precipice of doing something very stupid, barely aware of Sammy and Wilson standing behind him. Meghan and Lara watching from behind Tommy. No other guards around.

Tommy seemed to read Brent's mind. He smiled, winking at Brent.

"Wanna piece of me? Eh? Go for it, tough guy."

He laughed.

Brent charged at him, hands outstretched to grab the man by the throat and shove him to the ground.

Tommy laughed, sidestepping Brent's awkward attempt at bravery. As Brent stumbled past him, Tommy spun around then punched Brent hard in the ribcage.

He fell to the ground.

Tommy jumped on top of Brent, straddling him.

Before Brent could raise his arms to deflect the man's blows, Tommy's fists pummeled his face, so fast and furious that he was blinded by the pain.

Brent lost a tooth, and maybe swallowed it.

Tommy kept punching.

Black Beard came behind Tommy and pulled him off of Brent.

Brent could barely see, blood clotting around his puffy eyes.

"Enough!" Black Beard said. "These slaves have work to do, and we don't want Marcus pissed if shit don't get done. Stop fucking around."

"Sure thing, Wyatt," Tommy said, wiping Brent's blood from his chin with the back of his hand.

He held a hand out to help Brent up. He tentatively raised his own to take it, knowing it was a mistake before he did.

Tommy laughed, pulled back the offered hand, ran it through his hair, then looked from Brent to Ben and Becca before settling his gaze on Brent. He winked, blew him a kiss, then walked away.

Brent felt a brick in his stomach. He'd surely put a target on all of their backs. Tommy paused by Meghan and Lara and laughed, petting Lara on her head.

"We'll be seeing you later, baby. Maybe tonight we don't leave Mama alone." He turned to Meghan. "You up for that, honey?"

Meghan stared at the ground.

Brent wanted to kill every fucker behind the gates of Hell.

PAIN WAS the only thing reminding Brent that he was still alive.

As they waited in the container for nightfall, Brent tried to focus past the ache in his ribs and entire face, and pay attention to the game of Twenty Questions that Sammy was playing with the kids and Teagan.

Brent was thankful to the big man for stepping in with some cheer because Brent felt empty.

He wasn't the only one.

Wilson was staring at the ground, and Meghan and Lara were huddled together, crying. Whether it was over what they'd been through last night, the bodies they dragged into the grave today, or what might happen later tonight when the rapists returned, it was tough to tell.

The big man in the corner hadn't moved in more than twenty-four hours. He was clearly dead, and yet the bandits hadn't removed him. *Are they leaving him in here as a reminder not to fuck with them? Or are we going to have to drag him to the pit tomorrow?*

"Is it smaller than a potato?" Ben asked.

"No," Sammy said, "not even close, pal."

Brent saw something that moved his mind from both his pain and the game. Meghan was staring down into her palm, staring at something.

Oh, no.

Brent tapped Teagan, eyes wide, nodding toward the pair.

"Don't do it." Teagan whispered once she realized what the couple was contemplating. "Don't let them win."

"I have to," Meghan said. "I can't stand to be so … helpless. It's rotting my insides, and there's nothing I can do. Why *not* take matters into my own hands? At least I'd be *doing something.* You saw all those bodies. If we're all going to end up in the pit no matter what, why not *decide* when it's time, claim some control before those monsters do anything worse?"

Meghan turned from Teagan to her daughter. "Are you ready?"

Lara nodded, softly sobbing.

"I'll be back." Brent stood, rushed over to Lara and Meghan, then dropped down on his knees between them. He put one hand gently on the mom's arm, the other on her daughter's shoulder. "Don't do it. Please. Help is coming."

Meghan stared at Brent with hopeless eyes.

"Who?"

"A friend. She's outside now. She escaped when they caught the rest of us. She's bringing help."

"Help?" Lara asked, eyes suddenly hopeful. "How many?"

"I don't know how many, or when," Brent admitted. "But I'm sure they're coming. You don't have to do this."

Meghan said, "How can you be sure they'll come?"

"Because they've never let us down before." He shook his head. "I don't know how long it will take them to get here. But I swear to you, once they come, they will save us all. You can't do this. *Please.*"

Maybe everything would have been fine if Brent had had another few moments. But he didn't.

The door creaked open; lights shone on them and showed them the horror of Tommy sauntering inside.

"Who's ready for some fun?" He laughed. "Hey, Mamacita," he said to Meghan, "how about tonight you join me and your little peach in the passion pit?"

He licked his lips.

In a flash, Meghan lifted her hand to her daughter's throat, whispered, "I'm sorry," then sliced in a merciful yet vicious stroke.

Blood rained on Brent.

His hands flew to his face to wipe it away from his eyes. Through splayed fingers, he watched as Meghan raised the blade to her own throat and — without hesitation — followed her daughter to the grave.

Her body slumped forward, onto Lara's, sending them both to the floor; family blood blended in a single pool.

"What the fuck?" Tommy screamed, pulling out his pistol, aiming it at Brent and then Sammy.

Two bandits rushed into the container, shotguns drawn.

"Where'd you get the razor?" Tommy waved his gun back and forth across the slaves.

No one spoke.

They barely breathed.

Brent was closest, so Tommy approached him and pressed his pistol hard to Brent's temple.

He looked behind him, smiling at the pair of bandits

standing on full alert — Purple Hair and Skull Tattoo — then turned to the slaves. "Start talking, or I'll kill everyone, starting with Mr. Tough Guy."

Brent's heart raced as he stared into the helpless eyes of his family, and then to Sammy.

Sammy swallowed, looking like he was about to make a false confession, sacrificing himself for Brent. And as much as he hated to admit it to himself, there was a part of Brent — the part that needed to be here with his family — that was willing to let him.

Ben pointed to Wilson. "They came from him."

No hesitation: Tommy winked at Ben, turned to Wilson and shot him twice in the face, then looked down at Becca and Ben.

The kids screamed.

Tommy shoved Brent to the ground, beside Teagan and the kids.

Tommy dropped to a squat in front of them, met Ben's eyes.

"Good job, kid, you just saved your daddy."

Ben said nothing, sniffling back tears.

Tommy ran a hand through his hair.

Brent lurched forward, but Tommy's gun was in his face, as if he expected, maybe even was trying, to provoke Brent's response.

Gun in Brent's face, Tommy turned his gaze to Becca, licked his lips, and said, "How would you two kids like to come with us tonight?"

∼

THIRTY-TWO

Paul Roberts

"What the hell were you thinking?" Desmond yelled at Paul.

Desmond was usually smooth in his reprimands, not enraged. But as Paul stood there in the command center, Desmond wasn't holding back.

"I asked you a question."

"You wanted information, and she wasn't giving it. I improvised."

"That's what you call that — *improvising?*"

"You put me in a room with the woman who slit my daughter's throat and tell me it's up to me to find out where she is, where the rebels are, and you're surprised when I try to scare her?"

Desmond tilted his head to the side in his condescending way. "And how *scared* do you think she is?"

"I don't know." Paul shook his head. "Why don't you let me back in and find out?"

Desmond laughed. "Wow, Paul, you're really unraveling, aren't you?"

A small part of Paul wondered if Desmond was working him. Perhaps the tracking chip hadn't actually stopped working. Maybe Desmond was telling Paul so he would go hard on

Mary — even if he was acting upset that he'd been too rough. Desmond had to have known that Paul would do something like that.

A darker thought occurred to Paul: What if there never was a tracking chip? What if Emily had never been anything other than bait? Another worm to Desmond, and who cared what happened to a lowly worm?

Still, Paul had to find some way to stay on Desmond's good side and prove his value — just in case there was any chance of getting Emily back.

"No, I mean it," Paul said. "Let me back in. I laid the groundwork. I put the fear in her, even if she doesn't know it yet. When I go back in, she'll talk. It's like good cop, bad cop. You know the routine?"

"Yes," Desmond nodded, "but in my scenario, *you* were the good cop."

"And who was the bad?"

Desmond didn't have to answer. Paul saw it in his eyes. "Oh, you?"

"Yes, and now we have a situation with two bad cops, Mr. Roberts. Tell me, how do you think she'll respond to *two* bad cops? Think she'll open up, lower her guard?"

Paul took a moment to respond. "I'm sorry. I'll make it up to you. Just give me another chance."

"Well, fortunately for us, and your daughter, I happen to have a backup plan."

"And what if she doesn't talk?" Paul asked. "How will we find my daughter, or the rebels, if she stays the course?"

Desmond stared into Paul's eyes with a ferocity that Paul had never seen in the man. "Oh, she'll talk. One way or another, we will get our answers, Mr. Roberts."

THIRTY-THREE

Mary Olson

Mary wasn't sure when or how she passed out. Or if it was from exhaustion, blood loss, or something else. She woke, still lying down clamped to the table, hearing a buzzing sound, like a cell phone left on a nightstand.

A tickling sensation ran through her entire body.

Her eyes flicked open to darkness save for a blue sphere, roughly the size of a basketball, hovering just inches over her body.

What the hell is this?!

She squirmed.

Mary moved, and the ball of light loosened, like pieces of a tire coming off in every direction. They glowed blue, and after a momentary separation, pulled themselves back into the ball.

"I'd suggest you keep still," a voice said behind her. "We are repairing your wounds."

The voice was instantly recognizable, and boiled her blood.

Desmond!

She struggled to turn her head around, but it was impossible, strapped down as she was, to get a look directly behind her.

"Let me go, you fucker!"

"Now, now," Desmond said, his voice calm like a lover's, "save the sexy talk for later. You need to relax, Mary."

Suddenly, his hands cupped either side of her head, as if he were going to give her a scalp massage, though Mary was certain he held nothing loving in his intentions.

"Don't touch me!" she said, surprised as her voice cracked at the end.

She squirmed again and felt the ball of light buzz louder, disassemble, then reassert its form.

His hands went from a gentle caress to a vice-like grip, so tight she was certain he was about to squeeze her skull just to see it pop like a melon. Or at least let her know he *could*.

Desmond leaned in close, though she still couldn't see him, and whispered, "I said, *keep still.*"

Panic seized her entire body.

She'd been waiting for this moment so long, a chance to be in a room with him, to make him pay for Paola's death. She'd dreamed of the many ways she could end him, from a simple bullet in his skull to the more … *creative* methods. Tie him up and peel his skin bit by bit. Set him afire. Chop off his limbs one by one. She'd imagined so many details, like an athlete practicing for her biggest game.

But she'd never imagined this: him having her on a table, at his will, naked no less, unable to do anything. She'd never felt more helpless, save for the moment she cradled her dead daughter, watching the life leave her body.

Mary wanted to explode and take them both out in a fiery, violent death. Take out the whole fucking spaceship, too.

"Let me — "

He squeezed her head tighter. Mary cried out.

"Silent," he said smoothly, "and remain still until you're fixed."

She did as instructed. Desmond relaxed his grip enough

that he was no longer hurting her, but it was still tight enough to keep her in line.

After what felt like forever, the ball of light zipped away, out of the room through a sliding door to her right.

"There, there, all better," Desmond said, letting go of her head but still standing out of sight.

"I'm going to kill you." Though Mary was about as far from being able to execute her threat as one could possibly be, she meant it with her every molecule. And she believed it. She'd find a way to break free and deliver on her promise — even if it was the last thing she'd do.

Desmond laughed.

"Kill me? But why? I thought you loved me."

"You're *not* Desmond."

More laughter.

She heard his footsteps recede behind her, echoing off the walls.

"Oh, but Desmond is still in here with us."

"No, he's dead. Just like Paola."

"Yeah, that was a bit unfortunate, Mary. And for that, I'm truly sorry. If you remember, though, I gave you all a choice. I gave you a chance to live with us, to be part of something new, something big, something bold! But you and your little group of *roaches* thought you knew better."

"You are a fucking cancer! We will defeat you!"

"Mary, why are you so determined to avoid your destiny? This is the way forward. We don't have to be enemies. We can coexist."

"Liar! You do not coexist. You are nothing but parasites, killing everything you touch."

"No, *that* is the lie, dear Mary. That is the lie you people tell yourselves as you hold onto a crumbling past. As you run from a future you don't understand."

"Don't understand? We watched you wipe out most of a planet's population. Not once, but twice!"

"You are correct when it came to what happened on the other world, but we've since learned of our errors. We've learned of our true destiny."

"You've killed almost everyone on *this* planet, too!"

"No, we reduced the number to an ideal sum for all concerned. Going forward, our kinds will be intermingled in a way that will benefit both. An end to sickness, an end to war, an end to death, Mary. Don't you want to live in a world where we never die? Where Paola would never have died?"

"Don't you speak her name."

"Let me ask you something, Mary. You see us as parasites, bent on destroying your world, killing your people. But tell me, why aren't you this afraid of Luca?"

Mary said nothing.

"He is the same species as us."

"No, he's not. Where you kill, he sacrifices, gives of himself to save others."

"No, your precious so-called *Light* sacrifices *Luca's* body, but it isn't doing so out of the goodness of its heart. It is doing what we are doing. It is attempting to survive by any means necessary."

"No, you're wrong."

"No, Mary. It's you who are wrong. You accuse us of being parasites, yet we are no different than the alien in Luca. You see that Luca still has free will, yes? He is still acting of his own accord, right? Well, so are the others, Mary. We have hundreds of people coexisting with aliens just fine. And they get along fine with our free humans. Yes, Mary, we even let some people live free on The Island. Does that sound so horrible to you? Like we're the bad guys?"

"You lie." Mary continued the conversation not to argue but to buy time, to try and figure out Desmond's endgame, to see what he wanted from her. If she could find his lever, she could use it to get free. And if she could get free, she could finally take him out.

"Desmond is still here inside this body, Mary. It's true, ask him yourself."

Mary heard the sound of footsteps approaching.

Her heart raced. She wasn't sure how she'd respond when she finally saw Desmond face to face. Finally looked in the eyes of the man who was responsible for Paola's death.

His footsteps drew nearer.

It took every bit of her self-control to stay calm, to not pull at the binds holding her down.

He came around, into view.

She swallowed a painful knot in her throat.

"Hi, Mary," he said, his voice different. He'd gone from smooth and in control to apprehensive, unsure. "It's true. I'm still in here. The aliens saved me, gave me another chance."

She shook her head. "No. You're dead."

Desmond's eyes began to well up with tears. His shaky voice went on, "No, Mary, I'm here. And I'm so sorry for what he did to your daughter. He didn't mean for her to be shot. And I couldn't stop it."

Could he be telling the truth? Could a part of Desmond still be alive in there? This had to be a ruse. A performance to work on her sympathies. He was playing on her love for Desmond to find *her* lever. Mary refused to believe.

"Shut up!" she said, tears stinging her eyes. "You're dead."

"No," Desmond said. "*We're* not dead. We can live again. We can live forever."

We're?

She heard footsteps behind her.

Heard someone breathing.

"Yes," Desmond said. "Death isn't the end for us. We can all live together, forever."

The footsteps came closer.
Mary struggled to turn, to see who it was, but couldn't.
Then the other person spoke.
"We can live forever, Mom."

Episode 34

(FOURTH EPISODE OF SEASON SIX)

"The Reaping"

THIRTY-FOUR

Boricio Wolfe

Boricio was pretty sure his arms would fall the fuck off if he carried Luca much farther.

Keenan looked over and asked, "You ready to switch yet?"

"I got it," Boricio said, pretending his arms and back weren't burning. "Ain't no thing but a chicken wing."

"You sure? You look like you're about to pass out."

"I said I got it," Boricio snapped.

Keenan grinned. "Okay, you got it."

Boricio might not be Mr. Action Hero with hulking biceps like Ed Keenan, but he wasn't about to hand Luca over fifteen minutes into their trip and look like a pussy. A two-mile walk should take around forty minutes at their pace, carrying Luca. But fuck if fifteen didn't feel like fifty when you were carrying dead weight.

Lisa, walking with Barrow, Emily, and Jevonne behind them, laughed.

"My hero," she said sarcastically.

"Go fuck yourself, Lisa," Boricio said with a wink back at her.

"I could carry him for a bit," Barrow offered.

"It's cool," Boricio said.

Boricio wished Barrow had stepped up and offered in the first place. Dude was a fucking house, and dumb as the dirt it was built on. If anyone should be carrying Luca, it should've been the ox. Hell, the fucker could probably carry Luca the whole way without breaking a sweat. Except that the dude constantly sweated, like a politician on trial. Despite his sweatiness, he was good for lifting and brawling. But Barrow had failed to step up, so Boricio had taken the lead. Now Boricio wasn't about to let everyone think he wasn't leader of his fucking pack by being a bitch.

Despite his internal whining and groaning muscles, Boricio didn't mind carrying Luca. He'd never had a family worth a fuck, but in a lot of ways, Luca felt like the kid brother he never had. Opie Cunningham looked like *Cocoon*, but still, Boricio would do anything for the little man — even carry his scrawny bones through The Catacombs.

As they continued onward, Boricio noticed that Emily wasn't saying much at all. She'd gone from being an annoying, overly apologetic kid, to giving everyone the silent treatment, walking with a permanent scowl. That made Boricio think that Keenan was right when he said they needed to get her on their side. That meant an apology.

At exactly twenty minutes, which Boricio knew without needing a watch to tell him, he set Luca down and looked up at Keenan. "Okay, Agent Double O' Keenan, he's all yours."

"No, I got it," Barrow said, scooping Luca into his arms without a hint of effort.

Boricio scowled.

Keenan glanced over at Boricio and winked.

Boricio grinned and nodded. "Motherfucker."

Keenan laughed.

Boricio slowed to walk beside Emily then asked if he could talk to her.

Lisa looked back and exchanged a glance with Boricio as if she wanted to say "Don't be mean." Boricio rolled his eyes.

Lisa and Jevonne picked up their pace, walking closer to Keenan, Barrow, and Luca.

Boricio licked his lips, ready for crow.

"You all right?"

"Yeah," Emily said.

Boricio looked at the bandage covering the neck wound Lisa had created and stitched — nothing compared to the gash Mary had put in the girl's throat, but Luca had healed that. This one Luca wouldn't be able to heal given his current condition of being passed the fuck out.

"That hurt?"

"It'll be okay."

Her short responses and inability to meet his gaze wouldn't make this easy. But Boricio was nowhere near surrender. There wasn't a woman alive who didn't eventually succumb to the charms of his gentlemanly side, and this moody little tween wasn't about to be first. He'd find a way to make peace whether she wanted to or not.

"Listen, I wanna apologize for how I acted back there."

"It's okay," Emily said, still looking down. Boricio didn't think her avoidance of his gaze was a guilt trip so much as her not wanting to invest any more into a relationship that had already been abandoned in her head. Best not to get friendly with the people you plan to fuck over first chance you get.

"No, I was a major dick."

She laughed. Emily was probably still young enough that she wasn't used to an adult using such language in front of her. Her laugh reminded him of how Paola responded when he'd say things in her company that made Mary wince, while Paola and Boricio giggled like naughty kids.

"That lady, Mary, the one who did the — " Boricio stopped talking to make Emily look at him, another way to force a connection, then ran a finger across his throat and stuck out his tongue. Emily smiled. "Anyway, Mary wasn't always so … "

He paused, trying to think of the right word.

"Bitchy?" she offered.

Emily's smile turned uncertain, as if she wasn't sure if she'd offended Boricio by trashing his friend, or if everything was cool between the naughty kids.

"Yeah, that's one word." Boricio laughed.

Emily laughed, too. He could feel her warming up. Could see it in her body language, her smile, and how she was now looking at him again.

"She wasn't always like that, though. When I met Miss Mary, she was Wonder Woman. A single momma raising a girl about your age. Mary was smart and funny. Creative, too. She used to draw greeting cards, if you can believe it. An' they didn't even drop F bombs or have dead people on 'em. They also made a shit-ton of money without her forced to draw Garfield. You could see how much she loved her daughter. Mary wasn't one of these parents fucking their kid over because they're so busy chasing bullshit career goals. She always made time. She was the girl's momma, and her best friend. Now, I never had that kinda family, so seeing Lorelei and Rory was touching."

"Lorelei and Rory?"

"*Gilmore Girls?*"

No recognition in Emily's eyes.

"Shit, didn't you watch *any* TV? Anyway, then that fuck, Desmond, came after us. One of his men shot Mary's little girl, killed her right there on the spot. And I'm afraid that also killed Mary. She's not been the same since."

Emily stared ahead, processing Boricio's story.

"What was her name?" she finally said.

"Her daughter?"

"Yeah."

"Paola. She was a great kid. A lot like her mother but different in a lot of ways, too. You two would've been peas and carrots. I mean, I *think* you would've; I can't say for sure since I don't really know you all that well. But I'm trying to say I hope you don't hate Mary for what she did."

"I don't."

"I think part of the reason she did it was because you reminded Mary of Paola — well, the fact that Desmond had taken her — so she wanted to take something from the enemy."

"I understand."

"As for me, well, I love Mary, and I hate to see her in pain. So you being here, and seeing how it messed with her head even more, well, I got stupid. And, well, I'm sorry."

"What about the others? Do they hate me?"

"I don't think so. If they did, believe me, you wouldn't be with us now. That Keenan guy, and Lisa too, they're Terminators. If they didn't want you here, they'd tell you to get lost."

"So, do you think Mary's okay? I heard you say you wanted to go look for her."

"Mary's a big girl. We'll get her back, then I'll sit with both of you, and we'll have a heart to heart to heart. Trust me, everything will be fine."

Boricio thought about asking the girl if she missed her father. Maybe ask about her mom, but figured if he made her think too much about her family, she might miss them more and want to get back on The Island.

They walked in silence.

But the quiet was different. Boricio felt that Emily had come around, and was back on their side.

He hoped his intuition was right because once they reached the house, Boricio was heading out to look for Mary, no matter what.

~

THIRTY-FIVE

Emily Roberts

As the group marched toward their destination, Emily tried to telepathically find her father. While she no longer felt in danger, at least from the group, she couldn't stop thinking about her dad. She'd been trying to reach him for what felt like hundreds of times. At first, frantically for help, then to explain that she'd been rescued and was safe.

He had to be losing it by now, maybe even thinking her dead. Though the memories were fading, Emily could still remember a time when he thought he was going to lose her to the plague. He'd sit next to her bed, crying, praying to God. Losing his wife — her mother — had nearly killed him. If the plague had taken her, too, he would've been lost. He'd told her so many times.

She had to let him know that she was safe.

But at the same time, she knew there was no way he'd understand that she wasn't in a rush to come home. A part of her wanted to stay here, in The Wastelands.

Though there had been a point where Emily was scheming an exit from her captors, it wasn't a very practical plan. For one, she knew nothing of The Wastelands, or its many threats. As they toured the area in the shuttle before it crashed, their instructor — *God rest his soul* — had warned them of both the Ferals roaming The Wastelands and the deadly bandits. He'd not spoken of rebels like Boricio and his group specifically, but rather barbaric men and women who were reduced to animals in their savagery. *If they catch you, you'll wish you were dead.*

At the time, she'd wondered if the threat had been propaganda, something her father had taught her about in discussions of the Old Days. Propaganda designed to make the teens untrusting of others, to stay within the safe confines of The Island's community and never yearn to know what lay beyond — to never search for freedom, as freedom was too scary.

However, she'd seen enough in Luca's memories to know there were horrible people — and aliens — preying on the weak. So, yeah, Emily could probably escape the group, but she'd have nowhere to go.

Also, she didn't *want* to go.

Emily felt a connection to Luca that she yearned to understand. It wasn't romantic, or even familial, but it felt as strong as either of those, if not more so. It was as if their souls had touched in some transcendent way and were now forever linked.

Emily wondered if the alien in him — The Light — had burrowed its way inside her. Maybe this wasn't a magically heartwarming thing so much as a parasite working to compromise her.

Panic began to swell within.

Am I infected?

The thought of one of the aliens being inside her, *controlling her*, sent Emily's thoughts in a downward spiral. She'd rather die than be a host to the things.

But Luca's alien was different. In her brief glimpse of its true nature, she saw it wasn't this festering dark thing like the aliens on The Island or the ship. The Light was bright whites and blues, ethereal, intoxicatingly beautiful. Warm and welcoming, not cold and sinister.

Still, the thought of something inside her sent chills to Emily's core.

I don't think *it's inside me.*

She had a fairly good feel for her own mind. She could feel when her father was attempting to pick through her thoughts. She could feel when the aliens tried, too, though they'd been unable to do so with her or her father, or so she thought. Emily figured she'd know if there was someone, or *something*, hijacking her headspace. And she didn't feel anything in there.

And yet she felt *different*.

"We're here," Keenan said as they reached a set of concrete steps leading up to a strong-looking black metal door.

Keenan had his pistol ready as he knocked on the door, a series of raps separated by silence. She memorized the pattern, just in case she'd need to someday use it to gain access.

A metal panel in the door at eye level slid open, and a pair of eyes appeared cloaked in shadows.

The panel slid shut, then the door opened.

They were greeted by an old dark-skinned woman with long white hair. She wore a black trench coat over dark-red leather pants, a matching tunic and knee-high black boots, which made Emily think of her as some kind of kick-ass granny gunfighter or something. At her side was a black lab.

For a brief moment, Emily got a deadly vibe off the woman — that she'd been through a lot to survive, and didn't suffer fools.

She smiled, big and warm, completely changing her gruff appearance.

"Boricio!" She opened her arms and went right to him.

"Hey, Jazz, what's shakin'?" He lifted the woman into a hug. She gave him a kiss on the cheek.

"Not much; you come to cook us up something good?"

"You got the fixings, I'll melt your mouth, baby."

Jazz smiled slyly, "You're so bad."

"That's why you love me."

Emily stared in disbelief at the exchange. She'd not seen Boricio be this giddy with anyone, and yet here he was, putting on the charm for this old woman. Emily searched her memories, the ones Luca had given her, but only caught glimpses of Jazz, not enough to piece together a narrative, or a past relationship with Boricio.

Jazz went from flirty to worried at the sight of Barrow holding Luca.

"Wait a second … is that … *Luca?*"

Barrow nodded.

Boricio said, "Some bad shit went down, Jazz, and we need to lie low for a bit. Got room?"

"Got nothin' *but* room. The rest of the team is on a supply run outside The City, and I'm not expecting them back for another few days."

Jazz went up to Luca, still in Barrow's arms, and ran a hand gently over his cheek, saying, "Poor thing."

Jazz looked at Emily, her smile returning.

"We got a new member?"

Nobody else answered, so Emily nodded. "Yes, ma'am."

"Oh, you don't need to call me ma'am. The name's Jazz."

She held out her hand.

Emily reached out and met the woman's firm handshake.

"Is that your real name, Jazz?"

Emily didn't mean to snoop on the woman's thoughts but saw a flash of horrifying memories. Bloody. Jazz was a survivor, who'd lost plenty.

"I used to go by another name, but too many bad things happened to that woman. She was a victim. But Jazz, she's a fighter."

Emily nodded. "Nice to meet you, Jazz."

Suddenly, Luca screamed: "Mary!"

THIRTY-SIX

Mary Olson

No, it can't be.

Paola?

Mary listened as the footsteps behind her came closer. Then the girl stepped into view.

It *was* her!

"Paola?" Mary couldn't stop the tears streaming down her face.

Paola stood in a long dark-blue dress. She looked slightly different, slightly older, nineteen or so, but there was no mistaking her daughter: long dark hair, large brown eyes, small lips, trembling as she wept. It was somehow, impossibly Paola!

Paola collapsed onto Mary, hugging her as best she could with her mother naked and strapped to the table, crying in her ear. "I missed you so much, Mom!"

Her daughter's hair covering Mary's face, she inhaled the girl's scent, leaving no doubt that this was, in fact, her daughter, still somehow alive.

"I missed you, too. Oh, God, I missed you so much. *How? How are you still alive?*"

It hit her before either of them spoke. Paola was alive in

the same way that Desmond was — animated by the aliens. Likely hijacked.

Mary let out a scream. Paola jumped back, startled.

"You're not my daughter!"

Paola pushed her hair back from her tear-stained face, eyes wide, hurt. "What?"

"You're not my daughter! You're a corpse, pretending to be Paola."

"No, Mom, it's me!"

Mary stared at the girl, desperate to believe her, to *know* that somehow Paola was alive. But nobody could survive the gunshot wound she'd seen her daughter take to the head.

Mary closed her eyes. She couldn't look at this mockery to Paola's memory any longer.

"Please, Mommy, it's me. It's Paola." She reached out to embrace Mary again.

Mary screamed, flinching from the thing's touch, shaking her head, "Get away! Get away!"

"She *is* your daughter," Desmond said.

Now she had Desmond, speaking in his normal voice, and Paola, begging her to see them as the humans she once knew and loved.

She squeezed her eyes tighter, screaming to drown their voices, "Gettttttt ouuuuuuttttttt!!"

Mary screamed until her throat was raw, sore, and cracking.

She finally stopped. The room was silent except for her sobbing.

Are they gone?

Mary opened her eyes to an empty room. The abominations pretending to be her daughter and lover were gone.

Mary never thought she'd experience anything worse than Paola's death.

Now she knew how wrong she'd been.

THIRTY-SEVEN

Boricio Wolfe

"Mary!" Luca screamed, his body shaking in Barrow's bulging arms.

Boricio ran to help Barrow gently lower Luca to the ground just outside the Chandler House's basement entrance.

"Easy does it." Boricio placed a hand behind Luca's head and watched the old man convulse.

Boricio usually kept his eyes on two things when the Boy Wonder was making a maraca with his body: that the kid didn't hurt himself and that he didn't swallow his tongue. Now he was wondering why Luca was screaming Mary's name.

Was she in trouble? Did something happen to her? Was there anything he was supposed to do?

Boricio tried not to consider all the terrible things that could befall Mary out there. Yet all matter of awful atrocities started playing in his mind's lonely theater.

Karma, bitch, comin' to take the person you care about most.

Boricio told his inner voice to shut the fuck up.

Luca's body stopped shaking. His eyes opened.

Good, he's coming to. Kid can give me the spoilers.

"You okay, buddy?"

Luca's eyes looked up at Boricio, dizzy, confused.

"Luca? You with me?"

He stared at Boricio, still lost.

Fuck!

Boricio could feel the others crowding around him, watching, waiting anxiously to see if the kid was okay. He was the *one thing* that they all had in common, and maybe the *only thing* holding them all together. If, or when, Luca died, Boricio was damned sure the wheels would come flying off the Team Boricio Mystery Machine. And if that happened, Team Fucking Alien won.

"Come on." Boricio shook Luca, trying to wake him from his stupor. "Come on, buddy."

No response.

"What *about* Mary?" Boricio shook him harder. "Come on!"

"Hey, hey!" Keenan put a hand on Boricio's shoulder. "Easy now."

Boricio flinched and looked up at Keenan. "He knows where Mary is. We need to find out!"

"We won't know anything if you shake him to death!"

Boricio looked down. Luca's eyes were closed, out cold again.

"Fuck!"

Boricio laid Luca's head down gently then popped up and spun, searching for the first thing he could plunge his fist into. The tunnel's wall would work just fine.

Pain shot through his hand like a bolt of lightning.

Fuck! What's this fucking wall made of?

He held his hand, hoping he didn't break anything, and fell back against the wall. He closed his eyes, breathing in and out, slow and deliberate, trying to calm himself.

He heard the others, including Barrow and Luca, move into the Chandler House basement, giving him space.

He waited for silence then opened his eyes.

But Boricio wasn't alone.

"What?" he said to Emily.

"Maybe I can help."

Boricio laughed. "Yeah, how's that?"

"Maybe I can go in his head and see what he saw."

Boricio smiled then found a laugh.

He opened and closed his fingers. His knuckles were red and bleeding, and his whole hand felt like he'd punched Iron Man's crotch. But he didn't think there was anything broken.

"You think you can do that? I mean, you still ain't reached Daddy Dearest."

"I can't promise anything, but I think maybe I can't connect with Dad because I'm so far away. But Luca's right here. I've never tried going into someone who wasn't awake, but I want to help however I can."

Boricio looked at the girl's eyes, so wide and earnest. While she was hardly Paola's twin, something about her reminded him of Miss Mary's daughter. He had to be careful not to get too attached.

God gives me the old dick slap when I start to fucking care.

"All right, let's give it a shot," Boricio said, leading Emily inside the Chandler House.

~

THIRTY-EIGHT

Brent Foster

"How would you like to come with us?" Tommy repeated to Ben and Becca.

The children were silent, trying not to cry.

Tommy, still crouched, leered at them then smiled at Brent and Teagan.

Brent wanted to strike but couldn't stop what was happening and would surely die if he tried, maybe dragging them all down with him. He thought of his own razor, hidden under a clump of dirt a few feet behind him, and tallied his odds.

Tommy smiled wider and ran a hand through Becca's long, red hair. "How old are you?"

Becca flinched.

Ben's lip quivered like he wanted to say something but was afraid to.

Brent scooted back, slowly, inching his fingers toward the razor somewhere behind him. Purple Hair looked at Brent, called him a coward with his eyes, then turned his full attention to Tommy's show, his hand reaching down and adjusting his cock, or stroking it.

Brent wanted to cut it off. Cut both their cocks off and

then shove them down their throats. Brent couldn't conceive of how either of them could be even thinking about raping when the girl they raped last night, along with her mother, were still bleeding all over the container floor just inches behind them.

Tommy looked from Ben to Becca. "Which one of you wants to come with me first?"

When neither child spoke, Tommy turned to Teagan.

"Mind if I borrow your daughter?"

Teagan whimpered, clearly trying not to scream. Brent had to act, and had to act now. There was no way that he could let them take either of the kids out of the container. No way in hell.

Brent's fingers desperately searched behind him, fumbling over debris. *Where the hell is the razor?* He had to find it.

Purple Hair glanced over at him. "What are you doing?"

"I can't watch," Brent said, throwing his head into the crook of his right arm. He kept his left arm behind him, searching.

For the longest moment, there was nothing but silence save for Tommy's telling Becca what a pretty, pretty girl she was.

Brent prayed Purple Hair wasn't still watching him, or worse, coming over. He dared to peek over his arm, saw that Purple Hair's eyes had returned to the show, kneading the head of his cock through his pants.

Fucker.

Brent's fingers splayed as wide as they'd go, groping in the dirt, pushing dirt and debris aside, searching for the sharp edge of his blade.

Come on, where the hell is it?

Right hand still over his eyes. Brent stretched his left arm out as far as he could without inviting attention, or scooting any farther from Teagan.

"Your boyfriend says he can't watch," Tommy said to Teagan. "Can you?"

Suddenly, a moment of silence. Brent was sure he was busted. He pulled his hand back quickly to his side.

"Why you looking at him?" Tommy said. "Think he can save you?"

Brent looked up, knowing they were talking about him. He met Teagan's crying eyes. Then he looked into Ben's and Becca's, also wet. But they were too terrified to cry out loud with the bandits over them. They knew something bad was about to happen, even if they couldn't know *how* bad.

Teagan shook her head.

"He *can't*. Ain't nothing gonna save you but *you*, and only if you're smart enough to make the right choices. You wanna watch, or join in?"

Skull Tattoo shook his head, glanced over at Wilson's body, and clapped a hand on Purple Hair's shoulder. "Come on, let's get this guy out of here first. Dead bitches next."

The two bandits lifted Wilson's body, one at the armpits and one at the feet, and began to carry him outside.

Brent's fingers returned to their search and then felt the razor's edge.

Got it, fuckers!

Purple Hair stopped.

Skull Tattoo, holding Wilson's feet, said, "What is it?"

"Not sure," Purple Hair said, eyeing Brent.

Brent was frozen, doing his best to appear as though he was making eyes at the ground, without drawing attention to his left hand behind him.

Tommy looked back at them. "There a problem I should know about?"

"No," Purple Hair said. "Just do your thing."

Brent stayed frozen. The bandits continued to carry the body out of the container.

His hand closed around the blade, cold in his flesh.

He tightened it in his fist, hoping he wasn't slicing his flesh. He was so amped he might not feel it. He imagined plunging the blade into the pervert's eyes, one at a time before cutting the throats of the other two bandits.

But he had to bury his intention until the perfect moment.

"Hmmm … who's first?" Tommy ran his hand over Ben's head. "They're both so cute. You two did such a good job raising these little ones."

It took everything inside Brent not to lunge forward. Tommy moved his eyes from boy to father, daring Brent's response, a sick glee gleaming in his beady eyes.

Brent had to be careful. The wrong move would get them all killed.

He wondered if Sammy was ready to move.

He saw himself lunge, saw himself miss, saw the disaster he rained into the container. But he had to do something now. Could not let Tommy take the kids or Teagan.

He put both hands behind his back, passing the razor carefully from his left hand to his right — the one closest to Tommy.

Teagan lost it, screaming, "You leave them alone!"

Tommy laughed, slapped Teagan across the face, then caught her with his right arm as she slouched toward the floor. He came just close enough for Brent to finally strike.

Tommy's left fist balled, ready to assault her. The other two bandits dropped Wilson's body outside, running in.

Brent lunged at Tommy, razor tight in his fingers, aiming for Tommy's neck.

The pervert twisted like a sprinkler head as Brent tried getting the razor to his neck. He grabbed Brent by both wrists, shoving him back against the wall so they were both standing just inches apart.

From the corner of Brent's eye, he saw Teagan throw herself between them and the other bandits, screaming, "You stay away from my kids!"

It took both of them to grab her and contain her thrashing body.

Sammy started toward them, but Purple Hair put a pistol to Teagan's head. "Step back!"

Tommy's eyes burned into Brent's, laughing as he kept pressing him against the wall as if he was about to shove him through the steel container. "Ah, someone's balls dropped!"

The asshole squeezed Brent's wrists so tight that Brent thought maybe the man might snap them off.

Tommy's eyes widened as he realized that Brent was holding a razor. "You fuck!"

Something burned inside Brent. He tried to twist the blade to cut at Tommy's hand.

This ends now.

Whatever that meant.

"You're dead," Brent snarled.

"One of us is." Tommy gripped Brent's wrist tighter, pulled it forward, then slammed it back, repeatedly.

Pain shot through his wrist. Brent dropped the blade.

Shit!

Tommy's knee found Brent's gut, twice.

Brent groaned, falling forward, seconds from vomit.

Tommy dropped to the ground and grabbed the razor.

Teagan screamed louder, flailing and writhing in the bandits' grip. Becca was screaming, Ben was crying. The slaves all stayed frozen.

Brent looked and saw Teagan stomp on Skull Tattoo's foot.

He fell back, and Teagan made a run at Tommy, screaming as she grabbed his hair and ran him straight into the wall, face-first.

Sammy leaped into action, going after Purple Hair before he could fire at Teagan.

Purple Hair saw the big man approaching and turned the gun on him.

Sammy barreled forward, nearly swallowing the man.

Brent's eyes scanned for the razor that had fallen from

Tommy's fingers. He saw it, fell on it, and grabbed it. He looked up and registered two things at once: Skull Tattoo pulling Teagan off Tommy, and a gunshot thundering through the container.

Another two more followed.

Brent's ears screamed as he stumbled back, disoriented.

Sammy fell backward, bleeding from the chest and face.

Brent looked down at the razor then looked back up.

Skull Tattoo was holding Teagan at gunpoint.

Purple Hair was aiming at Brent.

Tommy glared, mouth bleeding, fists clenched, hate burning bright in his eye. He was going to make Brent pay. He was going to make them all pay.

"Want me to shoot him?" Purple Hair asked.

"No, no, no, I want him all to myself. I'm gonna fuck him up then make him watch as we fuck his kids and his girl."

Adrenaline and hate coursed through Brent. Sammy was down, Teagan had a gun to her head, and the kids were crying, huddled on the floor. It was down to him against the bandits. And not just the three in the container but the countless number waiting outside.

They wouldn't survive the night.

No way in hell.

Brent asked himself: *What would Ed do? What would Boricio do?*

His answer: *Survive as long as you can.*

He swiped the razor in a wide arc toward Tommy.

Tommy jumped back, smiling, bobbing and weaving like a boxer, eyes watching Brent's every move, smiling like a maniac.

"Try again, tough guy."

Brent did, this time leaping forward as he swung, aiming at the man's gut.

Tommy fell back but held his balance.

Brent barely had any and stumbled past him into the opposite wall, tripping over Meghan's and Lara's dead bodies.

Tommy delivered two blows at once, to both of Brent's ears.

Pain exploded in his ears and his head. He fell to the ground, dizzy, nauseated, and feeling like he was going to die.

His razor fell to the ground.

Despite Brent's ringing ears, he heard the bandits' maniacal laughter. Blinking through blurred vision, he saw them close in around him.

His heart was pounding; this was the end.

Brent imagined the horror of what they'd do: strip him naked, beat him senseless, force him to watch as they did the unthinkable to Ben, Becca, and Teagan.

Teagan.

Before Brent realized what she was doing — before any of the bandits realized what she was doing — Teagan grabbed Purple Hair by the back of the head and slammed him into the wall, just as she'd done to Tommy.

He cried out and dropped his revolver.

Teagan grabbed the gun.

He twisted on her, hands raised to strike.

She fired three times, twice into his chest and then into his face.

Purple Hair slumped down.

She turned the gun onto Skull Tattoo and Tommy, who both stared at her, flabbergasted.

"Let us go," she said, eyes wild, blood covering her face, chest, and arms.

"No." Tommy sauntered forward, gun still in his holster.

Skull Tattoo aimed at Brent's head. "Why don't you put your gun down, Missy."

"I'll shoot. I mean it!" Teagan's gun shook wildly in her hands.

"No, you won't." Tommy inched toward her.

"Stop!" she screamed as he drew closer.

What the hell is he doing?

Tommy said, "You ain't got no bullets left."

Teagan stared down at her gun in horror then pulled the trigger, repeatedly.

Empty.

Tommy grabbed the gun then swung, hitting her across the face with its butt.

Brent jumped to his feet.

Skull Tattoo pressed the gun harder into his head. "Sit, bitch; we ain't done with you."

Brent looked up to see more bandits streaming into the container. And in the middle of the pack, Marcus, the Reaper.

~

THIRTY-NINE

Emily Roberts

The basement was surprisingly large, divided into makeshift rooms, with many of the home's furnishings brought below to make the place feel more like home. Luca slept in the dark bedroom, with Emily lying beside him. Boricio sat in a chair at the end of the bed, waiting for Emily to "work her magic," as he'd said.

Seeing the hopeful look in Boricio's eyes, Emily wished she'd not made the offer to enter Luca's mind. She'd shatter that hope if she failed, and Boricio would probably be mad at her again.

But if I can do it, then maybe he can find out what happened to Mary. And if he brings her back, maybe she'll stop being mad at me, too.

Emily closed her eyes, feeling for the threads of thought surrounding Luca's aura, swaying like a sea of grass caught in currents of wind.

She had to find the right one, or *a* right one, to tug. Pull the wrong one, then all the thoughts would unravel in a spool of futility. Find the right one, and she could grip and pull herself inside, deeper into his mind.

She'd practiced a few times with her friend, Sami, one of her closest friends at school, and one of the few people she could be certain wasn't hosting an alien. Emily had never told him what she was doing, for fear he might think her a freak, but she'd been able to do it enough times to develop the skill.

Finding the thread was tricky enough in a serene environment. But here, in this basement, with a swell of emotions surrounding her — fear for Luca, fear of being caught, fear for Mary, and fear for herself, along with psychic stains in the walls of the house from years following the invasion — made her job all the more difficult. Traumatic memories competed with breathing thoughts, sometimes drowning them down to a barely audible echo.

Emily focused to find what she was seeking.

Then she felt it — a memory of himself walking along the beach. An old man selling lobster tacos. Will was his name.

Emily grabbed the thread with her mind and pulled herself into his headspace.

Then she was sharing the beach with Luca.

Unlike other memories she'd experienced through Sami, which felt artificial, fluttering with change and the imperfections of recall, Luca's memories were vivid enough to make Emily swear that her toes felt the sand, and her skin the kiss of a sun so bright she had to squint. Gulls cried. Boats bobbed in the distance. Music blared from radios. A salty scent stung her nostrils. She could even hear chatter from people. Not just chatter, but threads of conversations.

This wasn't now. This was *Before.*

Emily had never experienced anything so intoxicatingly immersive. There was a part of her that wanted to live in this memory. Spend the day with Luca, in his younger form, hanging out, talking — doing the sorts of things normal kids used to do. The sorts of things she'd never known.

Luca looked at her, surprised.

"Emily?"

"Hi, Luca."

"What are you doing here?"

"I need to find out what happened to Mary."

Luca looked up, as if trying to remember. Smiling, he said, "I don't know. Would you like a lobster taco?"

Her stomach growled, mouth salivating at the heavenly scent.

"Here ya go, ma'am." Will smiled and handed her a foil-wrapped taco.

Emily lifted it to her nose and inhaled. She'd never had lobster, but from the bright scent of its grilled flesh, she could tell it was going to be delicious before it touched her tongue.

This feels so real.

Emily took a bite of taco. Lobster and salsa, melting with avocado on her tongue.

Oh, my god.

"This is amazing," she said, surprised after she swallowed.

A group of girls walked by in tiny bikinis. Emily was surprised that neither Will nor Luca checked them out. More surprising was that she could smell coconut and other sweet fragrances as they passed. She could hear their thoughts. One of them, Missy, was thinking about Kim, and what a bitch she was being.

This can't be real.

I'm not really here.

I'm lying in a bed beside Luca in the basement of a house in The Wastelands. None of this is real.

Luca broke into a run. She was about to pursue him, but realized he was chasing a dog.

"He'll be right back," Will spoke into her mind.

Are you telepathic, too?

He smiled. *Yes.*

"This isn't real, is it? I'm not, we're not really on this beach, are we?"

Will took a bite of taco. *We are indeed here. Right now.*

"No," she said. "It's impossible. None of this is here.

These people are all dead. There are no radios playing music. This is a dream."

You're looking at time and space all wrong, young lady.

Emily's head hurt, trying to decipher the old man's odd words.

Luca came running up to them, the dog trotting at his side. He grinned, petting the dog between his big, fluffy ears.

"This is Dog Vader," Luca said. "He's not really a dog, though."

"Hi, Emily," the dog said, also in her mind.

No, this isn't happening. Luca is having the weirdest freaking dream ever. I'm caught inside and can't get out.

Emily felt dizzy, almost delirious. The world felt topsy-turvy. She reached out to grab the cart to settle herself but missed and stumbled backward.

Will caught her.

As he helped Emily right herself, she caught a whiff of a cologne her father wore *Before*.

Thinking of her father reminded Emily of her mission to find Mary.

"Luca," she said, "I need to know where Mary is."

He looked around, said, "I dunno," then bent to pet Dog Vader again.

Agitated, voice raised: "Come on, Luca, I need to know!"

The world moved beneath her feet. At first, Emily thought it was just her, then she saw Will and Luca swaying to stay upright.

"She's fading," Will said.

Emily had no clue what that meant.

"You need to hold on," he said, reaching out.

She tried to reach out then fell. Not to the ground but *through* it.

She sank fast then stopped, with the lower half of her body stuck in the ground like it was quicksand.

The beach was gone, replaced by a charred landscape

stretching as far as she could see in every direction. No trees. No greenery of any kind. The sky churned with a black mass of swirling clouds.

Something moved within them, sinister and staring back at Emily.

She struggled to move but couldn't.

Her feet were stuck, along with her hands, trapped in the earth.

"Luca!"

He wasn't there.

The clouds swirled faster, and red lightning erupted, spreading like a spiderweb in darkness.

Clouds roiled, creating a cone-shaped tip surrounded by bursts of red lightning. It gathered speed, its train engine's roar growing deafening as its tendrils swirled toward the ground.

A tornado!

It hit, in the distance, scattering debris. Pieces of earth, rock, and whatever else was on the ground soared into the funnel and became one, the tornado swelling in size.

The world turned into a chaotic maelstrom of screaming rain and wind, tearing at everything as Emily struggled to break free.

But the earth refused to lose her.

"Luca!" she cried out.

The tornado kept coming.

This isn't real!

This isn't real!

This isn't —

— and then Emily was back in the bed, with Luca, sitting up, gasping for air. Soaking wet.

"What the hell happened?"

Boricio stared at her. "Where did you go?"

"What do you mean?"

"You vanished. Where did you go?"

"I dunno. I was on a beach with Luca and an old man, Will. And a talking dog."

Boricio stared at Emily. At first, she thought he'd think her crazy. But his horrified eyes weren't suggesting insanity.

"You said Will and a *talking dog*?"

"Yeah."

"Did you see Mary?"

"No."

"Did you ask Luca where she was?"

"He said he didn't know. He seemed confused. It was a weird dream or something. Nothing made sense. Then I was in a burned field with a tornado coming at me, with red lightning inside it."

Emily shivered, her body ice cold. She looked down at her clothes, soaking wet and filthy.

"How long was I gone?"

"Just a minute," Boricio said. "I was about to get up and get the others when you came back."

She looked at Luca, still old, still in his same clothes. Still sleeping.

"Did he vanish?"

"For a moment, yes."

"He was there, too, but as a kid, with Will and a dog. *What just happened?*"

"I don't have a fucking clue."

Boricio not knowing scared Emily more than anything.

~

FORTY

Brent Foster

This was the end.

It had been almost an hour since Marcus had yanked the other bandits out of the container, demanding answers for what the hell happened.

As Brent, Teagan, and the kids waited, huddled together, quietly, he knew that whatever reprieve they were enjoying would be short lived. The question was what would happen next. Would the bandits come back and have their way with Teagan and the kids before killing Brent?

Or would they be shot by firing squad like the other slaves?

Then the door finally opened, and they had their answer.

"It's time to die," Marcus said.

They were marched single file, collars off. Oddly, that freedom meant that hope was gone because they were surrounded by at least five bandits, including the blonde who'd helped to catch them, guns aimed.

He stared up at full fat moon, cold and oblivious to their pain. The same moon he'd once stared at as a child, thinking the worst thing that might ever happen would be a life lived without falling in love.

But no, there were far worse things than that. Like finding

love and having it ripped away. Like watching your child's murder, helpless to prevent it. Like slitting your daughter's throat to end her suffering at the hands of evil men.

The moon didn't care about any of that, of course. It shone light down on good and bad alike, never intervening. Never caring. Not unlike God.

They followed Marcus down the cul-de-sac, through the fence toward the fields just inside the fortress perimeter.

There would be no last-minute heroics here unless God Himself intervened. Or Team Boricio. But Brent couldn't rely on that glimmer of hope. He had to prepare for his death, and the deaths of those he loved.

The only possible blessings were that at least Tommy and the others wouldn't rape and murder the children and Teagan. Marcus made it clear as he commanded them to leave the container that "the bullshit is over" and it was "time to end this."

Marcus led the way through the fence and out to a new, though smaller, freshly dug ditch.

Teagan was crying, softly. Ben and Becca were louder, but for the first time they weren't told to shut up.

They reached the pit's edge.

Teagan stopped walking. She turned back to Marcus and begged.

"Do whatever you want with me, but *please*, don't hurt them." She looked at Becca and Ben. "I'll do anything you want." She lowered her voice. "*Be* anyone you want. Just please, let them live."

"What makes you think I can't make you do whatever I want, *be* whoever I want, and still fill my pit with your mistakes?"

Brent finally found his balls and stared into Marcus's milky-white eye. "*Our* mistakes?"

Brent heard Becca whisper to Ben behind him. "Are we gonna die?"

"No. It's okay," Ben whispered back. "My dad will make everything better."

"Yes, *your* mistakes." Marcus twirled his fingers toward the clouds. "You done fucked up, Fishbelly. I'm trying to build a polite society here, give everyone a role to fill, and let the smart folks go about filling 'em, a spot in the world where people know their place and aren't prone to problems. You've gone and pissed in the pool."

Brent flinched.

"The world is a dangerous place. You all should be thankful that we brought you in. But no, you all gotta rock the boat. Cause some sorta rebellion. Got razors, dead slaves, and you killed one of my men. You've brought this upon yourselves."

"Are you kidding me?" Brent yelled. "You have *Welcome to Hell* written outside!"

Marcus gave Brent another rotten-toothed smile. "You never heard of a little color?"

"*Color?* They were going to rape our kids! Are you telling me that *you* wouldn't fight back if that was happening to your family?"

Marcus lost his smile. His eyes flinched.

Tommy yelled, "Goddamned liar!"

Marcus yelled, "Wyatt!"

Black Beard came over, and Marcus nodded toward Brent. "What's he talking about?"

"I don't know anything, boss."

"You don't know anything, or you've nothing to say?"

Marcus looked from Wyatt to Brent to the rest of the crew then finally to the bandits and back. Brent couldn't see Tommy or Skull Tattoo, and wasn't willing to dare a look.

Wyatt shook his head. "I don't know anything about nothing."

Brent clenched his fists, studying the Reaper's face, wanting to scream the truth even if it earned him a bullet.

Marcus said, "Anyone else have anything to say?"

No one spoke.

Marcus looked at Brent. "Tommy says you're lying."

"I'm not lying. This all started because they came in the middle of the night and started raping that girl, that *dead slave* you're so worked up over. The mom killed her daughter, and herself, to keep it from happening again."

Marcus shook his head and clucked his tongue. "Now does that really sound like something a sensible mother would do?" He turned from Brent to his men. "Any of this true?"

Shaking heads and mumbled nos.

Marcus nodded toward the pit. "Then let's go."

The kids and Teagan started to cry.

Brent prepared for his death, wondering if he should plead.

Cowards begged, but at least they lived longer.

But was it worth it? Brent could beg until he was blue, and they'd probably kill him anyway. At least closing his eyes and waiting for the bullet would leave him with a splinter of dignity.

No. He wouldn't beg. Pleading would make it worse for Teagan and the children. Brent would leave life like a man.

Brent squeezed his eyes tight and prayed to himself. If he was going to beg, it would only be to a God who wasn't likely to hear him.

Please, if You're there, I'll do anything You ask if You'll only do something.

Nothing happened.

Brent opened his eyes to see Wyatt whispering into Marcus's ear.

Smiling, the Reaper said, "Good point," then turned to Teagan and Brent. "Good news. We have room for one of your children in the main house. You see, Fortune wasn't so kind to our chef, Brother Bill. He's lost his child, and Sister

Liza's been wanting another ever since. So ... " he cast his eyes between them. "Which will it be? Jack or Jill?"

Brent swallowed to keep from choking. He couldn't believe it — a chance to keep one of the children alive. A chance that Ben might live.

And then, a horrible thought: *maybe Ben would be better off dead.*

Teagan stepped closer to Brent and touched his arm. "We can't." She shook her head. "You know what will happen."

"I want to be with my dad," Ben said. "You should go, Becca."

The briefest glimmer of hope died inside Brent.

Teagan moved closer to the Reaper. "You're not getting them."

Marcus stepped closer to Teagan and breathed what had to be death's stench into her face. "I must have given you the impression I was making a request."

Marcus snarled like a dog, walked past Teagan, and grabbed Becca roughly by the arm. "Jill it is."

Teagan lurched forward. Brent threw himself in front of her, wrapped his arms around her waist, then pulled Teagan toward him and held her tight.

"Don't, don't, don't, don't ... "

Over and over, Brent whispered, hoping to calm her before she got shot. Teagan was silent for seconds, until Becca screamed.

"No!" she echoed.

This is it.

This is the end.

If You're out there, our time is just about over.

Brent grabbed Teagan's hand, then Ben's. He pulled them both into a hug as Becca was dragged away screaming.

"Don't look. Don't look," he whispered to them. "Just close your eyes."

Teagan sobbed into Brent's shoulder, squeezing his hand.

Ben squeezed tighter, crying. "I love you, Daddy."
"I love you. Both of you." Brent said to them both.
"Finish this," Marcus said.
Brent closed his eyes.
Gunfire erupted.

~

FORTY-ONE

Teagan McLachlan

As they hugged, Teagan prayed to God to please save them.

Her body trembled as she heard Marcus give the order.

She hoped that Becca would be okay with them. Maybe they weren't all rapists, after all. Marcus had seemed genuinely surprised at the accusations. But how could he not have known? Wilson had said it had been happening for at least the four months he'd been there. And anyone could've heard the screams in the container.

Was Marcus a liar? Was he that blind to what his people were doing? Or was he turning the other cheek to keep things moving?

Please, God, protect Becca from these evil people. Please.

Teagan turned from Brent, hoping to catch a final glimpse of her daughter.

Her eyes found Becca.

Then the air cracked with bullets.

But it wasn't the firing squad.

Instincts took over, and she pushed Brent and Ben into the ditch.

They fell into the darkness.

Screams and gunfire erupted above.

Then silence.

Teagan's heart raced as she and Brent traded glances.

Ben was shivering, holding tight to his father.

Footsteps above, approaching the pit.

Oh, God, please save us.

And then a voice.

"They're dead."

Marina!

Teagan and Brent stood up to see Marina standing above them, a rifle in her hands, a sword on her back, blood coating her from head to toe, like a ghost in the moonlight. She held Becca's hand.

Thank you, Lord, for sending Marina back for us!

"Thank you for coming back," Teagan cried as Becca jumped into the pit, "Mommy!"

Teagan hugged her harder than she'd ever hugged anyone ever. "Oh, thank God you're okay!"

Teagan's world was foggy, barely aware of Brent holding Ben, the both of them crying. Only Becca mattered.

Then she heard Brent ask, "Are you hurt?" as Marina helped Ben out of the pit.

"No, it's *their* blood."

They climbed out of the pit, and Marina pointed farther back in the field, about fifty yards away. "Come on. There's a hole in the wall back there. We've gotta get out of here now. That big ox with the scar ran off. He'll bring everyone in camp, if the gunfire doesn't bring them first."

Brent scooped Ben into his arms and stood. "What about the others, in the containers?"

"I killed a couple of bandits then opened the containers. We can't be responsible beyond that. We've gotta go."

A siren screamed, and dogs started howling.

"*Now!*" Marina yelled then ran toward the hole.

The four of them followed.

Barking dogs and yelling men drew closer. Flashlight beams bounced, probing the gloaming, searching.

Teagan and Brent kept running, each holding their children's hands, until they reached the escape point. Brent pushed Ben through, then Becca. He held out a hand, ushering Teagan forward.

Light found her, froze her in place.

Someone yelled, "There they are!"

Gunshots hit the wall above Teagan.

Brent shoved her through the hole, "Go!"

She cried out as she fell through the hole and down a small slope. Brent was right behind her.

Just when she thought there was no way they'd get away from all those bandits and their dogs, she looked up and saw what God, through Marina, had provided, waiting in the clearing ahead.

Their horses.

They all mounted without a word, Becca in front of Teagan.

She held her daughter tight.

"Everything is going to be okay." Teagan whispered into Becca's ear. And for the first time in a long time, she believed it, as they raced through the woods toward the crumbled asphalt of the Pacific Coast Highway.

～

FORTY-TWO

Brent Foster

The trip back was quiet.

No one seemed willing to speak. Brent was grateful that Marina had come back to save them — he'd never really lost hope that she would — but was surprised to feel a fair amount of shame as well.

She hadn't returned with Ed, Boricio, and Lisa. She hadn't come back with that giant, Barrow. She'd come alone and done what Brent had never come close to being able to do — save his family.

She was like a zombie on her horse, practically catatonic. Yet still she'd galloped into Hell to be the hero Brent couldn't be.

They took a zigzagging route to avoid running into Marcus and his men, in the likely event they were searching for them. Eventually, mist turned to rain, and hooves squished in mud rather than clomping on dirt, until they finally found themselves at the bottom of the hill and almost to the highway.

Brent said, "I don't think we should travel PCH in the dark. There are a lot more bleakers closer to The City, and we'll never see them."

No one said they agreed or didn't. Instead, they fell in line behind Brent, including Marina, as if they were all expecting him to lead them wherever they were supposed to go next.

A half mile or so later, Brent saw a steeple peeking out in the distance — a not-too-subtle reminder of the hell the world had become. With a view that stared out over the sea, the church had surely once been beautiful, a natural sanctuary amid the receding forest behind it.

"We'll have to take the horses inside." Teagan's voice was scratchy, her throat probably raw.

"Let me look around first." Brent dismounted and headed toward the chapel entrance.

Marina spoke for the first time in miles. "I'm coming with you."

Though emasculated, Brent was grateful for her company. Besides, he had no weapons.

His body was on high alert, nerves tingling as they crept through the shattered threshold. Pews were askew and in splinters. Stained glass confetti glittered the ground. Jesus lay in pieces.

Brent said, "It doesn't look like this place has been used in forever."

Marina deadpanned, "This place is dead."

They cleared the chapel then ushered the horses and children inside.

"I haven't had anything to drink since yesterday," Becca whined.

Without a word, Marina unloaded supplies from a satchel on her mount: two apples, three sloshing canteens, and something that looked like dried meat in a brown bag. She handed an apple to each of the children and a canteen to Ben. "Share this with Becca."

She handed meat to Teagan, then meat and water to Brent.

Brent sipped, handed the canteen to Teagan, and tore into the meat.

"Thanks." The taste hit his tongue. "This is terrible."

Chewing, Marina agreed. "Sure is."

"What is it?" Teagan asked.

"I have no idea." Marina shrugged. "I stole it from Hell."

Ben said, "Maybe it's monkey."

"There aren't any monkeys around here," Becca said. "And besides, monkeys aren't gross enough. It's probably a dog."

"Gross!" Ben laughed. "I bet it's rat."

"Ewww!" Becca giggled.

Brent felt slightly warmer, the children's laughter telling him that they, and maybe everything else, might be okay.

"Thanks, Marina." He put a hand on her shoulder. "I never thought I'd hear them laugh … or anything … again."

She flinched, shrugged Brent's hand from her body, and nodded.

Away from the battlefield, Marina still had that hollow disposition. She refused their eyes and was stingy with syllables. Whatever hell she'd gone through — twice — to save them was undoing her mental state. He remembered when she first arrived, how she said she'd grown sick of fighting in The City. She needed a break from the unending violence.

Maybe this had pushed her over the edge.

He wasn't sure how the hell he could make this right for her, or thank her enough, but he would find a way once things returned to normal. She'd given them their lives back. It was their debt to make sure she got hers back, somehow.

"Yeah, I don't know what we'd have done without you. We were … " Teagan choked. "Well, that was the end."

"Did you happen to get a radio?" Brent asked.

Marina didn't respond.

"Because the men took all our supplies," he added.

With no expression, Marina stood, went to the horse, and

pulled a radio from the other side of her saddlebag opposite the pouch where she'd pulled out the food.

"This is it," she said, handing it to Brent. "I grabbed our supplies from one of their houses before I came to get you guys. You wanna do the honors?"

He smiled in disbelief. *Finally.*

Moments later, Brent had Keenan on the other side of the line.

His best friend left in the world, other than Teagan.

Everything was going to be fine.

"It's Brent," he said. "We lost The Farm."

~

FORTY-THREE

Boricio Wolfe

Boricio couldn't wait any longer. And it wasn't just because Emily's attempt to get into Luca's head turned into the fucking *Wizard of Oz*. Radio Bob had failed to check in this morning.

Radio Bob was a man stationed in the belfry at the First Lutheran Church in Las Orillas — a sanctuary for any lost rebels to meet if they should need help or get separated from any of the four teams.

Every morning at seven, Bob would radio The City's four rebel camps to let them know whether or not anyone had shown up. The system had been responsible for saving a few people, including Barrow a time or two when the big man had got separated on a mission. Boricio hoped to get a call that Mary had shown up this morning since she wasn't answering her radio. She could have made it to The Farm, which would be Boricio's next visit if she wasn't here. But given how Luca woke up screaming her name, and the fact that her radio was silent, only made Boricio more convinced that something was wrong. And he wasn't going to find her hiding in the basement of the Chandler House.

If Mary came around, like she usually did after a fight,

she'd probably return to the warehouse. When she found nothing but bullets, she'd likely freak the fuck out and head to the church.

But when Bob didn't call, or respond, Boricio got worried. It was too much for coincidence that both Mary *and* Bob stopped answering their radios, which only added to his reasons to head for the church.

Keenan and Lisa decided to accompany Boricio, just in case shit went down. They were his two best recon agents, able to get in and out of places without creating much of a clusterfuck — unlike the slightly clumsy, tank-like Barrow, who was staying behind with Jevonne and Jazz to look after Emily and Luca.

They left at a quarter past seven, on foot, keeping to side streets and alleyways so as not to attract attention from any bandits patrolling major roads in search of victims to plunder. They walked mostly in silence, commenting here and there on the low-hanging fog.

Boricio liked that Keenan and Lisa didn't pollute his air with bullshit. They knew they had a job to do and fucking did it. Some of the others turned into *The Fucking View* after ten minutes. Boricio was an amiable fucker, and didn't mind shooting the shit, but over the past couple of years, he'd learned to appreciate the quiet more than the assholes attempting to use the dictionary as a to-do list.

As they walked along a road in a neighborhood overrun with vegetation, he found himself wanting to chat. Boricio wasn't sure if it was boredom or not being able to do diddly dick about Mary, but he wanted to stir some shit into sauce.

"Hey," he said to Keenan or Lisa, whoever might be listening, "you two fuckin' yet, or what?"

"What?" Lisa turned to Boricio, giving him her usual sour face. As crass as she was, the bitch was a prude when it came to bumping uglies.

"Well, I figured, you two spend a lot of time together, one

thing leads to another, and before you know it Officer Keenan's beating you with his nightstick."

Keenan didn't even look back.

Lisa rolled her eyes then turned her attention back to the road.

Boricio smiled. "I guess that's a yes."

After another minute of walking, Keenan finally ate the bait. "We're out here looking for Mary, and checking on Radio Bob, and you want to ask if we're *fucking?* Really?"

"Inquiring minds."

Lisa turned, raised her middle finger, and smirked.

"Sorry, I didn't realize I was walking with the Pope and Mother Teresa."

Neither responded.

Now Boricio kinda wished he'd brought Barrow. That asshole was easy to rile. Especially when you fucked with him about his weight.

How come every other person is on the verge of starving in this alien apocalypse, and you're still Hurley? You sure you're not slipping away and eating people while out on runs?

And Barrow would attempt to give shit back to Boricio. But the guy was slow, and tended to say stupid crap that only made Boricio laugh harder. But it was all in good fun. Barrow didn't mind you poking fun at him, and Boricio liked the big fucker well enough.

Now that Boricio felt like talking, Keenan and Lisa were a silent film walking. Next mission: Barrow and Lisa. Boricio would instigate Barrow to make some joke about Lisa. She'd respond with a verbal beat-down. Barrow would shrink like a pussy. Good times.

Despite his need for distraction, Boricio was glad to be walking the apocalypse with the Boring Twins. If shit *did* hit the fan, they were the two motherfuckers, aside from Mary, he most wanted by his side.

Their radios crackled to life: Brent Foster, who'd been staying with Marina and the others at The Farm.

Keenan answered first.

"It's Brent. We lost The Farm. We need to talk with you."

"Lost The Farm?" Keenan said. "What happened?"

"Overrun with aliens. A few nights ago. I'll tell you about it when we get there. We're down to just five of us, and just got within radio range."

"Shit." Keenan swallowed. "Who's left?"

"Me, Teagan, and the kids. Plus Marina."

Keenan sighed. "What about Mary?"

"Mary?"

Boricio got on his radio and interrupted, "Yeah, Mary was headed to The Farm last night."

"Well, we haven't seen her," Brent said. "We were a bit off path for a bit, but we're sticking to the normal route now. We'll let you know if we run into her."

"Fuck!" Boricio yelled.

Brent said, "We're coming in. Where are you now?"

"We're staying with Beta Team at Station C 17," he said, giving Brent the code for Chandler House. "We'll meet you there once we're back from our current job."

They walked in silence for several blocks, no one remarking on the loss of more lives or what might have happened to Mary. No use dwelling on the maudlin. You had to shove that shit deep where it couldn't get you, pick yourself up, and carry the fuck on.

After another few blocks, they saw the belfry and steeple come into view over the treetops through the fog.

The belfry's stone walls and large wooden shutters concealed the bell and room, making it the perfect watchtower, and sniper's nest, if necessary.

As if tuned into the same thought frequencies, Keenan signaled for them to stop.

He raised his infrared binoculars to survey the belfry then slowly lowered them. "Nothing."

They continued forward, guns ready, approaching from the south, through neighborhood backyards abutting the church's cracked, overgrown parking lot.

The trio hid in the thick brush, Keenan scanning for signs of life.

"I got something," he said.

"What?" Lisa raised her rifle and peered through the scope.

Boricio squinted and saw something in the parking lot, sitting on the ground, but couldn't tell what it was. He'd mistaken it for a body — it wasn't uncommon to find corpses whenever they went on a run or recon mission. Of course, the bodies never stayed out long, either picked apart by carrion or carried off by cannibals.

"What the fuck is it?"

"A dog," Lisa said.

While it wasn't uncommon to see wild dogs, Boricio hadn't seen a mongrel just sitting there, hanging out like it wasn't the end of the world. They were usually twitchy, nervous, always on the move. This fucker was waiting for someone to pet him.

"He alive?" Boricio said.

Lisa nodded. "Yeah."

Boricio grabbed the binoculars from around his neck and looked. Sure as shit, it was a dog. Black and white, fuck if Boricio knew the breed, with blue eyes. And he — Boricio couldn't be sure without checking if it was male or female, but assumed it took balls to sit there — didn't look fucked up and dirty, or wild. He looked like a pet.

"I got a clear shot." Lisa said.

"No, don't shoot him," Boricio said.

Lisa turned and looked at him, eyebrows arched.

"He's not a threat."

"Oh, Jesus, you've gone soft. First the kids, and now the

dog. You sure you don't want us to take you home so you can apply your makeup?"

Boricio returned the bird she'd given him earlier.

Keenan turned to Boricio. "Okay, we don't need to kill him. But if he starts barking or comes at us, you're putting him down, got it?"

"Got it, *chief.*"

Boricio didn't mind Keenan calling the shots in the day-to-day, but he didn't like when the fucker thought he was Boricio's boss.

Ain't nobody the boss of Boricio, chief.

Keenan, as he typically did, ignored Boricio's tone and continued to search the surrounding area, a burned-down shopping plaza, and another handful of houses.

"Looks clear," he said. "Let's roll."

Keenan led the way into the parking lot and toward the church, guns drawn, prepared for any sign of enemies.

Lisa stopped, signaling trouble ahead.

"Two o'clock, possible bogey."

They all turned, though no one fired until Keenan determined the threat. The potential peril was a man shuffling along the street near the burned-out plaza. He was old, pushing a creaky garbage-filled shopping cart, seemingly oblivious.

Keenan shook his head.

They crept closer, now drawing the dog's attention.

The dog, who was sitting on all fours well past the entrance, looked up at them, ears perked.

Easy, boy. Don't make me have to put you down.

Boricio didn't aim his silenced pistol at the dog but kept it ready, just in case.

They were halfway toward the front doors, and the dog kept staring without a growl. No getting up, barking, or chasing them off, defending his territory. He just sat there.

Boricio kept watching the dog as they drew closer to the church entrance.

That's it, good boy. Shit guard dog, but good boy.

As Keenan and Lisa approached the wooden front doors, Boricio kept an eye on the dog to make sure it didn't suddenly charge them.

"Clear," Keenan said.

Boricio turned and followed them into the church, unable to shake the feeling that something was wrong, and that they were walking right into a trap.

~

FORTY-FOUR

Mary Olson

Mary wasn't sure how much time had passed. Somehow, she'd managed to fall asleep then woken to darkness, no longer confined to a table. She was lying in a bed, dressed.

What the hell?

Mary sat up, confused, trying to gather her bearings and maybe figure out how she got here, and where exactly *here* might be.

A light came to life above her, revealing that she was in a small room, almost like a ship's cabin, with its low ceiling and narrow claustrophobic walls. And she wasn't alone.

Paola — or rather, the thing wearing her daughter's body — was sitting across from Mary in a sleek, curved, black matte-finished chair.

Mary was going to get up but couldn't move after seeing Paola sitting across from her. She couldn't do anything but stare at the girl.

"Desmond let you up as a show of good faith," Paola said.

Her cool, calm speech indicated to Mary a lack of humanity. No emotion. No pleading. No tears. Matter-of-fact: *Desmond let you up as a show of good faith.*

Mary said nothing. She smirked at the creature.

Does it really think it's fooling me?

"I want to go home."

"You *are* home, Mother."

"Do *not* call me that." If glares could cause violence, Mary's would've eviscerated the alien.

"But you *are* my mother."

"No. And you are not … *her.*"

"Yes, I am. How can I prove it? Ask me something only Paola would know. Go ahead."

"I'm not playing games with you. Just because you're in my daughter's body, and can access her memories, doesn't make you my daughter."

The girl stared at Mary, her head tilted to the side as if lost in thought, or trying to understand something Mary was saying. Maybe it was attempting to mine the right tactic to change Mary's mind, to convince her that Paola was still in there.

The girl spoke, still with no emotion. "Why are you so afraid of the unknown? The different?"

Mary shook her head, refusing to answer. "I want to go home."

"Is it the alien inside me that disgusts you so much? Do you really think Paola is dead?"

Mary looked down, refusing to participate in its manipulation.

"Do you know what happens to the human body when it dies, *Mary?*"

Calling her Mary rather than mother was a confession, the alien no longer pretending.

She looked up and met its eyes. "No, please, enlighten me."

"There's a release of energy as your body shuts down, an energy your science isn't equipped to register. Some might call it a soul. Other species have different words. But it isn't really all that different from what you've seen of our scouts. Or from our true forms."

"Scouts?"

"Yes, this thing you've been calling The Darkness is part biological, part artificial intelligence, created by our species, sent to many planets, searching for those inhabitable to our kind. But we're not all that different, at our root."

"What are you saying?"

"These ... " The girl waved her hand in front of her chest to indicate her — *Paola's* — body. "These aren't us. They aren't *you*. They are husks. Shells. They are biological machines in which we, in our true forms, exist."

"What the hell are you saying? Aren't you The Darkness?"

"No, we are another species altogether, called Pruhm. We are *all parasites*, as you call us. You, me, even your precious daughter. We're all forms inhabiting a shell for a finite amount of time before we go on and inhabit some other form, or vanish into the Great Void. The only difference is that our species is advanced enough to leave *before* our hosts die. We can then find a new host to hold our identity."

"Are you talking about reincarnation?"

"That's the closest to your understanding, yes."

Mary tried to wrap her head around the alien's words. Something about them rang true, as if it were providing her with the secrets of life, but her human mind was too feeble for true understanding.

Or maybe they're trying to get me to drink the Kool-Aid, manipulating me into joining them.

"As I was saying," the alien continued, "when the human body dies, your soul remains for a while, until the organs sustaining the body's life finally die. Some souls can stay in a body for weeks after the shell is dead. But once the body is gone, the soul moves on, to the Great Void if it can't find another vessel."

Mary wasn't exactly buying the story, but her curiosity

couldn't be quelled. "What is the Great Void? Like Heaven or Hell?"

"Nobody knows for certain. It is believed that we all go there if we can't find a new body to host us."

"How do you know of this void if people, souls, whatever, don't come back?"

"Like humans, we all have our myths, Mary. But no there is no certainty of what happens next, which is why we cling to life for as long as we're able. Which is why we're here on your planet, to find a species to live with. From what we know of your kind, we can allow you to live practically forever. Isn't that a dream worth pursuing?"

"So, are you telling me that Paola really is alive in there? That you got to her soul before it crossed over into the Void?"

"Yes, I am."

Mary stared at the girl and shuddered. Her every fiber wanted to kill this conversation, to refuse the possibility. *Her* Paola was dead. There was no returning from that.

"You were both dead once before. Don't you remember? Killed in the dungeon of that cult leader's house? Luca, or *The Light* as you call him, brought you back. You know what I'm saying is possible. Your daughter's soul is safe and sound, in here with me. You can be together again, Mary. Only your fear of the unknown is stopping you."

Tears welled in the corners of Mary's eyes. The grief she'd driven into the depths of her soul — into a place where she could no longer feel — began rising inside her, consolidated in physical form as a giant ball in her throat. She swallowed, painfully, but could no longer drown her grief.

It felt as if her body was on fire, her flesh unknitting in the flames of her pain. Soon, there would be nothing left but a husk.

The alien stood, eyes boring into Mary's.

"You're hurting," it said in Paola's voice.

She wanted to look away, not give it the benefit of seeing its words undoing her resolve.

"You don't have to hurt any longer, *Mommy.*"

Her daughter's hand reached out, touched Mary's cheek.

She fell against the touch, into Paola's embrace. "It hurts so much."

"I can make it all better," Paola said, stroking her hair.

"How?" Mary pulled away. "You want to put an alien inside me? Take over?"

She covered herself with arms, hating the alien even more for using Paola to reduce her to such an emotional mess. For using her willingness to see her daughter alive to undermine her resolve.

She wished it would go away.

But at the same time, she wanted to hear more. Wanted it to tell her the one thing she could believe without feeling like a fool.

Give me a reason to trust you.

"You still don't trust us?" The alien stared at Mary as if reading her mind. Maybe it was in her head, even though she couldn't feel it.

Mary felt at a crossroads, that the next thing she said would choose her path forever. The wrong choice might be her death. She had to get ahold of herself, control her emotions, bottle the grief. She had to figure out what the alien wanted and play along enough to buy more time.

Buy time for what? You think Team Boricio is coming to save you? They don't even know you're here!

"It's okay." The alien nodded. "I think I can help."

The alien stepped closer.

Mary tensed, backed up again, her foot hitting the bed.

"It's okay." The alien smiled. "I'm going to show you that everything I said is true. Your daughter is still here, and you can be together again."

Paola began to yawn. At least that's what Mary thought at first. She fought back her own urge to do the same.

Her daughter's lips began to vibrate.

Mary couldn't do anything but stare at the light burning inside the girl's throat.

What the hell?

Dozens of tendrils of blue light spilled from Paola's mouth like floating filaments in a slow current, swimming past her lips, followed by the rest of the alien's body, a bulbous sheer sack of iridescent blue flesh rippling with thousands of tiny bright lights.

While The Darkness had been an almost inky, smoke-like creature, this thing seemed more organic, more like something you'd find in the deep sea, more fragile, lighter, dancing on air above them.

Mary was so entranced by the thing's wonder and beauty, she'd almost forgotten the point of the show.

Paola gasped.

Mary looked back at her daughter, choking, trying to catch her breath.

"Mom?" she cried.

Mary met Paola's eyes, and in a heartbeat knew she was no longer staring at some hijacked husk controlled by the aliens. No, this was her daughter.

Mary threw her arms around Paola and hugged her tight. "Oh, God, baby, I'm so sorry. I'm so sorry."

∼

FORTY-FIVE

Boricio Wolfe

They searched the entire ground floor and hadn't found any sign of foul play, or a note left behind to indicate that Radio Bob had headed somewhere else.

As they climbed the circular staircase in the back of the church toward the belfry, Boricio kept thinking about the stupid dog outside. Just staring at them, blue eyes, so peaceful. He wondered if the dog had any idea that the world had gone to shit. Maybe it was young enough that it didn't remember the world as it had been. For the dog, it had always been this — scumbags and aliens destroying everything they touched. As tough as it was to survive now, during some months in the beginning, Boricio's team had been on the verge of starvation before they'd learned to do some rooftop farming and got a bit luckier on food runs. This dog seemed like he was living on easy street.

Boricio wondered if the dog could be domesticated. Maybe Luca would like having a dog around. Maybe Emily would, too.

They reached the belfry and saw Radio Bob sitting in the darkness, his back to them, facing the wall. Shafts of light seeped through the wooden shutters, illuminating just enough of the short bald man to show it was him, but not whether he was dead or alive.

Boricio took the lead, approaching with his pistol drawn.

Closer, Boricio smelled piss and blood.

He reached the man but didn't bother to touch his shoulder. Instead, he circled and saw through the light streaming up at Radio Bob.

Fuck.

"His throat is slit. We need to get the hell outta here."

Boricio went to the closest shutter to look out, to check if either bandits or alien fucks were closing ranks.

At first, he saw nothing.

Then Boricio saw something he wished he hadn't.

The dog was no longer sitting there. It was lying on the ground in an awkward position, facedown in the parking lot, clearly dead.

Boricio wasn't sure what it meant but knew it wasn't good.

The sound of doors exploding inward erupted downstairs, followed by the all-too-familiar shrieking and clicking of aliens.

Double fuck!

Boricio went and looked along the north-facing shutters and saw something worse than the dead dog — a horde of aliens, too many to count, moving too fast to escape.

"Hey, guys," he said. "We've got a problem."

Keenan and Lisa raced to Boricio side and looked down.

"Fuck," they said together.

Episode 35

(FIFTH EPISODE OF SEASON SIX)

"The Belfry"

Prologue

EDWARD KEENAN

Two years ago
  First Lutheran Church
  Las Orillas, California

ED PUT the gun against his temple, ready to end it all in the belfry's heavy shadows.

But instead of pulling the trigger, he lowered the gun, hands shaking, sweat drenching his shirt.

Again, he couldn't do it.

He shook his head, disgusted with himself.

Why can't I do this? It's not like I'm afraid to die. Or have anything worth living for.

Why can't I end it?

Ed had once been known as a man without conscience — a black ops agent who could be counted on to act without hesitation. No matter the target, from obvious enemies of the state to a seemingly innocent person whose crimes Ed couldn't imagine rising to the level of assassination, the soldier followed orders and did his job. He pulled the trigger and did what had to be done.

He'd never been particularly proud of his reputation. Nor had he ever been ashamed, until some time before the end of everything, when he started to question his government's role as the good guy — after Ed realized he was working to perpetuate some of the very crimes his government claimed to be fighting. Until then, he'd never blinked before pulling the trigger.

There was a small part of Ed that *did* take some pride in the workman-like quality he brought to the job. He didn't break or get overly emotional on assignment or when odds were stacked against him. He kept his shit together whether he was being held against his will or facing insurmountable odds behind enemy lines. Ed got shit done. He was the perfect killer — be that to praise or damnation.

He'd once been celebrated, and feared. Now he was nothing — a shell of himself, a loner in the dark, contemplating the best way to end it all.

He looked up at the bell, which hadn't rung since The Fall, and fought the urge to ring it now. Announce his presence and let his enemies come — bandits, aliens, or hybrids — *come and fucking get me.*

That would be a proper way to go out, fighting, doing what he did best. Of course, he'd be putting the sanctuary at risk. And as the sole guard working it, he couldn't be that selfish.

The church served as a refuge — a place for rebels to go if they got lost in the field. It was usually manned by one person who kept lookout in the belfry and radioed the bases each morning with an update. *Yeah, we found your guy. Come and get him.* The rebels would send Luca and Boricio to make sure the rebel hadn't been compromised, or infected. It was a decent system that protected the hidden locations of rebel camps in The City. Keenan couldn't leave the job empty without risking the lives of others.

The last guy working the belfry had gone stir-crazy and

requested reassignment. Ed had gladly volunteered to take the open spot, even though his talents were wasted.

He thought working at the sanctuary would give him some desperately needed alone time. Ever since Jade's death, he'd found it harder to be around the others and stay civil. The church gave him space to rebuild what was left of his life.

But since he'd taken the position three months ago, Ed found that the solitary confinement had only hollowed him further. He felt scooped out like a gourd. And with that emptiness came a bleaker series of thoughts:

Why go on?

What was the point of fighting an impossible battle?

Weren't they all just delaying the inevitable?

Ed had no answers, and saw little reason to go on. At least not for himself. Maybe for Brent and Teagan. They had children to protect. And in a way, Ed felt responsible for their safety. But at the same time, how long could they delay the inescapable? Someday, death would come for the kids, for Brent, for Teagan. Death would come for them all.

The enemy was too many, and there weren't enough people to fight it. No matter how many aliens or bandits they managed to kill, there *always* seemed to be more.

There was no way around it. The end was as inevitable as the night.

And Ed didn't want to be there when it happened. He couldn't stand to see another situation where he was helpless to prevent the unpreventable.

As he sat there, gun in hand, an idea found shape. Ed would call home base tomorrow, tell them to send someone new, because he needed to follow a lead — he'd figure the specifics later. Then he'd go off, somewhere where he wasn't compromising their network's security, radio home one final time to let everyone know they shouldn't come looking for him, then he'd end it.

On his terms.

For the first time in two years, Ed smiled.

Soon, it'll all be over.

~

FROM HIS MAKESHIFT hunter's perch in the thick tree line, Ed scanned the slaughterhouse grounds, watching the alien shuttle land on schedule.

Once a month, the shuttle dropped off fresh workers for the slaughterhouse, one of the mainland's few structures with working power. The rebels had been wanting to hit the slaughterhouse for a while — to interrupt The Island's food supply. But following rebel attacks on factories and farms, the aliens had beefed up their security. Now the place was a fortress, turning any attack into a suicide mission.

Which, of course, was why Ed was here.

There were four towers, one in each corner of the high-gated perimeter. Three of the four were occupied by Guardsmen, with black helmets but no visors. The men closest to Ed, on the west side, were staring ahead. That left the man in the rear free to eliminate without Ed being noticed — hopefully.

He lined up his shot and squeezed the trigger, hitting his target with the first suppressed bullet.

The guard fell in the tower, thankfully not out of it. Ed scanned the other two towers, ensuring that neither man was alerted. Both were oblivious to their fallen comrade. Ed lined up his next shot, taking out the farther of the two men. Again, he hit his target with a single bullet. This Guardsman, however, fell forward and plunged to the ground.

Shit!

Ed swung the rifle's scope to find the final guard. The sentry's movements were panicked, raising the rifle and scanning his surroundings in search of the shooter.

If the operation had any sort of decent protocol, the man would be signaling for backup in seconds. Ed had to eliminate him before then. He planned to die, but Ed didn't want a wasted death. He intended to do some damage before going out in a blaze of glory.

He lined up his shot, fired, and missed.

The man spun around and fired blindly. Unlike Ed, the man's gunfire wasn't suppressed. Shots screamed in the twilight.

Well, so much for going in quiet.

Ed fired twice more and brought the guard down.

Seconds later, an alarm blurted out, a droning ring punctuated with two seconds of silence before its return.

Several Guardsmen flooded out of the main gate, racing toward his general direction. Ed considered picking off a few of them, but they were fast and erratic. Some wore the visored helmets, equipped to identify heat signatures, making Ed an easy target before he leveled major damage to the facility.

Ed swung his rifle strap over his neck, weapon dangling against his back, then scrambled down the tree.

Gunfire cracked behind him.

Debris spit up in front of him.

Shit. Shit.

Ed had nowhere to run. He cursed himself for not thinking through his plan more. He'd gone in rashly rather than deliberately. Now he was about to be shot dead like a dog in a field outside the slaughterhouse.

He swung the rifle around and fired, eliminating three of the Guardsmen before pain splintered his right shoulder.

Ed fell back, somehow managing to stay on his feet. He used his left hand to raise the rifle, but his right refused to cooperate, pain rendering it useless.

Fuck!

At least a dozen Guardsmen stopped ninety yards away, guns aimed at Ed, holding their fire, recognizing that he was injured, no longer a threat.

An amplified voice yelled out, "Put the gun down!!"

Ed shook his head. "Fuck you!"

A gunshot shattered Ed's right kneecap.

He fell to the ground, on his back, in blinding pain.

Ed winced, trying to raise his rifle and tag at least a few of the fuckers before he died.

He looked down at the gun and his useless hand, willing it to cooperate.

Thundering footsteps approached, as if in a herd.

Ed reached down with his left hand, finding grenades on his belt, ready to do what had to be done.

And then a flash.

He felt the grenade fall from his hand, but the explosion never came.

Suddenly he was back in the belfry, with Luca.

"Dammit!" Ed yelled, "What did you do?"

"I saved you," the young man said. "Now please, let me fix your wounds."

"Did you ever think maybe I didn't *want* to be saved?" Ed pushed the healer away.

Luca laid his hands on Ed's chest, warmth pouring from his palms, melting into Ed's body.

Ed tried to push him away again, but somehow Luca had him immobilized. Perhaps it was part of the healing process.

"Please," Ed begged, meeting Luca's eyes. "Please, don't fix me. I don't … I don't want to go on."

Luca stared at Ed then shook his head. "No."

"No? No what?"

"I'm not letting you give up."

Ed tried to move again but couldn't. He could feel the warmth repairing his wounds, in both his shoulder and his knee. The pain was still intense, but he'd seen Luca's handiwork enough to know he'd be right as rain in minutes.

Ed stopped resisting.

He closed his eyes, lying back and letting Luca finish healing him.

Luca finally let go, but Ed kept his eyes closed. If he opened them, he'd cry. And Ed didn't want anyone, let alone another guy, to ever see him crying.

Ed sat in silence until he felt like he could finally sit up and face Luca without breaking down.

Luca was sitting across from him in the rays of moonlight bleeding through the belfry shutters, cross-legged, his usual serene self.

"Why didn't you let me do what I needed to do?" Ed asked, his voice dry and raspy.

Luca stood, went to the supply box, and handed Ed a canteen.

Ed refused the water.

Luca set it down beside him then returned to his spot across from Ed and stared at him, as if disappointed.

"What?"

"Do you think Jade would want you to give up?"

"Jade's dead, kid. Doesn't matter what she'd want. Dead people don't have wants."

Luca nodded. "What about Brent? Teagan? The kids? I know you're close to them."

Ed shook his head. "I just can't do it any longer."

"Do what?"

"Watch people die."

Luca nodded. "Fair enough."

Ed expected resistance and felt tears welling from Luca's kind response.

He closed his eyes again, tilting his head down.

"It's okay to miss her," Luca said.

"I don't need you to tell me that."

"Would it help to know that the end isn't the end?"

Ed looked up, glaring at Luca, despite his blurry eyes. "You gonna tell me there's some Heaven or something?"

"No," Luca said. "Not in the sense that you think of it, anyway. But our souls do live on. Your daughter's is somewhere out there."

"You talking about reincarnation?"

"Something like that, yes."

"So this is supposed to be some kind of relief, knowing she's out there in this wretched hellhole?"

A horrific thought hit him. That Jade was reborn as a baby, somewhere helpless, family struggling against bandits, aliens, and all the other predators running the planet.

"Is she out there now? Do you know where she is?"

Luca shook his head. "She's not here."

"Where the hell is she?"

Luca was silent for a moment. Then he shook his head. "Not everyone comes back here. There are many dimensions, multiple worlds, infinite timelines she can be brought into."

"I want to be with her then. Can you do that?"

"We need you here."

"I don't *want* to be here."

"You are an important part of what's coming."

Ed hated when the kid started talking as if he knew the future.

"You can see these things, yet you couldn't warn me that my daughter was going to die?"

"I don't see everything. I only see some things. And what I can see, I can't necessarily stop. Fate has an odd way of asserting itself."

Ed laughed, unable to hide his contempt.

"So, what, I need to stay alive to play some part you've seen in your head? I don't get a fucking say over my life?"

"This isn't just about you. It's about the ripples you create in the lives of others."

"It's *my* life!"

Luca didn't respond.

Ed grabbed the knife from a sheath on his belt and brought it to his throat, sharp cold blade ready to slice. "I have free will. *I* choose when to die, not you. Not fate."

Luca stayed infuriatingly calm. "You can do it, but I'll bring you back."

Ed glared at him again then let the blade fall to the ground with a hollow clank.

"Trust in fate. Everything happens for a reason."

"Fuck fate. No reason can justify killing my daughter. None! How does killing her make for some greater good? And if that *is* the greater good, then fuck it, I could give a shit about the greater good."

"I can make the pain go away."

"What do you mean?"

"I can make you forget her. I can erase her memories so you won't feel the pain. If that would make things easier."

Ed wiped the tears from his eyes, regarding the offer.

"How would you do this?"

"I can go in and pluck the memories from your head, make it as if she never existed."

"No," Ed said, feeling violated by the thought of someone stealing his memories of Jade. "That's not right. I don't *want* to forget her."

"Why?" Luca asked, as if he didn't understand why a father would want to remember his only child. Ed had always thought Luca was a bit off, and maybe more alien than human after all.

"Because I love her. I don't ever want to forget her, no matter how much it hurts."

"Then why are you so eager to end your life? How can you remember and honor her if you're dead? Come on, Mr. Keenan, you're stronger than this."

Ed swallowed, wiping more tears from his eyes.

"I know it can't be easy for you. To have lost your wife and daughter. To watch as all these horrible things happen to people around you, and to feel helpless. But these people need you. *We* need you. Like a rock thrown in the water, your actions cause ripples that affect everyone. Give up now, and all those lives will have been lost for nothing. And shouldn't their lives count? Do you want that to be their legacy? That they caused you to surrender? Is that how you'll honor them?"

Ed looked down, ashamed.

Luca stood, walked over to Ed, and extended a hand to help him up.

Ed ignored the hand, trying to stand on his own. But his knee was still sore and wobbly. He didn't trust himself not to fall, or want Luca sapping another couple years from his own life to heal him, again.

Ed looked up at Luca, into the young man's eyes. There wasn't judgment. Only friendship, and the genuine offer of help.

Ed took his hand and allowed Luca to help him stand.

Once on his feet, and putting a bit of pressure on his wounded knee to make sure it wouldn't give, Ed said, "Thank you."

"No, Mr. Keenan. Thank *you*."

~

FORTY-SIX

Edward Keenan

"Lock the door, and keep them from getting in here," Ed barked at Boricio and Lisa. Radio Bob was dead, and they'd stepped into an ambush, trapped in the church belfry with enemies advancing below.

They had the firepower for a small engagement, but not enough to hold them off forever — especially if the aliens called for backup. Particularly if they called or attracted the attention of the aliens in the mothership. If Guardsmen in shuttles started appearing, they were done for.

They had to get out of the church, quickly, and retreat.

Boricio and Lisa pressed their bodies against the door in anticipation of having to hold it shut once the aliens made their way up the stairs. Ed looked at the wooden shutters running from floor to roof on all four sides, hoping they weren't as strong as they appeared. He kicked at the bottom of the closest one.

The shutter didn't break, but it cracked enough to let him know that if he kept at it, he could get through the belfry windows and lead the team out to the rooftop. It would be quicker to shoot the shutters, but the resulting cacophony would likely shatter their eardrums in such a confined space, so it would be best to break through without shooting.

"I'm going to make a hole, and I want you both to go through."

Neither was dumb enough to ask what next. Both knew better.

Ed hated leading civilians on missions because they turned into jelly when shit hit the fan. They forgot their training. They asked stupid questions, like "What do we do next?" They often became more of a liability than an asset in the field. Lisa wasn't a civilian, so he never worried about her. And while Boricio had no military or agency training, he was an experienced killer with instincts as sharp as a hunting knife. Both Boricio and Lisa knew that the plan right now was to be fluid, evaluate and adjust as required by the situation. Right now, their only priority was escaping the belfry.

Ed continued his assault on the shutters. The aliens must've heard him downstairs because his sounds were met with clicks, shrieks, and the thunderous sound of God knew how many aliens racing up the stairwell. No matter how immovable Boricio and Lisa attempted to be, they'd eventually get overwhelmed, and the door would come crashing down under the weight of a swarming horde.

"Fuckers are comin' up fast," Boricio said, as if Ed hadn't realized.

He kicked harder, faster at the shutters, splinters of wood flying back at him, nearly hitting Ed in the face. He closed his eyes and kept kicking.

The door rattled in its frame, hard, Boricio and Lisa doing their best to keep it in place.

Come on!

The wood finally broke free. He kicked out the wire mesh screen and opened a hole onto the roof.

"Go, go!" Ed called out.

Lisa ran first, sliding to the ground then scrambling out of the hole.

Boricio was still holding the door. Both men knew it would burst open and the aliens would pour in the moment he stepped away.

"I got you." Ed kneeled beside the hole, raising his AR15 and ready to fire low at the aliens' legs to fell them.

Boricio nodded then counted.

"One, two, three."

He scrambled toward Ed.

Boricio had made it halfway to the hole when the door exploded open.

Ed was afraid Boricio would hear the door blow off its hinges then turn, wanting to fight the enemy. But Boricio did as he was told and scurried through the hole.

Aliens loped in, four at once, stopping only long enough to fix their bulbous heads and black hole eyes on Ed.

Their mouths opened, full of flinty razor-sharp teeth, shrieking as one and creating an unholy echo like a knife in his brain.

Ed opened fire, aiming at their legs.

Aliens fell, but were nowhere near dead. The fuckers would crawl on their hands to reach him if he waited long enough. Ed had one hundred rounds in his high capacity magazine, but a hundred rounds went fast when spraying and praying. He couldn't waste shots killing them when more were already rushing in.

Knowing there was no way to switch magazines before getting overrun, Ed had to plan on how the hell he could get out of the room — there didn't seem to be a break in the influx of black beasties pouring through the doorway.

He backed up closer to the hole, still firing low, blasting the legs of every fucker he could.

Suddenly, movement above.

They were adapting, shifting strategy. No longer rushing

straight in. One jumped over his fallen comrades, coming straight at Ed.

Ed raised his rifle and fired in an arc, but not in time to stop the creature's trajectory. Hot black blood rained on Ed as the thing fell on his body, knocking him to the ground and sending his gun sliding across the floor.

Ed pushed, trying to get the alien off him, but its lithe body was too slippery, and its weight too dense.

Suddenly, he felt movement.

Its head was still, but its body struggled and writhed.

Is this thing still alive? Or are these its death throes?

The creature was still conscious enough to be deadly. Its sharp talons reached up, along Ed's right side.

No! No! No!

Ed tried pushing it off, but his right arm was pinned, outstretched, reaching for his rifle.

His world erupted in pain as talons burst through his ribcage and into his lungs.

He screamed.

From the corners of his eyes, Ed saw black flashes of movement. Shrieking monsters piled into the room to seize upon him.

This was it.

This was how he would die. Overrun by a horde, too many to fight off.

He remembered nearly killing himself two years ago in this very room, and Luca teleporting him here after his failed raid on the slaughterhouse. He'd been so ready to die.

Ironic then, that as he gasped for air and choked on blood, the last thing Ed wanted was to give up.

Trust in fate.

He heard Luca's words in his head. Was it an echo of that event, or calming words he was now somehow in Ed's mind as panic promised death?

A scream from behind, followed by gunshots.

Ed craned his neck enough to see Lisa coming through the hole, firing into the room, doing her best to fight back the mass.

Ed met her eyes and shook his head: *I'm too far gone.*

He coughed, coppery blood filling his mouth then spilling past his lips. "Go," he managed to say.

Lisa's eyes tracked down, likely seeing how much blood he'd lost. She suddenly seemed to realize there was little if any hope.

She stared as if unwilling to face the truth.

Boricio appeared beside her, his eyes now also lit with the truth.

"Go," Ed managed again, his voice weakening already.

Trust in fate.

His left hand reached down for the grenade at his belt. He was going to die, but not without taking as many of them with him as he could.

Lisa's and Boricio's eyes widened at his intention.

No time for goodbyes.

No final words.

No trips down Memory Lane, or reflections of a life devoted to country, sacrifices made, or family lost.

The last thing Ed wondered before the grenade detonated was whether he'd feel his body explode.

~

FORTY-SEVEN

Boricio Wolfe

The grenade exploded and forced Boricio and Lisa to improvise. And ad-libbing in this case meant leaping from the roof's edge — twenty feet high — to the grass below, while avoiding the overgrown bushes running along the church walls.

Boricio managed to land on the balls of his feet then roll to his side without harm.

Boricio rolled a hard eight, two strokes of luck in a row. That meant the moment he turned, he'd likely see Lisa on the ground with a broken ankle, or worse, because Lady Luck was a cunt. Getting away was gonna be a bitch and her sister already, and he could add the whole damned family if he had to flee with a wounded soldier. If Lisa was injured, Boricio would be forced to decide between fighting beside her and abandoning the broad to save himself.

Normally, it might not be too difficult a decision. But after losing Ed, and not being able to find Mary, losing Lisa would be a serious blow to the rebels.

He was surprised to turn and find her standing instead, looking down, hand out to help him up.

Boricio grinned, glad to see her in one piece, took her

hand, and hoisted himself up. He looked at the belfry's burning remains then down to the entrance where the aliens were already starting to flood out the door. It wouldn't be long before the chase was on. There was no time for a moment of silence for Keenan's sacrifice. They'd have to mourn later.

For now, they could only run before more aliens appeared.

Lisa pointed down the closest street. "That way."

Boricio never needed shit said twice.

They raced down the street, aliens clicking and shrieking like banshees behind them.

"This way!" Boricio cut through the yard of a pale-blue house, boarded like a brothel full of whores and herpes, leaping over a chain-link fence and through the backyard of another house.

His heart pounded, pushing his body harder, faster, crossing the street, ducking between more yards, over more fences, putting as much distance between them and their pursuers as possible. Lisa kept pace, staying a few steps behind Boricio the entire time.

They came to another fence, this one wooden. Now she was slightly ahead. Lisa leaped up, and just as she was about to hoist herself over, the fence crashed beneath her.

She cried out, "Fuck!"

Boricio went to help her, but Lisa was lightning on her feet, training her gun out at the yard, waiting for aliens to come bearing down upon them. They'd lost too much ground to run again. They'd have to stand and fight.

Unless …

Twenty seconds passed. Boricio and Lisa traded wide stares of disbelief.

"Did we lose them?"

"Fuck if I know," Boricio said. "But these Aliens are Predators. Shit don't seem likely."

"Maybe they didn't see us escape the church?"

"Maybe," Boricio said, listening for any sign of them. All

he could hear were the tree branches around them, swaying in the breeze as a storm seemed to be brewing in the clouds above. "So, what, they just happened to be burning calories in our general direction when we were making our adios?"

"I dunno. I mean, nothing else makes sense. Maybe they were running from the explosion."

"Well, let's not stand around chafing cock, waiting for them fuckers to find us."

Lisa checked her wristband compass then turned in a circle and scoped their surroundings. "We should probably turn around soon if we're gonna head back to the Chandler House."

"Not yet," Boricio said. "I think we need to lay more space between us and the uglies then circle back."

With Lisa turned at an angle and her jacket opened at an angle, Boricio noticed something — a red stain on Lisa's shirt, near her abdomen.

"What's that?"

Lisa looked down, pulled her jacket aside, and lifted her shirt enough to see the sliver of wood — same color as the fence she just fell on — jutting from her stomach. "Fuck."

Lisa kicked the fence with her boot. "Cunt!"

Boricio went to examine her wound. It looked like six random seconds from *Saving Private Ryan*. Blood gurgled from the wound, and as much as Boricio didn't want to upset her by stating the obvious, Lisa was a tough broad and likely knew what this meant.

"We need to take care of this, or you're gonna be Dracula's wet dream."

"Why don't you head back. I'll catch up."

"I ain't going back without either of the people I left with. What the hell do you think that'll do for morale on Team Boricio? Some captain, can't even keep his star players alive!"

Lisa laughed, as she usually did when he talked about *Team Boricio*. "Star players?"

"Yeah, you're two of my best."

"Shit, I need to have my agent negotiate a better salary."

"You and me both, Sister. I don't get paid dicksquirt considering some of the prima donnas I'm saddled with."

"Let's just keep going." Lisa smiled. "I'll be fine."

"No, we need to sew you up. You got a kit in your pack, right?"

Lisa nodded.

Boricio looked around, searching for the closest spot he could operate without worry of aliens, bandits, or wild animals coming along and fucking shit up. He settled on a terra cotta-colored house two yards up, slightly less shitty than the others.

"Come on, let's fix you up."

≈

FORTY-EIGHT

Mary Olson

Mary sat in her bed, staring at the locked door, waiting for her daughter's return.

They'd barely had time to catch up before Paola was called away by Guardsmen. Mary resisted, demanding that they let her stay in the room.

One of the two Guardsmen looked like he might smack her, though Mary couldn't tell for sure because they were both wearing helmets and visors. Paola intervened, stepping between the guard and Mary. "It'll be okay," she told her mom. "I promise. I'll be back as soon as I can."

Mary figured that was about two hours ago.

It took every ounce of restraint to not get up and scream, demand that they return her daughter. Mary had to play this cool. She'd assumed they were watching her — that Desmond was looking — via hidden cameras or maybe through the mirror over the dresser along the far wall across from her bed.

He's keeping her away to break me.

I can't give in.

Mary tried to keep calm. Yet the longer she sat there, the more her questions grew, chief among them: *Why did Desmond save Paola?*

Was there some part of him that cared about her and regretted having her shot, as he'd claimed? While a part of Mary wanted to believe that Desmond was still in there, like Paola was, her cool, logical part was too skeptical to buy the alien's act of sincerity.

No, he brought Paola back for some other reason. Leverage being most obvious. Use Paola to get Mary to roll over on her friends' location.

Before a few hours ago, they could never have broken her. They could've tortured Mary for days. Because back then, they could only hurt her body. Her mind was already too far gone to care what they did.

But now they had Paola. They gave Mary something to care about — not just something, but her daughter, the only thing in the world she gave a damn about, save for Boricio.

They gave her to me so they could take her away.

Let's see how strong you are now, Mary.

The scary thing was that Mary didn't know what she'd do if they used Paola to break her. For the past few years, she'd lived with the regret that she hadn't done enough to save Paola. That she could've done *something*. How many times had she wished for a do-over? How many times had she said that if she'd only been given another chance, she'd do anything to save her little girl?

And now they had this over her.

The door slid open.

Despite Mary's efforts to remain still, she launched herself out of bed, eager to see Paola again.

But her daughter wasn't at the door.

Desmond stood in the threshold, with an arrogant smile.

"Hello, Mary."

Her short, fat interrogator from before stood beside him: the man whose daughter she'd nearly murdered.

"We'd like you to come with us," Desmond said.

Mary held her tongue and nodded. She followed the pair

out the door and along the bright corridor. It reminded her of a hospital in many ways, down to the white-tiled floor chilling her bare feet. Mary navigated the hallways, making mental notes in case she needed to retrace her steps later.

Yeah, like you're gonna escape an alien ship! What are you gonna do? Jump off?

After several turns, Mary wondered how big the damned spaceship could be. It appeared massive from the mainland, but even so, it was hard to get a feel for its actual size. She wondered how many aliens, or hybrids, or even other humans were living onboard. Maybe she'd ask Paola when they were alone again.

If they let you be alone with her again.

They finally stopped in a long hallway, exactly like all the others.

Paul went to one of the doors and waved his hand in front of it.

The door opened to a pregnant woman lying in bed. She was nude, asleep, covered in a translucent blue sheet with hundreds of tiny lights blinking inside it.

"What is this?" Mary whispered.

"This," Paul answered, "is but one room of our maternity ward."

A sickness grew inside her, memories surging that she'd tried to keep down.

Paul continued. "Thirty women, each deemed an ideal specimen for birthing perfect children, or at least as close to perfection as we can engineer."

"Perfect children for what?" Mary asked, unable to hide her disgust.

"The children will serve as hosts. Clean bodies, not weighted with the psychological baggage preventing most humans from being ideal hosts."

"Why are you showing me this?"

Paul looked at Desmond.

Desmond nodded.

Paul took his cue and left the room.

The door closed, leaving Desmond and Mary alone with the sleeping pregnant woman.

"Tell me, Mary, what happened to our child?"

She wasn't sure which child he meant — the one the real Desmond had impregnated her with, or the one the alien had. "I lost the baby. I told you."

"No, not Desmond's baby. *My baby.*"

The way the alien said *My baby* sent a chill through her. He stepped forward, just inches from Mary, as if inspecting his bill of sale.

Her skin burned as she tried not to flinch or show fear. To give him the satisfaction of seeing the white-hot rage burning inside her.

"You killed it, didn't you?"

"It died."

Desmond's hand was quick as he smacked her hard across the face.

"Don't lie!"

Mary held her breath, trying to stay calm, trying not to give him whatever the hell he was looking to get. She glared at Desmond, wondering if he could tell how close he was to having her thrust her palm upward, into his nose, sending his bones straight up into his brain and ending him.

"I want to know what you did with my baby."

"I killed it," Mary said, meeting his eyes.

"You had no right."

"And you had no right to kill my daughter."

"But she's alive. I brought her back. Can you say the same about our child?"

"Don't call it a child. There was no way I was going to give birth to some alien *thing.*"

She hadn't meant to say it with such disgust, but it was too late to reclaim the words. She'd have to ride it out and gauge his response.

"It would have been a perfect child. A true hybrid, two souls born into a single shell. Not ... this temporary arrangement." Desmond waved his hand across his body. "With combined DNA, our child could have been a wonderful thing. The next step for both species."

"Well, it looks like you have your fill now. So, all that shit about humans and aliens living together as some sort of evolved species, sharing a body was bullshit?"

"No. I meant every word."

"These are babies whose bodies will be used by grown aliens. How will these children have free will?"

"It will all work out."

"Why are you showing me this? To guilt trip me over killing that thing growing inside me? It's not gonna happen. I already felt like shit, especially after losing Desmond's first baby, and worse after losing Paola. You think I *wanted* to take another life? I had to because I couldn't stand the thought of giving birth to the creature who betrayed me and caused me to lose my daughter."

He nodded. "On some level, I can understand."

"Good for you," Mary snapped, barely able to check her emotions. Years of simmering rage rolled to a fast boil, threatening to spill over.

"You asked why I showed you this. Yes, I have my motives."

Here we go.

"I want to let you and your daughter live here, freely, not as hosts."

"But?"

"But I need something from you in return. I want Luca's location."

Mary laughed. "Not gonna happen."

"Oh, I think it will. Let's not kid ourselves, Mary. We both know I have the upper hand. And there are things far worse than death for your daughter."

He looked at the pregnant woman.

Mary snapped.

She lashed out, aiming with her palms at his nose.

He was too fast, turning away, so Mary struck only his cheekbone. Desmond fell back with a yelp.

Mary did some damage, but her blow was far from lethal.

He looked up at her, eyes wild.

Mary remembered her favorite Niccolò Machiavelli quote: *Never do an enemy a small injury.*

She couldn't take the strike back. Now she'd have to kill him.

But Desmond was on her before she had a chance.

He thrust her against the wall, hands around her neck, squeezing tight. He glared up at her, eyes gleaming with hate.

"I should kill you."

Mary's instincts took over. She used her heel to stomp on the top of his right foot. The alien still had Desmond's pain points.

He screamed, releasing her throat as he fell back against the wall.

Mary didn't bother to run for the door. She came back at Desmond, ready to end this before he could counter.

She struck at his Adam's apple, causing him to reach up and grab his neck with both hands, gasping for air.

Mary made her fingers into a triangle and thrust them into his right eye, puncturing the socket, shoving his eyeball back into his head.

Desmond screamed an unholy howl, human and alien.

Mary was about to take out his other eye when she felt her entire body catch fire.

She fell to the ground, pain coursing through her: a shock from men who had entered the room behind her.

Two Guardsmen tended to Desmond while another pair grabbed Mary by the shoulders and hoisted her up.

"What do we do with her?" one of the men asked.

Desmond looked up, blood pouring from his injured eye, and screamed, "Take her to the chamber! And tell Glih we have a new host."

~

FORTY-NINE

Boricio Wolfe

Boricio stared down at the kitchen table where Lisa was sprawled following his impromptu operation. Bloody cloth and snippets of thread lay discarded on the floor.

"Well, look at that," Boricio said, admiring his handiwork. "It's like I'm Dr. Archibald Moonlight Graham."

"Who?" Lisa said. Then, "It's a shame we can't put those skills to use in a quilting bee or something."

She sat up with a grimace.

"You might want to sit a spell and let it heal a bit before we set out. And by the way, I'll have you know I can quilt like a motherfucker."

"Really?" Lisa arched an eyebrow.

"Do I look like a fucking fag?"

Lisa shook her head.

"I'm sorry, I meant, do I look like a fucking *homo?*"

"Oh, *soooo* much better."

"Just call me a kinder, gentler Boricio."

Lisa snorted.

"What? I'm a changed man. You should've known me before shit hit the fan."

Lisa's smile faded. "Yeah, I've seen flashes. And if I'd met you back then, I would've put a bullet between your eyes."

He looked down, a swell of guilt in his gut.

"Yeah, well, that me is dead."

"Is it really?"

"What's *that* supposed to mean?"

"Well, as you said before, Luca fixed you. But how do you fix someone so broken?"

"You saying you don't believe I've changed?"

"No, I believe it. I can see it. I think the old Boricio would've kept running if I got wounded. Or maybe he would've taken me inside and finished me off himself."

Boricio looked down again. If Lisa was trying to make him feel like shit for his past sins, she was doing a damned fine job. Hell, *Mary* hadn't given him this much grief. What the hell was Lisa's deal — he hadn't seen many of her memories in the cross dreaming, so he wasn't sure what baggage she was checking in with.

After an awkward silence, she said, "I'm sorry."

"No, don't be. I deserve it. Hell, I deserve whatever the hell I get, and more."

"Maybe," Lisa said. "But I've gotta treat you as the person you are now, not what you were."

"You speak about this like you have experience."

"My ex."

"What about him?"

"Let's just say he wasn't a nice guy. Met him when we were both in the Marines."

"Ah," Boricio said. "And did you kick his ass?"

"No." Lisa sighed. "The old me was a pussy. Well, at least where he was concerned. I could field strip any weapon in front of me. Could kill five unarmed men with my bare hands. But for some reason, I couldn't stand up for myself when it came to him. I had some guy friends who offered to kick his ass, but I didn't want to make trouble."

"I've seen that a lot. Were you in love?"

"Fuck if I even know what love is. Thought I was. But hell, who knows?"

"So what happened with you two? You leave him?"

"I took a job offer with Black Mountain, left his ass behind. We weren't ever married or anything."

"And that's it?"

"Well, then the world ended."

"Ah … think he's still alive?"

"Wouldn't surprise me if he was running with the bandits. He was always out for himself, so he'd fit right in with 'em. But I doubt it."

"Well, if we run into him, I'm sure you won't be so shy next time around."

Lisa laughed then winced, holding a hand over her wound. "No, I won't be so shy."

"And if you need some help, well, the New Boricio would love to atone for some of Old Boricio's sins."

"By killing?"

"Hey, if you're killing the right people, it ain't a sin in my book."

Lisa smiled.

Suddenly, Boricio had the distinct feeling that they were no longer alone in the house.

~

FIFTY

Emily Roberts

Emily was with Jake Barrow, watching over Luca.

She couldn't stop staring at the wobbly, wooden dividing walls and thinking about how flimsy the basement seemed, as if the room had been built as a hurried contest in one of her father's old reality shows.

Life on The Island was nice by comparison. Their walls were all wood or brick, with straight lines and sturdy materials. The basement Emily was hiding in now had been divided into separate rooms using portable walls. Everything felt so awkwardly constructed that Emily could imagine them falling over, one after the other, if Jake coughed too hard, given his size.

The thought made Emily laugh, and she had to cover her mouth. The big guy was more awkward than the walls.

"What did I do?" Jake asked.

"Nothing." Emily smiled, and he looked away.

She wondered if he was always this uncomfortable, or self-conscious, or whatever it was. Maybe it was only because he'd probably been told to watch her and didn't really know how to act around a little girl — not that he was all that much older than she.

Emily also wondered if Boricio had told him about her little teleportation event. And if he had, then how many of the others knew, too?

For some reason, it hurt her to think about.

Emily didn't want anyone to know. It was embarrassing. And beyond that, she barely felt like herself. Ever since the event, she'd felt somehow … less than who she'd been. Dizzy. *Lost.*

At first, Emily figured she'd teleported them away. But as time passed, she wondered if Luca had somehow done it even though he was unconscious. Yet that didn't feel right. Something inside her insisted that *she'd* somehow done it.

But how?

Was this a power she'd always had? Something that only manifested itself in a moment of stress? Or had Luca somehow changed her when they were in each other's head?

It was all so confusing, and not the sort of puzzle Emily could easily solve. She loved working out problems, just like her dad. But you needed to *see* the pieces before you could solve the puzzle, and Emily had never felt more blind. Nor did she think the answers were that evident, even if she knew where to look. Like much of life's great mysteries, you could spend an eternity wondering and still not know for certain.

If Luca had done something while inside her head, *why* did he do it? And what else had he done? Did he lay some alien seed inside her, waiting for the right moment to hijack her like the aliens on The Island and ship?

To make matters worse, she was stuck in a room with Jake, whose thoughts were practically shouting themselves at her.

He was scared, uncomfortable around her, and clueless around girls in general.

Does she think I'm big and fat?

She probably thinks I'm dumb.

I need to say something to make her not hate me so much.

But what? Everything I think of sounds stupid. What am I gonna say, "Hey, how about us all nearly getting killed?"

Why didn't Boricio take me with him? Leave someone else to watch over her and Luca?

Emily wanted to say something to put him at ease, if only so his pain didn't spread into her mind. But she didn't want to encourage him to stay.

Emily wondered if she could push a thought into his head without him noticing. Get him to leave the room so she could be alone with Luca.

She was pulled from her thoughts by a knock on the basement door and then heard Jazz shout, "Hello!" as if they were long-lost best friends.

Jake looked as relieved for the interruption as Emily felt. "Come on," he said, ushering her out of the room, leaving Luca alone, and into the living room of the basement.

As everyone hugged one another, Emily sank into a couch against the wall, feeling as awkward as Jake had been feeling a few minutes ago. She recognized the people from Luca's memories, but she didn't know their names.

A sad-looking man held the hand of a boy who looked like his tiny twin. A pretty redhead stood beside them with a girl who was surely her daughter clutching her hand. Behind her stood another woman who Emily thought seemed both sad and mean. For no reason she could identify, Emily decided that she didn't like that woman at all.

The children laughed as Jake scooped them into his big arms and swung them around, his awkwardness gone.

And suddenly, Emily felt an odd warmth, like she, too, was happy to see these people. Before she even realized it, Emily was suddenly standing, waiting for them to notice her. Or for Jazz or Jake to introduce her.

Emily wanted to run up and hug them. Wanted to play with the children.

Wanted to be *included*.

Emily wondered if these feelings were also somehow Luca's doing, like he'd imprinted these people onto her like animals sometimes did with people. Some sort of forced bonding among everyone Luca's Light had touched in some way.

She stared harder at the group, waiting for them to notice her, feeling like she didn't belong, and that she should stay on the fringes. Maybe even go back to Luca's room.

Emily's head started to hurt, and she noticed the room's colors getting brighter. She didn't always see auras around people. Usually, she had to focus, unless they were being very emotional. But as she watched the group, her sensitivity, along with the headache it was bringing, intensified.

Colors swirled around them, darker shades of red, purple, and gray, signs that something awful had happened. But of course, Emily figured, something awful *had* happened to most people living in The Wastelands.

She wanted to pry, to peer inside their minds to see what sorts of things they'd been through. Maybe she could find some way to relate to them better, whenever they finally noticed her.

But peeking into their minds would be wrong, so she shouldn't. *Couldn't.*

The sad man came close enough for Emily to hear him. He looked at Jevonne, "Are Boricio and Ed still out looking for Mary?"

"Last I heard. How'd ya know?"

"I radioed them earlier."

As the group caught up with each other's recent events, Emily sat back on the couch, focus elusive. Her head was swimming, stomach churning. She felt sick, and needed to leave. She decided to creep back toward Luca's room, hoping nobody would notice her.

But Jake grabbed her hand, raised it, and said, "Hey, everyone, this is Emily, the girl from the ship."

"Really?" The boy's face filled with wonder.

He left the sad man and came up to Emily. The little girl followed. "What's the ship like?" he asked. His aura was confusing — bright blue mixed with swirling darkness. Same as the girl's, indicating both happiness and either fear or grief.

Emily shrugged, not knowing what to say.

The little girl looked at Emily with big eyes. "You'll tell us, won't you?"

A bead of sweat dripped from her temple. Emily raised a hand to wick it away, wrestling her growing discomfort.

Something's wrong. I can feel it.

"I don't know … " she said, wanting to say nothing, desperate for Luca's room.

The children looked at her with hopeful eyes, wanting to hear her story, their hope a glaring contrast to the feelings she somehow felt *behind* their eyes — the feeling that the children had crossed through the other side of something awful and were looking to her stories as candy to numb their pain.

She started telling them about the ship, barely able to focus on her words, but somehow getting through.

" … It's *big,*" Emily finally finished, her head feeling like someone was plunging an ice pick into it.

"Big?" the boy repeated. "How big? Is it shiny inside? How fast can it go?"

The little girl kept looking from the boy to Emily.

"It feels bigger than The Island, even though it's not." Emily whispered because anything else would have seemed too loud. "There are a lot of really long hallways that turn in circles. It's easy to get lost."

Emily couldn't shake the feeling that something was terribly wrong. A tingle she couldn't explain, and had never felt before, crackled all over her body. Dad would probably say it was her gut talking. But what was it saying, and what could she do to make sure that she listened?

The girl's mom approached her, smiling sweetly. She held out her hand, and Emily took it.

"I'm Teagan," she said, shaking Emily's hand.

She looked behind Teagan at the boy's father then the children, looking at each in turn while the woman told her their names.

"That's Brent, Ben, and Becca. Brent is Ben's dad, and I'm Becca's mom." She glanced at the woman that Emily didn't like, though she still didn't know why. "That's Marina."

"It's nice to meet you," Emily said.

Still smiling, Teagan said, "It's nice to meet you, too."

Emily didn't know what else to say, so she let the part of her mind that was listening speak instead. "Why are you scared?"

Teagan blinked, seemed to think, then said, "Well, we were all scared, we all were. But I feel better now that we're here."

There was so much that the woman wasn't saying.

Emily asked, "Is that because you came from a bad place?"

"Yes," Teagan nodded, her face falling from pretty to almost ugly. "We came from someplace terrible."

"Let's talk about something else," Jazz said, interrupting the awkwardness. "Does anyone want to sit down?"

Everybody stayed standing.

The man and his children were looking at Emily in a way that made her uncomfortable, maybe trying to figure out why she was asking such odd questions. Had she not heard them tell their stories to Jazz and Jake? Truth was, Emily could barely pay attention. But she'd heard enough to know they weren't telling the whole truth — of the horrible things Emily sensed.

Emily felt them all looking at her. She smiled.

She sensed the woman — Marina — at the room's edge. Emily didn't know if she was imagining it, but she felt the woman's eyes on her, maybe wanting something, though she had no idea what that might be. Her aura was gray as well. But unlike the others, it was *only* gray, without a lighter emotion inside her.

There was something burning in the woman shared by no one in the room. Yes, they were all scared, but this woman was feeling something deeper, an emotion Emily couldn't quite place. It was like the woman was having trouble with her thoughts or her feelings, and that made her mad at everyone. Maybe, Emily thought, she'd been forced to do something she didn't want to do.

As Emily stood there listening to the kids, and then to Jake and the kids, she felt two things. First, her dizziness and headache began to subside, as if the kids' happiness chased her pain away. But she also felt Marina's eyes the entire time.

Why is she staring at me?

Emily tried to look up a few times, to prove that Marina wasn't looking. Each time she dared to do so, the woman was just staring blankly at the room in general, not specifically at Emily.

Like a ghost.

The more she thought about Marina watching her, the more Emily's headache begged its return.

I think it's her making me sick. She's so twisted up inside, I'm feeling it.

She had to leave the room. Hell, she had to get out of the basement. The woman's thoughts were contagious.

But then, as if Marina were reading Emily's mind, she told Jazz, "I need some air."

"You should go to the roof," Jazz said. "That's the best place to think, and breathe. I could use some air myself. I'd be happy to go with you if you'd like."

"No." Marina shook her head. "I need some time to myself."

She needs to get rid of the thing inside that's making her mad.

Marina left through a secret door leading from the basement to the house. Once the door closed behind her, Jazz said, "Man, what's wrong with *her*?"

"You have no idea." Brent sighed. "She seems cold, but believe me, Marina's been through hell."

Jazz said, "Sounds like you've all been through hell, but at least you didn't forget how to smile."

"Marina had it the worst," Teagan said. "She saved us twice. Once before we were taken prisoner, and another time after. We'd be dead if it wasn't for her. And it couldn't have been easy to do what she did. It's no wonder she's shaken. I'm sure she'll be fine, we just need to give her some time. Like she said, she needs some air."

With Marina gone, Emily felt suddenly better, no longer dizzy or sick to her stomach. She considered how odd that she'd feel so many of Marina's feelings. While she'd always been sensitive to people's emotions, and oftentimes influenced by them, she'd never felt it so strongly. Whatever hell Marina had been through must've been even more traumatic than anyone was saying. Maybe they'd share later, after the kids were asleep.

"Where's Luca?" Ben craned his neck toward the room where Luca was sleeping. Emily wondered what he'd looked like the last time the boy had seen him, and if he'd be shocked when he saw Luca again.

Jazz said, "He's sleeping."

"Can we see him?" Becca asked.

"Maybe later." Teagan tousled her daughter's hair. "But right now I don't think we should disturb him."

Ben turned to Emily, dragging Becca behind him.

Almost demanding, he said, "Tell us about the spaceship!"

Becca giggled. "Yeah, tell us about the spaceship!"

The children's sweet innocence reminded Emily of something she'd lost long ago and hoped to someday recapture.

She turned around, sat on the old sofa, and gestured for

the children to join her. As they sat on either side of Emily, she saw their auras turn brighter blue, dotted with hues of blushing pink.

Emily smiled, sinking into their happiness like a bath.

"Ask me anything," she said.

~

FIFTY-ONE

Jake Barrow

Jake was still in the basement, back in Luca's room, trying and failing to keep his eyes off of Emily. He was supposedly in charge of watching Luca, but all he could do was stare as Emily sat in the bed next to Luca, reading through a book she found on the shelf in the living room.

He knew she was only reading the book to avoid eye contact, and a part of him wanted to go back in the living room, maybe play with the kids or something, but hell if he could break away from the girl, trying to find the right words to say to charm her.

There was something about Emily that made Jake feel things he'd never felt. It wasn't like lust — he felt that plenty while thinking about Mary, and sometimes Marina, though he imagined Marina less with Mary around. Her hard body and *don't fuck with me* posture had a way of turning him on. There was something sweet about Emily that made him want to talk to her, touch her, know her — something that made him long for her to have the same feelings toward him.

It was a crush, plain and simple. And while he'd had countless impure thoughts since the days when he started needing moments alone, he'd never felt anything so perfectly innocent.

More than anything, Jake wanted to kiss her. But he was pretty sure she thought he was way older than he was. While the team thought Jake was sixteen, he was, in fact, only fourteen. He was just very big for his age. And he was sure if he'd told them his actual age when they first found each other, they'd never have let him do stuff with them. But now, he felt screwed.

He wondered if there was any way he could tell her his real age, so maybe she'd not feel so weirded out by him. Maybe he could finally tell the others, too. He'd already proved himself as a capable fighter, and it wasn't like there were child labor laws in the postapocalypse preventing him from still going out on runs with the Alpha Team.

She looked up, and he quickly looked down.

He felt twice his already giant size, six times as awkward, and as Boricio would say, *dumb as a dick hole.*

He kept trying to think of something that wasn't stupid to say. But hell if he could.

Jake heard Marina return to the living room, shouting.

He ran with Emily to see what was going on.

"I spotted Marcus out on the street," she said. "And he had Mary."

"What?" Jevonne jumped out of his seat. "The guy from that place you were all at?"

"Yeah, he must've somehow tracked us."

"How?" Teagan asked.

The kids clutched one another between her and Brent on the couch.

Jake felt like he should speak, maybe ask something that would prove his intelligence and ability to respond. Maybe impress Emily.

"What about other bandits?" Brent asked before he could.

Marina shook her head. "I only saw Marcus, and Mary."

Brent stood from his spot beside Teagan. "We need to get her."

She pulled at Brent's shirt sleeve and tugged him back to the couch. He barely resisted, and fell back on top of Teagan's legs.

"You're not going anywhere."

Brent stood again, and shrugged himself from Teagan's grip. "I'm going to help find Mary."

"No!" Ben said. "Please, Dad, don't go."

"No." Marina shook her head. "They're right. You need to stay here and protect the kids."

Brent reclaimed his spot on the couch, eyes sad, expression wounded.

Jake wasn't sure what was going on there, whether Marina was really saying he should stay here because it was best, or if she was caving to Teagan's and Ben's request.

Marina looked around the room. "Who else wants to go with me?"

Jake desperately wanted to go. He would definitely volunteer but hoped he'd be chosen. That would show Emily that he was one of the team, that he pulled his weight, that he was brave and valuable and worth having around.

Jake raised his hand. "I'll go."

Jevonne nodded. "Sounds good, Barrow. You and I will follow Marina. Jazz and Brent can stay here and handle anyone that shows."

"All right then," Marina said. "Are we ready?"

Without waiting for an answer, she turned and ascended the few stairs from the doorway into the house.

Jake grabbed his pistol and machete then turned and waved at Emily, and the others, smiling. "Bye, everyone."

Everyone said "Bye," but he only cared Emily's small farewell wave.

Feeling brave and worthwhile, he followed Marina and Jevonne into The City.

They walked several blocks, with Jake focusing on Marina's ass rather than the detritus of a dead world that littered the concrete hallways around them. Not a bad substitute. Jake had always thought Marina was hot. Specifically, she had a fantastic ass. Perfectly athletic. Mary turned him on, but she was almost *too* hard. Marina was slightly softer. Perfect, really. Not too fat, not too flabby, not too muscular. Nice and toned. He felt a flush of shame, wondering how he could go from thinking kind and sweet thoughts about a girl like Emily to dirty ones about these two women.

"Too bad you can't take a picture." Jevonne winked.

"Shut up." Marina was a half block ahead, too far to hear them, but being caught by Jevonne was bad enough. "I wasn't really looking."

Jevonne, who was in his early forties, but always gave cool conversation, laughed. "Dude, you couldn't have been staring harder."

"I didn't want to look at all of this shit." Jake waved his hand at the destruction around them.

"Hell, man, I don't blame you, I'm just calling it like I see it. You can stare at all the ass you want. Lord knows I do."

Jevonne smiled, clapped Jake on the shoulder, and made him feel like less of an idiot. Jake was surprised because usually Jevonne was friendly, and on the quiet side around the others. Not exactly someone he'd picture checking out booty.

Jevonne went on. "Ya see, the thing about ass … "

Marina stopped walking, and Jevonne fell silent.

"This is where I saw them go," Marina said.

Jake looked up at the sign: *Thomas Edison Middle School.* The school was mostly burned and broken, but there were still several parts, including the main entrance, which were serviceable.

Jake smiled at the sign in front of the burned-down school, wondering if it also looked like this *before* The Fall.

Marina stared into the entrance. "I'm going inside to

check it out. You two wait behind, and guard the doors. Radio me if you see anything suspicious."

"Shouldn't we go with you?" Jake asked.

"No, I'm quieter on my own. I'll come back if I need you. And this way, if they leave, you can catch them."

"Okay," Jevonne said.

Marina left. Jevonne continued.

"The ass is a lovely sight to behold, and the best part of the body because — as you know — you can stare without getting caught, and it gives you a reasonable estimation of what the rest of that woman's body might look like. If a woman has a nice ass and legs, you can bet the rest of her body will match. And you can stare without getting in trouble like you would if you got caught staring up top."

"I wasn't *staring*," Jake tried again.

"You don't have to deny it. This shit is biological. Men are designed to check out a woman's birthing hips and judge her to see if she can yield healthy offspring. That shit is half instinct. Boners aren't our fault."

Jake laughed.

The radio crackled.

"Jevonne," Marina said, "I need you in here now. Barrow, you stay behind, and watch the doors to make sure no one leaves."

"Okay." Jevonne's tone was back to business, his eyes serious. He fastened the radio to his belt. "You see both doors? There's one up close and another farther down that way." He pointed toward the tree line. "Don't lose sight of either door, no matter what. You got it? And if anything comes out, you radio us. And if we don't answer, then you take that fucker out and get Mary, okay?"

Jake nodded. "I got it."

"Well then," Jevonne said. "Yippee-ki-yay."

Jevonne inhaled, exhaled, then left Jake alone.

Jake told himself he'd die before allowing Marcus to take

Mary away. It was his job to protect his team, his friends, and he was grateful for the chance to prove himself. But Jake couldn't quiet the voice inside him that wanted to whisper all the ways he was sure to fuck up.

You're a lousy shot.

That wasn't true. Daily practice had made Jake a decent shot, and everyone knew he was unstoppable at close-quarters combat.

That's because you're the size of a house. You just have to stand there. You're shit, and you know it.

That wasn't true either. Jake could throw a punch because Ed and Boricio had both shown him how. Jake didn't hit like either of the guys, since they had different styles of fighting, but he'd learned to throw down his own way with their help. No matter what, he'd be able to take whatever was coming.

No, you can't. You're a coward. And everyone's going to see it.

Most of him wanted the excursion to go smoothly, for them to find Mary and return her to safety without any hiccups. Another part of him was hoping for a skirmish, nothing too big, just big enough to give him a chance to prove he was a decent shot, good in close quarters, and brave enough to use his courage as much as his size to help his friends when they needed him.

As time passed, the sun grew hotter in the sky, and shadows from the surrounding trees moved across the nearby asphalt. Every breaking branch sounded like bandits sneaking up behind him.

He turned, scanning the school in front and the woods behind, trying to keep an eye on both.

They'd been gone too long.

He wiped his brow and looked all around.

An ancient paper skittered across the road. A bird flew from the school's rooftop and sent something small falling.

And then a loud crack behind him.

Jake spun around, gun aimed, crying out, but saw nothing. Embarrassed, he gathered himself.

Gone too long. I should check in.

He hoped they'd turned their radios to buzz, in case the sound of his call drew unwanted attention.

"Anyone there?" he said into the radio.

No response.

He looked around again, unsure whether he should enter the school and abandon his post, or wait as ordered.

Jake looked around yet again, unable to shake the danger pressing on his mind and body.

If he climbed the school steps, he'd lose sight of the second door for sure — the one thing he promised not to do.

If the Reaper escaped, or worse, left with Mary, and fled through the same door Jake was supposed to be guarding, he'd never forgive himself.

And neither would anyone else.

Jake would rather die than disappoint anyone, especially Boricio.

Boricio had been a tormenting older brother and Jake's best friend ever since Boricio found him starving while wandering the streets. Boricio had relentlessly mocked Jake ever since that first day, burning through an endless litany of names, starting with Baby Huey, then Tank for a few weeks before finally settling on Truffle Shuffle.

Jake wasn't fat, just big, and Boricio knew it. He'd always had to put up with a lot of shit from other kids growing up, until he lost his temper one day and sent a kid to the hospital. No one even whispered about him after that.

But he never lost his temper with Boricio. Jake understood that getting shit from Boricio was like getting rain from a cloud. That was the way he talked, and that Boricio was busting Jake's balls because that's what guys did when they were friends. Despite Boricio's teasing, or maybe partly *because* of it, he'd made Jake feel like he belonged to something for the first time ever. Boricio had also taught him more than anyone. Every insult somehow worked backward, and made Jake feel more like a man. Every time —

Marina suddenly flew out the front doorway.

Alone.

"What the hell?" Jake said quietly to himself.

Marina approached him. Her eyes were big, concerned, not quite right. "Where's Jevonne?"

"What do you mean? I thought he was with you."

"No." Marina shook her head. "He came back out. You didn't see him come out?"

Jake looked around nervously.

I fucked up, and I fucked up in front of Marina. Must've missed him when I was looking in the woods. Dammit!

"Wait, is that him?" Marina's eyes widened as she pointed toward the trees.

Jake turned to look. "Where?"

Something sharp hit the back of his head, then everything went black as his body fell.

Jake never felt the ground.

~

FIFTY-TWO

Marina Harmon

The kid hit the ground with a dull thud.

He was huge, crashing to the road without any grace, like a sack of excrement.

It looked down as the life left Barrow's body. The human, Marina, wanted to feel something, but *It* kept her from feeling anything, lest her body revolt against *It*.

It looked down at the boy who was once named Jake but was now the remnants of a soul on the way to the Great Void.

It could feel Marina crying out, fighting for control of her body.

But it wasn't hers any longer.

Neither her body nor her mind. Certainly not her will.

That alien at The Farm had seen to that, just as it divided itself, leaving most of *ITS* body for her to kill as a show to the humans, and the other part wormed *ITS* way inside her.

Now the thing that was once Marina could only watch, helpless and afraid, as The Darkness planned to decimate her friends.

Please, she begged inside her mind. *Please don't do this.*

It laughed. *It* remembered that other part of *Itself* dating her, getting close, and trying to take over her father's church, trying to get the vials.

How do you feel now, Marina, to finally lose to the very Darkness *you thought you were destined to defeat?*

Marina screamed, trying to push *It* out.

But *It* held on tight, sending sharp pain through the host's body, until she stopped fighting.

Only after *It* felt her weaken did *It* start walking.

"Where are we going?" Marina asked.

It refused to answer.

But that didn't matter. She and the alien were one, and if Marina focused, allowed its thoughts to become one with hers, she could see the truth as if she'd felt it herself.

"No!"

Marina whimpered, seeing — *feeling* — the horrible truth.

"Please don't," she begged again.

It approached Chandler House, and sent out a message to The Collective.

I've found The Light.

~

FIFTY-THREE

Brent Foster

Brent wondered if he'd ever get used to the resilience of children. A day ago, they'd been living in a shipping container filled with filthy slaves under the constant threat of rape or death, with barely anything to eat or drink between terrors. They'd escaped Hell, and found their way to a home in The City. Now, barely a sunrise later, Ben and Becca were smiling while reading the few tattered books that Jazz had managed to scavenge.

Teagan took his hand. "Come on."

Brent looked from the children to Teagan. "Where are we going?"

"Upstairs. For some privacy."

"Oh, okay," Brent said, wondering if Teagan wanted to do what he didn't think she possibly would want to do for a long time. They went upstairs, leaving Jazz and Emily downstairs with the children.

Upstairs, her face grew more serious. "Are you okay?"

Brent nodded. He wasn't sure if he'd ever felt worse, or at least less optimistic. They were home but far from safe. Mary was possibly missing, and the aliens were a constant threat, along with the Reaper. Still, he sure as shit wasn't about to whine.

"We're okay," Teagan smiled. "We made it, you know. *He* saw to it."

"What do you mean, *He*?" Brent felt his agitation swell.

Teagan pointed to the sky.

"God?"

Nodding, she smiled wider. "I was praying that He would save us, and He did. Now we're safe."

Brent had prayed, too, a few times during the crisis because that's what you did when you were a few breaths from death, whether you believed in the bearded man above or not. But away from the wretched town and its wretched people, it was harder for Brent to buy stock in the fairy tale. He couldn't believe God had saved them, even if he wanted to.

"No," Brent said. "Marina saved us. Not God."

"Yes," she nodded. "You're right, Brent. Marina saved us, but only because that was part of His plan."

"Really, Teagan?" Brent dropped her hand and gestured around the room. "This is His grand plan? To flush the world down the toilet except for a few turds that refused to go down, then leave the rest of us here like rats fighting for scraps?"

That was probably enough. Teagan's jaw hardened.

"Some fucking plan, G!" Brent couldn't help it. "Great job and glory, glory hallelujah."

Teagan's expression softened, as if she were willing her anger away. She put an arm on Brent's shoulder; the smile returned to her face. Calm.

Her placidity was pissing him off.

"*He* works in mysterious ways."

Brent shrugged Teagan from his shoulder and took a step back.

"I thought you didn't believe in God. I thought your father scared the Good Lord right out of you."

Teagan looked at Brent, still calm, now patronizing.

"For a long time, I hated God because of what my father did — how he treated my mother and me. How he more or less made my sister kill herself. But now I understand; I see that we can't judge Him, or know Him, by the acts of man, especially by the acts of His misguided messengers."

There were a thousand things Brent wanted to say, but he didn't dare breathe even one. He'd say something he was sure to regret, probably about her having a mind of her own and not needing to use it for Scripture. Instead, he shook his head and reclaimed Teagan's hand.

"Let's just drop it, okay? We're going to disagree, and that's fine. We don't have to see eye-to-eye about everything."

"No," Teagan squeezed Brent's hands tighter. "I want to understand *why* you don't believe."

"No." Brent shook his head.

"Why not?"

"Because I don't want to be the one responsible for shaking whatever faith you have. If believing what you do makes you sleep better at night, who am I to fuck that up?"

"You think *you* can shake my faith?"

"That's not what I meant. I'm saying that *I* don't have it myself. All we've seen, all our horrible losses. I don't have it in me to believe that a loving, benevolent God would allow, let alone *plan*, for such things."

"It's not for us to understand His will. Or His plans."

"That's bullshit. That's something people say to justify that God's plans suck. You think my wife dying, Paola dying, all the other innocents — men, women, and children — that's all part of some grand plan meant for us? No way. That's selfish thinking. Dangerous, delusional thinking."

"Fine, Brent. Whatever." Teagan let go of his hand, turned, took two steps toward the stairs, then turned back. "I thought we could have a normal conversation, but clearly you're not ready to talk."

Teagan stomped down the stairs back to the basement.

Brent wanted to follow her. Instead, he collapsed into a chair in the main house, still fully furnished — a modernized yet classic mansion, nicer than any place he'd been in before The Fall, let alone after.

He wondered why he always had to be such an idiot. Brent tipped back in the chair, remembering the many times he'd had to beg Gina to see his side of an issue yet always caved, doing what she wanted him to, thinking like she wanted him to think. He wasn't willing to be the weak one again. Following Teagan, pleading, eventually surrendering — like he always did and always had.

No, Brent *had* to stand his ground. At least for now.

But then again, was it worth it? He'd be losing even if he won. He could let Teagan have her faith and stay in her good graces as much as possible. Be there for her without needing to *be right*. Besides, it wasn't like Brent was even sure what he believed anymore. Maybe she was right. Maybe God *did* save them. Who really knew? Just because he couldn't disprove something didn't make it false.

He could let Teagan have her faith without needing to share it.

He stared out the window, wishing Teagan was with him, knowing he'd apologize if she was. Brent blinked, wondered if he was seeing what he thought he might be, then leaned closer to the window and saw it again.

Oh shit.

Four shuttles were zooming right toward them.

Brent screamed.

∼

FIFTY-FOUR

Brent Foster

"They're coming!" Brent yelled, racing through the secret door and into the basement.

Jazz looked up and met his eyes as he crashed through the doorway. "Who's coming?"

He closed and locked the door behind him. "Guardsmen!"

Teagan rose from the couch. "You're sure they're coming here?"

Brent felt doubt creep in. He wanted to shrug. Instead, he said, "I don't know for sure, but there were a *lot* of shuttles headed this way, and it seems like too many for a random sweep."

The room crackled with nerves. No one spoke. Brent could hear the too-loud beating of his heart.

Emily stood beside Teagan and looked to Brent. "Can't we hide out here? This is a secret basement, right?"

Jazz shook her head. "Sorry, kid. While the basement is lined to protect us from infrared and stuff, if they somehow know we're here, they're gonna find us."

Jazz turned her back to Brent and addressed Teagan and the kids.

"You all need to get into the tunnel. And run. As fast as

you can without looking back. Brent and I will get Luca and catch up, okay?"

"What if you can't catch up?" Teagan asked.

Brent wished she hadn't.

Then maybe God will save us.

"We will." Brent could hear Jazz's lie through a crack in her voice.

"Be brave," Brent said, kissing Ben's head.

"I will," he said, surprisingly not crying as he led Becca and followed Teagan and Emily through the metal door, out into the tunnel.

"Wait, wait," Jazz said, running to the gun rack and grabbing two pistols. She gave one to Teagan then found Emily's hand. "You don't happen to know how to use a gun, do you?"

Emily shook her head. "Sorry."

Jazz still had her face turned from Brent, but he could imagine her smile. "It's okay, honey. Take it anyway, just in case. You best get going. We'll catch up."

He wanted to kiss them all goodbye, especially Teagan. Something insistent inside him warned Brent that this might be his last chance. He ignored the voice and told them all to go. They started running.

Glass shattered upstairs. Brent could hear splintering wood — the front door breaking down.

"Come on," Jazz said then led Brent into Luca's room.

The man who was only a boy lay like a doll on the bed, still out cold and barely breathing.

Jazz put her hand on Brent's shoulder. "You better at carrying or fighting?"

Brent looked at Jazz, felt embarrassed for what he was about to admit, then shook his head. "I'm not as tough as you."

"All right then, you take Luca into the tunnel. I'll stay behind and make sure they don't follow for as long as I can."

This was suicide, and Brent had seen too much death already.

"No way. You're coming with us. We can both go if we move fast."

"Don't argue with me, Brent. One of us needs to stay, that's nonnegotiable. Even if we can only buy a few minutes, those minutes are likely the difference between living and dying. And we don't need two people to hold them off."

"We can hold them off longer if I stay."

"Maybe, but not by much. And we both know I'm not the one with family in that tunnel."

More glass shattered upstairs, followed by something crashing hard against the basement door.

"It's not gonna hold," Jazz said, meeting his eyes. "You need to go *now*!"

Brent sighed, nodded, reluctantly scooped Luca into his arms, and headed out of the boy's room toward the tunnel.

Jazz grabbed a shotgun and didn't say goodbye.

Brent ran — awkwardly, as best he could carrying Luca — out of the basement and into the dimly lit tunnel. He raced forward, hoping like hell he wouldn't trip over any debris, thinking about how frail Luca's body felt in his arms, and how the boy had gone from old to ancient in so little time.

He heard Jazz bellow a war cry then open fire behind him.

He couldn't keep running.

Jazz was wrong: two people *could* hold them off longer than one, maybe much longer, maybe long enough to guarantee escape for Teagan and the kids.

Protecting Luca was their number one mission, but that didn't compare with Brent's need to keep his loved ones safe. He never signed up to sacrifice his family, no way in hell. He'd lost enough, he'd *failed* enough.

Brent laid Luca down against the tunnel wall then turned around and raced back toward the door, drawing his gun on the way.

He threw open the tunnel door, aiming into the room as he did, and found Jazz crouched behind an overturned metal table in a shootout with a pair of Guardsmen. A third lay dead on the stairs.

Neither Guardsman was expecting Brent at the door. Owing to regular practice, fierce determination, blind luck, or perhaps the God he didn't believe in, Brent managed to squeeze off a pair of shots and tag both men in the head, right through their visors.

As they fell to the ground, screaming or dying, another three Guardsmen rushed into the room, firing.

Brent ducked behind the metal table, shielding himself beside Jazz. The table's bottom was coated with Kevlar — as if the team had planned for attack. He wondered if any of the stuff back at the other team houses was similarly modified.

"Why'd you come back?" Jazz seemed furious rather than grateful.

"To help *you.*"

Guardsmen fired. Bullets thunked into the table and the wall behind them.

"I don't need help, Brent. *You do.* Where's Luca?"

"He's in the tunnel, against a wall."

More bullets. Brent hoped the table would stay in one piece, and that none of the Guardsmen had armor-piercing bullets.

Brent made to stand and squeeze off a couple of shots, but Jazz yanked him down. He heard a bullet whizz by above.

"Dammit, Brent. You were supposed to protect him. Now you probably got all of us killed."

Brent swallowed and said nothing, hating that Jazz was probably right.

She popped up, fired her shotgun, then fell beside Brent, her back pressed to the metal table.

Desperate to feel like a hero, Brent stood, quickly surveyed the room, saw that Jazz had managed to tag one of the three

Guardsmen, set his sights on one of the remaining two, and pulled the trigger.

Brent was certain he missed.

Both guards returned fire.

Jazz loaded her shotgun.

"Yeah, well," Brent said, "change of plans."

Jazz screamed, "You don't get to change plans, Brent! Get back in there, and get Luca to safety *NOW!*"

"No. We can take them."

Jazz rolled around to the table's side and blasted her shotgun again. Brent heard a Guardsman plop to the ground.

Assuming the Guardsman's attention would be with Jazz, Brent surrendered his cover and fired again.

This time, he hit the Guardsman. He grabbed two of their rifles and brought them behind the table and dropped them to the ground.

Another three poured through the door.

Jazz ducked back behind the table beside him, still looking furious, but less willing to argue.

"You said you saw how many shuttles?"

"I dunno, three or four."

"Then there are plenty still coming. Go!"

Jazz jumped up, but automatic strafing sent her back down.

She glared at Brent. "*Go NOW!*"

Brent looked behind him at the door. It was close enough that he could probably back away without getting hit and make it safely into the tunnel. But the minute he left, Brent felt certain, the Guardsmen would overrun Jazz and be right behind him moments later.

Jazz leaned around the table's edge, over Brent, and fired blindly into the room.

"GO! You're a shit shot, Brent. All you're doing now is helping to make sure that Luca's dead and that the

Guardsmen all follow. You want to be a hero, then get the hell out of my way."

It stung like his hand in a hornet's nest, but Brent finally got it.

"Sorry," he said.

"Don't give me that sorry shit. Just get Luca to safety."

"Sorry," Brent repeated anyway. "And good luck."

"I'll cover you," Jazz said, still irritated, not bothering to look Brent's way to say goodbye. "And shut the door on your way out."

She grabbed one of the rifles then sprang up on the opposite side for her final attempt at clearing the room, covering Brent while he scrambled through the door.

He slammed it shut behind him, feeling like he was leaving Jazz to her doom. No time for regrets: he scooped Luca up and raced ahead at full speed.

He kept racing, hearing the volleys of gunfire, thankful that Jazz was buying them time — more time than he thought she could. He kept going, gunshots fading, knowing that as long as they boomed in the distance, he had clear passage and maybe a chance.

He pushed himself harder, wishing he was in better shape, picturing how easy Barrow had made it seem, carrying Luca like a comforter on the way to the washing machine.

Suddenly, the gunfire stopped.

Brent hated himself, wondering if he should lay Luca down so he could run faster. The kid was nearly dead, but that didn't excuse Brent from being a coward.

Still, he had to save his family, *no matter what.*

Brent laid Luca down and raced into the darkness.

He made it about twenty yards down the tunnel, fear muffling his guilt, desperate to catch up to the others while simultaneously hoping that they'd run far enough that he'd never be able to catch them.

If he couldn't, then neither could the Guardsmen.

Brent rounded a corner and stopped dead in his tracks. Marina was standing with Teagan, Emily, and the children.

Brent was thrilled to see Marina. Maybe the two of them could hold off the Guardsmen long enough for everyone else to get away. Hell, Marina could probably do it herself.

Brent yelled, "They're coming!"

He noticed that neither Barrow nor Jevonne was present.

"Where are the others?" he asked.

Marina shook her head. Her eyes were sad, and something else. "They didn't make it."

Before Brent could wonder what that something else was, Marina raised her gun and fired.

A bullet burned through his gut.

Brent fell to the ground and saw Emily vanish.

FIFTY-FIVE

Boricio Wolfe

Boricio felt sure that someone was in the dilapidated house with him and Lisa.

He crept into the living room, holding his gun while looking around at the detritus of years. The house was decayed: rotting wood swallowed by cobwebs, the stench of dust and mold burning his nostrils.

Lisa stepped out of the kitchen and looked at Boricio with her eyebrows raised. "What has you so — "

Boricio shook his head with a finger to his lips and gestured around the house.

Lisa nodded, and together they searched. He could hear her racing heart next to his.

From nowhere, Emily flashed into existence.

Boricio jumped back, barely holding his scream.

Lisa spun around, aiming her gun on the girl.

"No!" Boricio yelled, grabbing Lisa's wrist, squeezing it tight and raising her arm in the air.

Emily looked at them with terrified eyes.

"They got them."

"What?" Lisa and Boricio asked together.

"The aliens." Her voice trembled. "They came and got them."

Boricio licked his dry lips. "Got who?"

A beat, as if she had to catch her breath then, "Everyone."

❧

Epilogue

One minute, Ed was in the belfry, waiting for the explosion. The next, he was surrounded by utter darkness.

He was in some kind of void, wondering if death was an absence of any sensation, and if it had claimed him. No God. No Heaven. No Hell. Only nothing.

But that wasn't quite the case.

Ed felt cold.

And suddenly, he was gasping for air.

A flicker of light above!

His body spilled into motion, acting on instinct, clawing at what felt like soil, pushing, pulling, himself upward. Only after his hands broke through the surface did Ed realize he was crawling out of the ground, like an undead monstrosity scrabbling up from the grave.

He stood and looked around, feeling an odd sense of déjà vu, even though he was certain he'd never been wherever he was.

Best Ed could tell, in what felt like dawn's early light, he was in some kind of grove. His *grave* was smack dab in the middle of a rich brown soil road running forever in two directions like the Yellow Brick Road leading to Oz. On either side of that road were flowering bushes with the largest, brightest flowers he'd ever seen, seeming to glow with an eerie incandescence.

Just beyond the flowering bushes were thousands of massive ancient redwoods that looked thousands of years old, climbing into the sky. Streams of sunshine flowed like a river through breaks in the canopy. In those streams, motes of dust, pollen, and other things too tiny to identify floated in what felt like slow motion.

Where the hell am I?

Luca must've teleported him away from danger, again, just before the grenade went off in the belfry. *Where's Boricio and Lisa?*

He looked down at his ribs, searching for the stabbing wound. But it was gone, as was any trace of blood. Ed was also wearing different clothes: charcoal pants, a white long-sleeve shirt, and a gray jacket. Clothes he'd worn more than two decades ago, when he'd first started on the job.

What the hell is happening?

"Luca?"

No response.

Ed heard a babbling brook to his right.

His feet decided to follow the sound before his mind had agreed it was a good idea. He stepped through a thick green bush with large purple flowers that looked like nothing he'd seen on Earth. Branches retreated as he stepped through, to protect the flowers or clear his way.

The environment's surreality caused his head to spin in confusion. Had Luca teleported him to some other dimension? An alien world? Ed wasn't sure what scared him more — to think that he was on some other world far away from everyone he knew, or ... another possibility. That he was dead, and this was some kind of afterlife — Heaven? Hell? Limbo?

He pushed himself to walk faster to find the water. The

answer that might be there. He couldn't get lost in this massive forest. If he did, Ed would certainly lose his mind.

Suddenly, he was no longer in the woods.

Ed was pushing through a hospital door.

He looked down to see himself in scrubs over those same clothes from before.

What the hell?

His wife was on the operating table. A nurse held something in her hands, turned away from Ed.

Oh, God.

Memories flooded back, intermingling with present.

Impossible. Surreal.

Wonderful. Awful.

The nurse turned to Ed, holding his baby.

"It's a girl," she said, showing him the tiny creature he was suddenly responsible for, then handing her to him.

Ed held her carefully, so afraid he'd be too rough, drop her, or something worse. She was so small, so fragile.

Her tiny pink fingers melted his heart.

And then she was gone.

Ed was back in the woods.

"No, I want to go back!"

He fell to his knees, screaming, eyes squeezed tight, crying.

Then a voice came from behind.

"It's okay, Daddy."

Ed turned to see his daughter.

Episode 36

(FIFTH EPISODE OF SEASON SIX)

"The End"

Prologue

Jacksonville, Florida

CHARLIE WILKENS WASN'T UPSET when he woke up to an empty world. In fact, it was the best damned thing to happen in his seventeen years on the planet.

He was frightened at first, of course, when he opened his eyes to an empty house, both cars in the driveway, and no sign of his mother or asstard stepdad, Bob. But after going door to door and discovering his entire block was as empty as his house, Charlie was many planets past the moon.

He tottered down the street on his 12-speed, stopping to knock at each house, considering its occupants and the offenses they'd committed against him over the years. He knocked on the bully, Eddie Houghton's, house, remembering the time the fat, redhead made Charlie eat dirt in front of his classmates in sixth grade.

A vague sense of déjà vu flooded Charlie's senses as he waited for Eddie to answer the door. He knocked, but Eddie wasn't home.

He's never home.

Hasn't been home any of the hundreds of times I've done this.

Charlie was confused.

He hadn't done this hundreds of times. At least not that he could remember. And yet the sense that he had was too overpowering for Charlie to ignore.

He got back on his bike and headed toward Josie Robinson's house, a girl he had a crush on since kindergarten. She'd been his friend until last year, before she started hanging out with Shayanne and the rest of the cheerleaders in the Bitch Clique. It was bad enough that she'd shunned him, but at one point, Josie had called him "pizza face" in front of half the lunchroom. It was all Charlie could do to keep from crying.

Bye bye, Josie.

Then there was that asshole, Mr. Lawrence, at the end of the block. A short, creepy dude who once hired Charlie to go door to door and hand out flyers for his painting business. Mr. Lawrence had promised Charlie $40 for the job. But after Charlie spent the entire weekend canvassing the neighborhood with ads, Mr. Lawrence claimed someone saw him ditching a box of the flyers in a dumpster at the Quick Stop (which was bullshit). So, he refused to pay Charlie.

Sayonara, asshole.

Charlie laughed, racing to the next block and repeating the process, growing increasingly giddy with every empty house.

"Goodbye, assholes! Fuckers! Motherfuckers!" Charlie shouted from the top of his lungs. It was an amazing release, even if no one was around to hear him.

"Who you calling asshole?" someone shouted.

No, not *someone.* It was Bob.

No, he's not supposed to be here.

Not yet.

Charlie tried to follow his thoughts, to figure out what they meant. Again, more indications that he'd been here before, that this had happened. But it hadn't. Had it?

Bob was standing in the street, wearing his greasy Sal's Towing uniform, staring at Charlie with his usual disdain.

Why is he just standing there? Where did he come from? Where is his truck?

Charlie looked around, confused, as Bob came toward him. Nothing seemed right. Everyone in the world was gone except Bob? What kind of cruel cosmic fucking joke was that?

No. There has to be others. It can't just be me and King Asshole.

"Why did you do it, Charlie?" Bob yelled as he got closer, face red with rage. Charlie could practically smell the beer on his breath.

He racked his mind trying to conjure Bob's imaginary crime. Had Charlie left the cap off the milk? Had he left his backpack in the hallway again? What was Bob torqued about today? And, more importantly, what would Charlie's punishment be?

"You little ungrateful shit!" Bob was on him in seconds, right in the middle of the street, not giving any fucks to possible witnesses.

As if anyone's left to see!

Despite his slurred speech and slower movements, Bob's fist flew fast and landed on Charlie's jaw.

Pain splintered through him like lightning, sending Charlie to the ground, writhing in pain.

Bob wasn't done. He kicked Charlie, hard, in the gut.

"What did I do?" Charlie cried, throwing his arms over himself and crawling into a fetal position on the ground to give Bob a smaller target, or at least protect his face, chest, and groin from the kicks.

This isn't what happened! What's happening here?

"You ungrateful little fuck!" Bob said, kicking again, this time, hitting Charlie in the spine. "I took you and your bitch mother in. I didn't have to do it!"

Something snapped in Charlie.

He stood up, despite the pain in his jaw, gut, and back.

He met Bob's red eyes, widening in response to Charlie on his feet.

"Not used to me standing up for myself?" Charlie grinned.

Bob, unwilling to tolerate such disrespect, took a drunken, misguided swing. Charlie sidestepped and watched Bob fly by then fall to the ground in an embarrassing heap.

Charlie kicked Bob in the back of the head, as hard as he could. Bob cried out, an incoherent wail.

"You didn't take anyone in. It was *our* house, asshole!"

Charlie kicked again, this time in Bob's back.

Bob screamed.

Charlie stood over him, fists balled at his side, wanting to pummel King Cunt, to take out years of frustration of being Bob's whipping boy, of being picked on by bullies at school. But how far could he take this? What was the next logical step? He couldn't kill Bob. Even though the man was maybe the biggest asshole in Florida — and given the state's reputation for assholes, that was saying something — no jury in the world would let him off for killing his stepfather, no matter how abusive the man was.

There are no juries left. Do it.

After a long moment of silence, Bob looked up at Charlie and apologized. "I'm sorry."

Charlie stared at the man, confused. He'd never apologized to Charlie, for anything. Ever. Charlie listened.

"You're right, kid. I can be a bit of an asshole sometimes. But it's not me, man. It's the booze. It's the stress of my fucking job. It's — "

"Oh, boo fucking hoo," a voice said from behind with a slight indistinct drawl.

Charlie turned, surprised to see a young man in all black standing behind him, swinging a bat as if preparing to take the plate. His hair was long, pushed back, eyes intense. There was something familiar about the man, but hell if Charlie could remember how he might know him.

"The only way to get power," the stranger said, swinging the bat and looking up in the sky as if he'd just cleared a ball from the park, "is to step to the fuckin' plate and swing your bat in its fat fuck of a face. That's how shit's done on Team Boricio. Fuckers who don't like it get squashed."

Team Boricio?

Charlie felt like he'd heard the man say that before. That he somehow knew this Boricio fellow.

"Who the fuck are you?" Bob asked, standing.

"Did I say you could stand?" Boricio said, staying in his spot and not moving to stop Bob. There was a confidence in Boricio's stance and swagger that Charlie loved, and longed to possess.

Bob marched forward, toward Boricio, fists ready to tangle.

Charlie stepped between the two men, emboldened by Boricio's sudden presence, even though he didn't know if this man was an enemy or ally. He sure as hell seemed like an ally, though, and if there was a Team Boricio of badasses, Charlie wanted his name on the roster.

Bob looked Charlie up and down then sniggered. "What are you gonna, do, boy?" He thrust a finger in Charlie's bird chest and pushed him back slightly — something he'd done in their house several times when Charlie dared to talk back even a bit.

So much for the apologetic Bob. Maybe that had been a ploy to disarm him, to stop Charlie from attacking, and buy Bob more time to come back at him harder and more brutal.

A part of Charlie wanted to apologize for letting this get out of hand. *Let's just go back to the way things were. I'm sorry, Bob. Please, don't punish me. Please, don't take this out on Mom.*

Charlie hated that part of himself.

He had to kill that part of himself. Now or never.

"Sit down," Charlie said.

"Or what, *boy?*"

"He'll make you sit," Boricio said from behind.

Charlie didn't turn to see the man but could tell from the disgusted reaction in Bob's beady red eyes and trembling lips that Boricio was probably wearing a smug and oversized smile.

Ooh, Bob is afraid!

Charlie grinned then yelled, "Sit down, Bob!"

Suddenly, Boricio was at Charlie's side.

Bob looked at the two of them, did the math in his head, and realized he was outnumbered and pretty much fucked. He blinked, a furrow in his brow indicating confusion before he verbalized it.

"Who the hell are you? What are you doing with Charlie?"

"The boy said *sit.*"

Bob reluctantly found a spot, smack in the road's center, and sat. He looked like a confused child trying to figure out how bad his punishment was going to be, terrified to do anything that might make everything worse.

Charlie turned to Boricio and wanted to ask who he was and why he was helping but couldn't bring himself to admit he didn't know who the man was. He felt like he should. Charlie felt like if he could just get past some block in his head, everything would make sense. Yes, he'd been here hundreds of times. It certainly felt as if this scenario had played out, though maybe not this exact one, more times than he could count.

An obvious realization came to Charlie. He was dreaming. He had to be. That's why nothing made sense, why the world was gone, and why he was suddenly able to stand up to his prick of a stepfather.

Boricio offered Charlie the bat. "You ready, slugger?"

So, if it's a dream, just play along, and see where it goes!

Charlie grabbed the bat.

"Now what?" he asked Boricio.

Boricio looked down at Bob then back up at Charlie, eyes darting back and forth. "Duh."

"Oh! You want me to hit him?"

Boricio smile and clapped. "How about that, Chuck, we've got ourselves a winner!"

Bob's eyes went wide. "No, please! Please, don't hit me. I'll do whatever you want. I'll leave your mother. I'll leave the house and never bother you all again."

Charlie considered Bob's offer. Were this real, he'd probably accept. Because all he really wanted was for the fucker to get out of their lives. All Charlie *ever* wanted was to see his mom happy again, like she'd been before his real father died.

But this wasn't real, and hell if Charlie didn't want to take out his frustrations on the bastard who had ruined their lives.

Charlie took a somewhat reluctant swing, hitting Bob in the arm.

Bob cried out, "Fuck!" Looked up at Charlie, rage painting his face red. He started to stand but stopped dead in his tracks when Boricio put a gun against his temple.

"No, no, no, Bobby boy, we ain't even close to bein' done!"

Bob glared at Boricio then returned his hateful stare to Charlie, mumbling something under his breath, likely vowing to get even with Charlie the first chance he got.

Fear bubbled in his gut. What if this *was* real? Not a dream at all? What would happen after he beat the shit out of Bob with a baseball bat? There was no way on earth the man wouldn't retaliate against him, *and his mother.* Whoever Boricio was, he wouldn't have Charlie's back forever, and eventually Bob would find him alone, and get revenge. Charlie would be helpless to stop him. Because in the real world Charlie wasn't brave. He was a scared kid, and Bob was a fucking bully. And the bullies *always* won.

"That's why you gotta end the game now," Boricio whispered in Charlie's ear.

"How did you —"

"Read your thoughts?" Boricio smiled. "Because, Charlie boy, we're connected, you and me. We're all connected."

"All?"

"Not now, Charlie Brown, we got a job to finish. Now are you gonna stand there and tickle Bob's berries, or are you gonna fucking *hit* him?"

Charlie hit him, in the arm, again, and still not nearly as hard as he could swing.

Bob screamed, as if it hurt more than it possibly could have.

"Oh, come the fuck on, put your back into it, boy!" Boricio said.

"I can't," Charlie whined.

"Why not?"

"I dunno. I'm confused. I can't tell if this is real or a dream."

Boricio, looking disappointed, reached out and grabbed Charlie's bat.

"I thought you were ready to play in the big league, Charlie. I thought you were ready to be Team Boricio's all-star hitter, but frankly, I'm not sure you have what it takes."

"Please," Charlie begged, "give me another chance."

Boricio's face relaxed into a smile. "You know what, you're right. I'm sorry. I'm expecting a bit much from a rookie. After all, you haven't even been to Boricio's spring training camp. I'm gonna show you how the pros play, all right? Now I want you to pay real close attention, okay, Charlie Brown?"

Charlie nodded.

"Now, the first thing is to get a good grip on your bat, like this, see? Not *too* tight, or you'll just fuck up your swing and end up limp wristed like little Wilma here, right?"

Charlie nodded again, watching Boricio's fingers tighten around the black tape wrapping the bat's handle.

"Now, next you wanna pay real close attention to the angle of your swing. You want to connect with the ball, or, in this case, Bob's fat fucking head, in just the right spot, like — "

He swung, hitting Bob right in the temple, hard.

The bat made a sickening thunk and sent Bob to the ground like a sack of potatoes.

" — this," Boricio finished.

Charlie stared, unable to do anything else, wondering what the fuck just happened.

Boricio continued his lesson, all smiles, as if he hadn't just murdered Bob.

"Now, that was a pretty good shot, but sometimes, what feels like it might go long winds up being a foul ball. And that's a dick in the mouth when you wanted a lollipop, so you need to brush it off and find the confidence to face the batter again. Get your head straight, tell yourself, *I'm gonna knock this bitch outta the park!*"

Boricio swung again, in a downward arc, smacking Bob in the back of the skull.

"And sometimes, you get a pitcher who thinks he's got you figured, and he's gonna make you strike out, but no, you keep swinging, foul tip after foul tip, until you find the right pitch to drive right down his fucking throat!"

And then again, and again, repeatedly bashing, fragments of skull, brain, and blood splashing up and covering Boricio.

"And you just keep fucking swinging, and — "

The bat broke in Boricio's hand. He stopped, looked down at the mess he'd made of Bob, all over his shirt. He had no expression. No revulsion. No surprise.

And then a huge smile.

Boricio raised both arms triumphantly. "Fuck yeah, grand fucking slam! In the bottom of the ninth, Team Boricio comes back and wins the game!"

Boricio dropped the broken handle then trotted around Bob as if running bases. He ran up to Charlie and grabbed him, blood and remnants now varnishing Charlie. Boricio scooped him up, swung him around, and started singing Queen's "We Are The Champions."

Charlie pushed himself away, looking down at his shirt, disgusted.

"You're a psycho!"

Boricio laughed. "Ding-Ding-Ding! What's that? Looks like we've got another winner, Chuck! Now let's show Charlie Brown what he's won."

Boricio grabbed Charlie, spun him around, and thrust him forward.

Suddenly, they were no longer on the street but rather in front of a grocery store. Boricio shoved him through the front doors.

Boricio was gone, and Charlie was back with Bob, hunched over in the dark aisles, searching for food, batteries, and any other supplies they could scavenge back to the house.

Bob looked over at Charlie. "What?"

This had to be a dream. Not just a dream but an unending nightmare. Yet it felt so real and … like he'd been here before.

Charlie remembered every heartbreaking moment that occurred after October 15. How they'd wound up on another world. And then, most importantly, he remembered her. The girl they'd met as she attempted to break into Bob's truck outside the store.

Callie!

Oh, God, Callie!

Charlie scrambled to his feet, to the store's front, and then through the broken doors, coming to a skid in the debris outside. There, parked in front of the shopping center was Bob's truck — Callie breaking into the cabin.

He flashed back on their original meeting, how he'd chased her, how Bob had hit and nearly killed her. He saw

Bob coming through the doors, bat in hand. Not just a bat, but the same bat that Boricio had been holding moments ago, but no longer broken.

"Hey!" Bob called out.

Callie looked up, surprised to see them, caught red handed.

She ran toward the woods in the distance.

No, no!

Charlie had to prevent the inevitable.

Instead of chasing Callie, he went after Bob, racing as fast as he could, a tightness in his chest as he pushed himself to catch up. Bob was about ten steps ahead, and closing in quickly on Callie.

Charlie focused on his stepfather's back, pushing himself fast enough to launch himself at Bob and bring the man down, stop him from catching Callie and hitting her with the bat. He noticed something moving beneath Bob's shirt, just between his shoulders.

Something fell back, hitting Charlie in the face.

He reached up, swiped it aside, then looked down in his hands to see a piece of Bob's skin and hair.

Disgusted, Charlie shook his hand until he'd rid himself of the flesh. When he looked back up, Charlie saw more scraps shedding from Bob, revealing something underneath: a black, oily-looking creature with hundreds of tiny lights inside its skin — an alien!

And just as he realized what it was, and how much danger it posed, the alien gathered speed and closed in on Callie.

Charlie screamed, "No!"

The alien turned on a dime, causing Charlie to smack into it.

They tumbled to the ground. The bat fell.

Charlie grabbed the bat, spun, and slammed it straight into the alien's giant face. Black goo gushed everywhere.

Charlie leaped away, lest the stuff touch him, then turned to search for Callie.

But she was gone. And suddenly he was alone, on a path, surrounded by giant redwoods on either side.

The dream was getting weirder.

Charlie looked up and down the path, which seemed to unspool forever, wondering how the hell he'd ended up on it. These weren't the same woods where he'd chased Callie.

Are they?

"Callie!"

Waiting for an answer, Charlie heard water in the distance.

He left the path, following the sound, creeping through the woods toward a clearing where three people stood in the shadows. One stepped forward from the trees.

"Callie?"

She smiled then ran into Charlie's arms. "You're finally here!"

"I thought you died. I mean, I saw you die."

She kept hugging him and whispered into his ear, "Death isn't the end, for any of us."

As he held her, another figure stepped from the shadows, an old man Charlie recognized from Black Island.

"Will?"

"Welcome, Charlie. We've been waiting for you."

~

FIFTY-SIX

Paul Roberts

News came back from the incoming shuttle, reporting results of the rebel house raid, and Paul felt his knees weaken.

"No sign of the girl," the Guardsman said over the transmission. "One male, one female, and two children. No Emily."

The Guardsman relayed a video of the prisoners, displayed on the window in front of them, momentarily replacing the view of Mary in her chamber.

Paul's heart sank when he saw these other faces, and not Emily's, on their way to the ship.

Desmond clicked off his shoulder communicator then turned to Paul, the only other person in the observation room overseeing Mary's cell.

"I'm sorry," Desmond said.

"*Sorry?* What? Is that it? You're not going to look for her?"

"I'm sure we'll get answers from the prisoners once they're onboard," Desmond said. "Let's not overreact."

Paul couldn't believe Desmond's manner, as if this were some minor mission failure that would be corrected in due time.

"She's my daughter. She's a child, Desmond. Alone in The Wastelands, with bandits, rebels, and Ferals *you* can't control. Do you understand the danger she's in?"

"I'm sure she's fine," Desmond said with his usual dismissive smile.

Paul crossed his arms, turned, and again stared through the window at Mary strapped to the table.

"She knows where Emily is."

"Maybe, but she's not talking."

"We haven't tried everything."

"Are you suggesting that I let you fail to get inside her head again? Or maybe you'd prefer another crack at slitting her throat?"

"I can do it this time. Before, she was strong. Now she knows we have Paola. Her resolve is weaker. I can break her."

Desmond stared through the window, arms crossed, chin resting in the nook of his thumb and index finger as he contemplated Paul's offer.

"You have Luca and the others, right? You've already got what you want. Let me try and get the info."

Desmond kept staring through the window. Paul tried reading his thoughts, but like with the other aliens, found little but static. He didn't dare press, lest they notice and kill him immediately.

Paul tried one more gambit. "You said you were going to use her as a host, right? But we both know you can't really do that until she's broken. She'd kill whomever you put in her. So if you already have what you want from her, and she's of no use as a host, you've nothing to lose. Please, Desmond. Let me try."

Desmond finally turned, met Paul's eyes, and nodded. "You're right, Mr. Roberts. Go ahead, see what you can get from her."

"Thank you."

Paul was about to leave the room when an idea struck him. "I think I know a way to break her. But I'll need you to trust me."

Desmond's head tilted ever so slightly to the side. "Whatever you need," he said.

~

FIFTY-SEVEN

Mary Olson

Mary's attempts to bar regret from her head failed almost immediately.

She'd refused to surrender the rebels' location, and now Desmond was making her pay. The longer she laid strapped to the table, now in a vertical position in the room's center, the more horrible her imagined scenarios became. Desmond had Paola and therefore possessed everything needed to hurt her.

She should have given the location. Yes, the group would be screwed, and many of them, including Boricio, likely killed. But at least Paola would have been safe. At least Boricio, Luca, and the others would've stood a chance. Even if caught by surprise, they would surely mount a defense. Mary had no power on the alien ship. And they had all the leverage.

After what felt like forever, but may have only been fifteen minutes, her chamber door opened, and Paul stepped in, alone. He slowly approached her, stopping about four feet away, staring at Mary, hands folded in front of him. She wasn't sure if this was an intimidation tactic or if Paul was deep in thought, perhaps trying to get back inside her head.

"Come back to slit my throat?"

Paul shook his head. "No. I don't need to."

Mary wasn't sure what that was supposed to mean and wasn't taking the bait. If he wanted to threaten her, he'd have to be more direct.

"Tell me," he said, remaining perfectly still, "what was it like seeing your daughter again?"

Mary said nothing, refusing to bite.

She felt him probing at the edges of her mind but pushed him out, easily.

"So, that's your tactic, eh? Get me to think about my daughter, weaken my defenses, and storm into my mind?"

"Pretty much. An opening move, to test your response."

She chuckled. "And?"

"As expected. Tell me, Mary" he began again, as if that was a hypnotic trigger word to get her doing whatever it was he'd programmed into her, "why didn't you take the offer?"

Mary tried not to think about the why, but that was almost impossible with a foot on the path. She could feel him pushing again, trying to use the known responses to regain entry.

Again, she pushed him out.

"You could've been safe. Desmond offered sanctuary, for both you and Paola. Yet you refused. And for what? To protect your allies?"

"Pretty much."

"But why? What do you think he's going to do to them?"

Mary chuckled again. "I know what you're trying to do. Figure if you push my thoughts enough in the right direction, you'll sneak past my defenses. It won't work."

"So, tell me, Mary, what *will* work?"

Doing something awful to Paola.

Even as Mary thought it, she tried not to.

A smile spread across his face.

Had he glimpsed her thought? Or was he trying to trick her? Mary could no longer tell if he was trying to break in. When someone tried consistently enough, you grew numb to the sensation. It was harder to tell the difference between a genuine attempt at intrusion and a psychic echo of a prior attempt.

"You turned down Desmond's offer for nothing, Mary. We have Luca, and the others. They're on the way now."

"Liar."

"Oh? Look in my eyes, and see."

She looked then turned her head away quickly. Another attempt to breach her defenses. Yet in that moment, Mary saw a flash of something she knew to be true.

"The Chandler House," he said. "In a secret basement. We have them. But here's the thing, Mary. Desmond has no reason to kill them. He'll offer them the same thing: a chance to live here on the ship, or on The Island, as one of us."

Mary shook her head, wanting to look back into his eyes again, to see if that was also true. That this war could be over that easily. Simple surrender. She could even keep her mind and body.

But didn't that doom the humans still fighting for freedom?

"You're thinking about those you'd be betraying, aren't you?"

Mary closed her eyes, pushing Paul out with everything she had.

"You'd only be dooming The Wastelanders, as if they had a shot in the first place, which they don't. Evolution is coming, Mary, whether you like it or not. We are the last of our species. There's something special about that: witnessing the next step without being killed by those replacing us. I'd say we're lucky. Well, some of us are. You, not so much. You chose wrong, Mary, and now you'll have to regret saying no."

Paul looked up at the mirror and shouted, "Bring her in!"

The door slid open.

Seconds later, a Guardsman stepped through, gun aimed at Paola, prodding her forward.

"Now," Paul said, "I'm going to give you one last chance to do the right thing."

Paola's eyes were brimming with tears, though she seemed to be doing her best to hold herself together. "Mom," she said, before the Guardsman at her back told her to keep quiet.

Paul looked at Paola then back at Mary. "I believe I have your attention now, right? This man behind your daughter, his name is Kurtis. He had a wife and family taken by the plague, so he's been through some shit. But he's not a bad guy. The alien inside him, however, now that's a different story. I'm not sure of his name, forgive me, but I do know he has little empathy for your situation. Way he sees it, you and the other rebels are only keeping his kind from finding new homes. He'd like this fight to be finished and is prepared to do whatever it takes. Am I correct, sir?"

"You are correct," the Guardsman said through his helmet's speakers.

"So, here we go. Since your friends are already captured, and you no longer need to protect the location of their *secret hideout*, I'd like you to tell me where my daughter is."

"I don't know."

"Kurtis, kill the girl."

"No!" Mary shouted.

Paul raised a hand to stay the execution then approached Mary. "Tell me where my daughter is."

"The last time I saw her, she was in the warehouse you all raided, not the Chandler House. I swear. I left because I was pissed off that everyone trusted her so implicitly."

"What do you mean?" Paul asked.

Mary wasn't sure how much she could say without risking Emily's or Paul's life. If she told him, in front of the alien, that Emily had wanted to leave, that she hated the aliens and wanted to stay with them, it could endanger them all. Or her calling Paul's daughter a traitor could piss him off. Maybe he'd snap and order them killed.

There was only one way to convey the information. She had to let him inside her.

Mary met his eyes and aloud said, "I was jealous that they'd taken her in, that they didn't see her as a threat."

As Mary spoke those words, she sent others into his head.

Look inside me. You'll see the truth.

Paul's expression changed for only a moment, but it was enough to see her message received. Mary felt him prodding at her mind's doors moments later.

This time, she opened them wide and let him in.

FIFTY-EIGHT

Paul Roberts

Paul entered Mary's head even though he was certainly stepping into some sort of trap. But what choice did he have? If she knew something about his daughter, he *had* to take the chance.

Usually, when Paul entered people's minds, he was in their present thoughts. If they were daydreaming about a beach, he found his toes curling in sand. Inside, he could go wherever he wanted, spy on whatever memories he found without permission. But he always started in their mind's current space.

But Mary was different.

When Paul entered her mind, he found himself in a small, dark vault, with her standing there, in all black, greeting him, like a guard determined to show him only permitted displays.

"What is this *truth* you want to show me?" Paul looked around at the vault's hundreds of lock boxes. A large circular door led to what seemed like another vault — perhaps where Mary held her deepest secrets. He had to admit it was an interesting, if not obvious, construct designed to safeguard her thoughts.

"I couldn't tell you in front of the Guardsman. If I did, you and your daughter's life would be in danger."

"*Really?* And why is that?"

"Emily doesn't want to be on this ship. She wants to be free."

"Liar!" Paul said. "What the hell did you do to her? Did you brainwash Emily, get her to buy into your rebellion?"

"We didn't do anything. See for yourself."

A flash, then the vault was a warehouse.

Paul watched as his daughter sat on the ground beside the old man-child that Desmond was obsessed with — Luca. The child with The Light, significantly aged.

Paul listened to them discussing The Island, her father, and a desire to be free of the aliens.

"So, what does this tell me? You took advantage of a confused little girl. She doesn't know anything about The Wastelands. She's an idealist without the first clue of the sacrifices I've made to keep her, to keep *us*, safe."

"I'm not judging," Mary said. "I'm showing you the truth. And no, we didn't *take advantage* of her. We told her to try and contact you on the ship, but she couldn't. Hell, *I* wanted to return her immediately."

"Where is she now?"

"Like I said, she was at the warehouse with the others. When your people attacked, I ran over to find out what was going on, and then you all grabbed me."

"So if she wasn't there, and wasn't at the Chandler House, where could she have gone? Could she have left with one of the others?"

Mary was thinking about someone. Now inside her head, he pulled at the frayed edges of that thought, hoping to unravel it and see for himself.

There was a man, Boricio. Mary's lover, also a sociopath. He'd taken a shining to Emily. He wasn't the male prisoner Paul had seen on the earlier video, which meant he was still down there, in The Wastelands — maybe with Emily.

"Where are they?" Paul asked, both hopeful and afraid.

"I don't know, but I do know one thing, Paul."

"What's that?"

"You better hope that nothing happens to me or Paola."

"Why is that?"

"Because you haven't seen anything when it comes to Boricio."

The second vault creaked open. From the other side, Paul heard screaming. Not just one or two bellows, but what felt like the anguished cries from thousands.

A fiery-orange glow painted the inside of their vault, as if this doorway led to Hell itself.

"W-what's that?" Paul's voice trembled.

"Why don't you have a look?"

Mary was now inches away. She spun him around then shoved Paul toward the open door.

As Mary pushed him closer, screams grew louder, men and women enduring things Paul's mind dared not imagine. He'd seen many atrocities since The Fall, but nothing was preparation enough for whatever waited inside the other vault.

Just when Paul thought the sounds couldn't get worse, something sent ice through his veins: the sound of a man laughing and … singing whimsically.

As they drew closer to the threshold, every fiber in Paul's being resisted.

He threw his hands out, pressing on the door, trying to keep Mary from shoving him inside.

"You wanted to see inside my head, right? Well, why don't you take a look into the mind of the man holding your daughter?"

"No!" Paul screamed, closing his eyes and throwing himself to the ground, making it harder for Mary to push him into the vault.

"Fine!" She slammed the door and silenced the screams.

Their vault was again dark and silent.

Paul looked up. "What was that?"

"That was a peek inside the head of the man with your daughter. I swear to God and all you hold holy, if anything happens to me or Paola, he'll make that seem like a children's birthday party in comparison."

Paul stood, trembling, staring at Mary, uncertain how to respond.

"I don't know what to do. I don't know how I can help you."

"You're going to find a way, Paul."

PAUL LEFT MARY'S CELL, afraid and shaking. What kind of monster was this Boricio? And how long could Emily possibly stay safe with him near? Further, what the hell did she expect him to do? Betray Desmond?

And do what, exactly?

It wasn't as if he could just set her, or her friends, free. Even if they did somehow get away, they were on a mothership with no less than one hundred armed Guardsmen aboard. And nearly a thousand aliens. The rebels were outgunned and outnumbered. It would be suicide to join them.

As he walked down the hall to the observation room where Desmond waited, Paul's fear gave way to indignation.

She wants to threaten my daughter? I'll show her. I'll find her precious Boricio and kill him in front of her.

Paul stepped into the cell.'

"So, what happened, Mr. Roberts?"

"I got inside her head."

"And?"

"A man has my daughter. His name is Boricio Wolfe, and he's very dangerous."

Desmond smiled. "I know this man well."

FIFTY-NINE

Boricio Wolfe

The girls were sitting with Boricio at the rectangular kitchen table, waiting for him to answer their question: *What do we do now?*

Boricio sat there, shoulders slumped, head in his hands, feeling **Fucked** with a capital F, bold, italicized, *and* highlighted.

It was the bottom of the ninth, and Team Fucking Boricio's entire squad was dead, wounded, or captured.

Mary was still missing, hopefully not gone forever.

Keenan was already rotting.

Marina had turned on them, likely hijacked by an alien.

Jazz was now just a body.

Barrow and Jevonne were both presumed dead.

And the alien cocksuckers had Luca, Brent, Teagan, and the kids.

The benches were clear, with zero pinch hitters on deck.

Boricio thought about putting a distress call to the other rebel teams, any who might answer, but all the best people were already dead or taken by the aliens. Only scrubs were left, and fuck a duck and watch it waddle if Boricio was going to war with scrubs at his back.

Lisa was a warrior, but she was also wounded, and Boricio wasn't sure how much she could take without ripping her fresh stitches and bleeding out all over the place.

He had to do this himself.

He had an awful idea, but you took what you had when you got it.

Boricio opened his eyes and answered the question.

"*What are we going to do?* We're going to do what we've always done. We're battered and broken, but we ain't dead and buried. We're gonna swing with all we have, and if that ain't enough to knock a fucker's head from his shoulders, well, at least we'll leave 'em ugly and scarred."

"Yeah, that's not exactly inspirational," Lisa said, sitting across from Boricio.

"Well, Hallmark fired me. You want inspiration, go dig up Tony Robbins and ask him to give you a ditty. This is all I've got."

"So, do you have a plan beyond *swinging with all we have?*"

"Yeah."

Lisa looked at Emily. "Do you believe this guy? Normally, you can't shut him up, but now that I want him to talk and give us details, he's all Silent Bob."

Boricio grinned. "I'm pretty sure you stole that line from me."

"I know who Kevin Smith is."

"You do?" Boricio was genuinely surprised. "I never pictured you as a cineffecianado."

"What *did* you picture? And that's not a word."

"I dunno. I figured you were a junior survivalist or some shit, learning to assemble rifles, hunt mammoth, maybe driving monster trucks, I dunno. And you knew what I meant; that makes it a word."

"You *so* don't know me."

Emily burst into their back-and-forth banter: "Will you

two get serious? What are we going to do? Luca and the others are in trouble."

Boricio turned to her. "I know. I'm just trying to shoot a few womp rats before heading to the Death Star."

Lisa sighed. "What's your plan?"

Boricio looked at them both then said, "You're not gonna like this."

"Come on," Lisa said.

Boricio turned to Emily. "Tell me, kid. Do you think you could teleport me, or you and me, onto the Death Star?"

"You mean the big ship?" Emily's eyes widened, as if the thought scared her. "I don't know."

"You teleported you and Luca somewhere, then you teleported away when the Guardsmen stormed the tunnel."

"Yeah, I did. But I couldn't control it either time. If I could have, I would've saved the others, too."

"Okay," Boricio said, "then onto Plan B."

Lisa said, "What's Plan B?"

"Me and the kid will head down to the docks. Guardsmen are always eyeing the area, as if someone would be dumb enough to boat on out to The Island. We'll be dumb enough and get ourselves caught."

"*Caught?*" Lisa asked.

"Yes, ma'am."

"Then what?"

"Not sure. I like to play things by ear."

"Going on the ship with no plan isn't playing things by ear, it's a suicide mission!"

"Ain't nobody bringing Boricio down."

"Okay, now you're just being stupid."

"Hey, it's got me this far in life." Boricio spread his hands wide to indicate their shitty surroundings in a rundown house.

"So, you're gonna get yourself caught and brought onto the ship. Then what? You think they're gonna hand you the keys to wherever the hell they're keeping Luca so you can walk in and escort everyone out? How do you know they won't kill you on the spot?"

"Because I won't let them."

Lisa turned to Emily. "What?"

"I won't let them. I can convince them to keep him alive."

"And then what?" Lisa asked.

"I don't know. They bring us on the ship, my father welcomes me with open arms, and I'll try and find some way to save Boricio, and the others, from the inside. Maybe we trick them into thinking that Boricio was trying to bring me to the ship in exchange for the others."

"They won't make an exchange," Lisa said flatly.

"I know they won't. But that could get us onboard. After that, we'll figure out what's next."

Boricio leaned back in his chair, turned to Lisa, and smiled. "Now *that* sounds like a fucking plan!"

He raised his hand to get a high-five from Emily. She stared at his open palm, clearly perplexed.

"It's a high-five. You never gave someone a high-five?"

Emily shook her head.

"Kids these days."

Lisa ignored him. "I don't like this. You're gonna get yourself killed. I'm going with you."

"So I can get *both* of us killed?"

"I won't take no for an answer."

"You're in no shape to come with us. That wound needs to heal before you're back in the field."

Lisa began to object, but Boricio shut her down.

"Sorry, princess. Me and Chewie are going without you. You're staying put."

"Here? In this house?"

"Well, we can't trust that our sites aren't compromised if the aliens are interrogating fuckers for information."

"What about your other teams?" Emily asked. "Aren't they compromised?"

"No, we don't have locations of any team other than Beta," Lisa explained. "They all operate as cells, more or less unaware of one another's identities and locations, to prevent a situation like this. I can call this in and report that the church is no longer a sanctuary, set something else up."

"Good," Boricio said. "You do that while I go see what I can scrounge up for you before we set out."

Boricio left the house and set out to find whatever food or medical supplies he could gather. Searching through the scant remains he could find, he tried not to consider his plan's many flaws.

He'd always rolled the dice and gone with his gut. He'd been joking when he said his cavalier attitude had got him that far in life, but there was plenty of truth to it, too. Sure, he was fucked up, but flying over the Cuckoo's Nest had kept him alive longer than most.

Others hemmed and hawed, analyzed shit for strengths and weaknesses. Boricio dove from the plane, parachute or no.

He'd find a way, like he always had before.

SIXTY

Brent Foster

Brent opened his eyes to the sound of Ben's crying.

His entire body, save for his head, was immobilized. He was also standing straight up, naked in a glowing red gelatinous goo holding him in place in some sort of black metal pod mounted to the wall.

He looked to his left, right, and across, seeing the others also confined in black pods, their entire bodies, save for their heads, in the glowing jelly-like material.

Ben was directly across from him, softly sobbing. Luca was between him and Becca, still asleep, if not dead. There was also a black metallic-looking brace around Luca's head, covering his mouth and nose, reminding Brent of Hannibal Lecter's mask in *The Silence of the Lambs*.

"It's going to be okay," Brent said to Ben, another in an endless string of lies.

Ben looked up. "No, it's not. They're going to kill us."

That drove Becca to tears.

Teagan, on Brent's left, said, "No they're not, honey. We're going to get out of this. Don't worry. You need to be strong. Can you do that for me?"

Ben sniffled, "I dunno."

Brent tried to help out. "We'll find a way out of this, guys. We always do. But for now, I need you to be quiet so I can think. Can you do that?"

They both nodded.

Brent surveyed their surroundings. They were in a long dark, narrow room that looked more like a corridor. The walls were black, red, and bumpy, with hundreds of small amber lights just under the surface. There were at least a dozen pods on each side, though the others were empty, of both people and jelly. He thought of the aliens' skin and how the walls seemed almost organic. He shivered, thinking of Jonah inside the belly of a whale.

The floor was a tough, bumpy black metal, like the roof. The room's only light came from the walls and the jelly holding them in place.

He strained to move his arms then found some momentary give. But then the jelly buzzed around him, seeming to tighten as if in response.

The walls began to make an odd swooshing that reminded Brent of the sound he'd heard when he went to the gynecologist's office with his wife and saw the ultrasound showing them Ben. The jelly in all of their pods began to pulsate, lights brightening and dimming in a pattern to match the swooshing.

"What is that?" Becca asked, starting to cry again.

"Nothing to worry about." Teagan's expression said she was merely hoping. Brent figured the kids could see through it.

He had nothing to substantiate his guess but spoke anyway. "I think it's keeping us hydrated and healthy. It's not trying to hurt us. If they wanted to hurt us, we'd be hurting already."

Ben said, "Maybe they're trying to fatten us up, to eat us."

And Becca, of course, cried. "I don't want them to eat me!"

"They're not going to eat us," Teagan assured her.

"How do you know?" Ben asked, probably disagreeing with Teagan to calm his fears.

Brent wasn't sure what to say. The way he saw it, Ben's assumption was as good as any other. Given what the aliens had already done to two worlds, their intent was surely malicious.

Still, that wasn't something they could tell the kids.

As the swooshing continued for another few minutes, Brent felt his exhaustion. Ben yawned, followed by Becca and Teagan.

Perhaps these pods weren't helping them after all. Maybe they were draining their energy.

Luca's pod glowed a brighter red than theirs. There was a sudden jolt as the cube came alive in a bright spiderweb of crimson lightning.

Luca's eyes shot open, and he looked up at them as if in shock.

Then, in an instant, his eyes closed again, and his head leaned lazily to the side.

The swooshing stopped, and the pod went dark again.

Brent had another theory. The pods weren't hydrating or keeping them healthy so much as using them as batteries to recover Luca's consciousness. And if that were the case, how long before they ran dry and were disposed of?

Brent watched the others drift off to sleep, trying his best to stay awake, as if doing so would keep anything bad from happening.

As if Brent could do anything at all.

～

SIXTY-ONE

Boricio Wolfe

It was nearing nightfall as Boricio and Emily navigated side streets and alleyways toward the docks.

Boricio carried a pistol, and a blade strapped to the small of his back. Emily carried a blade in a boot sheath, just in case they ran into any trouble along the way. In Boricio's experience, if shit could happen, it *would*, so as they drew closer to the docks, he found himself surprised that nothing had yet to stand in their way.

She'd spent the first half hour of their trek explaining the difference between the aliens they'd been calling The Darkness and the aliens who came on the ship, the Pruhm, all of it enlightening even if Boricio didn't quite know what to do with that info just yet.

"So, you really don't have a plan?" Emily asked.

"Nope."

"Are you always this impulsive?"

"Yep." Boricio grinned. "Before all the shit hit the fan, there were two kinds of men. Those who would spend months, or years sometimes, learning everything they could about something, never committing to anything until they knew every possible outcome. And then, and only if the situation was perfect, would they pledge allegiance to the plan. Then there were guys who didn't research shit. Guys who jumped into the fire. Guess which one I am."

"Interesting."

Boricio wasn't sure if Emily was being sarcastic or not and waited for her to say something else as they kept walking.

When she didn't say dick, he asked, "Really? You think that's interesting?"

"Yeah. I wish I could be that brave. I've spent years trying to figure out a way to get off the spaceship, a way that wouldn't cause problems for my father, and, well, I never would've done anything if you all hadn't come along."

"Well, don't feel too down on yourself. Hell, I'm not even saying my way's the right way for *everyone*. It just happened to work for me. There's something to be said for playing it safe."

Emily stared at him then said, "You don't really mean that."

Boricio grinned, "Nah, not really. Safe is for pussies. Fortune favors the bold."

Emily laughed.

Boricio liked the sound but told himself not to get too used to it. Soon, she'd be back on the ship, and the odds of her coming back with them were thinner than Kate Moss in a concentration camp.

"So," he asked, "let's say this all works out. You and your daddy figure a way to get us off the ship; what then?"

"I don't know. I was hoping we could come with you."

"You think your daddy's gonna want to leave his cushy spot in the sky for *this hellhole?*" He waved his hand across the torn-up roads, broken-down cars, and half-destroyed houses surrounding them.

"Then maybe we don't leave. Maybe we take the ship for ourselves."

Her eyes were bright and hopeful. Obviously, she'd been sitting on this idea for a while.

"Go on … "

"Well, as I said, there are a ton of Guardsmen and aliens onboard, so we're obviously outnumbered."

"So far, so good," Boricio joked.

"Well, I'm thinking they all answer to Desmond, right? I mean, there are aliens above him, but Desmond's basically running the show."

"Okay."

"And my father has a vital role. He's in charge of making sure the hosts are sufficiently softened when an alien takes over their body."

"Softened?"

"Yeah, the way he explained it is that the stronger a person's psyche, or the more messed up their life was, the harder it is for the aliens to stay in the body. After a while, the host rejects the alien. A lot of times, the host brain goes crazy and gets violent or suicidal. This doesn't just endanger the host but also the alien inside it. The Pruhm can be killed by stress from the host body. Dad uses his gifts to weaken resistance, to ensure hosts give the alien as few problems as possible."

Boricio nodded.

"So, in short, the aliens need my father. Maybe more than they need Desmond. So, what if we kill Desmond?"

"Oh, that's definitely part of my plan," Boricio said. "Let's say we do. What makes you think the aliens won't kill us? I mean, if Desmond's in charge, they must need him for something, right?"

"Desmond helped corral and control the Ferals after they killed most of the planet. He eliminated a lot of them, though I'm not sure how. Basically, he got them to stop reproducing and destroying all the resources, what they were designed to do. If he's done that job, then I'd say he's no longer needed, right?"

"Unless they still need him to keep these Ferals controlled.

If he's dead and these fuckers rise up, then everyone has a problem."

"I've been thinking about that," she said. "And I have a solution."

"What's that?"

"Luca."

"Luca?"

"Yes. I think I know why he's aged so much in a few years. I saw it in his memories when we were in each other's heads. He's been spreading himself, The Light, among the humans *and* the Ferals."

"What? When the hell did he do this? He's with us all the time."

"He's been leaving at night, when no one is watching. Teleporting out of your hideout, going out and spreading The Light. He didn't want to tell any of you because he was afraid you'd disapprove."

"That little shit."

"Are you mad at him?"

"Fuck no. I think Boy Wonder might just save this stinking rock!"

Emily smiled.

Boricio patted her on the back. "Remember that shit I said about people who think too much being pussies? Forget it, kid. You've got a great head on your shoulders."

"Thanks. And I didn't even tell you the best part of the plan."

"What's that?"

"I'm going to kill Desmond."

"You're *what?*"

"I'm the only one who can get close enough that they'd never suspect."

Boricio shook his head. "Um, I don't think so."

"What?"

"I don't like this part of the plan. It's like you promised me dinner and took me to Arby's. Everything else, perfect — but this, no bueno."

"It's the only thing that will work."

"No, we'll find another way."

"Why? Because I'm a kid? You think I can't kill someone?"

Boricio stopped in the middle of the street and turned to face her with his sternest expression. "You ever killed someone?"

"No, but — "

"No buts. It's a yes-or-no question, no qualifiers."

"I can kill him."

"Listen, you're a nice kid. You're smart, funny, and you've got balls. But you have no clue what it's like to end someone's life."

"He's not a person. He's an alien."

"Still."

"I'm not taking no for an answer! I can do it."

"Killin' ain't something you can do on a whim. It's either in you, or it ain't. You should leave the killin' to people who are good at it. Who have done it before. Who have a thirst for it."

"I have a thirst for it."

Boricio laughed.

"I do! These aliens killed my mother with their plague! They've taken over the bodies of kids I was friends with. I've spent the last year going to bed every night wishing there was something someone would do to get rid of them. And now there *is* something, something that *we* can do. That *I* can do!"

Boricio sighed, not wanting to consider Emily's offer but unable to help it. "I'll think about it. If there's no other way. But if there is another way, you've got to stand down and let the grown-ups take care of it. Ya dig?"

Emily nodded, though he felt like she was likely trying to placate him. He'd have to look out for her doing something stupid, which might ruin his hatching plan.

"I'm serious. You've gotta let me do my thing. And if I can't, then it's your turn. But if you try first, and fail, you'll screw this up for everyone. And they *will* kill you and your father, both. Comprende?"

Emily nodded again, lower lip jutting out, eyes on the ground. This time, as they continued on their journey, Boricio felt like maybe she understood.

After another ten minutes, they reached a clearing of scorched land stretching for nearly six hundred yards before giving way to the docks.

"That's where we're headed." Boricio stopped just inside the tree line and pointed to the docks. There were no boats, all of them either destroyed or taken to The Island. Yet Boricio routinely saw ships flying over the area, searching for those dumb enough to come. "You ready?"

Emily nodded.

"Now, we don't want to fight unless it looks like they're gonna kill us instead of bringing us in."

"Right." Emily nodded.

He met her eyes and said, "Thank you for doing this. I promise, one way or another, this shit ends tonight."

She smiled.

As they started crossing the field, Boricio heard the last sound in the world he wanted to hear: the galloping of horses behind them.

He turned to see ten of the ugliest motherfuckers this side of a *Mad Max* cast audition, approaching fast. In moments, they were circling Boricio and Emily, weapons drawn. Some had spears, some had swords, but their leader, at least judging from the number of his tattoos, was holding a rifle.

"Well, well, look what we got here, boys. A purty little thang, indeed."

Emily pressed herself against Boricio, unable to mask her fear. Unfortunately for her, fear was candy to assholes.

SIXTY-TWO

Will Bishop

Will didn't remember waking up early, leaving the cabin where the others were sleeping, or even walking to the Black Tree. Yet he was here, again, as he'd been nearly every morning since arriving in The Realm — the name he'd given the world where they woke after dying on Earth.

When he first opened his eyes here, Will had hoped he was in Heaven, not that he'd had much faith in such a place any longer. Yet when Will couldn't find his true love, Sam, he figured this couldn't be Heaven.

For a while, he thought perhaps this was some kind of purgatory, and he waited for some sign that he was ready to move on.

His first visit to the tree, that he remembered anyway, brought him visions of Callie, hiding from bleakers in a house, bleakers that only existed in her mind. He led her to the cabin, helped her get better and exorcise the demons plaguing her soul.

For a long time, the tree offered nothing more, even though Will found himself there every morning.

No answers as to where they were, or why they were there. It still felt like Purgatory to him.

Soon, other visits to the tree brought him Jade, then Ed. Callie insisted that they go out and search for Charlie. They had, but the woods and path both seemed endless in all directions.

So when the tree brought him visions of Charlie yesterday, Will felt like something was about to happen.

As he kneeled at the tree, Will looked up at its many skeletal branches reaching up to morning's first violet light.

Dread filled his veins as he placed his hand on the trunk, hoping he wouldn't see visions of Luca, Paola, or Mary. As much as Will would enjoy their company, their presence would mean they were dead.

A tremor moved under the tree's thick black bark. Beneath the bark, he saw the briefest glimmer of lights.

Will yanked his hand back, thinking of the last place he'd seen such lights: under the aliens' skin.

He stared at the tree, watching as light faded and the bark returned to its normal appearance. He hesitated touching it again — part of him afraid of what he'd see. Not just a part, *all* of him.

They'd grown comfortable with one another here. And something told him that was about to change. That this purgatory wasn't forever.

But what did that mean?

Touch the tree, and find out.

Will inched his fingers closer but couldn't bring himself to touch the bark.

You can't fight Fate. Touch the tree to discover what's next.

He closed his eyes and slapped his palm on the tree.

They came in a violent flash, bright and awful.

Will fell away from the tree and stared up at it, wondering how he would deliver the bad news to the cabin's crew.

~

SIXTY-THREE

Boricio Wolfe

If the bandit fucks had approached Boricio alone, he wouldn't have hesitated in the slightest to put each in a grave carefully crafted for their particular needs. But having to protect Emily limited his options considerably.

The group's leader looked down from his horse and asked, "What are you all doing out here on this lovely evening?"

Boricio's gun was in his holster. He could easily squeeze off a shot or four, but there were too many bandits to account for, surrounding them, with half of the ten riders behind him.

"We don't want no trouble. Just out looking for somewhere to stay the night."

"She can stay with me," one of them said, a fat man with long dark hair and an equally long beard.

The other men laughed. Some made lewd comments about how she could stay with them, too.

Boricio wanted to tear the tongues from their bodies, gouge out their eyes, and shove them right up their cornholes. But again, he was hamstrung by the kid.

"Tell you what," Tattoo Man said, "you put those weapons on the ground, and we'll let you go on your way."

Boricio looked up at the ugly fucker and smiled. "I put down my weapons, you'll gut me and take her."

More laughter from the *Mad Max* rejects.

"Or," said a man from behind, "we could gut you now and take her."

A revolver clicked behind him.

"Fine, fine," Boricio said, slowly turning to face the man who'd cocked his gun. Another big fat ugly fuck, with a broken nose and a face that even his mother would hate. Boricio wanted to crack a joke and ask how so many of them were fat enough for neck deodorant when most of The Wastelands struggled to find food. But that would just get him shot quicker.

Then Boricio remembered that he was with a girl who could teleport herself away when shit hit the fan. Maybe there was a way out, after all. Boricio pushed a thought from his mind, hoping Emily was tuned in. *If you can blink out of here, do it now.*

He drew his gun and made like he was about to set it on the ground.

Instead, he fired at the left front leg of the horse carrying Broken Nose.

And in a flash, Emily was gone.

Now it's party time!

The bullet hit, causing the horse to whinny as it reared up on its back legs and sent Broken Nose to the ground.

The other horses reacted as well — some rearing up, others turning to run.

Boricio raised his pistol and fired at the leader's horse, right in the chest.

The horse made a god-awful bray as it threw Tattoo Man off and crashed to the ground.

Boricio leaped on top of the man, shoved the pistol against his head, and fired.

Gunshots zipped past him, kicking up dirt to his left and right.

Only a matter of time before his targets stopped missing.

Boricio spun around amid the chaos of tromping horses, searching for the shooter, found the fucker standing thirty feet away, and fired two shots.

Boricio didn't miss either of them.

Boricio turned to find his next target when out of the corner of his eye he saw a big, black blur — a horse — coming right at him, with one of the bandit fuckers laughing maniacally.

The horse slammed into him then barreled over Boricio, trampling him as he went.

Boricio felt like he'd been hit by a truck, but there was no time to inventory aches or pains. He had to stand and fight.

But his pistol was gone.

He scanned the ground and heard galloping coming his way.

Boricio looked up in time to see that same fucker on horseback returning to finish the job.

He jumped out of the way, barely in time, and rolled to the ground.

Luck, for a change, was on Boricio's side.

He landed right beside his pistol.

He fired at the horse's ass — an easier target than the jockey — and watched the horse rear up with a piercing *wheeee*, sending the man from its back.

Boricio fired, missing at first, and kept squeezing the trigger until his magazine was empty and the fucker was down.

Boricio grabbed the blade at his back and spun around, searching for any asshole who wanted to step in the ring.

But the horses were all galloping off, and the bandits on foot were retreating.

Boricio laughed, dusting his hands off: a day's work done.

He looked around for Emily, hoping she hadn't teleported too far away.

Something moved behind him.

Boricio turned, just in time to see the bat flying at his head.

It missed, just barely, as Boricio fell to the ground.

The bandit, a giant ginger cunt of a man, swung again before Boricio could escape, hitting him hard in the ribs.

"Fuck!" Boricio screamed, and collapsed to the ground.

He flipped himself over, quickly, before Ginger Cunt could swing again.

But he wasn't swinging.

The man leaped on top of Boricio, straddling him, trading his bat for a hammer.

As the hammer came at his face, Boricio swung his left arm up to block it then came in with his right hand, holding the blade, stabbing it straight into the man's right arm.

Ginger Cunt screamed, yanking his arms back and dropping the hammer.

Boricio tried to retrieve his blade, but it was stuck in the man's arm. He threw two jabs into his gut instead then reached down to squeeze the asshole's nuts.

Ginger Cunt didn't back down. Instead, he pulled the knife from his arm and came at Boricio's throat.

Boricio moved quickly, almost blindly, raising his hands and seizing Ginger Cunt's wrists, stopping the blade just inches over his chest.

They were in a mortal struggle, with Ginger Cunt pressing down with all his weight, trying to plunge the knife into Boricio.

His mind scrambled, searching for some way to get the fucker off of him, but Boricio couldn't think of anything that wouldn't give the man the leverage.

Their eyes locked.

Ginger Cunt's bloodlust was deep.

Spit flew from his mouth as he growled, pushing harder.

Boricio's hands shook as the blade inched toward his chest.

Boricio grunted, trying to push back.

The blade pressed into his flesh.

No!

The man's eyes went wide with shock.

He released the knife and reached up to his head, where a knife was sticking out the back of his skull.

Emily stood behind the man, staring, horrified at what she'd done.

Ginger Cunt started to rise, as if he were going to pull the blade out of his head, turn around, and stab Emily.

Boricio's eyes spotted the fallen hammer, seized it, and brought it up fast, right into Ginger Fuck's cheek.

Direct impact with his eye socket.

The man screamed, falling back and off of Boricio.

Boricio leaped to his feet and brought the hammer down again and again, smashing Ginger Fuck's skull and face, over and over until he was sure the fucker was down, without any identifiable eyes, nose, or mouth.

Boricio's heart raced as he turned, searching for anything else that needed a killin'.

Then he heard the loud jet-like engines above, approaching fast.

Shuttles on their way.

Soon, he and Emily would be aboard the alien ship — assuming the Guardsmen didn't see his bloody body and take him for the threat Boricio was. In which case, he'd be put down like one of the horses.

~

SIXTY-FOUR

Paul Roberts

Paul watched as the shuttle doors opened and his daughter stepped out into the cargo bay, escorted by a pair of Guardsmen.

"Oh, God, Emily!" He ran and embraced her, tears rolling down his cheeks.

"You're alive!"

He kissed Emily all over her face, hugged her tighter, then pulled away, looking her up and down for signs of abuse.

"Did they hurt you? Did *he* hurt you?" Paul glared at Boricio being led from the shuttle by another two Guardsmen, hands cuffed behind his back.

Paul ran up to Boricio and got in his face. "I swear to God if you hurt her, I will kill you."

Boricio gave him an asshole's grin — the smug sort that said he thought Paul was all bark and no bite.

Paul would make him regret that grin.

"He didn't do anything, Dad," Emily whined behind him. "He wanted to return me, in exchange for the others."

"So, how 'bout it, Pops? You gonna let my friends go?"

Paul ignored Boricio, turned to Emily, and said, "We need

to get you to medical. You must be starving, dehydrated, and sleep deprived."

"I'm fine, Dad."

"Just the same, you need to get to medical." Paul needed to get Emily out of the room so he could deal with Boricio without interference.

"I'm fine."

"Take her to medical, get a full work-up," Paul told the two Guardsmen who escorted Emily from the shuttle.

"Yes, sir," they said.

Emily whined about wanting to stay, but Paul didn't have time for her mewling. She was back, and safe. These bastards would never hurt her again.

"Where do you want him?" one of the Guardsmen asked.

Before Paul could respond, Desmond emerged from the control booth, hands folded in front of him, pleased smile on his face.

"Take him to the chambers, with the others."

Paul watched as Boricio stared Desmond down. Such hate, so powerful, Paul could feel it wafting off the man in waves.

Desmond maintained a civil smile, though Paul could see a certain glee in his eyes at capturing this particular man.

～

SIXTY-FIVE

It

It stood in The Black Room, waiting for The Leader to show himself. *It* wasn't sure if the lack of chairs in The Black Room was a slight against *It*, or if the aliens kept the room free of chairs so as not to interfere with the energies coursing through the large circular chamber near the ship's crown.

The Black Room was named for its utter lack of light, except for the pulsating amber selvions buried within the walls and floors in the mid and upper levels. The selvions powered everything from the created aliens like *It* and the Ferals to the starship's organic sections. *It* was bioengineered on the aliens' home planet but was also sentient and helped in the aliens' replication.

It watched the lights pulsate faster and brighter, indicating that The Leader was coming.

Its heart raced faster.

The circular door slid open, and The Leader — largest and grayest of the centipede-moth creatures — entered, its spindly legs skittering along the black floor, lights pulsating beneath its body.

"Hello, Leader," *It* greeted the creature.

I'm told you have the boy.

"Yes, he is with the other prisoners. His mouth and nose are covered so The Light cannot escape. We finally have him. We're close to winning this war against The Light."

And how do you plan to do this?

"We will break him or coerce him by harming, or killing, the others. Then we'll get him to lure the Ferals into a trap. Herd them all into The Wastelands and blast that spot to hell. After that, nothing will stand in our way."

Do you think he can lure them all? Or is this only theory?

"The collective will answer to me, and the Ferals will answer to him. Between us, we can take care of them all."

Good. And once you're done, I want them all in The Cell. We can't risk The Light ever escaping.

"Of course."

The Cell was a pit in the bottom of the ship where no energy could escape. While it would serve as a perfect prison for their enemies, The Cell would also serve *Its* ultimate goal — to somehow turn The Light and absorb it into *Itself*. Then *It* would dispose of The Leader and his ilk before they inevitably turned on *It*.

The Pruhm wanted to enslave humans, no different than they've been doing for millennia. *It* planned an evolutionary leap to marry the best of both species.

Anyone standing in *Its* way would force themselves into extinction.

~

SIXTY-SIX

Boricio Wolfe

One minute, Boricio was being led away in cuffs; the next, he was waking up in some sort of pod in a long, dark chamber straight out of Hell.

He looked around, seeing the others: Brent, Teagan, the kids, and Luca. The kids were directly across from him, ready for Halloween in some sort of fucked-up masks.

"What the hell is this?" Boricio tried but failed to move in the alien marmalade.

Brent said, "My guess it's some kind of system where they're draining our energy to try and wake Luca."

"Is he alive? He don't look too good."

"He woke up once but then passed right back out," Teagan said.

Boricio looked at the kids, what he could see of their sad faces in the pods.

Poor bastards. What kind of fuckers do this to kids?

"How ya doing, Goonies?"

"Not good," Ben said, voice tired, eyes lacking any sign of life.

Becca didn't answer.

Last time Boricio had seen these kids on a trip to The

Farm, they were running around, laughing, somehow finding a way to *be kids* despite living lives in an alien apocalypse. Now they seemed as broken as their parents.

Boricio said, "We're gonna make these bitches hurt when they dookie."

"Do you have a plan?" Teagan asked.

Boricio wasn't sure if there were cameras, or any way to monitor them hidden among the alien flesh walls. So he winked and said, "No, but trust me. We *will* get out."

Brent asked, "Where are the others?"

"Well, let's see … Marina was infected and sold us out. Pretty sure she killed Barrow and Jevonne. Mary, I have no idea. Lisa either." Boricio left out details of Lisa's injury in case someone was listening, going right to the one that would hurt Brent and Teagan most. "And Keenan … well, he didn't make it."

Brent stared, tears welling in his eyes. "Dammit."

Teagan closed her eyes. Boricio couldn't tell if she was crying.

Becca cried, "We're all going to die."

Ben started crying, too.

This shit was too much for Boricio.

He didn't know which verbal treasures were apt to calm kids, especially ones as young as these. At least he could reason with Paola. But she hadn't been prone to crying tangents.

Boricio was trying to think of something a bit more inspirational than, "Kiss your asses goodbye, we're fucked," when the door slid open and Desmond entered the chamber.

Boricio turned to the alien cocksucker, glaring, but momentarily holding his tongue. He wasn't sure where Emily was with her part of the plan, if she'd pulled her daddy onboard or was still aiming to kill Desmond herself. He hoped not on the latter — that was a Hail Mary and a half sorta move, and he'd made that perfectly clear.

Either way, Boricio would have to watch his lip to keep

them all from getting killed. If he fucked up, then Emily's plan would fall apart faster than a bitch agreeing to "just the tip," whatever it was.

Emily's father stood behind Desmond. Boricio wondered if she'd had a chance to talk to him, convince him to help them out. Probably not. The schlumpy fuck was frozen, staring at them all, seemingly awaiting orders like one of Hitler's Youth.

Boricio tried to send another thought to Emily, wherever she was.

Did you talk to your daddy yet?

He tried sending a visual of what they were dealing with, their collective confinement in pods on the wall.

He had no fucking clue how this telepathy shit worked. He'd experienced it a couple of times but had never felt like he could control it, or direct the conversation. And that was with Luca and Paola, people he was connected with. Not Emily.

Hell, he wasn't even sure if it was his message that got her to teleport away when he decided to go for broke with the bandit fucks.

He waited to hear some kind of response, hoping to hear the girl's voice in his head.

Nothing.

Desmond walked over to Boricio, smiling his toothy fucking grin. "Ah, if it isn't the infamous Boricio Wolfe! Finally, my collection of Luca's pets is complete."

Boricio glared at Desmond, biding his time.

Keep talking, fucker. It's only gonna make what I do to you all the worse.

Desmond looked Boricio up and down.

"You were one of our favorite bodies to be in, despite the destruction in your mind. So, so messed up."

Boricio finally bit. "Sorry. Why don't you hop back in and give me another chance?"

Desmond laughed. "Nice try. But I think I'll stay where I am."

Desmond paced, looking at them all as if making internal calculations.

"Why don't we just cut to the chase and you tell us why we're all here?" Boricio said. "You looking for the best place to shoot it?"

"You're here, Mr. Wolfe, because you are all going to help me convince Luca of what he must do."

"Ah, well, why didn't you just say so? Wake him up, and let's chat. Then we can all be on our merry way."

Desmond looked at Boricio, no indication in his eyes of what his plans for them might be after he got what he wanted. With most people, you could tell by their reaction if they intended to kill you. Most people, save for crazy fucks like Boricio, would look away, if even for a fraction of a second, like they couldn't quite come to terms with the horrible shit they intended to do. But Desmond was a blank slate. Hard to tell if he'd have any remorse for killing a couple of kids. Hell, the aliens probably didn't regard humans any better than humans regarded insects: pests to be dealt with. Your boot didn't flinch for the roach.

Desmond said, "Yes, let's get on with it."

The walls pulsed red, and a loud swooshing echoed in the room. Almost immediately, Boricio felt his energy fading. Within twenty seconds, staying awake was nearly impossible. He remembered Brent's comment, that the boxes were a way to give their energy to Luca.

Brent, Teagan, and the kids nodded off — at least Boricio hoped they were only nodding off and not dropping dead — within another minute.

Boricio yawned, trying his best to stay awake.

Do not fall asleep.

Stay the fuck awake.

"What the hell is this?" Boricio asked.

Desmond answered, "We're waking The Light."

Suddenly, a scream.

Luca was awake.

~

SIXTY-SEVEN

Emily Roberts

Emily sat in the doctor's room, waiting for Dr. Blaire to return and complete her examination. The doctor was one of the few people who worked on the ship that Emily didn't think was hosting an alien. But that didn't make her trust the woman any more than the others.

After checking her vitals, Dr. Blaire had asked Emily a series of questions pertaining to her time with the "rebels."

While Emily had tried her best to pretend that these people were her enemies, for appearances' sake, there must've been something she hadn't managed to hide — something that tipped the doctor off. The woman excused herself almost immediately, telling Emily she'd be right back.

Emily stared at the door, wondering if she tried to open it if she'd find it locked.

Get out. Now, before she comes back.

No, stay put, play it cool. If I get up, I'll screw everything up.

Emily hadn't even had time to talk to her father, and needed to get him alone and figure out how to help Luca, Boricio, and the others — or kill Desmond.

She'd spent the past half hour or so since arriving in the

doctor's office trying to come up with a way to get her father to help. It would take convincing, but Emily was hopeful that she'd be able to sway him. He played the loyalist well, but Emily knew that if he could see a way to end the alien occupation, he'd do it. His biggest concern, of course, would be protecting her. He wouldn't want to do anything that might endanger his daughter, like betraying Desmond and the aliens.

But if he thinks we stand a chance at toppling them. If I show him what Boricio is capable of … maybe.

She thought of her father's overreaction to Boricio when they got off the shuttle, how he'd stormed over, an embarrassing, overprotective father who didn't know what he was talking about. She was furious but had to hide that fury lest her sympathies be too evident.

How do I get past his rage? He must be so scared.

Emily had only one option. She had to show him everything that Luca had shown her.

If he sees that, if he sees the good in these people, and what they'd been through, there's no way he'll deny my request. He'll have to help. Yeah, we'll need to figure out how to kill Desmond, but if I can convince him of the need, he will find a way.

The door opened.

Emily turned, startled, certain she'd see a Guardsman with the doctor. Or heck, maybe Desmond: *We're onto you, Miss Roberts. Come with us, please.*

But the doctor was alone, carrying a transparent box with four bottles of clear liquid.

Emily tried to hide her relief. "So, doc, how am I?"

"Good. You're a bit low on electrolytes, but otherwise, fine. I'm going to give you some liquids."

She handed them to Emily. "Drink one a day, along with your normal rations, then come back and see me. Okay?"

"Okay." Emily stood, eager to leave the office. "Thank you."

Emily rushed as fast as she dared without drawing attention, searching for her father. She figured he was either in his office or busy with the prisoners. Emily was hoping for the former so she could get to him before he went in to see them, and maybe work out some sort of plan.

Emily made her way to the elevator, and as the doors closed, tried sending a message to her father, letting him know she was coming.

She commanded the elevator to take her to his floor.

The door hissed shut.

Then something stopped the door from closing.

Marina, wearing Black Guardsman gear except for a helmet, stepped into the elevator. The door closed, trapping Emily in the box alongside her.

"Hello, Emily. You got away from me once today. That won't happen again."

"I don't know what you're talking about."

"I've told Desmond about your alliance with the rebels."

"What are you talking about? I was a prisoner."

"I heard you talking."

Emily wasn't sure if Marina was bluffing, or if she'd been around when Emily was talking to them about not wanting to be on the ship. She couldn't remember what she said or who was around.

Emily decided on a bold approach, one she'd seen her father take a few times with people attempting to get on his bad side. "I don't know what you *think* you heard, but I would've said anything to keep them from killing me. Why don't you come with me to talk to my father so we can straighten this out?"

"We never cared much for your father ... or talking."

A quick movement, so fast Emily didn't register what it was until the blade entered her gut then drove up.

"Help!" Emily gasped, dropping the bottles of electrolytes.

Marina pushed the blade higher, eyes boring into Emily's, watching her slump to the ground, consciousness fading, a blur spreading from the edges of her vision.

The elevator opened.

Marina turned and left Emily dying on the floor.

SIXTY-EIGHT

Luca Harding

Luca woke to see the enemy staring at him, his friends all held captive, a mask fitted tight to his face.

His head swam in confusion, dull with pain. Everything was blurred and double. A horrible swooshing sound wreaked further havoc in his head.

The Darkness in Desmond's form approached, eyes wide in delight.

"Now," Desmond said, "before you get any thoughts of teleporting away, or teleporting your friends out of here, know that doing so will kill them."

Luca wasn't sure if Desmond was bluffing, or how exactly teleporting them out could get them killed. But he wasn't about to take any chances.

Luca nodded.

Emily's father stood behind Desmond. Luca recognized him from her memories. He'd been brought here to decay Luca's resolve, to get him to do something. Luca could feel it on the man's thoughts, which were practically bleeding into air around him.

He looked up to see Boricio struggling in the jelly that held him in his pod. He could feel the man's anger rolling from his body.

Relax, Luca thought to him. *Save your energy.*

It was tough to tell if Boricio heard the thoughts. He kept glaring at Desmond, black waves still roiling in fumes.

Desmond stared at Luca then looked at the others. "Why are you obsessed with saving humanity?"

Luca asked, "Why are you so obsessed with *destroying* it?"

"I'm *not* destroying it. I am supplanting it. Their time is over. It's time for a new species to take custody of this planet. It's not like they were taking care of this world, right?"

Desmond went over to Boricio, grabbed him by the hair, and yanked his head up to face him. "You've seen how these animals treat one another. And yet you side with them over your true nature?"

Luca knew that Desmond wasn't talking to him, but rather The Light.

But The Light wasn't responding. Luca couldn't sense it inside him at all — the first time in a long while that he hadn't. Sure, he'd felt it less and less during the last few months, but it was always present. Now, he felt alone in his body, unable to feel the connection to his friends.

What's happening?

Are you there?

Nothing. Could The Light have died? Or was this pod somehow restricting The Light's presence?

Desmond shoved Boricio's head back, then turned away from him. "What was it you hoped to do, spread your seed around this barren wasteland? Did you think you could save them from their fate? Did you think you could stop evolution?"

"You are not evolution," Luca said. "You are annihilation. There is a distinction. In your world, humans are hosts with no free will. Vessels. No lives worth living."

"Says the alien residing in a boy. Wait, not residing in, but *parasitically thriving in.* And how is that working out for poor Luca? How old are you supposed to be? Twelve? Yet you have the body of a withered old man. Tsk-tsk. Your hypocrisy knows no bounds, *Light.* You call us *Darkness,* as if we're different. But we both know that's a lie. You are no different than us. You *are* us, but too blind to see it. We are one and the same, created by our masters with a singular job — cultivate this species into something they can use."

Luca's headache turned into an ice pick.

Someone was trying to get inside his head.

He looked up to see the guilty party: Emily's father. That's why he was standing there. While Desmond distracted Luca, the man was probing, picking at the edges to find a way inside.

Luca pushed him out. Whatever Desmond wanted couldn't be good for any of them.

Paul flinched, shaking his head, momentarily rattled by Luca's resistance.

Desmond looked at Paul. "Can't get in?"

"Let me try again."

"I have a better idea." Desmond touched the communicator on his shoulder and said, "Bring the girls."

Girls?

Luca and Boricio traded a glance. The swooshing held its incessant drone. They were all asleep, except Boricio. Luca could feel their lives slipping away. These pods were designed to sap their will, feeding their energies into him.

"Turn off the machine!" Luca demanded. "You're going to kill them."

"Again, with the interest for these insects. We wanted to make sure you were awake enough to do what we need you to do."

"I mean it," Luca said, staring Desmond down. Though his body was frail and he hardly had the energy to speak, much less intimidate, he did his best to sell his sincerity. "I don't know what you want, but if you kill them, you won't get it."

Desmond looked at Paul.

Paul nodded.

Moments later, the swooshing stopped, likely controlled by Desmond's mind.

The machine was off, but everyone other than Boricio was still unconscious. Which was probably a good thing for their sakes. He hated that the others, particularly the kids, were here, being used as leverage for whatever plot The Darkness had.

The door opened, and a dead girl entered.

Luca stared at Paola, unable to believe his eyes.

She and her mother were marched in at gunpoint, both of their hands cuffed behind them, a Guardsman standing with a mean-looking rifle.

Boricio gasped. "What the fuck?"

Desmond turned, "Yes, when you all left poor Paola for dead, we saved her. Yes, that's right, *we* saved her, the big bad Darkness, when your precious *Light* failed you. She's been living with us, happily I might add, ever since."

Boricio said, "What kinda beer-battered bullshit are you trying to pull?"

"Go ahead," Desmond said, "tell him."

"It's true," she said, nervously.

"It is." Mary looked at Luca then Boricio. "It's really her. She's back."

Luca tried connecting with Paola, the girl who had momentarily served as a vessel for The Light. The girl who had been the first life he'd ever saved. They had an unbreakable bond, yet he had failed to sense her. He'd assumed she was dead, and yet here she was.

But when he couldn't connect, Luca wondered if maybe this was some sort of trickery — or beer-battered bullshit — as Boricio said.

Maybe he couldn't connect for the same reason he couldn't sense The Light inside him. Something about this room was dampening his abilities. Or … The Light was gone.

Please, answer me, he called out to anyone who might hear him — The Light, Boricio, Paola, someone to let him know that he wasn't as alone as he felt.

"Now," Desmond said, "this is what's going to happen. I want you to connect with the Ferals and send them to the church you were all using as a sanctuary. You know the location, correct?"

Luca nodded.

"Good. You do that, and I will allow all to live. If you refuse, I will kill everyone you are trying so hard to protect, children first."

Luca's heart raced. Panic bloomed inside him. He couldn't even connect with The Light; how on earth was he supposed to connect with the things he'd spread The Light into? He couldn't even feel them.

"I can't call them."

"Please, Luca, don't lie. I really don't want to make you watch Paola die again. They say the third time's a charm, right? Afraid it won't be for her."

"I'm not lying. I can't feel The Light."

"Guard," Desmond said.

The Guardsman aimed his rifle at Paola.

"No!" Mary yelled, throwing herself between them.

Desmond reached out, grabbed Mary by the shoulders, spun her around, then threw her against the wall, hard.

Mary was down, faced away from Luca, blood pooling from under her long hair.

"Mom!" Paola screamed.

She tried running to her mom, but Desmond grabbed her by the hair, holding her in place as the Guardsman aimed his rifle at her head until she stopped trying to move.

"You fuck!" Boricio screamed, face boiling red, spittle flying from his mouth.

Desmond laughed. "Ah, not so big and scary now, are you? Just another insect with little brainpower and impotent rage."

Desmond turned back to Luca.

"So, Luca, would you prefer to keep lying, or are you willing to do what I requested?"

Please, Luca cried out again, *answer me*.

And then he heard Emily.

~

SIXTY-NINE

Will Bishop

When Will returned to the cabin, Charlie and Callie were sitting on the porch swing, arm in arm, deep in conversation, as happy as two lovers could be.

He hated what he had to do next, particularly when these people — Charlie and Callie; and Ed and his daughter, Jade — had barely reunited.

He passed Charlie and Callie, went inside and found Ed sitting at the kitchen table, eating breakfast with Jade.

"Hey, guys," he said. "We need to talk."

Ed looked up, a wary look in his eyes that seemed to know that this thing — whatever they thought it might be — was about to end.

"What is it?" Jade asked.

"I'll tell you all at once."

Will didn't wait for anyone to stand. He turned and headed out the front door, down the steps, so he was facing the home's front when Ed and Jade emerged.

Charlie and Callie sat up straighter, sensing that their attention was needed.

"Guys," he began, "I'm not sure how to say this, but we have to leave."

"Leave?" Charlie said, "I just got here."

"Me, too." Ed hugged his daughter.

Jade, purple hair hanging over one eye, asked, "Go where, Will? I thought we were in Heaven, Purgatory, or something."

"It's not what you think it is. And we can't stay any longer."

Charlie stood up, "If it's not Heaven or Purgatory, what is it?"

"It'll be easier to show you," Will said.

He retraced his steps to the tree, knowing the others would follow.

This was the first time Will had ever been conscious when he walked to the Black Tree, and was surprised how close it was to their cabin, even though he'd never seen it in any of his walks around the woods. Not that reality held any sway in this place.

He arrived at the tree to find the half-there, half-not girl with curly brown hair and big green eyes.

He knew her name even though he didn't know her. He'd seen her in the vision.

"Emily?" he said.

She looked up, surprised to see him.

Will could hear the others, who had been slow to follow, finally arriving. He didn't bother to turn. He knew that they were seeing what he was — this girl in front of the massive black tree.

The tree had no leaves, just thousands of blood-red roses.

"Are you Will?" She looked at the others. "Charlie, Callie, Ed, and Jade. I saw you all … in Luca's memories."

She looked around, saw the tree. "Why am I here? Am I dead?"

"Not quite," Will said, knowing she was close but not quite there. He saw in the vision what had happened to her body. He also saw the room where Luca and the others were being held with the abomination.

Will swallowed. "You're here to send a message to the others."

~

SEVENTY

Luca Harding

As Emily's voice spoke in his head, Luca noticed that Paul and Boricio were staring into space, eyes wide, as if they were receiving her words too.

Daddy, I'm dying. But whatever you do, don't let Desmond know.

Desmond looked at Luca. "So, are you ready to do what I want, or are you going to watch these people die?"

He aimed the rifle at Paola's head.

Mary begged him not to hurt her daughter. "Please, kill me. Not her."

Emily's voice told them each what they had to do.

Luca's job was the hardest and easiest of all.

He only had to die.

SEVENTY-ONE

Paul Roberts

At first, Paul thought it was some sort of trick, but when Emily flashed a vision of herself lying on the elevator floor, bleeding out, it was too real to dismiss.

He thought back: *What happened?*

It doesn't matter. All that matters now is that you do exactly what I tell you to do. And you can't question it. The man said if you do this, I'll live. But if you don't, we'll all die.

Desmond was asking Luca if he was ready to do what was required. Paul was only peripherally aware, attempting to focus on Emily's words over the sudden fear overwhelming his system.

Telepathic connections were difficult to maintain in even the calmest conditions. Having his daughter dying on the ship, telling him that he had to do exactly as instructed, only added to the choppy waters.

When Boricio distracts Desmond, you must kill Luca.

Kill Luca?

You have to. It's the only way. Please, Daddy, tell me you'll do it.

Paul stared at the old frail body. He had no qualms killing to save his daughter, particularly an enemy. But a small part of him was afraid that this was a trap — that Luca was somehow getting in his head, posing as his daughter. He could be walking right into a ploy that would get him and Emily both killed.

Boricio screamed, "Don't do it, Luca! Don't give this alien fuck what he wants. He's just gonna kill us all anyway!"

Desmond turned, glaring at Boricio. "Shut up."

"Or what?" Boricio said, "You gonna kill me? You can't fucking kill me, and you know it. If you coulda, you woulda. But your bosses won't *let you*, will they? Might wanna pull up your panties, Dez, your little pink pussy is showing."

Desmond pulled back the gun, swung, hit Mary in the head, and sent her to the ground.

"You want to see what I can do?"

Boricio screamed, "Big fucking man, attacking a woman and her child! Why don't you fucking come at me? I'll kick your ass even with my body in this pod!"

Emily's voice screamed in his head.

Now, Daddy!

Paul watched as Desmond and the Guardsman both went toward Boricio. It was time.

He slipped the blade from his belt and walked toward Luca slowly, uncertainty racing through him.

It's a trap. Don't do it!

They're going to kill you both!

Paul crept closer.

He heard Desmond punch Boricio in the face.

Boricio laughed.

"Is that all you got? My grandmother hits harder than that, Twinkie, and that ole bitch is dead. Come on, give it all you got, Desmond Do Right!"

Paul looked up at Luca's eyes.

They were soft and kind, a serenity in them that Paul had only seen in his wife's.

Luca nodded.

Paul brought the knife up to Luca's throat, sliding it under the mask designed to keep his soul inside him.

As the blade found Luca's throat, Paul struggled to find the will to plunge it into the old man's neck.

It was one thing to silence a threat. This was a helpless old man.

Or someone laying a trap.

Doubts screamed in his head.

Don't do it!

Don't do it!

Suddenly, behind him, he heard Desmond shout, "Paul!"

He turned to see the Guardsman aiming the rifle at him.

Paul froze, paralyzed by fear.

"Step away from him, Paul, or he will shoot you."

Do it! Emily's voice screamed inside his mind.

He saw a flash of his little girl on the elevator floor. Then another flash of Emily under the canopy a large black tree with bright-red roses rather than leaves. There were others there. None of it made sense.

"Drop the knife!"

Please, Daddy. I'm dying.

Paul swallowed, staring at the rifle aimed right at him, waiting to rip him to shreds.

He had to follow his instincts.

Had to follow his heart.

Paul plunged the knife into Luca's throat.

Gunfire tore into his body a half second later.

～

SEVENTY-TWO

Will Bishop

Lightning pierced the clear blue sky, striking the black tree in a cataclysmic clash, blinding them with brightness and deafening them all with its roar.

When Will's vision finally returned, he saw light pouring through cracks in the tree, spreading fissures that seemed to be unknitting the branches before them.

Though his ears were ringing with a high-pitched whine, he turned and yelled, "This is it, folks! Time to go!"

Charlie shouted a muffled and barely audible, "I don't want to! I want to stay here!"

"Here isn't a place," Will said. "We are inside Luca. And now he's dying. It's time to go."

"Go where?" Ed shouted.

"Into the light!" Will pointed at the growing fissure in the tree's center, where Emily had vanished.

Will marched forward, hoping they'd follow.

~

SEVENTY-THREE

Boricio Wolfe

The Guardsman opened fire, riddling Paul's body with bullets until it had an English muffin's nooks and crannies, buttered in his blood.

A bright flash of light came from beneath the surface of the jelly of Luca's pod. It looked as if the old man's chest was ripping open and something bright was pushing its way out, growing larger as it came.

They all stared as the first light made its way through — in the shape of a man. Though the man was all light, Boricio thought he could sense features within it.

Ed Keenan?

Another light stepped through, until five human-sized and shaped lights shone from Luca, standing in front of Desmond, fists tight at their sides.

Desmond screamed, grabbed the rifle from the Guardsman, and fired wildly at the shapes.

The Light immediately shattered into a thousand brilliant beads, scattering in every direction, spinning and spreading in arcs like an electric spiderweb, countless streams blinking on and off, strobing: light, dark, light, dark.

Desmond, without a solid target, turned his rage on Mary

and Paola, both lying facedown, hands still cuffed behind their backs.

He aimed at Paola's back and fired.

Her body bounced in the hail fire of bullets.

Mary and Boricio both screamed, neither able to do anything.

Desmond turned to Mary and fired, shooting her in the back and head.

Every ounce of despair and anger coursed through Boricio, leaving his body in an unholy wail.

Desmond turned to fire at him.

SEVENTY-FOUR

Emily Roberts

Emily had never felt so alive.

The Light coursed through her, knitting and healing her flesh.

But as she stood, Emily also felt death. Not hers, but her father's. She could feel his pain as the bullets tore through him. Could hear him cry out, *I love you.*

Emily had to save him. If The Light could bring her back, then maybe it could bring him back, too.

She was about to order the elevator to her father's level, but a voice corrected her.

The old man, Will.

She couldn't see him but could hear him as if he were right beside her.

Emily, your job isn't done. You have one more thing to do.

She stood in the closed elevator and looked at the black metal walls. An image flashed in her mind of something behind the walls. The ship's black flesh.

Get to it.

She clawed at a seam in the wall's metal panel until her fingers found purchase.

It took every ounce of strength, but the metal loosened.

"Come on!" Emily grunted.

The wall went slack then fell to the ground with a clang. There, in the exposed space, Emily saw the elevator's flesh.

Driven by instincts not her own, she thrust her hand into the wall. It was slippery and hot inside, as if she'd shoved her hand inside a living animal. Disgusting.

Lights under the ship's skin burned bright red in response.

Emily closed her eyes, suddenly knowing what she was meant to do.

~

SEVENTY-FIVE

Boricio Wolfe

As Boricio's rage left his body in one focused wail, Desmond opened fire on him.

Boricio felt the bullets pierce through the jelly, straight into his flesh and internal organs with blinding pain.

This was it.

This was how he would finally die — helpless like a caged animal.

Then The Light coalesced into a mass of swirling tangled streams of blue-white lightning, hovering above Desmond's head.

Desmond dropped the gun, staring in awe at his enemy's form. Guardsmen ran from the room, scared shitless.

The room grew brighter. At least that's what Boricio *thought* was happening, until he realized that The Light was coming straight toward him, gathering mass, sharpening itself into a point, before driving itself right into his wide-open mouth.

Boricio felt as if someone had turned his entire body into the Fourth of July. Except this wasn't a pain so much as a jolt of energy coursing through his body.

He could feel The Light inside him. Not just The Light,

but those souls collected by The Light: Luca's, Ed's, Jade's, Callie's, and even —

No, no way.

Well, fuck me with a corncob, it's Charlie!

Boricio could feel his old friends flowing through him, becoming a part of him, making him stronger.

Turning him into a god.

He looked up at Desmond as the fucker's gun went empty.

Boricio smiled and sent a blast of energy from his hands.

The jelly fell away from the pod, and Boricio stepped out, naked and covered in goo, but his body healing quickly.

He locked eyes with the enemy.

"You better run," Boricio said.

Desmond turned and did exactly that.

~

SEVENTY-SIX

Emily Roberts

Emily had seized the ship's flight controls. She didn't know how to drive a car, let alone a spacecraft, and yet was willing the craft toward the mainland.

Outside the elevator, she heard banging on the door.

Guardsmen shouted. "Let us in!"

Emily didn't answer.

She had to focus on steering the ship, and keeping the aliens from seizing control.

Marina's voice outside: "Let us in."

Emily continued to ignore the demands.

Gunfire erupted, slugs plinking into the metal door, leaving dents. Soon, the doors would disintegrate.

Emily tried to will the elevator up, but it was stuck in place.

Something slammed into the black fleshy wall in front of her. The first of the bullets to break through.

~

SEVENTY-SEVEN

Mary Olson

One moment, Mary was on the ground, feeling the world around her fading away — helpless, again, to save her daughter.

Just as The Darkness had swelled and she was certain there was nothing left, a warm, golden light appeared all around her.

She looked up to see Boricio standing naked above her, his body burning brightly as if he were a walking embodiment of the sun.

He looked down at her, spread his hand.

Tendrils of light danced at his fingertips then circled downward toward her.

She felt The Light enter her body.

Not just The Light but a soul attached to The Light — the girl, Callie.

"It's going to be okay," Callie said.

Boricio leaned over and broke her shackles.

Mary sat and felt her body healing. She watched as Light poured from Boricio's other hand into Paola, healing her daughter as well.

Boricio walked over to Paul and healed him, too. Then he sent sparks of Light into the pods, waking Brent, Teagan, and the kids, frying the jelly that held them in place.

They slipped out and fell to the ground, naked, covered in the pod's jelly, and shook up, but otherwise fine.

~

SEVENTY-EIGHT

Boricio Wolfe

Boricio stared at them, a motley fucking crew if ever there'd been one, but this was what was left of Team Boricio. But that was okay because he could feel the souls of Keenan, Will, Luca, Charlie, and Callie working with and through them. If that wasn't an all-star lineup, fuck if he knew what was.

But first, Boricio needed to figure out what to do as they sat in the cell with Desmond on the run, probably calling for backup like a bitch.

Brent, Teagan, and the kids huddled together. Mary and Paola, too.

Paul was standing there, confused. Boricio could feel The Light working its way through him, bringing him up to speed, healing him.

"What now?" Mary said. "We've got to get Desmond. But we also need to get these people to safety."

He didn't answer her question, suddenly overwhelmed by images flashing through his mind. It was as if The Light had turned on a hundred live feeds at once, showing things on the ship, on The Island, on the mainland, a god's view of everything, through the eyes of many that The Light had spread into.

And there were many more eyes than Boricio would've imagined.

Oh, this is good.

But what was the point of these fucking images? How the hell was he supposed to make sense of them or know what the hell to do? What good was seeing everything if you couldn't make sense of it?

Focus, Luca said inside his head.

And then Boricio saw what had to be done. He knew his job. And what the others needed to do.

Then he looked at Paul. "Can you get clothes for us?"

"Yeah," Paul said.

"Good, we've got work to do."

He met Mary's eyes. "I'm so fucking glad to see you again."

Boricio kissed her, hard on the mouth.

Paola said, "Whoa, what the F?"

"Long story," Mary said, laughing.

Paola stared then laughed.

"Sorry to break this happy reunion, but there's shit to do before we get off this ship."

Boricio cleared his throat. "All right, gang. This is it. I know we've been through a shit ton of fuckery, but we've got more to shovel before we're back home and happy. The good news is we've got friends. You all might not be able to see them, but I can feel them inside us, right now, and they're gonna help us bury these alien fucks. You all with me?"

A pitiful response, a few halfhearted yeahs, particularly from the scared ones, Brent, Teagan and the kids, all still huddled together thanking God they weren't dead.

"Come on, I wanna see those fists in the air and hear a 'Fuck yeah!' On three, Team Boricio, I wanna hear a fuck yeah. One. Two. Three."

The little girl, Becca, raised a fist and shouted "Fuck yeah!"

The room erupted in laughter.

Paul came back with a bunch of cult wear. All-white outfits and no shoes, but at least they wouldn't be running around the ship dressed for an orgy.

"Good, everyone put on the Kool-Aid Collection, then line up so I can tell you each what you'll need to do. You wanna live, you'll listen to me. Because I've been handed these directions by The Light itself, amen, hallelujah."

Mary was first in line. "What do you need me to do?"

~

SEVENTY-NINE

Mary Olson

Boricio delivered team assignments, short and to the point, kind of like Ed used to be. Mary was certain that Ed was now operating through Boricio, so instead of getting colorful job descriptions such as *keep fucking them till their assholes fall out*, she got a simply worded mission: *kill Desmond.*

But Mary was no longer with Callie alone.

She could feel Luca inside her, urging her forward.

A part of her wanted to stay behind to make sure Paola was safe, but Boricio said he needed her for a "very special" mission.

Mary raced out of the chamber, down the halls, following the trail of Darkness like a wolf chasing prey. She could feel Desmond running, scared, calling out for The Darkness to join him.

Guardsmen came at her, guns aimed, firing, but Mary was too quick, evading their shots, ducking, dodging, and weaving with a speed and fluidity she'd never thought possible.

As she closed the distance between herself and them, The Light transformed her hands into large glowing yellow claws of brightness. She sliced through their armor and dropped them in seconds.

She continued on, the scent stronger. The hunger to end him, to end The Darkness, made *her* stronger, faster. As she navigated more halls and enemies, Mary felt countless volts of electricity coursing through her.

Nothing could stop her.

She came to a dead-end hallway.

Except it wasn't a complete dead end.

There was a hole in the ground, a long chute leading deeper into the ship's bowels. Mary sensed his scent all over it.

This is where he went, where he was hiding.

She didn't think twice before jumping.

EIGHTY

Emily Roberts

Chunks of the door were vanishing fast, shrapnel whizzing by her, tearing at the backs of Emily's arms and hitting her in the back of her head.

She ignored the sharp metal stings.

She dared not turn around.

She felt that the ship was now over the spot of earth The Light wanted it to be.

Now to land it.

The elevator doors shattered behind her.

No, not yet!

Emily turned to see Marina storming in, shotgun raised, aimed right at her.

She'd been saved once by The Light, but Emily knew, somehow, that it didn't make her indestructible.

She pushed into Marina's mind, a sharp blast of pain that momentarily startled the woman.

And in that moment, Emily turned her attention back to landing the ship. Instead of lowering it slowly, she let it drop.

As the ship plummeted, Marina dropped the shotgun and tumbled forward, straight into Emily, sending her back into the wall's soft flesh.

Marina grabbed Emily by the hair, pulled her forward, then slammed her head into the wall.

Emily cried out, kicking, but doing no damage.

The ship crashed to the ground, a thunderous boom reverberating through the ship.

Lights stuttered, power disrupted.

Marina reached up with both hands around Emily's throat, strangling her.

Emily tried to push the woman away, but she was too strong.

"Please," Emily cried, staring into the infected woman's eyes. "Stop."

Something shifted in Marina's eyes. Her fingers released their grip on Emily's throat.

She looked at Emily and through a cracked voice, said, "I'm sorry."

Emily stared, confused. Had she somehow broken the alien's control over Marina?

A gunshot exploded.

Hot blood erupted all over Emily as Marina's body slumped dead on top of her.

Emily screamed then saw the gunshot's source standing over her.

"Daddy!" she shoved Marina aside and jumped into his embrace.

He hugged her tight, "Oh, God, I thought I lost you."

Emily looked down at Marina watching as a black shape poured from her mouth.

Emily's father pushed her aside, into the arms of Brent, standing with Teagan and the kids. He stretched his hand out toward the dark alien shape as it rose.

Suddenly, his hand was surrounded by a bright-white glow. A blast of light shot out, into The Darkness, disintegrating it.

"Whoa!" Emily said, staring at her father. "How did you do that?"

"No time to explain. We need to get out of here."
"Where are the others?" Emily asked.
"They'll meet us. Come on!"
They ran. To where, Emily didn't know, but at least she was with her father, knowing he'd protect her.

~

EIGHTY-ONE

Boricio Wolfe

Bullets rained on the control room glass in a torrent as Paola shoved her hands deep into the control panel's black flesh, keeping the ship's cargo bay doors closed. They couldn't let anything off the ship. Yet.

As she continued to hold the cargo doors closed, more Guardsmen lined up, firing more weapons.

Tiny cracks spread across the glass. It was holding up remarkably well, but Boricio wasn't sure how much time they had left. It could give way any moment. Then the Guardsmen would bring them both down, open the cargo bay doors, and make their hope disappear.

Boricio held the control room door as best he could. He watched through the glass as chaos unfolded in the cargo bay — Guardsmen and giant ugly centipede-moth-like aliens racing toward the shuttles, trying to escape as the ship tilted and rocked, lowering to The Island.

Several Guardsmen hammered at the door with fists, weapons, and large sledgehammers, trying to break it down.

Boricio glared at the enemies, laughing. "Not by the hair of my chinny, chin, chin!"

He flashed back to the belfry door, remembering his

forced surrender, and how Ed lost his life as the door gave in and Boricio escaped onto the church roof.

Sorry about that, Boricio thought to Ed, also in his mind.

Forget about that. Focus on this! Ed snapped.

"Yes, sir!" Boricio cracked.

Paola turned, "What?"

"Nothing. How's it going?"

"I can feel someone trying to override the controls, but I'm holding it down."

"Good. Just hang in there. I'm calling for backup."

Boricio reached out in his mind, calling for help. Connecting with every human and alien that Luca had poured The Light into over the past four years.

Come. Take the ship.

The door burst open.

Boricio's connection to the others broke as he was snapped back into the moment, just in time to see an old man with bushy eyebrows standing outside the door with a giant square weapon-looking thing that must have broken the door's seal.

Behind him stood the biggest, ugliest red centipede-moth-like creature.

They stormed the control center.

~

EIGHTY-TWO

Mary Olson

Mary fell for what felt like forever.

After finally hitting the ground, she found herself in a large black circular room that reminded her of a fighting arena.

The floor and walls were made of the same black flesh with embedded amber lights. Desmond stood in the red glow, smiling. His eye was already healed, but Mary was sure he was still pissed and wanting to lash out.

"I knew one of you would follow me."

Above her, Mary heard metal sliding.

"Now you're trapped."

"We're both trapped then."

"You forget, Mary. We are many. We cannot be contained to a handful of bodies. We are nearly a thousand strong on this ship alone, with thousands more out there in the world. And you are what? A handful of people?"

Mary glared at him.

"That's all we need." She thrust out her palm, surprised as an electric arc of light sliced through the air and sent Desmond back.

She ran toward him, feeling The Light working through

her, transforming her fist into a golden blade of light, eager to finish him off.

As she leaped at Desmond, he opened his mouth, shooting out dark swirls of matter.

The Darkness hit her in the gut, sending her flying back.

Mary hit the ground hard as The Darkness disintegrated then jumped back into Desmond's body.

The ship rocked, sending Mary sideways, sliding toward the wall.

"Looks like the ship is going down!" She smiled, feeling The Light working to land it, though she wasn't yet sure about the rest of its plan.

As she started to stand, thick ropes of Darkness shot out of Desmond's mouth, wrapped around her ankles, and yanked her back hard.

Mary hit the ground hard, knocking the breath from her lungs.

Desmond's Darkness reeled her in, pulling her in too fast for Mary to counter the move as she panted and puffed, catching her breath.

His hand formed a dark blade when he reached her. As the dark tendrils snapped back into his mouth, he sliced down, straight into her gut.

Unable to scream, Mary gasped.

∾

EIGHTY-THREE

Boricio Wolfe

As the eight-foot red alien shoved the old man with bushy eyebrows aside and burrowed through the doorway, Boricio's fist burned bright, forming a sharp triangle-like blade. He brought it up, straight into the fucker's underbelly, and sliced up.

Boricio used his other hand, also burning bright but still in its human form, to tear into the insect's flesh, ripping out guts and chunks of goo, screaming as he did.

The alien fell to the ground, black liquid pooling from its maw.

No, not liquid, but the alien's essence — its soul, seeking a home.

"Take that shit outta here!" Boricio yelled, thrusting his open palm toward the thing.

A bright-yellow spark of lightning shot from his hand and fried the fucker.

Bushy Eyebrows came at Boricio, no longer holding the big square thing but instead holding an assault rifle.

"Enough!" the old man screamed, firing.

Bullets smacked into Boricio, but he wasn't going down like that.

He raced forth, even as the gunfire tore into flesh, driven forth by Charlie and Keenan's white-hot anger.

Bushy Eyebrows looked up, startled, wondering why the fuck Boricio wasn't falling.

Boricio grabbed the gun, snatched it from his old fucking hands, and spun it around, fired point blank into the old man, tearing his organs apart.

Boricio kicked the old man back from the doorway then looked up to see a line of Guardsmen, weapons aimed at him.

He raised his rifle, fired, screaming, "Die, motherfuckers, die!"

"Kill them!" one of the helmeted voices screamed.

Gunfire erupted, tearing into Boricio's flesh. He fired back, taking out as many of them as he could before they brought him down, hoping they wouldn't hit any vitals.

The ship rocked, sending Boricio and the others skidding along the floor, again starting to take off.

Boricio grabbed the doorway, pulling himself back into the control room.

"Someone's overriding the flight controls! They're moving the ship!" Paola screamed.

Shit! Fuck!

"Can you keep the bay doors closed and land the ship?" Boricio asked, unable to look back as the Guardsmen scrambled to their feet and opened fire on him again. Boricio returned their shots but was taking too many himself.

"I'm trying!" she cried out.

"We need to land before we open the doors," Boricio said. "So land this fucker, now!"

"We're too high!" Paola said.

"Find a way!"

The ship rocked again.

Guardsmen and giant insect fucks alike slid and fell.

Boricio dropped the rifle then grabbed both sides of the

door, struggling not to fall, or die, as blood poured from his dozens of wounds.

Guardsmen found their feet and aimed their guns to finish Boricio off. Gunshots tore into his body.

He staggered backward with each shot's impact, struggling to hold tight to the doorway, standing as a makeshift barrier to keep anyone from getting Paola.

The ship lurched downward then hit the ground, sending Boricio's enemies back to their feet.

The landing was hard, but not enough to hurt the fuckers. Just momentarily disable them.

"Get out of the doorway!" Paola cried. "The ship's landed! Lemme open the doors!"

Boricio looked up and down his bloodied body. Gunshots pocked his chest, legs, arms, and gut, gushing blood.

"No, not yet. We're not ready!"

More gunshots came at Boricio as the Guardsmen continued shooting, even from their positions lying on the ground.

Boricio could see dozens of shuttles lining up, hovering in the bay, light burning beneath them, waiting to flee the ship.

You fuckers aren't escaping.

More gunfire as the Guardsmen regrouped, charging at the control room. If he wasn't responding to gunshots, they'd come and physically remove him from the doorway. No way he could fight them *all*.

Lightning erupted randomly from his body, like an instinctual defense system, hitting some of the Guardsmen, knocking them back, and frying a few. But there were too many gunmen firing.

Chunks of flesh ripped apart.

Bones were breaking.

His kneecap exploded.

Boricio fell then pulled himself up, doing his best to keep shots from getting inside and hitting the girl.

Boricio wasn't sure what was holding him together and keeping him alive, but it couldn't last forever.

Why won't these fuckers give up? Charlie screamed inside him.

Something had to give.

Outside, Boricio heard what he was waiting for.

They're heeeeere.

He turned to Paola. "Open the cargo doors!"

"Which ones?"

"All of them!"

A bullet found Boricio's left eye, half blinding him. The pain was intense, like a dagger through his pupil, screaming into his head.

The sound of heavy machinery and the loud banging of opening cargo doors drew the Guardsmen's attention away from Boricio and the doorway. They turned, running to join the exodus.

"Boricio!" Paola screamed, leaving the control panel and dropping to his side as he fell into her arms.

Boricio watched the shuttles race toward the bright daylight.

Shit, we didn't stop them!

But then a smile spread across his face as a beautiful realization dawned on him. They weren't running into the brightness, but rather into The Light.

Thousands of Light bleakers — the black aliens that Luca had infected now burned with a radiant white-hot light — flooded the exits, slamming into the shuttles and blocking their escape.

The Light tore through the shuttles, alien insect fucks, and Guardsmen like a tsunami of Light.

"You need to go!" Boricio said to Paola, blood pouring from his mouth.

"No, I can't leave you here."

She tried to lift him, but he was too heavy, and unable to help her.

"Go!" he yelled again. "They're going to destroy this ship!"

"No!" she cried. "I can't leave you."

Boricio looked up into Paola's crying eyes, and saw something he never thought he'd see again — love and friendship.

But he couldn't let that love get her killed.

He still had something to do, and couldn't if she were with him. He had to get Paola to her mother.

"Luca!" Boricio screamed. "Get her out of here!"

And then, in a flash, Paola was gone.

EIGHTY-FOUR

Mary Olson

"Why do you keep fighting me, *Light?*" Desmond raised his Dark bladed arm, with Mary stuck to it like a speared fish, and stared into her eyes. "You cannot win. And yet you keep fighting."

He jerked his arm, slicing deeper into Mary's guts.

Blood poured through her shirt. Intense pain flooded her body. The pain was dizzying, and she could barely hang on.

She longed to let go, to taste the sweet embrace of an endless abyss.

Come on, Mary, said Callie's voice. *You've gotta fight. Gotta fight for your girl.*

If she let go, The Darkness would finish her off. And that would be that. Desmond was right: The Darkness was many, The Light were few.

She fought to keep her eyes open, determined not to let the smug fucker win.

Just close them for a second. One sweet second.

No, Will's voice commanded. *We are not done. We will not give in.*

A high-pitched scream came from above, followed by the sound of metal tearing.

Mary looked up groggily and saw hundreds, if not thousands, of bright aliens pouring into the room in a wave of what looked like pure light.

Desmond's eyes widened: now he was outnumbered.

The swarm of brightness gathered around them, though not yet attacking. Desmond looked to Mary, confusion knitting his brow.

Mary, reinforced by hope, felt the tide turning. While she was tempted to act on the years of rage and hate that had been building within her, she then thought of Paola.

Act on love, not hate, a collective voice said within her.

Mary thought not of revenge for all The Darkness had done to her and everyone she loved. She thought of protecting Paola. Of never letting The Darkness anywhere near her daughter again. To do that, she had to end it, once and for all.

Mary looked down to see her hand and arm engulfed in a brilliant-white light. She stretched her fingers, entranced by the beautiful drops of light dancing around her fingers.

She met Desmond's eyes then looked down at his bladed arm in her gut.

She swung her bright hand down and severed his arm.

Desmond fell back, blood and black liquid jetting from his appendage.

Though he'd been holding her up, Mary didn't fall when she sliced his arm off. She floated in air, as if lifted by The Light swelling behind her.

She looked back to see the Light bleakers stacked atop one another, hundreds upon hundreds, if not thousands.

She could feel them buzzing, awaiting her command.

She ripped his claw from her gut and threw it to the ground where it dispersed into dark swirls.

Desmond met her eyes. "No, Mary, please."

The voice he used was more like the Desmond she once knew. Tears streamed down his face. Was the real Desmond truly trapped, a hostage in his body? Could he be saved if so, with only the alien killed?

The Light brightened behind her.

"I don't know what to do," Mary said, feeling as if she could either send the mountain of Light down on this man and end both him and the alien, or maybe try to remove The Darkness.

"Please, Mary," he begged again. "Don't kill me. The Darkness is gone; I swear it."

She flashed back to holding Paola's dead body. Seeing her shot in the head. Mary knew she couldn't take any chances. Could never trust another word from Desmond's mouth.

She met his eyes and felt two things at once — a genuine sadness for the loss of the man she once loved and relief to finally end the threat that had destroyed the world, and nearly killed her daughter.

"Goodbye," she said.

And the wave of Light rolled forth, consuming all in its wake.

~

Epilogue

Six months later
  Washington State

IN HER DREAMS, she'd saved Boricio.

In her dreams, she'd made it to the mainland with the others, watching the ship explode on The Island, finally destroying The Darkness. The difference between dreams and reality was that in her dreams she'd found Boricio after The Light teleported him to safety.

In reality, she felt him on the ship as it exploded.

He was gone with The Darkness.

Also gone, from all of their lives, was The Light, which had become such a deep part of them. It had moved on after the ship exploded.

And it was that realization, and that reality, she woke to every morning, feeling slightly empty.

But her bed was never lonely.

Paola slept beside her.

Mary watched her daughter's eyes roll behind their lids, wondering if she was having more nightmares. They all had them for several months after defeating The Darkness. The kids, including Paola, often woke in the middle of the night, screaming, thinking The Darkness had returned to claim their family.

Which was why Paola slept with her mother, for now.

Mary didn't mind. She was glad to have her girl back. Glad that they'd been able to build a new community in Washington. It was small, just over one hundred men, women, and children — all people she trusted. Paul and Emily were living among them, their telepathic powers still strong, even if neither Mary nor Paola felt anything *extra* running through them. Paul and Emily were in charge of ensuring the people in their community, called Hope Springs — Paola's corny suggestion — were good people.

Every now and then, they heard from Lisa, who was out on the road, doing what she could to help the teams working to rebuild life after the aliens. It wouldn't be easy, but Lisa was up for the fight.

The scent of bacon roused her stomach. Someone was making breakfast, and Mary was famished.

She looked at Paola, wondering how long the girl would stay sleeping. She gently shook her. "Want breakfast?"

Paola made a noise and rolled over, pulling the covers over her head.

"Fine, I'll eat yours," Mary joked then got out of bed.

She slipped out of her shorts and into some jeans then headed out of her room, downstairs into the kitchen she shared with Brent, Teagan, the kids, Paul, and Emily. They all lived in the compound's main house, with fifteen other groups and makeshift families sharing neighboring homes on the ten acres of farm and woodlands.

"Good morning," Teagan said, getting up from her spot beside Brent and heading toward the stove to get food for Mary. "Is Paola awake yet?"

"No, she was up late last night." Mary turned to give Ben

a look. "Someone kept her up playing Uno until one in the morning!"

Ben giggled.

"One?" Brent asked. "Why were you up so late?"

Ben shrugged his shoulders. "I'm not a kid anymore, Dad. I like staying up on Fridays."

Brent shook his head. "I'm sorry, Mary. If I knew, I would've sent him to bed."

"It's okay, Paola loves the kids. And she looks for any excuse to stay up."

Mary, with a plate of bacon, eggs, and fresh muffins, sat to eat.

Emily poured her a glass of orange juice from the pitcher on the table between them.

"Thank you," Mary said, smiling.

She was so glad that what started off as a rather rocky relationship — her slitting Emily's throat, then Paul trying to return the favor — was now so close-knit.

Teagan excused herself from the table without warning, suddenly rushing away.

Mary looked up at Brent. "Is she okay?"

He nodded sheepishly. "Yeah."

Mary looked at him, sensing his secret.

Emily looked at Brent, a smile spreading across her face. "Oh, my God."

Brent looked at her, eyes wide as he realized she'd peeked into his brain.

Emily threw her hands over her mouth, realizing she'd messed up. "Oh, I'm so sorry, I didn't mean to. I swear, I wasn't prying. It was just coming off you, practically screaming."

"What?" Ben and Becca asked together, staring at Brent, waiting for an answer.

"What?" Becca repeated.

Brent wiped his mouth with a napkin. "Really, Teagan should tell you."

Teagan returned to the kitchen. "Tell them what?"

Brent's lips pursed. "I think we should tell them. The cat's kinda out of the bag."

"What?" Teagan asked. "What do you mean, kinda?"

Brent pointed at Emily. "She saw my thoughts."

"Sorry," Emily said sheepishly.

"I'm sorry," Paul echoed then joked, "I'll be sure to lock her in the dungeon for dinner."

Teagan took her seat next to Brent and told the kids to come over.

They ran over.

Mary watched, knowing what was going to come, feeling her eyes well up with tears.

"How would you two like a baby brother or sister?"

"What?" Becca looked like she'd been offered a pony.

"What?" Ben seemed less excited, but not upset.

"We're pregnant," Teagan said.

"You're *both* pregnant? I thought only girls had babies," Becca said.

Everyone laughed.

"No, just Teagan."

"YAY! I hope we have a sister!" Becca danced around the table.

"And," Brent said, "we're not sure how we'll do it, what with there not being any judges or preachers or anything these days, but we'd like to get married."

Emily started crying. "Oh, I'm so happy for you all!"

She went over and hugged Brent and Teagan, then the kids.

Mary went over and hugged them, too. She was happy for them, even though she was thinking of Boricio, and what might have been.

Paola slunk into the kitchen, sleepy eyes, hair a rat's nest. "What's everyone going on about?"

Becca yelled out, "My mom is marrying his dad, and we're gonna have a brother or sister!"

"How long was I sleeping?" Paola joked.

Mary went over to Paola and hugged her. "I love you."

"What's that for?" she asked.

"Because I haven't told you yet today."

Epilogue Two

Six months ago
The Island

Boricio sat on a grassy hill in the distance, watching the mothership's remains burn in a bright-white fire. The music of bending metal collapsing into itself, organic material withering amid shrieking aliens that had yet to be killed, and those compromised by The Light, all leaving Earth in The Light's fire: a chaotic melody, music to Boricio's ears.

His body was still repairing itself, but at least he was no longer dying. Once certain that the aliens were all dead, he'd go find Mary and the others.

Two bright shapes materialized on either side of Boricio. He was about to jump, ready to rumble, when they found familiar forms: Luca, as a kid, and Will.

They sat on the hill, watching the ship burn. Their bodies were half-normal-looking, half light, partially transparent, like illuminated ghosts. For a moment, Boricio wasn't sure if he was hallucinating.

He sat back down. "Are you all here, or am I seeing shit?"

"We're here," Will said, putting a hand on Boricio's back, "for a little bit longer."

"Where's the others? Ed? Charlie, Callie?"

"They had to move on," Will said.

"Move on? To where?"

"We don't know what's next," Luca said. "Another life on another world. Maybe they come back here. No one can say."

Boricio felt a bit of The Light inside him, coloring his gaps of knowledge — *when the body dies, the soul moves on to another form.*

"So, there ain't no Heaven or Hell? I've been Ned Flanders for nothing?"

Will and Luca laughed.

It felt good to hear them.

Boricio had a disturbing thought. "Wait a second, if we all die and come back, are you saying these alien fucks are getting a sequel?"

"Everything comes back, but not always in the same form," Luca said.

"How the hell did you get so smart, Boy Wonder?"

Luca shrugged.

Boricio tousled the boy's long hair. "It's good to see you as a kid again. That old fucker was depressing the hell out of me." Boricio looked at Will. "No offense, Grandpa."

"None taken." Will smiled, his eyes still on the burning ship.

Boricio had what he thought was a damned good idea. "Hey, can't you all jump in the body of some fuckers here and live inside 'em? There's a lotta assholes out there wastin' the skin they were born in."

"No," Will said, "we need to go. I feel The Void calling."

"Well, fuck, we just got the gang back together, and you're gonna leave?"

"I'll miss you," Luca said.

"I'll miss you, too, kid. Come here, and give me a fucking hug."

Boricio hugged the boy, surprised that the ghostly apparition had any substance. It felt like hugging someone under water. Not that Boricio had ever done that.

Strangled someone under water, maybe.

"I'm proud of you," Will said, coming over and shaking Boricio's hand.

Boricio wasn't sure which version of Will this was, the old man on this world or the one on the other who'd adopted the other versions of Boricio and Luca. The Light said it was the one from this world.

The ground began to give way under the ship, causing seismic tremors in the land beneath them.

"Whoa," Boricio said, jumping up, glad to find his knees steady after being healed by The Light.

Will and Luca stood, staring at the ship as it descended into a massive crater, kicking up dirt and rocks all around it.

Boricio saluted the sinking ship. "Sayonara, cocksucker."

The ground continued to shake, and for a moment, Boricio thought the entire island might go under.

But then, as the last of the ship melted into the ground, everything stopped.

The ship's dying gasps sputtered out.

Boricio approached the mound for one final look.

A hand appeared, pulling something from the hole. A dark hand belonging to an alien.

"Motherfucker." Boricio's fists tightened as he approached the thing fast.

He heard Luca and Will coming up fast behind him.

He reached the mound as the alien pulled itself over the crater's lip. Boricio saw The Darkness, completely shed of its human form, clinging to life.

The alien looked up at the three of them and hissed, sharp teeth rattling in its wide mouth.

"What does it take to kill you fuckers?" Boricio asked, ready to finish it off with a stomp.

Will put his hand out in front of Boricio. "I don't think you *can* kill the last of it."

Boricio turned to the old man. "What?"

The alien hissed again and reached out a hand, trying to swipe at him, but it wasn't close enough.

"Looks like it's dying just fine," Boricio said.

"Yes, but we can't allow its soul to escape," Luca said.

Boricio looked down at the alien and saw it was a bit different from the others. It didn't have a hundred or so tiny lights under its skin. It had millions, moving fast, like sperm through a busted rubber, swirling in The Darkness.

Will looked at Boricio. "This is all that's left of The Darkness. If you kill this creature, its soul will escape. It will return and reproduce, not stopping until *It's* destroyed this planet and everything on it."

Boricio felt like the bull's eye of a cruel joke. "So, what the hell am I supposed to do? Lock it in a cage? Put up a sign: *Do Not Feed The Alien?*"

"No," Will said. "You must do something else."

Boricio didn't like the conversation's direction. "What are you talking about?"

Luca looked up at Boricio, hope in his eyes. "You need to absorb it."

"What? The fuck I will!"

"We did all we could," Will said. "The best we could to neutralize most of The Darkness. But this bit will not die. It cannot die. We can only hope to contain it."

"You think I wanna be bodysnatched? I don't fucking think so!"

"You're the only one strong enough," Luca said. "And you still have some of The Light inside you to keep The Darkness at bay."

"No." Boricio threw up his hands and turned away. "I didn't sign up for this shit. It's done. It's over. I'm going back to find Mary and the others. I deserve my own Happily Ever After!"

Boricio started to walk away.

Will and Luca appeared in front of him.

He walked through them, pushing what was left of their bodies out of his way.

Will pleaded behind him. "If you don't do this, The Darkness will return."

Boricio spun on the old man. "What's the difference? If I put it in me, and let's say for shits and giggles I can somehow contain El Feo, what happens when I die? It's just gonna get out and do whatever the hell it wants, anyway."

"No," Will said, putting a hand on Luca's chest. "That's the thing. You will live for a long, long time."

Boricio looked back at the pit to make sure the alien wasn't slipping out of its shell as they spoke. It was struggling, trying to stand. Not yet a threat.

Boricio turned to Will. "So, what, I'm Methuselah?"

"You will live long enough to keep it from ever harming anyone."

Boricio shook his head. "I know this might come as a surprise to you, but I kinda like myself after Boy Wonder here fixed me. How do I know this thing won't turn me back? Won't this only make me worse?"

"You are strong enough to fight it," Luca said. "I believe in you."

Boricio laughed. "First time someone believes in me, and it's 'cuz they want me to take one for the team. Take a hard one, too. I mean, shit, if I do this, I can't ever be around Mary and them, right? How can I trust that it won't try and kill them? It seemed to have quite the hard-on for Mary and her little lamb."

Will met Boricio's eyes. "I don't think you should be

around any of them. Don't allow The Darkness strength to gather."

Boricio scowled. "*Bullshit.*"

Luca said, "You love them, don't you?"

Boricio stared at the alien, tears stinging his eyes. He never would've guessed how much this could hurt — the very idea of never seeing Mary or Paola was a sharp blade through his tender heart.

"Yes, of course I do. And I hate you for making me love them. Shit was easier before you forced me to give a fuck."

"Sorry." Luca looked down at the ground.

"It's okay," Boricio said with a deep sigh.

"So, what happens if I do this? Is there any danger it's gonna jump in the driver's seat and take over, like it did with the other me?"

"No," Will said. "The Light is too strong. It might fight you over time to try and wrest control, but I have faith you'll be able to fight it. You've already come back from so much."

Boricio looked out over the mainland. He could feel Mary and his friends, too far to see.

"Can't I at least say goodbye?" Boricio asked.

The alien gasped, choking as it fell back to the ground.

"Looks like it's dying," Will said. "I'm sorry, Boricio. If you're gonna do this, you need to do it now. Kill the alien, then suck his soul into your mouth."

Boricio looked at the mainland then back at the alien.

"Fuck it," he said. "Let's do this."

~

Eight months later ...
Washington State

Boricio stood along the mountain ridge, training his binoculars down at the wedding taking place in the valley behind the church.

"Well, looks like Brent finally found his nuts," he said, staring down at Teagan's swollen belly.

Mary and Paola stood behind Teagan, wearing the ugliest fucking bridesmaid dresses Boricio had ever seen — orange as a rotten tangerine.

Boricio laughed.

Despite the ugly dress, Mary couldn't have looked more beautiful. His heart ached at the sight, the first time he'd seen her since The Island.

He longed to descend the mountain.

"Go ahead," The Darkness whispered in his ear. "Let's go."

"Fuck you," Boricio said.

Living with The Darkness inside his head, seeing his every thought, was tough to get used to at first. But in time, Boricio mastered his ability to shut it down. It was like throwing an unruly child into a locked room. They could scream and cry all they wanted, but Boricio held the key, and he wasn't giving in.

Of course that didn't stop The Darkness from trying to woo him, pretend they were long-lost friends, lure him back into killing. And while Boricio wasn't averse to killing fuckers who deserved it — he wasn't about to give in and go back to his old ways. The Darkness would find a way to take over if he did. But even if that weren't the case, Boricio didn't ever want to hurt an innocent again. Fortunately, the world didn't have many innocents left. And he could keep killing bad fuckers who deserved to be killed.

In a way, Boricio enjoyed having The Darkness where he could watch it, keep it under lock and key, knowing it would never get out and hurt the people he loved.

He watched Mary, again wishing he could go down and see her.

She suddenly looked up, toward his spot on the mountain. There was no way Mary could see him, especially with the sun at his back, but for a long moment it felt like she could.

"I love you" he said, even if his Miss Mary couldn't hear him.

He had to go. It was too much, and if Boricio didn't leave, he'd lose his willpower, head down, and crash the wedding.

He left the woods and sent a thought to the only other person who knew he wasn't dead.

"Thank you for letting me see this, Emily."

You're welcome, she thought back.

"I'll see you all around. Watch over them, will ya?"

You know it. Bye, Boricio.

"Bye."

Boricio kept walking until he found the road winding through the valley below and back up toward mountains. He looked north and south, unsure where to go.

The Darkness asked in his head, "Where are we going?"

Boricio reached into his pocket, found a quarter, and flipped it.

"Wherever the road takes us."

A Note from the Authors

Thanks for reading *Yesterday's Gone: Season 6*

If you enjoyed this book please write a review on your favorite bookselling site so other readers can enjoy it too. Just a couple of sentences would mean a lot to us.

Thank you!

Sean & Dave

About the Authors

Sean Platt is an entrepreneur and founder of Sterling & Stone, where he makes stories with his partners, Johnny B. Truant, and David W. Wright, and a family of storytellers.

Sean is the bestselling author of over 10 million words' worth of books, including the Yesterday's Gone and Invasion series. Sean is also co-author of the indie publishing cornerstone, Write. Publish. Repeat. and co-host of the Story Studio Podcast.

Originally from Long Beach, California, Sean now lives in Austin, Texas with his wife and two children. He has more than his share of nose.

~

David W. Wright is the co-author of edge-of-your seat thrillers including the best-selling post-apocalyptic series *Yesterday's Gone*, the paranoid sci-fi *WhiteSpace* series, and the vigilante series, *No Justice*, as well as standalone thrillers *12*, and *Crash* which was recently optioned for a movie.

David is an accomplished, though intermittent, cartoonist who lives in [LOCATION REDACTED] with his wife and son [NAMES REDACTED.]

He is not at all paranoid.

He is "the grumpy one" on the *The Story Studio Podcast* with fellow Sterling and Stone founders, Sean Platt and Johnny B. Truant.

David writes about books, TV shows, movies, and video games he enjoys; his struggles with anxiety and OCD; writing; and posts the occasional drawing at his personal blog at davidwwright.com

You can email him at david@sterlingandstone.net

We swear, he almost never bites. Unless you feed him after midnight.

For a full list of his most recent books visit sterlingandstone.net.

Also By Sean Platt

The Dead World Series

Dead Zero

Dead City

Dead Nation

Dead Planet

Empty Nest

The Beam Series

The Beam Season One

The Beam Season Two

The Beam Season Three

Robot Proletariat Series

En3my

Robot Proletariat

The Infinite Loop

The Hard Reset

Cascade Failure

Reboot

The Tomorrow Gene Series

Null Identity

The Tomorrow Gene

The Tomorrow Clone

The Eden Experiment

Karma Police Series

Jumper

Karma Police

The Collectors

Deviant

The Fall

Homecoming

Yesterday's Gone

October's Gone

Yesterday's Gone Season One

Yesterday's Gone Season Two

Yesterday's Gone Season Three

Yesterday's Gone Season Four

Yesterday's Gone Season Five

Yesterday's Gone Season Six

Tomorrow's Gone

Tomorrow's Gone Season One

Tomorrow's Gone Season Two

Tomorrow's Gone Season Three

Available Darkness

Darkness Itself

Available Darkness Book One

Available Darkness Book Two

Available Darkness Book Three

WhiteSpace

WhiteSpace Season One

WhiteSpace Season Two

WhiteSpace Season Three

Stand Alone Novels

Burnout

The Island

Crash

Emily's List

Pattern Black

Devil May Care

The Secret Within

Also By David W. Wright

Cold Justice

Cold Justice

Cold Reckoning

Hidden Justice

Hidden Justice

Hidden Honor

Hidden Shame

Hidden Virtue

No Justice

No Justice

No Escape

No Hope

No Return

No Stopping

No Fear

Karma Police

Jumper

Karma Police

The Collectors

Deviant

The Fall

Homecoming

Yesterday's Gone

October's Gone

Yesterday's Gone Season One

Yesterday's Gone Season Two

Yesterday's Gone Season Three

Yesterday's Gone Season Four

Yesterday's Gone Season Five

Yesterday's Gone Season Six

Tomorrow's Gone

Tomorrow's Gone Season One

Tomorrow's Gone Season Two

Tomorrow's Gone Season Three

Available Darkness

Darkness Itself

Available Darkness Book One

Available Darkness Book Two

Available Darkness Book Three

WhiteSpace

WhiteSpace Season One

WhiteSpace Season Two

WhiteSpace Season Three

Stand Alone Novels

12

Crash

Emily's List

Threshold
The Secret Within